ALEXANDER'S

Novels

SACRED TRUST

"Alexander is great at drawing the reader into her story line
and keeping them hooked until the resolution of the plot."
—*Christian Retailing*

A KILLING FROST

"Running dialogue and a few twists will keep romantic
suspense fans coming back for more."
—*Publishers Weekly*

DOUBLE BLIND

"Native American culture clashes with Christian principles in
the freshly original plot."
—*Romantic Times BOOKreviews*

GRAVE RISK

"The latest in Alexander's Hideaway series is filled
with mystery and intrigue. Readers familiar with
the series will appreciate how the author keeps
the characters fresh and appealing."
—*Romantic Times BOOKreviews*

FAIR WARNING

"The plot is interesting and the resolution filled with action."
—*Romantic Times BOOKreviews*

LAST RESORT

"The third novel in Alexander's Hideaway romantic
suspense series (after the Christy Award-winning *Hideaway*
and *Safe Haven*) is a gripping tale with sympathetic
characters that will draw readers into its web.
The kidnapped Clarissa's inner dialogue may
remind some of Alice Sebold's *The Lovely Bones*."
—*Library Journal*

Other books by
HANNAH ALEXANDER

Love Inspired Suspense

Note of Peril
Under Suspicion
Death Benefits
Hidden Motive

Steeple Hill Single Title

Hideaway
Safe Haven
Last Resort
Fair Warning
Grave Risk
Double Blind
**A Killing Frost*

Love Inspired Historical

Hideaway Home

*Hideaway novel
**River Dance novel

HANNAH ALEXANDER

SACRED TRUST

Steeple
Hill®

Published by Steeple Hill Books™

be aware
sold and
the
ook."

STEEPLE HILL BOOKS

Steeple Hill®

Recycling programs
for this product may
not exist in your area.

ISBN-13: 978-0-373-78651-0

SACRED TRUST

Harlequin Enterprises Limited/2009

First published by Bethany House Publishers

Copyright ©1999 by Hannah Alexander

www.SteepleHill.com

Printed in U.S.A.

To the Great Physician,
the Author and Finisher of our faith.

In memory of our fathers:
Johnie R. Cook & Ralph B. Hodde

We wish to thank Joan Marlow Golan and her excellent staff for giving us this opportunity to share our books with a new reading audience.

SACRED TRUST

Prologue

Frankie Verris held the plastic cup in his trembling left hand and stared out the bedroom window. Broken limbs from winter storms littered an unmowed lawn. Weeds lay flattened in the vegetable garden. The jonquils and tulips, which Doris had always loved so much, had refused to bloom this spring. It pretty well summed up Frankie's life over the past year, with Doris gone. Another sleepless night, filled with pain and loneliness, had brought him to this despair.

He looked at the easy-open prescription vial in his right hand, cherishing even the look of his wife's name on the white label. Why hadn't he cherished her more when she was alive?

With unsteady fingers, he flipped off the cap and poured the pills onto the dusty chest beside the window. They had helped Doris sleep. Would they work for his pain?

He gagged on the first swallow, but it finally went down. He sank into the bedside chair and took two more. They went easier. He watched the silent flight of a hawk as it winged over the horizon of forest past the yard. Everything seemed to remind him of Doris these days. She'd loved the hawks because of "the poetry in their wings." She'd loved so many things. She'd loved him, unworthy as he was.

She'd loved God most of all.

For years Frankie had been jealous of God, often resentful because of the special relationship Doris seemed to have with Him. And now God had taken her and there was nothing left.

He swallowed two more pills, then kept going, two at a time. It grew easier and easier.

The drug was fast acting, and he appreciated that. He didn't want to sit around and wait for it to work. In fact, he thought he might be feeling the first effects already....

Jacob Casey gripped the telephone receiver hard, fighting back another wave of pain in his upper thigh. "Hello, emergency room? This is Cowboy again. I'm coming in with another injury." It had been a few months since they'd seen him, and he'd never been there in the daytime. Maybe today's would be a different staff, and maybe this time the doc on duty wouldn't give him the familiar three-hour sermon about being careful around wild animals.

He grimaced as the secretary questioned him. "Nope, no ambulance. I'll do it myself." He'd called an ambulance once—last year when the bison had kicked the paddock gate over on him. It had taken him longer to get to the hospital then than ever before or since.

He looked down to find more blood dripping from his thigh. "Can't take the time to talk. Just be ready for me. My pet cat bit me. No rabies, so don't even think about shots." Leonardo was well vaccinated.

With a short grunt Cowboy hung up the phone and

reached for his hat. The room started to go black on him, and he lowered his head. *Must be losing more blood than I thought.* Forget the hat. He picked up his keys from the kitchen table and flung one last, angry glance out the window toward the cage outside where Leonardo the lion paced from end to end. Let him go hungry if he was going to behave like this.

At this rate there would be blood all over Cowboy's beautiful vintage Mustang. That cat had a lot to answer for.

Frankie stood up unsteadily from his perch at the un-curtained window. The sun had passed the tree line and now blasted through the bedroom with unrelenting force. Dust particles danced in the sunbeams, and Frankie stared at them for a moment, fascinated. The neighbor kids would want to see this. He'd have to show them the next time they came over....

No, he wasn't planning to be here to show them. He was going to be with Doris by then.

He would be with Doris, wouldn't he? She was dead and he'd be dead, in the ground.

His mind worked through that thought slowly. Doris had never believed she would just end up in the ground. She was sure she was going to heaven. He'd gotten sick of listening to her talk about heaven so much. But it sure had comforted him after she was gone.

Frankie's hands felt numb. He wiggled his fingers and tried to shake the muzziness from his head, but it just made him dizzier. *Man, oh, man, this drug is working fast.*

Maybe he didn't want it to work so fast. What about the kids next door? He hadn't thought about them. What if this drug worked and he died, and those little kids found him?

He did not want that to happen.

Using all his strength to force his feet to move, he walk-stumbled from the bedroom toward the living room. He'd better try to reach that phone. He could call 9-1-1 and stop all this. Then, even if he died, the kids wouldn't be the ones who found him.

Ivy Richmond sat on the chair closest to the front door and listened to the siren. Soon the ambulance would pull up outside. They'd take care of everything. She pressed her hands against her chest and tried to breathe slowly, as if that would help normalize the crazy rhythm of her heart. This was not a heart attack. She wouldn't let it be.

So what was it? Stress? She could get philosophical about it and say she had a broken heart. It would be true. Her heart was breaking more and more every day, but she hadn't expected to get so physical about it. She'd experienced grief before, but maybe it was different every time. Maybe it dug deeper each time until it finally destroyed either the mind or the body. Or maybe she was just being melodramatic. She needed to snap out of this.

The siren stopped as the ambulance pulled up outside. She could see the reflection of the lights against her living-room drapes. Time to let them in.

She stood up and opened the door just as they stepped up to knock.

"Mrs. Richmond?" It was the big guy she'd seen before.

She nodded and stepped back. "This way. She's in the first bedroom." She gestured down the hallway, and her hand shook.

The man stopped in front of her. "Are you okay?"

"I didn't call for me," she snapped. "It's my mother. Cancer. Get her to the hospital!"

* * *

Frankie never realized how much effort it took just to walk. He could not concentrate long enough to form his steps. He finally leaned against the wall and pulled himself down the hallway that seemed to stretch for miles. If he could just get to the phone…

Doris would be so ashamed of him, trying to buy his way out of life like this. He couldn't do it. He wanted her to be proud of him when they greeted each other again.

Would they ever see each other? What if she was right about heaven and hell?

He needed time to think about it. He had to reach that phone.

There it sat on the end table. Frankie teetered as he stepped away from the wall and reached forward. His foot caught on something, and he fell as if in slow motion.

Yes, he should have thought about this to begin with. He could crawl so much easier than he could walk. He inched across the remaining space on his elbows and knees and raised his hand toward the phone. He knocked off the receiver, and it fell next to him. He squinted at the face of the dial pad and realized he'd lost his glasses. He peered closer, fighting the heavy darkness that rushed in toward him like a hard wind. He hit the first button: nine. He found the one and poked it, then raised his finger to hit it again, but the black wind grabbed him.

The receiver slipped from his hand, and his head and shoulders slumped helplessly onto the carpet.

Chapter One

A delicate carpet of spring-green crept across the central Arkansas-Missouri border. The buds of serviceberry and dogwood had clothed their trees in pristine white just in time to welcome Dr. Lukas Bower to his new place of residence in Knolls, Missouri. He refused to call it home yet. After his most recent experiences in the job market, he couldn't place his trust in these strangers. Nevertheless, nestled between patchwork properties of Mark Twain National Forest, this Ozark community of ten thousand promised to meet the needs of a country boy who loved the outdoors, especially hiking. When he had driven down from Kansas City to check out the area, the first order of business, before interviewing for the position of full-time emergency room physician, was to count the logging trails and off-road-vehicle paths that crisscrossed the forest. He'd even followed several of the trails in his Jeep. By the time he'd appeared for the interview with Mrs. Estelle Pinkley, the hospital administrator, he was sold on the place.

He was just finishing his usual morning repast of

grease and eggs in the hospital cafeteria when the phone rang for him. He recognized the voice of an emergency room registered nurse.

"Dr. Bower, this is Beverly. We have a man by the name of Jacob Casey on his way here in his own car. He says he's been bitten by his pet cat. He sounds pretty excited about it."

Lukas frowned. "His cat bit him?"

"I gathered that the bite was pretty bad," answered the RN.

"Rabies?"

"He specifically said there were no rabies. From the way he talked, the secretary thinks he's been here before."

"Okay, Beverly, I'll be there shortly. Would you please pull his chart?" How much damage could a house pet do?

"But I've got good news," she said. "We'll have double nursing coverage through the noon rush."

"As far as I know, this cat bite *is* the noon rush."

Beverly chuckled. "Don't worry, when Lauren and I do a double-coverage shift together, we always have some excitement."

"I'll trust your judgment." Lukas hung up and took the one-minute walk to the emergency room.

He stepped in to find everything quiet. "Beverly, did Mr. Casey estimate how long it would take him to—"

The sudden blare of a car horn interrupted him and continued, obnoxiously loud.

"What on earth...?" Beverly walked through the open E.R. entrance and disappeared down the hallway. In less than fifteen seconds the honking stopped. Beverly came running back.

"Dr. Bower, Carol, I need your help." She reached for one of the two gurneys sitting just inside the entrance.

"There's a man parked in the ambulance bay who looks like he's bleeding all over the place. He's alone." She pushed the gurney out the door, with Lukas and Carol, the secretary, close behind.

By the time they reached the bay, the forty-odd-year-old man had opened his door and now clung to it desperately as he tried to get to his feet.

"Can't seem to stand up," he grated in a deep voice. His face was the color of recycled paper, and even his lips looked bloodless. "Cat bit me."

Lukas, Beverly and Carol grabbed him and eased him onto the gurney.

Beverly gaped at him, then at the blood around his upper right thigh. "A cat did this?"

He held out a set of keys to her. "I always wanted a beautiful redhead to drive my Mustang. Take good care of her." His eyes shut and his head dropped sideways.

"Let's get him inside." Lukas closed the car door. "Beverly, give those keys to Carol. She can drive this car out of the way and park it as soon as we get him transferred to a bed."

"Oh, come on!" Beverly protested. "He told me I could take care of it."

"He needs you worse than his car does." Lukas held out his hand as they pushed the gurney through the automatic sliding glass doors. "The keys, please."

Beverly curled her lip at him, but handed over the set of keys. "I've never driven a Mustang before."

"Thank you." Lukas handed them to Carol. "Would you do the honors? Beverly, let's get an IV established on this man immediately, and we need to get his clothes off and see where the blood is coming from."

While they worked on him, the double-coverage nurse arrived. Lauren groaned when she saw Beverly. "We'll be swamped." Even as she spoke, the ambulance radio blared. She pulled her long, blond hair into a ponytail and fastened it as she sat down at the desk to take the call.

In fifteen minutes, the emergency room was nearly full. The man in exam room seven had a deep laceration in his right forearm from an industrial accident. Lukas called industrial accidents his "graveyard specials," because they happened most often during the predawn hours when the need for sleep was at its highest. Lukas used them as an example when arguing against twenty-four-hour shifts for emergency room physicians. This patient had worked since midnight, having had no sleep the day before. Dangerous?

A high school track student in room two had a possible broken wrist. The E.R. staff was waiting for parental consent to treat, enduring endless telephone calls from classmates to check on the patient's progress while the track coach searched for the completed consent form. Naturally the parents were out of town for the day.

A baby in room three had a red ear, and Lukas was still trying to decide if it was serious enough to treat with an antibiotic. The young mother had come in crying almost as loudly as her baby, and for a while no one had known which of them was here for treatment.

Two unwashed females stood out at the reception desk complaining loudly because they hadn't been treated yet for their head lice.

"No, you did not 'wimp out,' Mr. Casey." Lukas stood beside the bed of their first arrival, thirty minutes after they'd wheeled him in. The man still looked weak, although his color had improved. "You lost a couple of pints of blood. Your loving pet nicked an artery in your thigh." He indicated Casey's bare leg.

Lukas traced the stablike wounds on the inside of Casey's right thigh. "That's some cat."

"This is just a love bite, Doc. My name's Jake, or Cowboy, but don't call me Mr. Casey."

"A love bite?"

"Male African lion."

"A pet?"

"Had him for four years, since he was a cub. I raise exotic animals for parks and zoos, but I kept Leonardo. He's good company."

"When he's not eating various parts of your anatomy. You must live alone."

"How'd you guess?"

Beverly entered the trauma room to recheck Cowboy's vitals and help Lukas finish irrigating the wound.

Covered in nothing but a towel, Cowboy's whole body blushed. "Uh, Doc, I'd be grateful if you could spare one of those skimpy hospital gowns. It'd cover a whole lot more."

Lukas grinned at him. "I think that could be arranged." He glanced at Beverly. He had already seen the way Cowboy looked at her—and the way she looked back. "Maybe I should help him dress."

"You don't have time," Beverly said. "I hear the ambulance phone now, and we have a mom out in the waiting room with three children she wants to have checked out for sore throats and earaches."

"How long before our surgeon arrives?" Lukas asked.

Beverly wrote down Cowboy's vitals on a clipboard. "Any minute now, Dr. Bower. He laughed when I told him who it was. He says he's had this patient before." She grinned at Cowboy. "I hear you're pretty adventurous."

He returned her smile and blushed again. "The folks I work with aren't always predictable. Dr. Wong took care of a gash I got in the head when a scared zebra kicked me." He looked at Lukas. "But why do I need a surgeon for this bite? Can't you just sew me up and let me get home? Leonardo will be hungry before long, and he's probably worried."

"Good," Beverly said. "Let him worry. Maybe he'll remember this the next time he confuses you with a beefsteak."

"Sorry, Cowboy," Lukas said. "Leonardo bit into a deep artery. That's surgeon territory."

"But you've stopped the bleeding."

"With pressure. When we remove the pressure, we'll be leaving an unstable wound that can burst open at any time. You've lost enough blood already. You can't afford to lose more."

"But, Dr. Bower—"

"Listen to your doctor." Beverly laid a hand on Cowboy's arm. "He knows what he's doing. Besides, if you're too eager to get out of here, we'll think you don't like our company." She winked at him. "You never want to offend your local emergency department personnel. You can't tell when you'll need them." She dug into her pocket and pulled out the set of keys she had retrieved from Carol. "I'll make a deal with you. If you'll let me drive your car and give me some instructions, I'll go out to your place when I get off work and feed Leonardo for you."

Both men stared at her.

"Uh, Beverly," Lukas said, "you do realize we're talking about an African lion."

"I heard through the crack of the door. Besides, I've read the chart."

"Sorry," Cowboy said in his gravelly voice. "No way am I sending a pretty female out to do the job I should've done. Get a man to feed Leonardo, and you can drive him out there in my car."

Lukas expected Beverly, with her obviously independent spirit, to spit fire. Instead, she gazed bemusedly at Cowboy and nodded. "I'll see what I can do."

Someone approached the trauma room entrance. "Dr. Bower?" It was Lauren's voice.

"Oh, Doc, please," Cowboy said. "I'm still practically naked here. Don't give me an audience."

Lukas slipped through the partially open door, leaving Cowboy his privacy. "Yes?"

"We have an elderly man in exam room one who has just been brought in unresponsive."

"I'll be right there." He rechecked Cowboy's wound, then crossed to exam room one, where Lauren was rushing through the vitals of an unconscious, toothless elderly man in his pajamas, who was already hooked to a monitor and a nonrebreather oxygen mask.

A worried-looking woman in her thirties stood at the patient's side, her eyes puffy and red from crying.

"Hello, I'm Dr. Bower," he said to the woman. "Are you his daughter? Granddaughter?"

"No, I'm Shelly, Frankie's neighbor. My children go over to see him every day, and today they found him like this on the floor of his living room. I think he'd been trying to call someone, because the telephone receiver was off the hook and lying beside him."

"Did you bring him in by yourself?"

"Another neighbor helped me get him into the van. We should have called an ambulance, but I just didn't think. We only live four blocks from the hospital!"

Lukas adjusted his stethoscope and did a quick auscultation of the man's chest. He had mild tachycardia and slow respiration. His skin was pale and cool to the touch. A quick check of his head and upper body revealed no signs of injury. Lukas didn't smell alcohol.

"Lauren, let's get a bedside glucose on him."

"Yes, Doctor. We have a new patient in room eight who needs you next." She lowered her voice. "It's cancer. She's a DNR."

Lukas grimaced. Those were the hardest. "Okay, thank you, Lauren." He checked Frankie's eyes. The man had good papillary sparing. Lukas quickly but gently turned the patient's head, holding his eyes open. The eyes remained fixed on the ceiling. Positive doll's eyes told him that this was either drug related or that there was bilateral brain swelling.

"Shelly, has he been ill recently? A cold? Flu?"

"No. Yesterday he was fine. He always brags about never getting sick."

"Does he ever drink?"

"You mean liquor? Never." She held out two prescription bottles. "I brought these. I found them on the bureau in his bedroom. His bottle is almost full, but the other one is empty. It belonged to his wife. She died last year."

Lukas took the bottles from her and glanced at the names of the drugs. Both were benzodiazepines for sleep. He glanced at the patient and didn't like what he was thinking.

"Blood sugar's 125, Dr. Bower," Lauren said.

"Thank you." He glanced again at Shelly, hating to ask his next question. "These are tranquilizers. Is it possible he might have taken an overdose of his wife's prescription?"

Her eyes widened with alarm. "On purpose? No way! I don't even want to consider it. He's so good with the kids, and he never seems depressed. He was doing so well after his wife, Doris, died."

Lukas was also reluctant to believe this kindly looking older gentleman would do anything so drastic. He'd probably flushed his wife's pills after her death. But what if he hadn't?

"He hasn't talked about going to be with his wife lately?" he asked Shelly.

"No."

"Has he displayed any changes in his normal habits, like changes in sleep time or amount? Changes in eating habits? Has he given any of his personal items, such as jewelry, to friends or neighbors?"

"Nothing that I know about."

"How long ago did his wife die?"

"About eight months ago. Long enough for him to show signs of depression if he's going to, I would think."

"Not necessarily. A wedding anniversary could have set him off, or her birthday, anything of significance to him." Lukas was well aware of this because his own father had gone through a similar depression after Mom's death. So had Lukas, though not as severe as Dad's.

"But they had just celebrated their wedding anniversary before she died," Shelly said. "And her birthday was two weeks before their anniversary. We celebrated it with them."

"Okay, thank you, Shelly. Lauren, set him up for a CBC, a comprehensive chemistry panel, a portable chest, and a drug screen. Then set up a heplock. I want him to have a milligram of Romazicon at 0.2 milligrams per minute. We'll repeat the dose after twenty minutes."

"What's that for, Doctor?" Shelly asked.

"Romazicon is the antidote for benzodiazepine overdose, just in case." At her blank look, he explained gently,

"He may have taken too many of these tranquilizers. I don't want to dismiss the possibility and take a chance on being wrong."

He glanced at Frankie's prescription bottle again. Dr. Robert Simeon had prescribed the drug. "Lauren, also put a call in to Dr. Simeon's office. He's the family doc. I'm going to check on Cowboy, then look in on the cancer patient. Would you see if that permission to treat has come in for the track student? We'll need a CT head scan on Frankie if our workup is negative."

Dr. Wong entered the E.R. and greeted Lukas with a cheery smile and warm handshake. "Lukas, I hear you have one of my favorite patients visiting with you this morning."

"Yes, and your patient is already asking for some clothes. Beverly will assist you."

As soon as Cowboy was settled with his new doctor, Lukas heard Beverly's cajoling voice through the door.

"Dr. Wong, you're a kindhearted person," she said. "What time do you get off?"

"Um, excuse me? Hold it, Beverly, you know I'm married."

"I know that, silly. How would you like to help out a hungry house pet?"

"Forget it. I know all about Cowboy's house pets. He just happens to be here because that 'pet' mistook his thigh for a drumstick. Isn't that right, Cowboy?"

Lukas chuckled as he walked back to the central desk. Beverly wanted that Mustang.

His laughter died when he entered exam room eight with a chart for Mrs. Jane Conn. The eighty-six-year-old woman lay moaning in pain in spite of the morphine Lauren had just injected at Lukas's order. A smooth, shiny sheath of mottled scar tissue obliterated half of Mrs.

Conn's face and showed up plainly beneath the nonrebreather oxygen mask she had received upon arrival. She
had been brought here from her daughter's home about
thirty minutes ago, her pain unresponsive to oral medication or morphine suppositories. Lauren had established
an IV where dark bruises attested to the failure of the new
paramedic to do so.

Since Lauren and Beverly were both busy, Lukas
checked the blood pressure himself. It was going down,
and the heart rate was dropping, probably due to a
decrease in pain—or Mrs. Conn was dying.

Lukas found Lauren and gave instructions for blood
tests and X-rays. "You did say Mrs. Conn had filled out
a do-not-resuscitate form for her family, didn't you?"

"Yes, but we haven't received it yet." Lauren wrote his
instructions down on a sheet. "Her daughter, Ivy
Richmond, should have it."

"I'll need to get it from her, or we'll have to take
measures to resuscitate if…" He shrugged, hoping they
would have no trouble getting the DNR form. He'd been
forced to run codes on late-stage cancer patients before,
and it had been very painful for everyone, especially for
the patient.

As Lauren ran orders for the tests, Lukas listened once
again to Mrs. Conn's chest. He glanced up, and to his
surprise, he saw her one unaffected eye watching him.

He took her hand. "Mrs. Conn, we're trying to reduce
your pain. How does—"

"Let me…" her damaged mouth twisted in an effort
to form the hoarse words "…go." Her eye held him a few
seconds, then glazed over and closed.

Sadness overwhelmed Lukas as he watched her. He
hated to see the pain, had always hated to see suffering

of any kind. It was one of the things that had driven him to be a doc in the first place, and ironically, it had been one of his worst hindrances in premed vertebrate physiology. He'd always been physically sick afterward, even though the animals were anesthetized and even though he reminded himself over and over again that human lives would be saved because of the sacrifice.

Mrs. Conn's moaning had stopped. Lukas placed a hand on her frail arm, then looked over to find the eye watching him again. He couldn't read the expression, for there was little expression to be displayed on the harsh mask.

She moved her mouth.

Lukas leaned closer to hear her.

"Ready." The word wasn't even a whisper, but a breath of sound that barely carried past the barrier of the transparent oxygen mask. "I'm…ready."

When he looked at her eye it was closed again. For some reason, some infinitesimal sign relayed itself to him—some lightening of expression on that scarred mask? He felt almost…a peace…assurance. Or was he just trying to comfort himself? Cancer was the hardest of all to take since Mom's days of suffering. *Lord, help her.*

"Dr. Bower?"

He turned to find the X-ray tech waiting to do the portable chest. Lauren stepped into the room behind her.

"Lauren, where is Mrs. Conn's daughter?" he asked.

"She's in the private waiting room. I'm surprised Dr. Mercy isn't already with her."

"Dr. Mercy?"

"She's Mercy Richmond, Ivy Richmond's daughter and Mrs. Conn's granddaughter. Dr. Mercy is a nickname a lot of her patients and staff members called her to keep from confusing her with her father, who was also a physician.

He was Dr. Cliff, she was Dr. Mercy. If you haven't met her yet, you will. She hasn't had an E.R. shift in a couple of weeks. She has a family practice across the street."

"Good," replied Lukas. "We can call her when we need to. But I'm going to need to see Ivy Richmond soon. I need that DNR sheet, and she needs to be prepared."

Lauren stood gazing at Mrs. Conn. "This has been a rough one. Everyone knows and loves Mrs. Conn. She used to do a lot of volunteer work here. Her daughter Ivy has made several large contributions to the hospital in the five years since her husband died."

The X-ray tech finished her work in the room, and Lauren took Mrs. Conn's vitals once more. "Down again. BP is 95 over 55 with a 90 pulse."

"Thanks, Lauren. I'll go have a talk with her daughter as soon as I check the test results."

"Okay, I'll go see Frankie again." Lauren gave Mrs. Conn another sad look and walked out of the room.

Had there been time, Lukas would have sat with the patient, but he had to return to reassure the mother with the sick baby, talk to the girl with the sprain, and check on Frankie. Where was Mrs. Conn's daughter, Mrs. Richmond? Why wasn't she in here? More than likely she was exhausted and had found a sofa or chair on which to sleep.

When Lukas finished his round of the patients, he returned to Mrs. Conn and read the test results. As expected, they looked normal for an elderly woman with late-stage cancer. She continued to rest peacefully, but her blood pressure and respiration were falling.

He found the E.R. secretary at the central desk. "Carol, would you please call Dr. Richmond's office and advise her of her grandmother's condition? I'm going—"

Carol raised a hand. "Wait a minute, Dr. Bower. We

received permission to treat Cindy Hawkins with the injured wrist. Also, I have Dr. Simeon on the line. You wanted to talk with him about his patient, Mr. Verris?"

After a quick consultation with Dr. Simeon, Lukas made arrangements to have Franklin Verris, the possible suicide attempt, admitted to ICU, then went back to check on the seventy-three-year-old gentleman one more time.

Shelly kept her vigil at her neighbor's bedside. Lauren stood at the other side of the bed, adjusting an IV line.

"Any change, Lauren?" Lukas asked.

"I'm not sure. There's no difference in his vitals, but his breathing seemed to change a moment ago. It's been twenty minutes, and I'm getting ready to give him the next dose. Do you want me to go ahead with it?"

Lukas bent over Mr. Verris and gently raised his right eyelid. He took out a penlight and shone a beam directly at the pupil. There was a faint reaction. The man didn't look as pale as he had looked before. But according to Dr. Simeon an overdose was highly unlikely. He had disagreed with Lukas's request for Romazicon. However, Lauren was prepared for another dose, and since Lukas had already given the order, he decided to carry it out.

"Go for it, Lauren. I need to stay and watch him, but I also need to talk to Mrs. Richmond. I'll be back."

Chapter Two

Lukas opened the door to the private waiting room and saw a tall, slender woman pacing the floor. Her casual attire of jeans, jogging shoes and a "Hiking is Life" T-shirt skewed the impression he'd formed in his mind of a wealthy, polished benefactress of the hospital.

Mrs. Richmond's long, dark brown hair was pulled back into a ponytail at the nape of her neck. She turned to face him, and he saw that the hair was liberally streaked with gray around the temples. Her large, dark eyes met his with deep gravity. She was at least sixty, and the gaunt face told him of recent weight loss. The prominent dark circles under her eyes told him she probably hadn't slept well for weeks.

"Mrs. Richmond?"

"Yes." Her voice held fear.

"I'm Dr. Bower, the emergency room physician on duty today. I need to speak with you about your mother."

Mrs. Richmond nodded. "I should be in there with her, I know, but the moaning…I just couldn't handle it, had to get away from it for a while." She resumed her pacing.

"She moaned all night. I gave her morphine suppositories twice as often as…" She turned back. "I'm sorry. I'm rambling. It's just so hard to think straight these days."

"I understand. Have you had an aide helping you with your mother at home?"

"No. I didn't want my mother thinking I'd abandoned her to a stranger."

"So you've been taking care of her yourself?"

"My daughter helps when she can."

"I'm sure that's very hard on you, Mrs. Richmond."

"Call me Ivy. Is she still moaning?"

"She was peaceful when I left her a few minutes ago. We gave her an injection. We ran some tests to see if there might be a pneumonia or something else causing her deterioration." He paused. "I'm sorry, Ivy, but none of the tests show a secondary problem. I'm afraid the cancer is taking her."

Ivy nodded slowly. "Hard to believe a little mole on her cheek could do such damage. Melanoma, you know."

"Yes. I'm sorry. Her oncologist is in Springfield?"

"Yes, but it's no use calling him. He'll just increase the morphine." Fatigue sharpened her voice. "She's not worth his time. She's just an old woman."

"We want to make her as comfortable as possible. I understand you have the DNR request she signed?"

Ivy grew still as her eyes flashed back to his face. Her chin lifted a fraction. "Why?"

"Would you like to sit down?"

"I'll stand."

"I know you must be tired. I want to honor your mother's advance directive, and to do so, I need the DNR sheet. This is all just legalities, and I apologize for having to ask you for it at a time like this."

"You mean to just let her die?"

Lukas flinched at the harsh tone of her voice and the sudden, angry-suspicious expression in her eyes.

"If her heart should stop," he said gently, "we wish to honor her request not to restart it."

"What's this 'we' business? You're the doctor. You call the shots. I don't want my mother's heart to stop, and if it does, I want you to start it again."

He held her suddenly angry gaze for a moment. She couldn't know what she was saying.

"Mrs. Richmond, I thought you understood about your mother's request."

"My mother is not capable of making that decision now. I have power of attorney, and I don't want you to just let her die like some worthless old woman. She's a living human being with a soul."

"Of course she is." He hadn't foreseen this. How could he get through to her? "I'm not talking about euthanasia. I'm talking about allowing nature to take its course, allowing your mother to retain her dignity and keep her from unnecessary pain. I've asked a nurse to call your daughter, Dr. Richmond, and she should be here—"

"You did what?" Her dark eyes flashed, and fatigue tightened the tension in her voice.

Lukas blinked at her helplessly. This was not going well. She was clearly, and understandably, irrational from lack of sleep. There had to be some way to make her see, without becoming too graphic.

"I specifically delayed calling my daughter because I wanted to put her through as little heartache as possible," Ivy said. "She's been through enough. You had no right to call her."

"I'm sorry you feel that way, but Mrs. Conn's condition is getting worse. I felt family needed to be here."

"Not yet!" She paused with a gasp, placing a hand on her chest.

He stepped toward her. "Are you okay?"

"I'm fine." Lowering her hand, she took a deep breath and held his gaze. "I don't care what the DNR form says. I have durable power of attorney, and I want you to do everything for my mother. She's not ready to die. She's not…"

"I didn't mean for this to be so difficult." Lukas kept his voice gentle, resisting the urge to ask if he could examine her. He'd seen this kind of family reaction before, during his oncology rotation, when a caregiver was so exhausted that they became confused and combative. They often blamed the physician for the pain of their dying loved one. "I will contact Mrs. Conn's family physician and clarify the matter." He turned to leave.

"You don't believe I have power of attorney?" she challenged, her voice rising a decibel.

He paused with his hand on the door. *Lord, give me compassion.*

But what about Mrs. Conn? She would suffer even more pain if they managed to resuscitate her.

He turned back to face Ivy, and he tried to keep his voice gentle. He knew his words were not. "What I believe is immaterial, Mrs. Richmond. For instance, I believe that to impose heroic measures onto a patient suffering the last stages of advanced carcinomatosis is not only transferring much-needed care from the living to the dying, it is inhumane to the dying."

"Only if you don't believe in hell."

"Mrs. Richmond—"

"Ivy! My name's Ivy!"

"I'm sorry, Ivy. I do believe in hell. I also believe that

your mother is at peace about this. She told me she was ready to go."

"What do you mean, she told you?" Ivy snapped. "Mother hasn't spoken in days. What are you trying to pull here?"

Be gentle. Be patient. But what about Mrs. Conn? "Ivy, to try to resuscitate your mother at this stage would only cause greater, unnecessary suffering. And for what? A few more minutes or hours for the family to say goodbye? What about your mother's feelings? She's made her decision already."

There. He'd done it again, him and his bad habit of stating his opinion to the wrong people at the wrong time. But if there was the slightest chance Ivy would listen…

She bent her head, her eyes closed for a moment. He watched her hopefully.

She reached into the right back pocket of her jeans and drew out a folded three-page form. "I had hoped it would never come to this." The strength had left her voice. She unfolded the papers and held them out with shaking hands. "I have the power of attorney. Are you satisfied?"

Beverly caught up with Lukas as he reentered the E.R. proper. "That Mustang's mine!"

Lukas struggled to work up some enthusiasm. "Don't tell me you cajoled Dr. Wong—"

"Nope." She jingled Cowboy's keys. "Sweet-talked one of the new EMTs to help me. Buck likes animals."

"Yes, but did you tell him this wasn't a gerbil?"

She grimaced. "He knows it's a big animal."

"Horses are big animals. How will you feel if your helper comes back in here on a stretcher?"

"Awful." She shrugged. "Dr. Wong's finished with Cowboy. Got any patients for me?"

"Have I ever." He gestured toward the charts at the desk. "Enjoy."

He left her staring at the sudden overload and stepped back into exam room one to check on Mr. Verris. Shelly still sat there beside his bed, and Lauren entered behind Lukas, as if geared to his location by radar.

"Any change?" Lukas asked Lauren.

"Test results are in."

Lukas checked the printouts. Nothing. Everything was normal. Even the drug screen was not helpful, because all it showed were benzodiazepines, and that was to be expected for someone who occasionally took them to sleep. Lukas could have done a quantitative drug screen, but that would have taken too long.

"BP's gone up just a little, but not much," Lauren continued. "Pulse and respiration are the same. They've called from upstairs to let us know they're coming to take him to ICU."

"Let's make sure they know he still needs a CT scan." Lukas did his own assessment. Was it his imagination, or was the man breathing more deeply? As he watched, Frankie's head moved a fraction of an inch.

Lukas looked up to see if Lauren had noticed. "Has he moved like that before?"

"I don't think so."

He watched a moment longer. It was probably just a stimulation of the limbic system, a common event in a coma patient.

Lukas did an auscultation of Frankie's chest one more time, then shook his head. With a nod at Shelly, he left the room. He was feeling more and more frustrated as the day progressed.

Lauren stepped out of the room behind him. "Dr. Bower? Some of the staff are getting together after this shift over at the cantina across the street. Want to join us?"

"Uh…sure. Yes, I'll be there. Thank you for asking." Lukas nodded and continued down the hall, knowing he would be kicking himself tonight when it came time to show up at the cantina. He would be starving when he got off, as usual, and since he always ate out anyway, this would be a good way to get better acquainted with the people who worked here. Unfortunately, he knew that by the time he arrived at the restaurant, he would be feeling so awkward about meeting with a group of near strangers, he would have lost his appetite. Almost.

Moving to a new place was lonely business, especially for him. Funny, he could face patients and coworkers all day long with no problem, but when his time was not regimented, he had trouble forcing himself to reach out to others. It wasn't that he didn't like people, because he did. The youngest of three boys in a loving Christian family, Lukas was the only shy one in the bunch, and he had often been teased about it. The teasing had only made him more self-conscious, turning him inward, and now his family despaired of ever seeing him married. But this was a new place, and no one here knew about his shyness. It was time to dig himself out of the rut—or pray that God would move him out.

He took Mrs. Richmond's papers to the secretary. "We'll need copies of these, Carol. Please call Dr. Richmond back and tell her that she needs to be on standby. Her grandmother is holding her own at the moment, but she could deteriorate fast, and she's now a full code."

"Yes, sir." Carol grabbed the papers from him, dark eyes glowering as she spun around to the copier. She muttered something under her breath.

Lukas watched the characteristically cheerful secretary in surprise. "Carol, are you okay?"

She put the first sheet into the copier and pressed the button. "Fine, just fine," she mumbled. "We're swamped, we've got patients dying back there, and all I hear are complaints that we're not seeing people fast enough." She indicated the waiting room. "Griping because you haven't looked at their scalps yet. They'd be in here right now, except one of them had to step outside for a smoke. I get so tired—"

"Have they been signed in?"

"No, I've been too busy with these other—"

"I'll take care of them." Lukas glanced out the door, where one of the women he'd seen earlier stood smoking, talking to the other. He strolled out to join them.

"Hello, ladies, I'm Dr. Bower. I hear you're unhappy about our service. What's the emergency?"

The smoker quickly shoved her half-smoked cigarette into the receptacle like a school kid caught by the teacher.

"We need to be treated for head lice," the nonsmoker said.

The patio was deserted, Lukas noticed. He took another step forward, carefully looked at first one over-permed head of hair, then at the smoker's long, stringy brown hair.

He took out a notepad and a pen and wrote the name of a shampoo. He held it out toward the smoker. "Wash with it once, then wait a week and wash again. You can buy this at your local pharmacy."

She stared at the note in his hand. "No prescription?"

"You don't need a prescription for this. The two of you can share a bottle."

"But we'll have to pay for it."

Lukas felt his skin tingle with growing irritation. He inhaled slowly, counting to ten as he placed the note on the top of a trash can nearby. It had suddenly become a stressful day, the worst he'd had in a long time. He couldn't blame it all on these two misguided souls.

He turned and opened the heavy glass door. "Ladies, the shampoo costs less than a pack or two of your favorite brand of cigarettes."

"But we have Medicaid cards," the smoker called after him. "We can report you for refusing to treat us!"

He stopped midstride and slowly turned back toward them. "Feel free," he said, keeping his voice calm. "I feel I should warn you, however, that when a card carrier tries to use the card in the E.R. for nonemergency care, she can lose her card. It's called Medicaid abuse. I think you'll find that shampoo works very well as long as you follow the directions." He stepped inside and let the door close silently behind him.

There were other Medicaid cardholders—for instance, the little baby in exam room three—who needed treatment today, not next week, and Lukas saw to it that they received good care. Lots of Medicaids used the emergency room here because many family practitioners refused to take assignment. Those who did still limited their patients. Medicaid paid so little that a physician who took too many could go broke. The system didn't work. Many times the people who behaved with integrity got left out entirely—both the honest Medicaid recipients and the honestly compassionate physicians. Greed was the culprit on all sides. Lawmakers spent their time writing more laws because people kept figuring out ways to take advantage of the system. It was frustrating. Lukas had to keep reminding himself not to blame the patients who sometimes misunderstood the constantly changing rules.

Lukas glanced around at the emergency department. He liked this little ten-bed setup. The exam rooms surrounded a large central station. Each room was well equipped. Five of the ten rooms had excellent cardiac equipment. There was a separate ambulance entrance and two physician call rooms.

Mrs. Estelle Pinkley, the hospital administrator, had done a remarkable job when she'd convinced the county to pay for this upgrade. Lukas had jumped at the chance to receive a dependable salary with benefits so far away from the congestion and stress and corruption of the city. Yes, he knew corruption was everywhere, but right now, with specific, damaging events so fresh in his memory, Kansas City represented everything painful.

Carol met Lukas as he entered the E.R. proper. "Dr. Bower, Mrs. Conn is getting worse. Lauren said to notify you."

"Thanks, Carol. Please call Dr. Richmond back."

"Lauren already did so."

"Get ready to call a code if necessary."

"Dr. Richmond will have a fit about that, you know."

"Maybe she can do more about it than I was able to."

Chapter Three

Mercy Richmond ran the block from her medical office to the hospital, not bothering to remove her lab coat. Mom had promised to call when the time came, but she hadn't done so. Instead, Lauren had been the one to break the news.

Shoving open the glass doors into the emergency room reception area, Mercy barely slowed her stride. "Carol, where's Grandma?"

"She was in exam room eight, but they called a code and moved her to trauma room one."

Mercy stopped and wheeled back. "What? There's not supposed to be a code!"

Carol shook her head in sympathy. "I'm sorry. Dr. Bower called it. He had to."

"We'll see about that." Mercy swung back on course. First, administration had arbitrarily decided to bring in a full-time E.R. doc from Kansas City, and now this hotshot doc had decided to ignore a perfectly legal DNR request. Perhaps he'd never learned to read.

She pushed through the swinging double doors that

pretended to lend privacy to the open emergency room. A secretary manned the central station. All other hands were gathered in the trauma room, six people altogether, including Grandma's frail, still body on the bed. Others worked with quick efficiency, responding without question to the soft-spoken commands of a slender, brown-haired man in green scrubs. He knew the drill well.

"Get me a blood gas…. Push the epi now, Lauren…. Any pulse…? Continue CPR."

Mercy stopped just inside the doorway as a nurse from upstairs pushed methodically against Grandma's chest and another bagged her.

"What's going on here?" Mercy demanded. "Doctor, what are you doing to my grandmother?"

He looked up, his blue eyes behind gray-framed spectacles holding her with gentle concern. "You must be Dr. Richmond. I'm sorry, but as per your mother's request, we are attempting resuscitation." He turned back to the table.

"Stand clear," he called as he prepared the paddles to send a jolt of electricity through Grandma's chest. He placed one paddle above her right breast, and the other paddle he placed to the side below her left breast.

Mercy stood in stunned horror as the frail body jerked, arms flying out, legs up. Mercy had done the same procedure herself many times during her shifts in E.R. but not on someone she loved like Grandma.

"Check pulse," Dr. Bower said.

Lauren gently felt the carotid artery for a moment, then shook her head. "Nothing, Doctor."

"Continue CPR. Prepare more epi, and I need lidocaine, 1.5 milligrams per kilogram. What's that blood gas?"

"Not back yet, Doctor."

Mercy stepped toward him. "Dr. Bower, I'm her granddaughter. Stop this code."

He was barely taller than her five feet eight inches, but his expression held calm authority. "As I said, Dr. Richmond, your mother—"

"I heard what you said, but my grandmother signed a DNR form weeks ago. Surely that has some bearing on this case."

"You know that form does me no good. Believe me, I wish it did." Dr. Bower's voice betrayed frustration. He lowered his voice. "Your mother showed me her papers for legal power of attorney. Her order is to resuscitate."

"Forget that order. As a fellow physician—"

"I can't break the law, Dr. Richmond."

"Don't abuse this patient any more than she has already been abused!"

Dr. Bower grimaced at her words, sighed and shook his head. "I'd love to comply, but I can't. If you want to sway the decision, please talk to your mother. I tried." He turned back to the table. "Stop CPR."

The monitor showed an irregular, sawtooth pattern. Grandma's heart was in ventricular fibrillation. Mercy hoped it would not change back.

"Where is my mother?" she asked, her voice heavy with frustration.

"She was in the private waiting room when I left her." Dr. Bower shook his head at the monitor. "No change. We need to shock again."

He charged the defibrillator to 360 joules. "Clear."

Mercy stepped back and almost turned to leave, but she couldn't. A sort of morbid amazement held her there, watching the scene of horror play out before her. She gripped the door frame. A loud pop and flash preceded the stench of burned flesh. An electrode had blown. Lauren and Dr. Bower checked for signs of life while another nurse replaced the electrode.

"No change," Dr. Bower said.

Mercy felt sick. Mom should be here to see what her crazy order was doing to Grandma. But then, Mom, too, had suffered enough.

Again they shocked, and Mercy could not bring herself to leave. CPR resumed. The longer they worked, the more convinced she became that Grandma was already far past their so-called help. And that meant she was also past any more pain.

Dr. Bower called a halt a seeming eternity later. Mercy did not move until he pronounced the time of death.

She stepped from the doorway as the code team cleaned up the mess of scattered monitor strips and plastic wrapping that had been tossed on the floor during the code. One by one, they filed out past her, some avoiding her eyes as if ashamed of the work they had just done.

Lauren stopped and laid a tanned, slender hand on Mercy's shoulder. "I'm sorry, Dr. Mercy." Tears filled her pretty green eyes.

"So am I, Lauren. Thanks for calling me over."

"It was Dr. Bower's request. Your mom told us not to."

"Figures." Mercy was thirty-nine, and Mom had still not overcome the need to hem her in with maternal over-protectiveness. Often it rankled. It showed lack of respect for Mercy's ability to cope. For goodness' sake, she was a doctor.

Dr. Bower paused for a moment at the bedside, his hand resting gently on Grandma's arm, his head bent and eyes closed. When the last team member had left the room, Mercy walked over to stand beside the man and gaze into Grandma's silent, scarred face.

Dr. Bower raised his head and looked at her. "I'm sorry, Dr. Richmond, I've been told she was a much loved lady." He had a kind voice, deep and masculine, but with a gentle quality.

Mercy nodded, dry eyed. "She was."

"I apologize for my abruptness. I could have handled the situation better."

The sincerity in his voice disarmed her. She'd been prepared for battle when she came in here. Now she felt spent. Empty. "I wouldn't let you." She shook her head. "I had always sworn that I would never do to another doc what patients and families have done to me, and here I led the pack—aided by my mother, of course. I know the law, Dr. Bower. It's just that she's my grandma." Her voice caught, and her professional demeanor abandoned her for a moment. Her throat ached with tears she refused to shed. She was grateful for the man's thoughtful silence.

"My mother died of metastatic breast cancer three years ago," he said after a few moments. "I remember the feelings of helplessness and anger. I wanted to do so much more for her, and there was nothing more to do except keep her comfortable. Had we revived your grandmother…"

"I know."

There was another pause, then Dr. Bower asked, "Would you like me to go with you to tell your mother?"

Mercy took a final look at Grandma and turned away. "No, thank you. It'll be best coming from me."

He hesitated. "Did you not have a chance to discuss the DNR form with your mother?"

"I tried. Mom wouldn't talk about it."

"It's a difficult subject to discuss. I gathered that your mother was the main caregiver."

"Yes. I tried to help more, just to keep her from exhausting herself." Mercy shook her head. "Mom can be stubborn and self-sufficient. She's lost so much sleep lately…she hasn't been her usual, rational self—not that she's ever been a perfect example of rationality." Why was she talking to this stranger like this? And a man, to boot.

"I know what you mean," he said. "My father was the same way after Mom's death. Be patient with your mother. This kind of grief and exhaustion can do strange things to the mind. And it can last a lot longer than anyone expects."

"Let me talk to Mom." She forced a smile and looked again into those blue eyes. "It'll be easier for all of us."

A few moments later, after taking a drink of water from the fountain and a few deep breaths to compose herself, Mercy opened the door to the private waiting room. The first thing she saw was Mom standing there in the middle of the floor, glaring in her direction.

"Where is that blasted doctor? I told them not to call you yet." Ivy Richmond turned to pace across the room toward the thickly cushioned sofa on the far side, then back again. "It's been over an hour, and no one has seen fit to tell me anything. Do you know that man came in here and asked for permission to just let Mother die?"

"Grandma had an advance directive, Mom."

"How can he just take it upon himself to decide who is and who isn't worthy to live? Mother couldn't have known what she was doing when she signed that form." Tears filled Ivy's eyes. "Oh, Mother."

Mercy's eyes grew moist, too. She'd thought they would have been drained of emotion months ago, but the stages of grief had continued to batter them. Right now confusion ran high, and Mercy knew Mom was exhausted and weak from too many nights of sleeplessness.

Ivy jerked another tissue from the box on an end table and blew her reddened nose. "I wish they hadn't called you against my wishes."

"It's a good thing they did."

Ivy stiffened at those words.

"She's gone, Mom."

Ivy's face twisted into a mask of pain. "Mother wasn't ready to die."

Mercy closed the door behind her and took a seat on the nearby recliner, perching on the edge with her hands in her pockets. "We're the ones who weren't ready."

Ivy turned away. "I can't believe my own daughter, the learned doctor, cannot grasp the reality of an afterlife."

Mercy suppressed a sigh. Now was not the time to bring up that old argument again, but if Mom had found peace in her so-called God these past few years, where was that peace now?

Ivy reached up toward her chest with both hands and bent forward, as if on a sob.

"Mom…?"

Ivy shook her head.

Mercy stepped up and laid a hand on her mother's shoulder. "Mom? Are you okay?"

Slowly Ivy straightened and turned around. Her face was as gray as the clouds gathering outside, but she nodded and patted Mercy's hand.

"I'll be fine. This just brings back so many memories."

"I know." Mercy's father had also died a lingering, painful death five years ago. That was when Mom had suddenly started babbling about "finding Jesus." At the time, Mercy was sure she would get over it, but she hadn't. Where was her Jesus now?

Ivy took a deep breath and squared her shoulders. "That doctor is dangerous. He doesn't hold human life sacred. He tried to manipulate me into allowing Mother to die. He was going to go over my head to keep from doing anything for her. Did he even try to save her?"

"He called a code. I saw it."

"How hard did he try?"

"He did everything to resuscitate her. He had already begun when I arrived."

"And he didn't revive her at all?"

"No."

"Is that normal for someone whose heart has just stopped?"

"It would be hard for me to say, Mom. Everyone is different. Most of the codes I get have been out for at least fifteen minutes."

"I think he could have bought us more time. Do you know that he as much as told me he had other patients who needed him more than she did and that doing more for her would be inhumane?" Ivy put a hand to her chest again, then quickly dropped it.

Mercy held her mother's dark gaze and said nothing.

"Jarvis didn't want this new doctor here in the first place, did he?" Ivy asked. They both knew that Dr. Jarvis George, E.R. director, had been bitterly opposed to bring in a full-time physician for the E.R.

"No, and neither did I. But to be fair, I disagreed with the code, too. I even tried to stop him. He did what he felt he had to, and I can't blame him for that. Granted, he could have been a little more tactful with you, but…"

"I'll have a talk with Jarvis. Maybe he can put my

mind at ease about this guy, but if he can't, I may have to have a talk with administration."

Lukas Bower could find his way around an unfamiliar hospital or a forest trail almost by instinct. Let him loose in a strange town, however, and he would be lost the moment he stepped out the door. By the time he entered the front door of the cantina—little more than a house with a small unlit sign in the front yard—where he was supposed to meet the others Wednesday night, the tiny place was nearly empty and a Hispanic waiter was clearing the tables. It still smelled wonderful, full of smoky spices and warmth.

Lauren waved at him from the far back left corner, where two smaller tables had been pushed together for a larger group. Much larger. Only Lauren was left.

"You're late," she called out, still waving for him to join her.

Lukas stood, staring at her in dismay. He had no desire to be rude, but he also had no desire to have dinner alone with a nurse who worked with him. Was he that late? Where were the others? Still, how could he turn around and walk out now?

He stepped hesitantly toward the back. "Sorry. I had to finish my charts; then I had to find this place. That turned out to be more of a challenge than I'd expected." He glanced at his watch. It was eight-thirty and the shift had ended at seven. Okay, so he was pretty late. "How long have you been waiting?"

"It's only been about twenty minutes since the last person left. Carol and Rita had to get home to their hubbies as soon as they ate. Connie and Ron, the ambulance team on duty tonight, got a call. Beverly and Buck had a lion to feed, and I know for a fact that Beverly took that Mustang by the car wash to clean it out." Lauren indicated the cluttered stack of plates that had not yet been cleared. "Sorry, you're stuck with just me." She signaled the waiter and kicked out a chair across the table from her. She had released her long, blond hair from its rubber band, and wispy tendrils framed a face devoid of makeup. "I ordered for you, and they've been keeping it warm in back."

Lukas wished she hadn't done that. "Could they make it to go? I'll just take it with me. There's no reason for you to have to sit—"

"Sorry, too late." She gestured toward the waiter, who carried out a sizzling platter of chicken, onion and peppers, and a steamer with hot flour tortillas. "I overheard you telling one of the patients today how much you loved authentic chicken fajitas, so I took the liberty of ordering them for you. Come on, sit down. They won't taste nearly as good cold."

This had been a stupid idea. Why had he agreed to come? But Lukas was hungry, and that hunger overrode his sense of caution. And this wasn't a date. He pushed the chair back in that she had kicked out for him, and instead he took the chair next to it, in spite of the mess of cluttered dishes he had to move aside. He would not get lured into an intimate dinner for two, or even the appearance of one.

If Lauren took offense at his small act of rebellion, her expression hid it well. She leaned back and rested her feet on the rail of the chair he had discarded. "Dig in, Doc. I know you're hungry. I don't think you've eaten anything since lunch, have you?"

"Breakfast, actually. Late breakfast." He bent his head in a short, silent blessing, then looked up to find Lauren nodding with approval. Big deal. The nurse in KC had pretended to approve of his faith, too, at first, until it got in the way of other things she wanted.

"Found a church yet?" Lauren asked, watching Lukas overstuff his first tortilla.

"Not yet. I haven't had a chance." He took a large bite, the force of which pushed half the meat and veggies back onto the plate from the wrap. The smoky heat so filled his mouth and senses that for a few seconds he didn't realize Lauren had resumed talking.

"…Covenant Baptist, just about four blocks from where you live."

Lukas shot her a wary glance as he chewed and swallowed. "You already know where I live?" He'd just been there a few days.

"Oh, don't worry, I'm not checking up on you. The real estate agent who sold you the place is a friend of mine," she explained as he took another bite and washed it down with water. "You don't grow up in a small town like Knolls without getting to know most of the other natives. Everyone's talking about the new full-time E.R. doc, and they probably all know where you live."

Lukas gulped another bite without comment. He, too, was from a small town, and because of that he knew he probably wouldn't be accepted here as one of them for twenty years.

"So do you think you'll come?" she asked.

He stopped chewing and looked at her.

"To church Sunday."

"I'll probably go somewhere." He built another fajita, this time with less filling, while Lauren chatted on about the hospital.

He learned quite a few interesting facts about his new

place of employment, such as the doubled volume of patients seen through the emergency department since Mrs. Estelle Pinkley took over as administrator five years ago. The lady had, according to Lauren, brought the hospital out of the computerless dark ages and out of debt for the first time in over a decade.

"But you'd better watch yourself," Lauren warned as Lukas finished his last bite of chicken. "The E.R. director doesn't want a full-time physician working here."

"Why not?"

She shrugged. "With Dr. George, who knows? He fought Mrs. Pinkley about the computers, too. He's about ready to retire, and he doesn't like change."

Lukas glanced around to find the waiter flipping around the Closed side of the sign in the front window. "Looks like we should be leaving. Will they give us a ticket at the cash register?"

"Don't worry, I paid it already."

Lukas reached into his pocket and pulled out a ten-dollar bill. He smiled as kindly as he knew how and placed the money on the table in front of her. He knew as he left that he was behaving like a jerk. It bothered him. Lauren seemed like a good, caring person, and she was probably just being kindhearted to a newcomer. Still, he wasn't going to take any chances.

Chapter Four

Thursday morning Lukas arrived at work later than usual, dripping with dew from the light rain outside. He could have kicked himself for oversleeping. The shift change would just have to be with the emergency department director, Dr. Jarvis George.

"Morning, Judy. Any patients waiting?" Lukas asked as he checked his mail cubicle.

"Good morning, Dr. Bower." The E.R. secretary for today's shift turned from her computer and smiled at him. "Dr. George is in the laceration room sewing a nursing-home patient who was injured when she became combative. We've got an irritable child in five and a possible sprain or fracture in seven. Dr. George hasn't seen them."

Lukas glanced at his watch. Even though he was ten minutes late, he had time to change into his scrubs. The patients weren't critical, and Dr. George would want to finish his own sutures. "Thanks, Judy. I'll be right back."

He glanced into the emergency room and glimpsed the director bent over his patient. Jarvis George's gray-white hair, army-cut short, could have depicted a kindly older gentleman who loved his patients and whose patients trusted and loved him. Maybe that was the case. Lauren's warning about Dr. George echoed from last night.

When Lukas walked into the laceration room a few moments later, he was friendly and upbeat.

"Good morning, Jarvis. Do we have any patients you want me to take?" He glanced at the elderly female who lay prone on the table, her nearly fleshless tailbone and hip exposing a small gash beside a partially healed bedsore.

The older man straightened from his work and pierced Lukas's friendliness with a glare. "I don't know how you were taught to address your superiors in your Kansas City hospital, Dr. Bower, but I prefer a little less familiarity, if you don't mind."

Lukas managed not to stare. "Excuse me, Dr. George. I meant no disrespect. I guess I am accustomed to a more casual atmosphere." Wow, Lauren was right. There seemed to be a problem here.

Dr. George returned to his sewing. "You can see to the whiny kid in five. He's got an earache. The patient in seven has a probable sprained ankle. I've been busy sewing, and since you came in late, I haven't had a chance to— Ouch!"

Lukas had watched it happen, had seen the needle pierce the glove in the palm of the man's left hand, and winced as he imagined the puncture.

"Can't believe I did that," the director muttered to himself. He shot a quick look toward Lukas, as if blaming him for the distraction.

Lukas stepped out of the room. "Nurse," he called and found redheaded Beverly coming from the child's room. "We need a needlestick protocol in here, please."

"I beg your pardon," Dr. George rumbled as he stepped around the laceration table and out toward Lukas. "Nurse, ignore that request," he said, not taking his gaze from Lukas.

Lukas cleared his throat, staring back at his new director in dismay. "I'm sorry, Dr. George, I didn't mean to offend. I've just been reading about protocol, and—"

"I'm aware of protocol, Bower," Dr. George snapped. "I helped write it."

Lukas winced. He was not winning a friend here.

The director waved Beverly away, still glaring at Lukas. "If you will kindly take care of your patients and leave me alone with mine, I'll be able to get home sometime this morning."

"Yes, Dr. George. Sorry. I'll go see my patients now." Lukas hustled away, resisting the urge to ask the director if his tetanus was at least up-to-date.

The sprain turned out to be a hairline fracture. The earache did not require antibiotics. After Lukas had splinted the ankle and convinced a distraught mother that the medicine she requested could actually set her child up for a more resistant strain of ear infection later, Lukas finished his charts and checked for more arrivals.

"Think I'll go to breakfast now, Beverly," he said when he found no other patients listed on the schedule board. He started down the hallway, then turned back. "Oh, by the way, where are the incident report forms kept?"

Beverly raised a brow at him. "They're filed in the secretary's cabinet. Tell me you're not going to report Dr. George."

"Rules are rules. Even if he doesn't follow protocol, I'm required to make a report. It's plainly listed in the little booklet I received the other day."

"You're going to find that we don't always follow the rules to the letter around here."

"Thanks, Beverly, but safety comes first. There's a good reason for those rules." He'd gotten into trouble before when he'd been lenient with a nurse and over-looked a break in protocol when she had violated a direct order from him. It gave her a chance to falsify the record.

"He'll find out. He knows everything that goes on around here," Beverly warned.

He waved and left for breakfast.

Theadra Zimmerman—Tedi to anyone who valued life—couldn't concentrate. She could barely keep her eyes open even to look outside, where the rain fell as if God had decided to wash off the new leaves and speed the growth of the grass.

Good thing she sat behind Jeff McCullough in class. His broad shoulders would cover her from Mrs. Watson's probing eyes and catch-you-off-balance questions. The fifth-grade teacher always seemed to ask Tedi more questions than anyone, and she even expected better answers from Tedi than she did from Abby Cuendet, who always got straight As.

Tedi leaned her chin down onto her fists on the desk as Mrs. Watson droned on about new discoveries regarding the rings of Saturn.

Dad and Julie had fought last night, the first time Tedi had heard them fight since they'd begun dating two months ago. Julie didn't like Dad drinking so much. Big surprise. Tedi didn't like it, either, but that didn't stop him. Last night she'd sat up in the hallway, eavesdropping, wondering if maybe he would listen to Julie, even though he wouldn't listen to anyone else.

When Julie finally left, she'd slammed the front door behind her. Apparently Dad had not listened to her, either.

Tedi felt a weird combination of disappointment and satisfaction. Why should a near stranger be able to do something she herself had tried to do for such a long time?

And what made Julie think that just because she was blond and pretty and wore a lot of makeup…

"Tedi Zimmerman, I asked you a question," came Mrs. Watson's sharp voice.

Tedi jerked. Her chin slipped off her fist.

Jeff's shoulders shifted as he turned to look at Tedi along with the rest of the fifth-grade class. This gave Mrs. Watson a clear view of Tedi trying to straighten up and look alert.

Mrs. Watson gave her that "I've had it with you, kid" look and shook her head.

"Class, I want you to read the next few pages on Neptune. No talking while I'm gone. Tedi, come with me."

For a moment Tedi sat and stared at Mrs. Watson. "Where?"

"Now, Tedi."

This was new.

"Theadra Zimmerman—"

"Okay." Tedi didn't look at anyone else as she got up and followed Mrs. Watson out the door. She could imagine Abby's smirk behind her back, but who cared? Nobody liked Abby.

Mrs. Watson closed the door on the classroom and turned to face Tedi, arms folded in front of her. "Ordinarily I would send a sleeping child to the nurse's office to take a nap, but you are not an ordinary child. I've had high hopes for you, but you've done more daydreaming, talking and disrupting than you've done homework in the past few weeks. I want to know why."

Tedi stared at her teacher's frowning face. She didn't look mad, but she wasn't happy.

"Are you taking me to the principal's office?" Tedi asked in a meek voice.

Mrs. Watson sighed and leaned against the hallway wall. She studied Tedi's face. "Does your father help you with homework?"

Uh-oh, she is going to drag Dad into this. "He's been really busy lately."

"How about your mother?"

"I don't see her every night." And she wasn't about to waste time on homework during visitations.

Mrs. Watson put a gentle hand on Tedi's shoulder. "What's going on at home?"

Tedi looked away. "Nothing."

Another sigh. "Look, I'm trying to be fair about this, but your parents are paying a lot of money to send you to this school, and—"

"My mother is paying the money."

Mrs. Watson nodded thoughtfully. "Nevertheless, this is an accelerated class, and you're falling behind. We need to do something about it."

Tedi didn't know what to say. She hadn't done all her homework lately. Dad wasn't there to nag her about it much, and it was just easier to read or watch TV.

"Come on."

Tedi's eyes widened. "Where are we going?"

"We're going to call your father. Maybe he can help us find out what the problem is."

Tedi drew back. "Why don't we call Mom? She's the one—"

"Your father has custody."

Tedi didn't move. "I still have a mother."

Mrs. Watson continued down the hallway. "Fine, stay there. Your father will find you there when he comes to get you." She turned around. "Unless you want to talk about it."

Tedi shrugged. "I guess he'll find me here." *Then he'll kill me. My blood and guts will be all over the hallway when class gets out. Hope it makes Abby Cuendet throw up.*

But then what would happen to Mom and Grandma Ivy?

At least an hour later, Tedi saw Dad coming down the hallway from the principal's office. She held her breath until he reached her. His neck and face were flushed all the way up to his short blond hair.

The bell rang, and classroom doors opened all along the hallway.

"Let's go," Dad said.

Tedi breathed again, following him out the side exit. She ignored the other kids as they rushed out of class. Dad ignored them, too, which probably broke Lyssa Cole's heart. She had a crush on him. She was weird.

After Tedi stepped into the passenger side of their red BMW, Dad slammed the door so hard she went cold all over. Yep, he was mad.

Her hands gripped each other tightly in her lap as the engine roared into life and the car sprang forward. Why had she been so stubborn with Mrs. Watson? She'd refused to even go back into the classroom and get her books. Now she'd not only be in trouble, but she would be making trouble for herself for later.

But she wasn't trying to be stubborn. Not really. She just hadn't wanted to face the class.

Okay, maybe she was a little mad at Mrs. Watson. Why did she expect so much?

Tedi glanced sideways at Dad. Was that alcohol she smelled?

He made a turn too fast, and Tedi fell against the door. She didn't have her seat belt on. She reached up and pulled it down and fastened it. Just in time.

Dad slammed on the brakes, screeching the tires for at least three feet.

Yes, that was alcohol on his breath.

Tedi looked at him. He had "patriotic" eyes—red, white and blue. She'd heard Mom use that term about him often enough that it wasn't funny anymore. Especially now.

He stared straight ahead. "You think I'm a reckless driver?" he demanded.

Reckless was a stupid word. Made it sound like you could never have a wreck. Dad was "wreckful," not "wreckless." He'd had several accidents to prove it.

"No, Dad, I don't think you're reckless. I just forgot to put my seat belt on when we got into the car. I always wear my seat belt. Mom makes me wear it. When you turned—"

Dad gunned the motor and sped along Highway F toward home. "I get your point."

How could he get a point she was trying not to make?

She glanced sideways at him again. "Um, Dad, would you please slow down a little? This is scaring me."

"You should've thought of that before you made that airhead teacher of yours call me."

Tedi grimaced with growing anger. "I didn't make her call you. I fell asleep in class, and she made a big deal out of it."

"That's not the way I heard it from her. I heard this isn't the first time you've caused trouble in class lately. Do you know she had me paged from an important luncheon meeting with some prospective buyers for the Reynolds Ranch? Do you know how much commission I stand to lose on that deal?" He turned into their drive at home.

Tedi wondered if that was one of those martini lunches she'd heard about. "Sorry I'm such a pain to you, Dad."

He didn't even catch the sarcasm in her voice. "If I lose that sale, we may think about taking you out of that fancy school of yours."

Tedi gritted her teeth. Why should he care? He wasn't paying for it.

He got out and slammed his door. She did the same with hers, pushing the door with as much force as she could. It made a satisfying *WHOMP!*

Dad just walked on up the sidewalk toward the front entrance.

Tedi opened the car door wide, then slammed it even harder. "I hate you," she said under her breath, glaring at Dad's back. "I hate you, hate you, hate you."

He unlocked the house and turned to wait for her.

She continued glaring.

He just waited.

Her glare wavered. Grandma Ivy said that hatred destroyed everything it touched. Tedi didn't really hate Dad. She just wanted him to stop drinking and stop saying bad things about Mom.

Dad kept waiting, and Tedi finally went in.

He closed the door behind them, slowly and quietly. He did that when he was really mad and trying to keep from losing his temper. He'd lost his temper and kicked a dog so hard once that he broke its ribs. He'd broken windows with his fists and kicked holes in walls. Always he'd been drinking when he did it.

"Can I go up to my room?" Tedi asked. "I'm tired."

He raised a brow at her. He didn't act drunk now. "Why are you tired? You went to bed early enough last night. Besides, you slept in class today, didn't you?"

His sarcastic tone made her madder. "Only because your fight with Julie kept me awake last night," she snapped. "I'm falling behind in class. Mrs. Watson thinks there might be something wrong at home. She asked me if you helped me with my homework, and I told her you were too busy." Tedi knew she shouldn't be saying all this, but she couldn't help herself.

"So I'm supposed to be doing your homework for you now? Is there something wrong with trying to make a living for my family?"

Tedi narrowed her eyes at him. "But you don't."

He stood for a long moment, glaring at her as red color once more crept up his face.

She glared back at him, heart pounding. She felt now as she did when she argued with Abby Cuendet during lunch—mad enough to say just about anything.

But Dad was bigger than Abby, and Abby didn't drink.

He took a step toward her.

"Can I go to my room now?" Without waiting for a reply, Tedi pivoted away from him.

His left hand came down hard on her right shoulder, and he jerked her around to face him, his thumb and fingers digging painfully into her flesh. His other hand drew back. Way back. His angry eyes burned out at her.

"Daddy, don't!" Tedi ducked.

She caught her breath and braced herself, tensing for a strike that didn't land. She remained braced for a long time, then raised her head to find Dad frozen in position, eyes wide, face drained of color.

He released her shoulder and lowered his hand, but

the pain still spurted down her arm. "Go to your room, Tedi." He took a deep breath and let it out. "I'm going back to work."

The spacious corner office that Dr. Jarvis George had used at Knolls Community for the past twenty years reflected the passion of his life: hunting. A moose head overlooked his credenza. The head and rack of a twelve-point buck peered out from between two glass-fronted bookcases filled with outdated medical texts. A rich, dark brown leather couch and two overstuffed chairs were situated so that visitors had a chance to peruse several hunting pictures taken in the field.

At the moment, Jarvis found no pleasure in his surroundings. He sat behind his massive oak desk and stared at the report. That insolent new doctor had decided to fill it out after that stupid needlestick incident this morning. The RMQA—risk management and quality assurance officer—was a personal friend. Dorothy had seen fit to call this to Jarvis's attention. Unfortunately, this was not the only copy. The administrator and chief of staff would know about it, and if anything came of it… But of course, nothing would.

Jarvis crumpled the sheet into a ball and threw it into the trash. "Big mistake, Bower."

He glanced at his left hand, flexed it. He'd scrubbed it well after the needlestick. There was nothing more to do. You don't catch Alzheimer's from contaminated blood, and that was this poor old gal's problem—increased dementia over the past weeks. Alzheimer's.

Someone knocked on the door. "Jarvis? You in there?"

The sound of Ivy Richmond's voice lightened his expression as he jumped up from his chair and rushed over to open the door for her.

His frown returned when he saw her face, drained of color and lacking its usual smile.

"Come in, dear, come in." He gently took her arm and led her to the leather couch, where he sat beside her. "How are the funeral arrangements coming? Do you need any help?"

Ivy shook her head and disengaged her arm from his grip. "Got it done. It'll be tomorrow at ten at my church. Will you sit with the three of us? No other family is coming."

"I'd be honored, Ivy. Pardon me for saying this, my dear, but you could do with some rest. Are you feeling okay?" He reached up and felt her cheek with the back of his hand.

She leaned her head back on the couch and closed her eyes. "Maybe some chest congestion…or something. I don't know. I'm just tired, Jarvis."

He eyed his stethoscope over on his desk, but before he could decide to get it, Ivy opened her eyes and fixed him with an intent look.

"I'm worried about something, and I don't know if I have a valid complaint. I'm just confused. I've gone through this grief process before, and I know what it can do to your mind. I think it's working a number on me, but I just can't tell."

Jarvis took Ivy's right hand in both of his. "Why don't you tell me about it? If there's anything in my power I can do to help, I'll do it. You know that."

She nodded. "But I'm not sure it's fair to drag you into it—not fair to you or Dr. Bower."

Jarvis tensed. "Dr. Bower?"

"I shouldn't even be talking to you about him. I know you didn't want him here."

"I still don't." And the whole thing was getting harder to swallow as time went on. "We don't need a full-time doctor here." And especially not Bower. Already two of Jarvis's regular patients had been treated by the younger doctor in the emergency room, and their glowing reports about Bower's compassion and kindness hit a raw nerve. He could be a horrible diagnostician, write scripts for all the wrong drugs, but as long as he had a "good bedside manner," he was praised as a good doctor. Sounded like slick politics. What about good, honest medicine? How long would it take Bower to convince administration to get rid of all the older docs and replace them with fresh grads who cared more about covering their tails from lawsuits than they cared about human beings?

Ivy pulled her hand from his.

Jarvis released her, shrugging off the bitter thoughts. "I'd like to think I'm enough of a professional to be objective. I think I can make a sound judgment call, especially for your sake."

She shook her head and sighed. "I may be stirring up trouble for nothing."

"Hey, I've been practicing objectivity as long as I've been practicing medicine. You trust me as a friend, don't you?"

"Yes."

"Then let's figure out this Bower business together."

Ivy took another deep breath, let it out and leaned forward, elbows on knees. "I had to fight him to get him to try to save Mother yesterday. I felt as if he wanted to dismiss her as just a dying old woman. Maybe it was my emotions talking, I don't know, but I question his ethics, Jarvis. I don't think he holds human life sacred. That's important to me, especially in my financial relationship to this hospital." She spread her hands "What do we know about him?"

"Just the basics. What do you want to know? I'll try to find out for you."

"For instance, what is his background? Where did he come from? I know he's a Doctor of Osteopathy. Is he an experienced emergency room physician? How does he feel about abortion and euthanasia?" She shook her head apologetically at Jarvis. "I'm sorry, but these are questions I really want answered."

Jarvis frowned. Okay, maybe he was going to have more trouble with objectivity than he thought. It was too tempting to play on Ivy's suspicions, but it wouldn't be fair to Ivy. He didn't care about Bower.

"I don't know much about him," Jarvis said. "His credentials are obviously in order, or our administrator would not have cleared him to treat patients here. She's conscientious. I've heard that Bower comes from Truman Medical Center in Kansas City, so he's obviously had some good experience."

"Is he board certified?"

"I don't think so. Most docs will include that with their title, and he hasn't. He would at least have done his internship before he could practice medicine in Missouri, so I'm sure he has a permanent licensure."

"Did he bring any references from Truman?"

"I'm sure he did, but no one has seen fit to share them with me. Remember, I'm just the director." Jarvis didn't try to keep the resentment from his voice. It had even been suggested by the hospital's chief financial officer that this new upstart should receive the director title since he was going to be the only full-time physician on staff for emergency room. Even the gung ho administrator had refused to consider that—for now. She'd suggested that they try this guy out first and see how capable he was. These people had no loyalty to their tried-and-true medical staff.

"Jarvis, did you hear me? Do you know anyone at Truman? I would think after all these years and all the medical seminars you've attended—"

Jarvis straightened. "Of course. One of the advanced trauma life-support instructors is a trauma surgeon at Truman. I've taken the course with him several times, not that I couldn't teach it myself if I were so inclined."

"Would he have worked with Dr. Bower?"

Jarvis got up from the couch and went to his desk. He fanned out a business card file. "Dr. Sal Probstfield just happens to be a duck hunter. Ducks aren't my forte, of course, but you get a couple of hunters into a room with 150 golfers, racquetballers and tennis jocks, the hunters will tend to find each other. Ah, here it is." He pulled out a card with a mallard printed on it.

"Don't tell me that a trauma surgeon hands out business cards."

"For his guide service. During duck season he takes groups out on hunting trips. It's what he plans to do with his time when he retires in three years."

"Sounds like you know him pretty well."

Jarvis reached toward the speakerphone and punched his numbers. "Well enough to get information from him about Bower."

They reached Dr. Probstfield at home. After a few preliminaries, Jarvis asked, "Sal, we have a new full-time doctor down here. Does the name Lukas Bower mean anything to you?"

There was a pause, then a low whistle. "So you're the guys who stole our whiz kid."

Ivy raised a brow at Jarvis. She mouthed the words, "Whiz kid?"

Sal continued. "He's awful at hospital politics, so his colleagues tend to resent him. He's great with patients and diagnoses and he puts on a good show of confidence, so his colleagues tend to resent him." He chuckled at his own attempt at humor. "Give him time. He's not obnoxious. He's just got a small problem with social graces. He's not as cocky or self-confident as he seems."

Jarvis saw the relief in Ivy's expression.

Sal's voice came again. "Those guys over at Cunningham Memorial lost themselves a good internist when they kicked him out of the residency program."

Ivy's head jerked up.

Jarvis stiffened, trying to control the surge of hope he felt. "What?"

"You know he's not board certified, don't you? That's why. The hospital's board of internal medicine decided he was endangering patients, and they fired him. He never got into another residency program. I know the trainer Bower had over there. Vicious man, very vindictive. He didn't like being shown up, and I'd hazard a guess that Bower did so without even realizing it. The director of internal medicine backed up Bower's trainer. They even tried to block Bower's permanent licensure. I hear he had to take them to court to get it through."

"I see," Jarvis muttered, glancing at Ivy. "Is that all you know about it, Sal?"

There was a pause. "I've heard other rumors, but nothing was substantiated."

"How did they feel he was endangering patients?"

"You'll have to get that information from somebody else. Remember, I liked the guy. All you have to do is ask Bower about it. He's an innocent, and he's never learned to keep his mouth shut."

"Thanks, Sal, I owe you. See you soon." Jarvis hung up and looked at Ivy. "I know some people at Cunningham. I'll give them a call later and see if I can come up with more info."

"Why don't you just ask Dr. Bower?" Ivy suggested.

Jarvis shot her a skeptical glance. "I'll call Cunningham."

Chapter Five

Lukas didn't often visit a patient after admitting, because he didn't want to interfere with the family docs. Friday morning, however, he'd received a special request from ICU that he could not refuse.

Mr. Franklin Verris had apparently just awakened from his mysterious deep sleep late yesterday evening, and he wanted to meet the doctor who, according to Dr. Robert Simeon, had probably saved his life. Dr. Simeon must be mistaken, and Lukas intended to tell Mr. Verris that.

Mr. Verris looked different in a hospital gown, but someone had been kind enough to bring him his teeth and help him comb his full head of white hair. His skin appeared pink and healthy this morning. Shelly had probably been by to see him already.

"Mr. Verris?" Lukas said quietly as he stepped up to the bed. "I'm Dr. Bower. I saw you in the emergency room Wednesday."

The man glanced at Lukas, nodded and reached up to take Lukas's hand in a firm shake. "Call me Frankie. My doctor tells me you kept me from doing something terrible. I thank you." He looked away. "I don't...don't know what got into me."

Lukas bent closer. "Frankie, did you take too much medication?"

There was a slight pause, then the man nodded, still not looking at Lukas.

"But your prescription bottle was almost full."

Frankie sighed. "I know. Tuesday evening I was going through the medicine cabinet for the first time since...since my wife died. I came across her bottle of Xanax. She used it sometimes to help her sleep when her arthritis acted up."

"So you did take hers." Lukas had noticed that the script was for sixty pills.

"She'd used about half the bottle before she died." Frankie closed his eyes for a moment, then opened them and looked at Lukas. His eyes were pale gray. It made him seem more vulnerable. "Tuesday was the sixtieth anniversary of our first date. When I saw that bottle, it occurred to me that I enjoyed life with Doris so much more than I enjoy life now, I just wanted to be with her again. I didn't want to live." He shrugged. "No reason to. No children or family."

"I'm sorry you felt that way. You do seem to have some neighbors who care about you a great deal." Lukas could have kicked himself for not trusting his own instincts. "How do you feel now?"

Frankie considered the question for a moment. "I've been thinking about Doris a lot today. When I allow myself to believe, as she insisted, that her spirit still lives, I feel better." A gentle smile lit his face.

That was it. Lukas realized that the lines of this man's face held humor. That was another reason why Lukas couldn't believe he had tried to kill himself when he came into the emergency room the other day.

"Was Mrs. Verris a Christian?" Lukas asked.

"Yes. Oh, I know a lot of people claim to be Christians, then live like the devil, but my wife...my sweet, giving wife..." The man's eyes filled with tears. "She lived it." He looked out the window for a moment and waited for his eyes to clear. "How she put up with an old reprobate like me for so long, I don't know. When the drug started taking effect the other day, it occurred to me that I probably wouldn't follow her anyway."

"Why is that?"

"God would kick me out of heaven."

"He doesn't kick His own children out. You don't share your wife's faith?"

Frankie continued as if he hadn't heard Lukas. "My wife was the most beautiful woman in the world." He said it softly, as if he were recalling her face. "She was beautiful inside, as well as outside, and she just grew more beautiful over the years." His attention returned to Lukas. "I want to thank you for giving me another chance."

"I'm glad I was here to help." Lukas paused, then cleared his throat. "There is a way to make sure that you follow Doris when you do leave this earth."

Frankie shook his head slowly. "I could never be the kind of person Doris was."

"You don't have to be. God created you as you are, and He wants you as you are."

Frankie continued to shake his head.

"Tell me," Lukas said, "would Doris be silly enough to worship a useless God?"

Frankie glanced sharply at Lukas. "My wife was a very wise lady. She wasn't silly."

"Then wouldn't the God she worshiped at least be able to love you and accept you as generously as she did?"

Frankie watched Lukas for a moment. "You're a Christian."

"Yes, I am."

"You talk just like Doris used to." His eyes filled with tears again. "Sure do miss her."

"Then why don't you start making your travel plans— and not the way you did Wednesday. Why don't you make sure you can be with her again? Get to know her Savior personally. Then when the time comes, in His time, not yours, He will see to it that you find her. Meanwhile, Frankie, He will be with you here, and He'll give you peace you never believed you could have…or deserve."

"What makes you think He'd do that for me?"

"He did it for me, and He keeps forgiving me every time I mess up. I keep asking Him to use me, and He sent you my way at just the right time. He loves you and wants you to join Him."

More tears filled Frankie's eyes, and this time he let them fall. "Give me some time to think about it."

"Okay, Frankie. Meanwhile, I'll be praying for you." Lukas laid a hand on the man's arm and squeezed, then said a silent prayer for him as he walked back to the emergency room.

Beverly was on duty that morning, and she met him as he entered. Stereotypical as it seemed, Beverly had a quick, impulsive temperament to match her flaming red hair. At the moment, the color of her face also matched her hair.

"Dr. Bower, there's a very obnoxious patient in three who has threatened to sue if I don't personally escort you to see him now." She lowered her voice. "His father is Bailey Little."

At Lukas's blank expression, she explained, "You know, Bailey Little, the attorney. He's the president of our hospital's board of directors."

"So the son is in the E.R. throwing his father's weight around?"

"Yes. I know you want to get to that funeral."

"But you don't think this one can wait." All he needed was a difficult patient whom Dr. Camp might refuse to take over when he arrived. It had been hard enough to convince someone to let him off a couple of hours, especially since he wasn't sure himself why he felt the need to attend the funeral of a stranger.

He glanced at his watch. It was only eight o'clock. If all the ancillary services would cooperate, he could take care of this patient and still make the service.

"Okay, Beverly, what's his complaint?"

Beverly lowered her voice. "He's out of his stuff, if you ask me."

Lukas raised a brow at her. "Drug seeker?"

She nodded, folding her arms across her chest, her thick, red brows drawn together in a disapproving glower.

"Okay, I'll come willingly. What does he say is the problem?"

"Headache. Again."

"Again? He's been in for this before?"

"Yes. At least twice when I was on duty, and I think he's been here a lot more than that, according to the secretary."

"Which doctor treated him?"

"Dr. George."

"And he got the drugs?"

"Dr. George believed his story. Dwayne is a good actor. Besides, Dr. George is good friends with Dwayne's father. Dwayne even calls him 'Uncle Jarvis.'"

"Pull Mr. Little's old chart, will you?"

"Sure thing." She turned to go, then hesitated and turned back. "I wouldn't cross this guy, Dr. Bower, not unless you can afford to lose your job. I know I can't."

"Thanks for the warning, Beverly."

She watched him for a moment. "I mean it. I heard about you turning in Dr. George for the needlestick. Bailey Little can get us both in trouble, and I've got kids to support."

Lukas frowned. "You're not going to get into trouble for doing your job."

He found the clipboard for room three at the central desk, then added a copy of a special form he had brought with him from KC.

The patient who perched on the doctor's exam stool in the darkened room didn't look like a typical drug abuser. Lukas wondered if Beverly had just been irritated by the man's personality. The young man, in his early to midtwenties, sat cradling his forehead in his hands. He wore a dark brown suit. His hair was short and neat. He looked clean. He glanced up when Lukas entered, then put his head back down and groaned.

"Hello, Mr. Little, I'm Dr. Bower." Lukas placed the clipboard down on the counter and remained standing. "I hear you have a headache this morning."

"Yeah, Dr. Bower." The man continued to rub his forehead. "It's the worst I've ever had."

"Then you've had headaches like this before? Any nausea associated with them? Fever?"

"I've had some before, but not as bad as this. I'm puking my guts out."

Lukas knew from checking the chart that the man's temperature was normal. "Have you ever seen a doctor for headaches before, Mr. Little? Ever had a CT head scan?"

"Not yet." The man leaned forward and pulled a card out of his back pocket. "Here. I'm supposed to go see a Dr. Pippin next week in Springfield. He's a neurologist."

Lukas took the card and glanced at it. It was a blank appointment card, one anybody could pick up from a front desk of a busy office. Lukas was not impressed.

"What time is your appointment? Maybe I can call for an earlier—"

"I don't have an appointment yet, okay?" the man snapped. "Look, I've had this thing for two days, and it's getting worse. Are you going to help me, or—"

Beverly rushed into the room. "Dr. Bower, we just put an asthma patient in six who sounds really tight. She's not panicky or anything, but—"

"I'll be there." Lukas reached for the clipboard.

"Hey, hold it a minute!" Little came halfway off his stool. "What about me? I want to know about my headache."

"Sorry, Mr. Little, I'll be back," Lukas soothed. "We have an emergency." He knew the irony of his words would be lost on this guy.

In exam room six, a woman in her forties sat forward on the bed with her legs dangling over the side. She wore a clear face mask attached by six feet of tubing to an oxygen regulator on the wall at the head of the bed. Lukas saw that her oxygen was running at 12 liters. Good. Beverly knew her stuff. The patient wore a pulse ox gauge on her right forefinger. It looked like a plastic clothespin with a thin cable attached to a small box on the bed.

Lukas glanced over Beverly's shoulder as she hurriedly took the woman's vitals. The O_2 sat had been 87 percent before the mask. Not good.

He stepped around to the other side of the exam table. "Good morning, Mrs. Knight."

"Miss. I'm Darlene," she said between breaths.

"Thank you, Darlene. I'm Dr. Bower. I'm going to listen to your lungs to get a better idea about what's going on." He pressed his stethoscope against her back and heard a soft, musical wheeze, both inspiratory and expiratory. She was moving very little air.

He straightened. "Beverly, do you have the vitals yet?"

"Yes, Doctor. BP 130 over 90, heart rate 120, respiration 36, temp 100.6."

"Okay, thank you." He gave orders for IV treatment and reassured Darlene. While Beverly carried out the orders, he went to the desk and ordered a stat respiratory therapy, blood tests and a chest X-ray.

Beverly had the IV established and was pushing the Solu-Medrol when he returned.

He glanced at the chart. "Darlene, we'll have someone here in a few minutes to give you a breathing treatment. It's going to help."

She nodded, not looking at him, still fighting to breathe. "Thanks."

Lukas frowned at her for a moment. Interesting. Her eyes were bloodshot, and dark circles shadowed them— not the typical signs of an asthmatic. She avoided eye contact. She acted as if she had other things on her mind. Other asthmatics watched every move he and the nurse made, desperate for help, needing their reassurance and attention.

He sat down in front of her. "After we get your breathing improved, then we'll need to do some tests to check you out." He glanced at the chart again. Beverly had only had time to do the vitals, not a complete assessment.

"Do you take any medicines, Darlene?"

She shook her head. "Supposed to take theophylline and two inhalers, but I haven't lately. I ran out. Can't afford refills."

Lukas nodded. "Any drug allergies?"

She shook her head.

"Any chance of pregnancy?"

This got her attention. She shot him a very startled look, blushed, shook her head. "No."

"Sorry, I had to ask. We're doing an X-ray."

She shot him another startled look. "Do you have to? I don't have insurance."

He considered it a moment. He'd like to see an X-ray, but with the other tests, it may not be necessary. "Okay, we'll put a hold on that for now, but we still may need it, depending on what the other tests show." That could be what was bothering her.

She looked slightly relieved.

"Hello." There was a knock at the open door, and Kaye, the respiratory tech, walked in. "Are you Darlene Knight? I've got orders to make you start feeling better, or I lose my job. Got a few minutes?"

Lukas smiled at her. "Thanks for coming so quickly, Kaye. Darlene, I'll be back after your treatment." He braced himself to face the man with the migraine.

"Do you make a habit of abandoning your patients in this emergency room?" Mr. Little demanded as Lukas walked back in and laid the clipboard down on the counter.

"Not if we can avoid it," Lukas said calmly. "Would you mind stepping to the bed?"

"Why?"

"If I'm going to treat you, I'm going to check you out. Please move to the bed. If you need some help, I can—"

"I don't need help," the man snapped, then grudgingly obeyed Lukas.

Lukas checked heart, lungs, reflexes. Normal. Then he lowered the lights and checked the eyes. Bingo. They were pinpoint, no dilation. In this dimly lit room, that didn't fit.

He picked up the chart. "Mr. Little, it says here that you're allergic to Imitrex and Reglan. Those are our drugs of choice for migraine. What medications have you taken before?"

"Demerol and morphine work best."

"But I can't in good conscience give you a narcotic without running some tests to make sure you're not in danger. I need a CT and a urine—"

"What?" Little brought his hands down from his head and glared at Lukas. "What're you trying to do to me? I just want some simple pain relief! No urine test."

Lukas checked the time. Forty-five minutes until Camp took over. No problem with this patient; he was about to leave. Federal law had to be satisfied first, though. Lukas knew the regulations well. Unfortunately, Little probably did, too, if he was habitual.

Darlene was another problem. For some reason, Lukas wanted to finish her himself.

"Okay, Mr. Little, I'll send the nurse in with a shot for you."

The man visibly relaxed. "It's about time."

Lukas had Beverly take a dose of Toradol to Mr. Little in room three while Lukas looked for and found the young man's old chart at the central desk. Very interesting—eleven E.R. visits in four months, all for pain shots and pills. How many other area hospitals had records on him?

"Carol, please call the area emergency departments

and check to see if Mr. Dwayne Little has visited them recently for pain medication."

Carol raised a brow at him. "Yes, Doctor, but you know who he is, don't you?"

"Yes. Thank you for your concern."

Lukas returned to Darlene in room six.

She still wore her mask and the finger probe. Her O_2 sat was still low, but better. Her arterial blood gas turned out to be better than Lukas had expected. He checked her breathing.

The wheezing was louder. Good. That meant more air movement. She was still working for her air, but she was holding her own.

"Well, Darlene, you're doing better, but we've got a way to go yet. You're still doing some inspiratory and expiratory wheezing. I can't send you home like this."

Her eyes grew wide. "Please, Doctor, don't put me in the hospital. I can't stay."

"We'll see. I want to give you a couple more treatments. How long have you been breathing this poorly?"

"Not quite a week. It didn't get really bad until yesterday. I know I should have come in sooner, but I already feel much better."

The woman was slightly more animated than she had been a few moments ago, but not much. Lukas would guess by the circles beneath her eyes that there were other things going on he hadn't discovered yet. Stress could bring on an asthma attack, especially when exacerbated by lack of sleep.

"Dr. Bower," came Beverly's flustered voice from the doorway. She glanced at Darlene, then back at Lukas. "The patient refuses the shot."

Lukas excused himself with Darlene and walked with

Beverly to the central desk. "Of course he refuses the shot," he said. "It's not a narcotic. He probably requested Demerol."

"His usual," Beverly muttered.

"Please make a notation on your chart that pain relief was offered and he refused it. Did he give a reason?"

"Said he'd had it before and it upset his ulcer." She looked around and lowered her voice. "I don't think it's a good idea to mess with this guy. He could cause a lot of trouble for all of us. I told you, I can't afford to lose my job."

"We could cause him a lot of trouble, too. It doesn't change the treatment plan. There's no record of ulcer history or medication. Time for our trump. Would you please call for Kaye to give Darlene another treatment? Then I need you to join me in room three. I need a witness."

"For what?"

"You'll see. Carol, what did you find out?"

The secretary bit her lip and glanced toward the room where Little waited. "He's been to at least three different places several times each in the past two months."

"Thank you. Call them back and warn them that he may be a drug seeker and he may be headed their way soon."

While Beverly called for Kaye, Lukas filled out his part of the form he'd placed with Little's chart earlier. They went together to room three.

"Mr. Little, so sorry to hear about your ulcer. Is it still giving you trouble?"

"That's not what I'm here for," the patient snapped.

"Sorry. You're not allergic to morphine in any way, are you?"

The man couldn't hide his surprise. "No."

"Good. I think we can fix you right up." Lukas couldn't resist a glance at Beverly. She gaped at him in shock mixed with relief. He grinned. "First, Mr. Little, I have a form for you to sign." He pulled out the sheet he'd just filled out and put it at the top of the papers on the clipboard. He placed it under Little's nose. "I need you to read this over first, of course. It states that you are aware of the nature of the drugs I am going to give you, and that you understand the effects Narcan has on you if you are an addict. It will precipitate violent withdrawal symptoms, up to and including death."

The man's mouth flew open. "Narcan!"

"Yes. Maybe you're familiar with it? It's a narcotic antagonist. You'll still get good pain relief from the morphine, but you will not have to put up with the resulting high. I was sure you would approve." He pushed the sheet forward. "Your signature, Mr. Little."

The man jumped from the bed. "You're saying I'm a junkie!"

"Not at all. I'm saying that if you aren't an addict, you should have no problem with this course of pain relief. If you do have a problem, we can get you into a drug treatment prog—"

Little stomped toward the door, shouldering Beverly aside. "I'm getting out of here. You people are crazy." He turned back and pointed a finger at Lukas. "You won't get away with this, Bower. Do you know who my father is?"

"Does your father know you're here looking for drugs?"

Little swung away and stalked out of the hospital.

"Dr. Bower!" Beverly exclaimed. "You don't listen very well."

"He was a drug seeker. What did you want me to do?"

"He could get us both into a lot of trouble."

"How can you get into trouble for doing your job and following the doctor's orders?"

She stared at him, shaking her head. "Those shots could have killed that man."

Lukas nodded. "Don't worry. I've never had anyone take me up on the offer. Where do we keep the AMA forms? If he's going to refuse medical advice, we need to fill one out, and we both need to sign it."

Beverly stared at him a moment longer. "They're at the central desk. I need to check on Darlene, so just have Carol get it out for me to sign later."

Darlene's numbers still weren't up to acceptable levels when Lukas checked her again. She wheezed only upon expiration now—a good sign. But Lukas didn't yet feel comfortable.

"I feel so much better, Doctor," Darlene said. Healthy pink tinged her cheeks now, and her posture was more relaxed. "Can I go home?"

"I'm sorry, Darlene, but I can't make any promises at this point. I'll cut your oxygen down and see how you do. I'll waive the X-ray. But we have to watch you awhile longer before I can decide."

She stared at him rebelliously for a moment, as if she might check herself out against medical advice.

Lukas glanced at his watch. Thirty minutes until Camp got here. Lukas completed some charts, then returned to Darlene's room and took her off the oxygen to see how she would do on room air. Then he went to change out of his scrubs. He would be cutting it close, but he still didn't feel right leaving Darlene.

After fifteen minutes on room air, Darlene did a peak flow test. She registered 250, which was not enough for her age, weight and sex.

"I'm sorry, Darlene," Lukas said. "We tried."

She moved halfway off the table, her eyes wide. "Please, can you give me another treatment before you make your decision? I can't stay."

He went into his usual spiel. "I know it's never convenient to be sick, but—"

"I'm not talking about convenience." Her whole body radiated tension. "I have to go home. I'll be fine."

"Is it worth risking your life? You can work out a payment plan with the hospital. Asthma can be fatal if not treated properly."

"I'll take care of it," she snapped.

"You weren't taking your medicine before. I don't think you realize how—"

"Please, Dr. Bower! I have a brother at home who needs me. He doesn't have anyone else to help him. I didn't even want to leave him this morning, but I just couldn't breathe anymore."

So that was what was going on. Lukas sat down. Time to find out more. "What's wrong with your brother?"

Her warm hazel eyes shimmered with tears. Her finger worried the pulse ox probe as if she'd like to slip it off and falsify the reading. "Clarence is very sick, and he won't see a doctor."

"Sick?"

"He's extremely obese. The last time he got on the scales, he broke them. He made a big joke of it, but that was two years ago. He's gained continually since then. He doesn't leave the house, and these past few weeks, I've had to take his meals to his room. The only place he goes is to the bathroom."

"He won't see a doctor?"

She shook her head as tears flowed down her cheeks. Lukas set a Kleenex box beside her on the bed.

"He's given up. He's tried so hard. He was such a hard worker, so proud of his mechanic skills. He helped me buy my house, then he lost his job because of a layoff. Which meant he lost his insurance. Then he developed pneumonia, went into the hospital, and used up the last of his savings to pay the bill. He had to give up his own home and move in with me, which really hurt his pride. He went into a deep depression, and he just kept gaining weight."

"You can't convince him to see a doctor?"

"He knows I can't pay for it. Even when I worked outside the home as a bookkeeper, I couldn't put him on my company insurance. I ended up having to quit my job and stay home and work as an indexer on computer so I could take care of him."

"Surely he qualifies for disability." Lukas couldn't believe his own words, but if anyone truly needed state aid, this family did.

"He wouldn't consider it."

"But doesn't he see what he's doing to you?"

"He can't help it. He's just waiting to die. That's why I have to go home. I don't dare leave him alone for long. Please let me go. We don't…we aren't close to family."

"Are you sleeping at night?"

"Not well."

"You need more help. This is too much of a strain on you. Would you consider counseling?"

She pulled a single tissue from the box and dabbed at her face. She took another tissue and blew her nose. "I don't have the money."

"There are local agencies that can help. We can make some calls for—"

"No."

He sighed in frustration. "Darlene, sometimes we all have to ask for help. That's why those agencies are set up, for people like you, who are really struggling, trying to make an honest living for yourself and your brother. There is no shame in—"

She burst into tears. "Please let me go home, Dr. Bower. I can't ask those people for help. Clarence and I were second-generation welfare kids. We grew up on handouts. We swore together when we left that mess that we would die before we asked for help again. We meant it."

Lukas bit his tongue. Clarence might indeed die. Darlene obviously knew that.

He gave her a spare inhaler, some antibiotic samples, and a theophylline tablet, then gave her a script for that, and for Vistaril to help her sleep.

"These are fairly inexpensive," he told her as he handed them to her. "Take them. You really need them. Remember that you're not going to be able to care for Clarence if you end up back here."

She stared at the bounty he had given her, then looked up at him. "You mean you're letting me go home?"

"Against my better judgment. I wish I could do more to help you. If you need someone to talk to, call me."

For the first time since she'd arrived, he saw her smile. She reached out and grabbed his right hand with both of hers. "Oh, thank you, Doctor. Thank you."

Chapter Six

Dad backed the red BMW out of the drive, with Tedi safely buckled in, just like on any other school day. This day, however, Tedi was getting out of classes. For the first time in her life she would rather be going to school.

Granny Jane had been sick almost for as long as Tedi could remember, and Tedi had felt so bad for her. It hurt to watch someone suffering the way Granny Jane had suffered, and Tedi knew it had been really hard on Mom and Grandma Ivy. That's why she had to go to this funeral. She wanted to be there for them.

"I'll drop you off in front of the church," Dad said as he turned onto the highway from their street.

"Fine." Tedi didn't look at him, but she felt him looking at her. Last night she'd hid out in her bedroom when he came home, and he hadn't bothered her.

This morning Dad had fixed her favorite breakfast: French toast and fruit, with powdered sugar and hot maple syrup. Dad could cook when he wanted to, and this morning he'd done almost as good a job as Grandma Ivy. Almost.

"How about a trip into Springfield this weekend?" he asked. "We can go to the mall and get some summer clothes, then catch a movie, maybe do the zoo while we're there. They've got a new baby elephant."

Tedi didn't stir from her inspection of the roadside scenery. "You go ahead, Dad. Maybe Julie would like to go."

"Julie doesn't like elephants. You and I do."

Tedi shrugged. "I'm not in the mood."

Dad sighed. He slowed the car and pulled to the side of the road. He turned on the flashers, then turned in his seat to face Tedi.

"Aren't you even going to let me try to make up for yesterday? I should never have scared you like that."

"You were drinking." She watched a robin hopping along the wire fence beside the road.

"That's no excuse."

Tedi turned to look at him then and almost gave in at the pleading look in his eyes, the sorrowful expression on his face. But she knew that could all change in a second. She was tired of it. "I'm not excusing you, Dad. I'm telling you that your drinking scares me. I'm still scared. I don't know when it's going to happen again. I never know. That was a good breakfast this morning, and Springfield could be fun, but nothing makes up for being scared of my own father. You get mad too easy when you're drinking."

His intent blue eyes held hers for a moment. "What'll make it up to you? How about I lay off the booze for a while?"

She bit her lip and took a deep, long breath. *Here it comes.* "How about I go live with Mom until you're off the booze?" She continued to hold his gaze so he'd know she meant it.

He looked away first, but not before she saw a flash of anger in his expression. Big surprise. She braced herself for another temper tantrum.

"She doesn't want you," he said quietly.

Tedi caught her breath. She hadn't been braced for that. "Why not?"

He didn't look back at her. "She's too busy with her job." His voice was bitter. "Got to make the almighty buck. You'll just slow her down." He turned off the flashers and signaled to pull back onto the highway.

"You're lying! If I ask her to, she'll take you back to court for custody."

A break came in the traffic, but Dad didn't take it. His face lost color until it nearly matched the shade of his short, light blond hair. "She'll be sorry if she does." He looked down at Tedi with narrowed eyes. "Don't forget why I have custody in the first place—mental patients don't make good parents."

Tedi almost said, "Neither do drunks," but she remembered yesterday.

"And public opinion matters here in Knolls," he continued. "She's spent these past five years trying to rebuild her practice after the last custody battle. She won't thank you if she loses it all again." He pulled out onto the road at last.

Tedi said nothing more until they reached Grandma Ivy's church—Covenant Baptist—at the edge of Knolls. Grandma and Mom stood outside the building waiting for her. She waved at them, then released her seat belt and opened the door.

Someday she would learn to shut her mouth and keep it shut, but not today. Today she was mad.

"You know, Dad," she said as she stepped from the car,

"if Mom lost her job, we'd all be in big trouble." She slammed the car door as hard as she could and turned toward the church.

Seconds later, Dad gunned the motor. The tires spun on blacktop.

Tedi waved at her mother and grandmother and wished her father would drive out of her life forever.

Lukas Bower hated the term "backseat Baptist." It implied a person one step away from backsliding. Although Lukas always preferred to sit at the periphery of the congregation, he by no means felt himself to be at the spiritual edge of God's family. Just because he was shy did not mean he was not a sincere Christian.

On the other hand, he knew he had a lot of growing to do before he was a mature Christian.

It was a moot point in this church today, since this was not a worship service.

The first strains of soft organ music reminded him of the circumstances leading up to today's funeral, and he had the typical critique session with himself. He could have shown more compassion to Ivy Richmond during Mrs. Conn's final hour. He could have tried harder to reassure Mrs. Conn during those short moments of lucidity—if indeed she had truly been lucid.

He could not, however, have been more aggressive with the code. Ivy Richmond probably disagreed, but he could do nothing about her sentiments, much as he would like to. She obviously possessed a great deal of power at the hospital, and he didn't have enough insight into her character to know how she might play that power. She was strong willed, much like another, younger woman with power whose influence had affected his career with devastating ease. Best not to allow his thoughts to wander in that direction.

Lukas couldn't decide whether to approach the Richmond ladies with his condolences after the service or to leave them in peace today. The latter course looked more favorable as more and more people filled the auditorium, and the old, familiar prickling of self-consciousness made him wonder why he had even bothered to come. No one would have expected him to. He'd lost other elderly patients and hadn't felt it necessary to see them off. Doctors didn't do this kind of thing, especially not for someone they didn't even know.

Dr. Mercy Richmond, however, was a colleague, and although she had covered her feelings well on the day of her grandmother's death, he had identified with her loss. He'd had several recollections of his mother's death three years ago. Maybe that was why he was here.

A shadow loomed low outside the window near his seat, then pulled up at the last second—a robin on a strafing run. Her aerodynamics put modern technology to shame, just as God's design of the human body made modern medicine look like kids playing with a chemistry set from Toys "R" Us. Lukas felt that way sometimes, as if he were playing games with the lives of his patients. But he wasn't playing. Some people had even complained that he took things far too seriously, and perhaps they were right. But how could he behave any other way?

The robin sidled along the roof guttering, oblivious to Lukas and the rapidly filling auditorium. She used her beak to toss rotted leaves out onto the yard. Then she selected some good stems she could carry and flew to a neighboring tree.

Maybe Lukas could entice the robins to clean out the

guttering on his new house. Guess one could say the guttering had gone to the birds, he spent so little time there. He'd never been good at home maintenance, mostly because he seldom paid attention to his surroundings. He'd spent too much time in hospitals these past few years. But home was lonely and had been for a long time.

He needed to force himself to get out and meet people, take part in some activities, find something that would interest him in community service. Knolls was a nice, peaceful little town, complete with a town square that surrounded the courthouse. As a center of industry, Knolls drew people from the surrounding area for employment. The population nearly doubled on weekdays, thus increasing the need for more restaurants and shopping centers—and a full-time physician in the hospital emergency room to take care of accidents.

"Dr. Bower?"

Lukas looked up with a start to find Lauren McCaffrey standing expectantly beside the pew where he sat.

"Yes?"

"May I sit here?" She gestured around the nearly full sanctuary. "There aren't many places left."

He couldn't help a slight hesitation before scooting over. She took the place he vacated while he struggled to hide his discomfort with a smile.

"I didn't expect to see you here," she murmured under cover of the organ music.

He raised a brow at her in query.

"Everyone knows you didn't hit it off with Ivy."

"I don't think there's a problem just because—"

The funeral director chose that time to usher in the family.

It was a small group, and since this was a Baptist

church and not a funeral home, there was no private room for grieving. The family consisted of both Richmond women and a little girl with long, chocolate-brown hair and serious brown eyes who looked like a small reproduction of Mercy. Mercy, in turn, looked like a younger version of Ivy. Dr. Jarvis George accompanied the ladies.

Dr. George presented another reason for Lukas to keep his mouth shut, his head down, and get out as soon as the funeral ended. The man had made his antipathy to Lukas quite obvious, and since he held the directorship for the emergency room, he was Lukas's immediate supervisor. Not a good situation.

"Dr. George was partners with Ivy's late husband, Dr. Cliff Richmond," Lauren volunteered quietly. "He's always been close to the family."

Lukas nodded. Just great.

"Poor Tedi," Lauren whispered.

In spite of himself, Lukas raised a questioning brow.

"Mercy's daughter," Lauren explained, leaning closer. "The little girl. She's ten, and she's a darling, very precocious. Her dad's not a darling, and he's had custody since the divorce five years ago. He doesn't mind causing trouble for Dr. Mercy, and he isn't above dragging Tedi into it to keep Mercy from defending herself."

Lukas cleared his throat. "Um, perhaps I don't need to know this."

"If you don't, you'll be the only person in the county who doesn't. Dr. Mercy doesn't smile and laugh like she used to, and I miss that. She used to be a warm, outgoing lady, always ready with a joke or a one-liner to make the patients laugh and relax."

Lukas glanced sideways at Lauren. She wasn't exactly a gossip. She was just filling him in on some inner workings of the community she apparently felt he needed to know. He didn't feel the same way.

"Ivy's kind of a loose cannon," the nurse continued, apparently unaware of Lukas's discomfort with the conversation. "Everyone loves her, just like they did her mother, but she can sometimes go off on a harebrainer. Three years ago she decided she wanted to backpack the Appalachian Trail."

"And did she?"

"She hiked for two weeks and got through part of Georgia before she got a stress fracture in her left leg and had to call Mercy. As usual, Mercy flew to the rescue. Ivy can be outspoken about a lot of things, and she takes a special interest in the hospital since she helps support it. The problem is, she sometimes throws her financial weight around. I think she means well, but the administration has trouble convincing her to trust them and keep out of politics." Lauren paused and waved at someone across the aisle.

Lukas was rescued from any more information by the pastor, who rose from his seat on the stage and bowed his head to pray.

Mercy stood for a moment at the casket after the service, tears sliding down her cheeks. She heard Tedi sniffling beside her and laid an arm around her daughter's shoulders.

"I can't believe he came," Mercy heard Ivy mutter as they filed out of the church behind the casket.

"Why not, Mom?" The question came out more sharply than Mercy had intended. Ivy Richmond was one of the most stubborn people in Knolls, and she wasn't afraid to express her views. She was obviously still laying blame at Dr. Bower's feet for Grandma Jane's death. "He seems to be a caring doctor, and he was very concerned about Grandma. He's not her murderer."

Ivy shushed Mercy, then glanced pointedly at Tedi, who walked ahead of them.

Mercy shrugged. "Just because the two of you disagreed on ideology doesn't mean he's a bad person. May I remind you I agreed with him."

"You didn't try to force me or manipulate me into changing my mind. Besides…you don't understand my reasoning. Not really."

"You expect a stranger to understand something your own daughter doesn't?"

Tedi glanced up at her mother as they reached the vestibule. "It's because Granny Jane wasn't saved, Mom. Grandma Ivy was concerned for her soul."

Mercy sucked in her breath in a sigh of irritated frustration. That again. This Christian business was just going too far, and Ivy never wasted a moment in her attempts to try to indoctrinate Tedi into every aspect of it.

As they turned to greet the first of the funeral attendees, Mercy had no time to comment.

This part of the funeral procession was the most trying to Mercy, as it had been five years ago at Dad's funeral. As with Dad, it looked as if the whole town had shown up to pay their "respects." Mercy had learned long ago not to trust what people said to your face. At times like this, they were all high on emotionalism. Try them later, when you were fighting for custody of your child and needed a friend, or you lost your practice and needed patients.

She saw Dr. Bower coming toward them, walking beside Lauren McCaffrey. He probably didn't realize it, but his expressive face showed his discomfort clearly. So why was he here? He didn't even know Grandma. And he didn't seem like the politicking type.

He took Mercy's hand gently. "Again, Dr. Richmond, I'm sorry." He seemed sincere, his clear blue eyes steady and earnest as he spoke. When he reached Ivy he hesitated.

To Mercy's surprise, Mom took his hand. "Thank you so much for taking the time out of your busy schedule to attend Mother's funeral."

If he caught the sarcasm in her voice, he didn't show it.

Then Jarvis spotted him. "Hello, Dr. Bower. Who's watching the shop?"

"Dr. Camp agreed to spell me for a couple of hours. Today's his day off."

"You might consider going through me next time."

Jarvis's tone held no rancor, but Mercy tensed. She would not allow Jarvis to reprimand one of his staff right here at her own grandma's funeral.

"Sorry, Dr. George," Dr. Bower said quietly. "I tried to contact you."

"No harm done. Camp's a good doc."

To Mercy's surprise, Jarvis shook the younger man's hand and even smiled, though it looked more like a grimace.

Later, as the four of them rode in the limousine to the cemetery, Mercy overheard her mother speaking to Jarvis quietly under cover of the soft gospel music that floated over them.

"What's up between you and Dr. Bower?" Ivy asked. "You waiting for him to hang himself?"

Jarvis tugged at the collar of his starched white shirt— probably the only starched shirt he had. "He's too smart for that. Do you know he ranked third in his class when he graduated from Kirksville?"

"You checked his personnel file?"

"Yes, and I called Cunningham today to find out more about the little contretemps Sal mentioned to us yesterday. I have an old friend who works there. Nurse. Great gal."

"And she told you about Dr. Bower?" Ivy asked.

"She told me what she knew, which wasn't much, except that about the rank, and the fact that Bower never dated, had very little social life at all, and spent most of his spare time—which was rare—at the hospital working and learning. She liked him. I mean, she really liked him."

Mercy suppressed a smile at the hint of frustration in Jarvis's voice. Ivy's brows rose in surprise. "So isn't that good news?"

"Of course it is," he said just a little too brightly.

"Are you still going to check him out?"

"June will call me when she has more info. She said something about a lawsuit, but no explanation." Jarvis reached over and patted Ivy's hand. "We'll get this thing figured out."

"Mom?" Tedi said softly, just loud enough for Mercy to hear.

Mercy leaned sideways and put an arm over her daughter's shoulders. "Yeah?"

"How's…the practice going?"

"Great, honey. Just great."

"You still doing some E.R. shifts to fill in on your days off?"

"Some. Not as many since the new full-time doctor joined us."

"Oh." Tedi frowned and glanced out the window for a moment.

Mercy watched her daughter, whose dark eyes were even darker than usual. Mercy hadn't forgotten the slammed car door and the squeal of tires on blacktop when Theo dropped Tedi off at the church before the funeral.

"Everything okay at home?" Mercy asked.

Tedi grimaced, still looking out the window.

Mercy repressed the urge to demand what that puny excuse for a father had been doing to make Tedi so unhappy. Just watching her daughter made her want to choke Theodore.

"So I guess you're pretty busy," Tedi said at last.

Mercy quirked a brow at her. "Busy? Do you have something in mind? You know I'm never too busy for you, Theadra Zimmerman."

Tedi made a face at the sound of her full name. "Oh, I don't know…maybe we could go to Springfield some weekend. You know, like to the zoo and to a movie or something."

"Sounds great. And maybe we could go to Bass Pro Shop and eat at Hemingway's."

"Yeah, and hike at the nature center and watch the deer and squirrels and birds eat. And maybe we could even take a whole week and drive down to the Boston Mountains in Arkansas."

"We could camp out," Mercy said, playing the little game they had always played, with their dreams and wishes getting bigger and bigger and more unreachable. "And maybe we could take a whole month and go to the Grand Canyon." She had forgotten how heartbreaking this little game could become as she named the things she most wanted to do with her daughter.

"And no one could find us, except we would know where we were," Tedi added. "And maybe you could set up practice in Arizona, and we could call Grandma, and she could come and join us, but no one else would know."

"Maybe we could, honey." Mercy leaned closer and kissed her daughter's forehead. "First we'll concentrate on getting to Springfield. Do you want to talk about it?"

Tedi turned and looked seriously into Mercy's eyes. The all-too-grown-up expression made Mercy's throat choke with tears.

"Would you, Mom? Would you do it for me?"

Mercy's eyebrows rose in surprise. "Why wouldn't I want to spend time with the person I love more than anyone on earth?"

Tedi shrugged. "I don't know…I guess I thought you might be too busy."

"Where did you get that—" Mercy paused, and a flash of fresh anger accosted her. She reached out and touched her daughter's shining dark brown hair. "Tedi, don't ever let anyone tell you that I don't have time for you or that I don't love you." The anger grew. The day's grief and the past weeks of struggle with Grandma's cancer had taken their toll. Mercy struggled for a moment with tears; then she gave up and let them fall.

Tedi watched Mercy for a moment, her own eyes growing larger. She reached a hand up and caught a tear and held her mother's gaze. "Don't cry, Mom. Really. It's going to be okay."

Mercy pulled a Kleenex tissue out of her purse and blew her nose. Her own daughter shouldn't be having to comfort her.

To Mercy's surprise, Tedi's spirits seemed to lift after that. She smiled when her grandmother and Jarvis teased her, and the smile was real. It was as if Mercy had reassured her of something vital. The mood relaxed until they reached the cemetery.

As the limousine driver held the door for Ivy, she clutched her chest and stumbled.

Mercy scrambled forward. "Mom!"

"Grandma!" Tedi cried.

Ivy caught herself against the seat as her face grew pale. Jarvis eased her back.

"Relax, it's okay," she said. "I just got a little dizzy." She breathed deeply through her nose, then exhaled through her mouth. "It's okay."

"You grabbed your chest, Mom. I saw you grab you chest. Does it hurt? What's wrong?" Mercy demanded.

Jarvis leaned toward Ivy. "You weren't feeling well yesterday, were you? You mentioned chest congestion. Are you still feeling ill?"

"Apparently so," Ivy snapped.

"Mother, why haven't you seen a doctor?" Mercy asked.

"Very funny. I've seen more doctors in the past two days—"

"That's not what I mean, and you know it." Mercy's voice carried more volume than she'd intended, and other arrivals at the cemetery turned to look through the open limousine door with concern. She lowered her voice. "How long has this been going on?"

"For pete's sake, don't lecture me like a—"

"Stop it!" came a ten-year-old voice.

All three adults turned in time to see Tedi's eyes fill with tears. Her lower lip quivered. "Grandma, you're scaring me."

Mercy quickly wrapped her arms around her daughter. "It's okay, honey. You know how stubborn your grandma can be sometimes." She cast a reproachful look at her mother, who did not hold her gaze. Good. She felt guilty.

"Now that we know she's sick, we'll take care of her. I know she doesn't want you to worry. Do you, Grandma?"

"No."

Tedi sniffed and smeared tears over her face with the back of her hand. "But what's wrong, Grandma?"

The color had already begun to return to Ivy's cheeks. She eased herself back more comfortably on the velour seat. "Nothing serious, I'm sure, Tedi. Sometimes I just get the hiccups, but it isn't in my throat. It's deeper in my chest."

"Do you think it's your heart?" Fresh tears formed in Tedi's eyes. She'd heard her mom talk too many times about heart attacks and the dangers of heart disease. Mercy wished she'd never discussed the subject in front of her.

"I don't know, honey," Ivy said.

"We'll know soon enough," Mercy said. "Mom, we're going straight to my office as soon as we leave here."

"No, we aren't. I don't feel it's ethical for a daughter to treat her own mother."

"Then we'll go to my office," Jarvis said. "You're not getting out of this, Ivy Richmond."

"And you're not getting your stethoscope on me, either, Jarvis George. I'll go to an unbiased doctor who doesn't know me and doesn't have preconceived ideas about the care I should receive. The two of you would have me trussed up like a full backpack and never let me out of the house again." Her color continued to improve, and Mercy relaxed. Tedi's tears had done more than any amount of browbeating could have done, and whatever was wrong with Mom, she was recovering for now.

Chapter Seven

At eight o'clock Friday evening, Lukas completed his patient charts and sat back with a sigh. As usual, the evening rush hour had hit with a vengeance, making up for a midafternoon lull. He'd seen twenty patients today, several with high acuities—two chest pains, one asthma, a surgical abdomen, and a broken leg. Not bad for a day's work when you also took into account the numerous flu, strep, pneumonia, sprain and workmen's compensation patients he'd also seen. He'd had to fly one heart attack out via chopper to the trauma center at Cox South in Springfield. There was just so much this small, class-four facility dared to handle without sending some patients to a place with more specialized equipment and medical expertise.

Lukas decided not to wait until he got home to call his father, but opened his cell phone as he changed from his scrubs to his street clothes. He smiled when Dad answered in the middle of the first ring, then frowned at the sight of his rumpled clothes in the mirror. He had to start using hangers.

"Hey, Dad," he said after the preliminary greetings, "I'm off this whole weekend. What do you think about that?"

"I don't believe it," came his father's musical baritone voice. "It's been months since you had a Saturday and Sunday off in a row. How'd you manage that your first week there?"

"I'm the only full-time physician working at Knolls Community E.R. Since most of the other docs practice family medicine during the weekdays, that's when I work. Mrs. Pinkley warned me that once she wins her battle with the number crunchers, she'll be hiring more full-time doctors in the E.R. and then I'll have to share my cushy hours."

"What did you tell her about your problems in Kansas City?"

"The truth. I told her that I had personality differences with my trainer during my residency, and—"

"Did you also tell her you weren't the only one who had trouble with him? Did you tell her that he and a nurse lied on the witness stand about your actions?"

"No, I just showed her the court papers where my name was cleared and the hospital was forced to stop blocking my license. She checked my references and told me that was good enough. She also said that it was her opinion that docs were worse about professional jealousy than attorneys. I guess she was satisfied, because she hired me. She's quite a lady."

"Is she married?"

Lukas sighed and rolled his eyes. "Yes, Dad, she's married, and she's retirement age."

"Doesn't hurt to ask. Found a church yet?"

"Not yet."

"Just think, you might even have time to join the choir and actually be there every Sunday for a change."

Lukas shook his head. Dad had never come to grips with the fact that his youngest son could not carry a tune. "What are you doing this weekend? I thought I might drive up. It's only about a two and a half hour trip to Mount Vernon from here."

"We won't be home tomorrow. We're driving to Roaring River with the Goennigs for some fishing."

Lukas stifled his disappointment. There was plenty to do this weekend. "Still feeling like a newlywed?"

"I still *am* a newlywed. It's only been a year."

"How's Beth?"

"Busy as ever." Besides being the church librarian, Lukas's new stepmom, Elizabeth, was on the kitchen committee at church, and she helped out at the senior citizen center and delivered food for Meals on Wheels. She'd been good friends with Mom and Dad before Mom got sick, and she was there for them throughout the chemotherapy and radiation. After Mom died, Beth had been there for Dad as a friend. She, too, had lost a spouse five years earlier, and Lukas had always been glad of her friendship. She'd fit perfectly into the family, and she was good for Dad.

"I wish you'd called sooner," Dad said. "We just made the date with the Goennigs today."

"That's okay, Dad. I probably need to stay and settle in, anyway."

"Oh? Don't tell me you actually have furniture now. That tiny apartment of yours barely had room for a bed and a couch."

"I had a small kitchen table, too."

"Does your new house have a kitchen?"

"Of course."

"Have you found your way into it? I bet your refrigerator isn't even hooked up yet."

"I don't have a fridge here."

"It figures."

"I haven't had a chance to get one. I've only been here a week and I've been working. I'll probably pick one up tomorrow somewhere."

"Do you have a stove?"

"The house came with one, yes."

"Let me guess. You don't even know if it's gas or electric, do you?"

"I specifically remember the gas flames when they showed me the house."

Dad sighed. "Do you have any new kitchen utensils? Last time I checked, all you had was that skillet and spatula Beth gave you for Christmas last year."

"I eat out a lot. I used to keep cereal and milk when I had that little fridge in KC, but most of the time the milk got old before I had a chance to drink it."

Dad clicked his tongue. "You've been a bachelor too long, Lukas. You need a wife."

"I haven't had any volunteers."

"Any possibilities? Any dates lately?"

"No actual dates…"

"But…?"

"But nothing. One of the nurses invited me to eat with some of the staff, but I was late and everyone else had left. She's been nice so far, but I just don't—"

"Son, you have to get over what happened in KC. You can't let one woman's actions hurt your own growth."

"Dad, that woman's testimony in court almost destroyed my career. All she had to do was cry sexual harassment when I wouldn't go out with her, and seduction when she turned up pregnant, and they listened! If it hadn't been for that DNA test—"

"But you're not in jail, and your career has not been destroyed. God is faithful."

"I know, but people aren't. There are some pretty vindictive people in this world."

"That's why you always count on God, not people. You're a good doctor, Lukas. Don't forget that. And you're a wonderful person. You deserve a loving woman, someone who shares your ethical standards—someone who shares your faith. Don't give that one misguided nurse the power to color all of your relationships with all other women for the rest of your life."

Lukas hesitated, glancing at his watch. "I guess I should go get some dinner before everything closes. Have a good time tomorrow, Dad, and tell Beth I sent my love."

There was a loud sigh over the phone line. "I'll tell her. Take care. Our prayers are with you every day. And, Lukas? One little date with a nice Christian lady wouldn't kill you."

After Lukas hung up he pulled on his jacket, grabbed his bag and walked out to the car. Sometimes he wished he'd kept his mouth shut about the Kansas City court case, but Lukas had never been able to keep secrets from his father. Besides, being fired from the hospital and kicked out of the residency program had left Lukas without an income for several months, until his permanent medical license had come through. During that time, not long after Mom's death, Lukas had gone home to stay with Dad and work as a respiratory tech at St. John's in Joplin.

Enough wallowing. Though he was disappointed about his immediate plans falling through, the weekend still beckoned ahead like a long holiday. There were hiking trails to explore and a river nearby. He'd heard one of the EMTs—Buck, the guy brave enough to try to feed Cowboy's lion—talk about how he liked to fish. Fishing didn't measure up to hiking, but the company would be nice. Of course, Lukas hadn't been invited.

Ten minutes after leaving work he parked on the town square by the courthouse, took a picture textbook out of his bag to study while he ate and walked down the street to the only place on the square still open this late, Little Mary's Barbecue. He liked this café, not only because they served his favorite food, barbecued ribs, but also because of the homey atmosphere and the fact that they pitched their homemade dinner rolls to you from across the room, just like at Lambert's up near Springfield. Lukas carried his book with him over to a corner table, ordered a plate of ribs and proceeded to read about dermatological medicine, his latest in a series of subjects he wanted to know better. His two-week dermatology rotation had bored him to death, but sometimes a case would crop up in the E.R. He wanted to hone his knowledge.

He smelled the sharp, smoky aroma of ribs as the server set the platter on the table. Then he heard a quick intake of breath, but by the time he glanced up from his reading, the server was stalking away—and "stalking" was the word for it. She shot him a glance over her shoulder as she neared the kitchen, and he could have sworn he saw offended animosity in the look. What was wrong with her?

After a quick, silent blessing, he reached for a rib and resumed reading, with the book lying flat on the table. He was careful not to get barbecue sauce on any pages. He did, however, become a little concerned when another woman came out through the swinging kitchen doors and walked toward him. She, too, did not stop, but gave an offended gasp as she rounded his table and returned to the back, where the first waitress stood glaring at him with her arms folded across her chest.

Lukas looked down to see if he had barbecue sauce smeared all over his shirt. Nope, nothing. His clothes were wrinkled, but that shouldn't— He looked down at his reading material and went cold with mortification. The particular case about which he was so innocently and intently reading involved an area of the male anatomy seldom discussed in mixed company outside the medical realm. It included pictures. He shut the book with a snap, smearing red-brown sauce all over the cover. Time to leave.

Maybe he did need to get that refrigerator and stop eating out so often.

Sunday morning, Lukas sat in a middle pew halfway over from the aisle at early service at Covenant Baptist Church. Saturday had been almost a bust—he always considered his day a failure when he spent it catching up with laundry and dishes and mail. He'd even worked up his nerve and tried to call a couple of guys from work to see if anyone wanted to go to a movie or something. No one did. Worse, he didn't even get a fridge, because a storm kept him inside. Some wonderful weekend this was turning out to be.

An elderly gentleman in a baggy suit and tie greeted him and shook his hand, as many had done when Lukas first walked through Covenant's front door. It was nice to meet the people like this before services began, but since Lukas rarely arrived anywhere early, he hadn't had much experience with this kind of thing. What he had experienced was that churches invariably singled out newcomers and embarrassed them during welcome time, either by making them stand when everyone else was seated, or remain seated while everyone else stood. On several other occasions when attending a new church, he had purposely arrived late to avoid the "first-time visitor" greeting; then the next time he came, he couldn't be mistaken for a first-timer. Antisocial, maybe, but it made things easier for a shy person. Besides, he wasn't as interested in seeing all the friendly Sunday school faces as he was in watching the nitty-gritty-business-meeting faces. Now *that* was something that could show the character of a church body. He was also interested in seeing how many people attended evening services.

Why he'd come to Covenant Baptist, he didn't know, except that it was close to home and he'd already been here once for Jane Conn's funeral. True, it probably meant that Ivy Richmond might be a member, and that wouldn't be comfortable, but he had to start somewhere.

A familiar voice reached him from the aisle. He jerked around to find Lauren talking with some teenagers beside the pew on which he sat, and he nearly groaned aloud. He hadn't thought of the possibility of running into her here. Before he could turn back around she spotted him, and a huge grin spread across her face. Oh, great.

"So! You decided to come!" She didn't ask permission this time but plopped right down beside him and laid a hand on his shoulder. "I'm so glad."

"Yeah." He forced a smile. One did not get up and leave before services even began. "I didn't know you attended here."

"Of course you did. I told you, remember? At the cantina the other night."

No, he didn't remember. He was probably too busy

behaving like a paranoid idiot then, too. This was crazy. She was obviously a member of this church and was only being friendly to a newcomer.

"So are you all settled in now? Got your stuff moved?"

"What there was of it."

"Good. How about a picnic down at the river this afternoon? I've got a couple of fishing poles and some good bait. Moving to a new place must be awfully lonely, and—"

"Actually, Lauren, I don't think so." He refused to lie and tell her he had something better to do, because he didn't, but why did he feel so guilty for turning her down? Was it the sudden expression of hurt and embarrassment that crossed her face and was gone in an instant? Or was it Dad's warning the other night that it was time to forget the past? "Thanks for the offer, but no."

"Sure." She swallowed, and the smile returned. "Well, anytime you want a fishing buddy, let me know. I can show you the best spots in the county."

After the service Lukas went home, changed into his hiking gear, and looked for the nearest forest trail. Lonely wasn't so bad. It never hurt to take things slowly.

Chapter Eight

At six-thirty Monday evening, two weeks after the disappointing weekend off, Lukas Bower watched with envy as the day shift prepared to leave, all except for him. He glanced at the clock and grimaced. He was stuck here for another full twelve hours, compliments of scheduling by his beloved director, Dr. Jarvis George. Lukas hated twenty-four-hour shifts. Amazingly, there were no patients in the emergency department at this time, and this was usually the evening E.R. rush hour.

Carol and Lauren chattered as they prepared to walk out together.

The ambulance radio buzzed. "Knolls Community Hospital, this is Knolls 830. Come in."

Beverly leaned forward and pushed the button and told them to continue.

"Be advised this is a code-red response." Beverly caught her breath and turned to glance at Lukas. It was a disaster code. The voice continued. "We are currently leaving the scene of a head-on MVA. A large sedan with three occupants struck a minivan with two adults and three children. You will receive eight patients."

Lukas started to call to Carol and Lauren, but he saw they had both stopped and put their purses back under the central counter.

"Looks like we're in for some overtime," Lauren said as she edged closer to the radio.

The ambulance report continued. "We are currently inbound with two class-one patients. The first is a Caucasian male, late twenties, who was the driver of the sedan. His vitals are: BP 80 over 45, heart rate 142 and weak, respiration 52 and labored. His initial O_2 sat was 68 percent. He has absent breath sounds over the left side. He is responsive only to pain. He is intubated and is being ventilated. We have two large bore IVs established, and 1000 CCs of fluid are being bolused to the patient."

Lukas began his mental note-making as he listened.

"There is prominent bruising to his chest," the paramedic continued. "He moans when chest is palpated. His O_2 sat has increased to 87 percent. Does medical control have questions or orders at this time?"

Lukas leaned forward and pressed the Talk button. "Wish to be advised if this patient has been secured on a long spine board with full c-spine immobilization."

"Affirmative."

"Acknowledged. Is patient showing signs of tracheal deviation and/or jugular distension? Also, is he having muffled heart sounds?" Lukas waited for a long moment.

"Sorry, the backboard and c-collar prevent my checking tracheal deviation or venous distension. Background noise drowns out heart sounds to an extent."

Lukas frowned. This was not a very aggressive ambulance crew. "Please continue with report on second patient."

This evening shift was not looking good. Time to start getting ready. Lukas pushed the talk button as soon as he received the report. "Knolls 830, what is your ETA?" How much time would they have to prepare for this deluge?

"About eight minutes. Does medical control have further questions or orders?"

"Affirmative. Is second patient intubated?"

"Negative, medical control. Are unable to intubate patient at this time but are assisting patient with bag mask ventilation, rate of 20."

Lukas frowned again. "Copy, Knolls 830. Increase respiratory rate to 24." He cleared and signed off, then released the switch, making mental preparations. "Sorry, Lauren and Carol, we need to keep you here for a while." He turned to the night secretary. "Rita, please call medical and surgical backup and be prepared to do a disaster code. I'll have to wait and see what the report is from the next ambulance unit."

"Where do you want me?" Lauren asked.

"And me?" Beverly asked.

Lukas gave them instructions, then turned to the secretary. "Carol, see if we can get some additional nursing staff down here, and then make sure radiology is on standby."

"Gotcha."

"Beverly, also check on air flight availability. Sounds as if we'll have to fly some of them out. Request standby at this time."

"Okay, Dr. Bower."

"Lauren," he called, "better make sure we have some mannitol set up in trauma two. We've probably got a head injury with a classic Cushing's reflex. Make sure there's an intubation set up in there, too, because I'll have to tube him."

He turned to Rita. "Have you been able to reach our medical and surgical backups yet?"

She hung up the receiver she'd been holding. "No, Dr. Bower. I've beeped both of them."

"Good. I'm sure they'll call right back. Ask them to come as soon as possible and warn them that this is a disaster code."

Once more, the ambulance radio blared to life. "Knolls Community Hospital, this is Knolls 832. Knolls, come in please."

Lukas pressed the talk button. "This is Knolls Community medical control speaking. Go ahead, 832."

"Knolls, we are currently inbound to your facility with two class-two patients. Be advised, two additional ambulances will be en route to your facility, with short ETAs. One will have a class-two patient who requires extrication."

They gave information and vitals on a female and a male, one with possible neck injury and one with possible back injury. With an ETA of approximately six minutes, he knew he had to get the nurses back to work quickly.

"Does medical control have any further questions or orders?" the paramedic asked.

"Nothing further at this time," Lukas said. "Keep us advised of any further changes in the patients' conditions. We will expect you in about six minutes. This is medical control out." Lukas pressed the button and turned to find Carol standing behind him. "Call the disaster," he said. "We need more help, and we still haven't heard about the children. See how many more helicopters we can get on standby. I don't know how many we're going to need yet."

Carol nodded and grabbed the phone.

"Rita," Lukas continued, "do we have more nurses coming?"

"Yes, the floor says they can spare one."

"Just one? This is a disaster code. They'll have to spare more than that. Lauren, is the needle decompression ready?"

"Yes."

"Okay, I'll be setting up in trauma one. Let me know if you need anything. Everyone glove up and get your goggles and trauma gowns on. Rita, will you see to it that any help that arrives receives trauma gear?"

"Yes, Dr. Bower."

"Have we received any calls from our backup docs yet?"

"Not yet."

Lukas frowned. What was going on here? Didn't the Knolls docs respond to emergencies? "Call them again, please."

Dr. Mercy Richmond stifled a yawn as she walked through the quiet second-floor corridor of Knoll's Community Hospital—quiet, because it was 6:45 p.m. Monday evening and census was down. All the other doctors had done their rounds and gone home. With census down, staff was down.

There was only one more patient to see tonight. Mom.

Just as Mercy stepped to the nurses' station, she heard her name paged over the speaker.

"Lucky you," Zelda, the floor charge nurse, teased. "It's what you get for your dedication. Probably someone wants you to cover their night call again." She punched the switchboard number and handed Mercy the phone.

"This is Dr. Richmond. May I help you?" She knew by the code paged that she would directly receive her incoming call.

"Yes, Mercy, this is Robert."

Mercy frowned. "Hi, Robert. Is everything okay? Is Mom—"

"Other than the fact that your mother is as stubborn as you are, she's not too bad right now. She actually showed up for her appointment today."

Dr. Robert Simeon, an internal medicine specialist, had been the one to do Mom's physical this morning. Mom had insisted that was the earliest she could take the time to go in. She'd just wanted to put it off.

"It's a miracle," Mercy said. "I've nagged her for two weeks."

"So that's why she was in such a bad mood."

"How bad?"

"Nothing serious. She wasn't happy when the treadmill stress test turned up a problem, and tried to say it was an artifact in the machine. Then she reminded us rather forcefully that she's not senile yet, and not to go running to you with a report."

Mercy sighed. "What's the report?"

"Her cholesterol is 163, blood pressure 120 over 70, fasting blood sugar is 87. Ivy's in good shape for sixty-six."

"Mom's in great shape for *thirty*-six. Why is she having chest pain?"

"I would take a stab at rate-related left bundle branch block."

"Rate related? But she nearly passed out at the cemetery just getting out of the car. She hadn't been running a marathon."

"She was burying her mother. That would account for an increased rate, don't you think?"

"But a near faint? I don't think a bundle branch block would account for that."

"Of course it could, especially if it brought on a vasovagal. She's been having this for a while, and it's sure to stress her when she feels it coming on. I'm sending her to a cardiologist against her wishes, and who knows whether she'll keep the appointment or not. I finally had to warn her that if I didn't see that she got excellent care, you'd turn me into a leather coat. I think I appealed to her maternal instincts."

"So she agreed?"

"She tried to laugh it off, but I think that's what convinced her in the end." There was a pause. "Mercy, you do realize she's still planning to go on her June hiking trip to Colorado, don't you?"

"Oh, no, she's not."

"That's what I told her." He chuckled. "I don't want to be around when you two clash."

"No, you don't. We had plenty of practice when I was growing up."

"Who won?"

Mercy grimaced. "Mom, usually. She can outtalk an Ozark auctioneer."

"Why don't you drop by later and we can discuss—"

"Code red in the emergency department," came an

urgent voice over the speaker just down the hallway. "Code red. All available personnel report stat."

"I've already started cooking, so don't tell me no," Robert continued. There was a pause. "Mercy?"

"Huh?" Code red was the disaster code.

"Dinner? My place in about an hour? We can discuss it then."

"Yeah, sure. Sorry, Robert, there's an alert. Gotta go." She watched the charge nurse send an aide and another RN from the floor, then hung up and rushed toward the elevator. This couldn't be a drill, could it? Nothing had been approved through the QA team. Mercy would know. She was on it. This had to be the real thing—disaster code.

Lukas stood in the middle of the room, surveying the "patients" being carried in from the ambulance. His first glimpse of bloodred mulage paint on Buck Oppenheimer, a supposed accident victim with tension pneumothorax, had given it away. This was a drill. Relief mingled with a little disappointment—not that he wanted anyone to be hurt. His adrenaline did a quick nose dive. He approached Buck's litter. The big fireman-EMT with short hair and big ears was covered in fake blood and had a note taped to his arm. He pretended to be unconscious, but Lukas could see his eyes open slightly a couple of times—and that gave him the idea for a little harmless fun.

Lauren's triage was right. Buck's injury was the worst. Lukas stopped at a utensil shelf just long enough to pick up a couple of things he needed. As he chose his pieces, another group entered the E.R. with one young woman holding a camcorder, and an older woman giving orders.

Lukas recognized her as Dorothy Wild, QA nurse and drill coordinator.

Before they could approach Lukas, he turned and started Buck's way. Buck started gasping for breath. Good acting, but how long could he carry it?

"Nurse," Lukas said, turning to Lauren with a slight smile. "Would you please hand me a fourteen-gauge needle?"

Her eyes widened, and she started to make an obvious protest, but Lukas winked and widened his smile.

She raised a brow and eyed him skeptically, but did as he requested.

"Thank you, Lauren." He took the syringe and lowered it from Buck's sight, removed the stainless-steel needle, and replaced the plastic cover.

Buck's eyes weren't shut quite so tightly now, and he'd forgotten that he was a patient in a serious struggle for breath.

Seconds later, Lukas held the syringe up again, raised it above Buck's chest, and started down with it.

Buck stopped breathing. His eyes bugged open, and his thick, muscular arms that were unsecured to the backboard flew up. "Wait!" He tried to scoot away but was held fast by the backboard and c-collar. "Hold it! No needles! I'm with the drill, Doc!" He held out his arm. "See? Fake blood. Mulage paint. This is all just a disaster drill, not the real thing!"

Lukas frowned to keep from laughing.

Buck took some deep breaths. "Does this sound like a tension pneumothorax? I'm fine. I'm just taking part in the drill. Please, no needles. I hate needles."

Lukas raised the syringe and flicked the flimsy

catheter tubing that jutted from the end of it. "Does this look like a needle?" He grinned wickedly. "I'm not going to waste all that steel on a healthy ox like you."

Buck exhaled a sigh of relief and gradually returned the grin, which made his ears stick out even farther from his head. "Oh, boy, Doc, you almost had me there."

"How'd they keep word from leaking out about this one?" Lukas asked. "Usually everyone knows about a drill before it happens."

Buck shrugged. "You got me. Can I get up now? Wanna undo those straps so I can—"

"Hold it." Lukas took the description sheet that had been taped to Buck's arm. "You're still hurt, remember? In fact, you're supposed to be unconscious, responsive only to pain." He gestured toward the observation team. "Over here. We have emergency chest decompression. This would be the first patient in the triage." He continued to describe his plan of treatment. "We would fly this one to at least a level-two trauma center," Lukas said, finishing with Buck as he unfastened the securing straps. "According to triage," he said, stepping toward the next patient, "this one is the patient I would treat next. I would be ready to intubate if necessary. He is showing signs of Cushing's reflex, elevated blood pressure and low heart rate caused by increased intracranial pressure. I would order a cross table c-spine, a one-view chest, a CT—"

"Excuse me, Dr. Bower." Lauren stepped in front of the camcorder operator and held up her hand. "I'm sorry to interrupt, but we have a patient in room five who—"

"Lauren, don't interrupt," Dorothy Wild snapped. The stocky, deep-voiced woman with salt-and-pepper hair stepped between Lauren and Lukas. "You've done your triage. We're recording Dr. Bower now."

"I'm sorry, but this is a real patient," Lauren said.

"They can wait a few minutes while we finish this."

"No, Dorothy," Lukas said, "I'm sorry, but real patients don't wait for drills." He turned to follow Lauren. "What seems—"

Dorothy stepped in front of him. "You can at least find out if it's critical before you put all these people on hold."

Lukas frowned at Dorothy as he stepped around her. "Don't worry, Lauren would not have come to get me otherwise. She's a good nurse."

Dorothy gestured to the camcorder operator and followed Lukas into the trauma room. "Fine, this is for PR. Let's give them some good PR."

Lukas turned to stand in the doorway. "I'm sorry, but it's a violation of federal regulations to film a patient without his written consent. Our patients are our first priority, Mrs. Wild."

Dorothy moved to push past him. "Fine, we'll obtain consent later, but we're getting this on film for—"

Lukas fought his irritation as he blocked her way once more. "No, you're not."

Mercy heard the sirens as soon as the ancient, incredibly slow elevator opened its doors for her on the first floor. She should know by now to take the stairs. The disaster code announcement had rattled her.

She raced toward the emergency room as the ambulance entrance doors flew open and admitted a stretcher with Rod, a paramedic, and Mike, an EMT, in attendance.

"Got another head," Rod called toward the E.R. entrance. He glanced at Mercy. "Hi, Doc. Decide to join the fun?"

Beverly, the RN, came out to the hallway, obviously to triage. She caught sight of Mercy. "Oh, thank goodness, Doctor. We need you if this thing's going to fly. We're double covered except for Dr. Bower. He's on for a twenty-four, and we can't get a response from any other docs."

"Why not?" Mercy glanced once more—this time suspiciously—at the head wound on the stretcher. There was a typed note attached to the shirt of the seemingly unconscious patient.

A drill? This whole thing was a drill! What was going on here? No one had warned her.

In disgust, Mercy turned to lead the way into the emergency room. A small group of observers stood staring toward exam room five, their attention on Dr. Bower, who stood nose to nose with the drill coordinator, Dorothy Wild.

"No footage." His voice was firm but not raised. "This is a real patient."

"Dr. Bower, part of the reason for this drill is to improve public rela—"

"Not with this patient." Bower moved to block the camera's view of the man lying on the cot. "We've received no permission to tape, and he has indicated that he wants his privacy. Kindly step from the room."

Mercy stepped forward and nodded at Dorothy, who was retreating from the room, face flushed, eyes narrowed, chin set. Bower was obviously not counting on a long career with Knolls Community Hospital.

"Dr. Mercy." The stocky, grim-faced woman spoke

sharply, then took a deep breath and rearranged her expression, as if concentrating on her favorite relaxation technique. "Maybe you can help us. We need Dr. Bower in this drill, and he is not being cooperative. If another doctor were to take the patient he is with now, and no one else chooses this time to come barging in with an emergency, we might get something accomplished."

Mercy stared at her. Who on earth had ever decided that Dorothy Wild would be a good PR representative for this hospital? "I'm sorry you're having so much trouble, Dorothy." She tried to keep the sarcasm from her voice. "I wasn't even aware of a drill scheduled for tonight. Is this a test of some kind specifically planned by our administrator for Dr. Bower alone?"

"Well...no...not exactly, but he is our first full-time emergency room doctor, and—"

"Who ordered it?"

"Excuse me?"

"You're the drill coordinator, not the whole committee," Mercy said. "Who ordered the drill? Why wasn't it sanctioned by the rest of us first?"

Dorothy's mouth opened slightly.

"Did Dr. George have something to do with this?" Mercy asked.

Dorothy's suddenly sheepish expression gave Mercy her answer.

"Thank you. I'll discuss this with Dr. Bower." She left Dorothy standing in the middle of the room with her camcorder and entered exam room five, where Lukas Bower and Beverly were bent over a supine male figure on the bed.

"Dr. Bower?" Mercy said tentatively. "I heard the code

and just happened to be in the building. Is there something I can do to help?"

"Sure," he said without looking up. "It would be great if you would help with the drill. I'll be out when I finish here."

"Well…since you're the doc in the limelight, according to Dorothy, I thought maybe I could take this patient for you and you could go back to playing doctor for the film crew."

He glanced up briefly from his perusal of the man's pupils. "Thank you for the offer, Dr. Richmond, but the crew will just have to wait. I'm the doc on duty, and this is my patient, my responsibility."

"I understand. But you must understand that the PR team is merely trying to learn how best to serve real patients better. It's what drills are all about, and they are a vital function of this hospital."

"Thank you for your input, Dr. Richmond, but I'll take this patient first."

Scowling, Mercy retreated from the room. None of this should have happened tonight. "Dorothy," she called as she approached the central desk, "I might as well help with the drill while I'm here. Lauren, do you have a patient for me?"

"Wait a minute, Dr. Mercy." Dorothy held up her hand. "We're on hold until Dr. Bower comes back. I was hoping you could help out with his patient so he could join us more quickly."

"Sorry, he's the doc in charge, and he chooses not to release to an off-duty doctor. I don't blame him. So what about the drill? What do you have?"

Dorothy frowned. "Thank you, Dr. Mercy, but I have a specific request to let Dr. Bower do this exercise alone."

"A request by Dr. George, no doubt."

Dorothy shrugged and turned back to the desk. Mercy had been dismissed.

Chapter Nine

"Does Jarvis George suddenly think he's God?" Mercy muttered as she stalked into the first call room she came to. She had never known her father's old partner to pull a stunt like this. Sure, he was opinionated and cranky, but his interests had always been with his patients and this hospital…before. Lately Jarvis had been behaving differently. In fact, only these past few days he'd been reprimanding E.R. staff for little things they did while under the direction of Dr. Bower.

Jarvis seemed to resent Lukas more as time went on. Beverly had complained that she was afraid to work with Dr. Bower anymore because Jarvis had grilled her two days ago about the younger doc's judgment, as if she had something to do with the medical decision. The problem was, the staff also seemed uncomfortable working with Jarvis. In Beverly's opinion, Jarvis didn't have the quality of medical judgment he used to have.

Mercy entered the call room and closed the door behind her. She immediately spied a doctor's traditional black bag—which she knew belonged to Dr. Bower—and a bomber jacket tossed over the chair back. Rumpled bedclothes told her he had already tried to get some sleep to keep alert on this twenty-four-hour shift.

She didn't leave. He was busy with a patient, and she wanted to make a private call.

She punched Jarvis's office number on her cell and waited. No answer. She hadn't expected one. She disconnected and dialed his home number, which had not changed in twenty-five years.

He did not answer.

She refused to disconnect. He was there, and she knew he was just being his new, obnoxious self.

On the fifteenth ring, he picked up and said testily, "Yes, what is it?"

"Jarvis, this is Mercy. Why don't you come and join our disaster drill party?"

"No." His voice was cold.

"Then would you at least call the coordinator and withdraw your order about Dr. Bower completing the drill himself? I'd like to help out."

There was a pause. "Why? You don't…owe him anything."

Mercy frowned at the sound of his voice. She must have awakened him. "He has a real patient, that's why. Besides, a drill is to test the mettle of a whole team, not just one person. These things are expensive and time consuming for all concerned. And disaster drills are supposed to come through the quality assurance committee. This one didn't."

"Don't start with me…about protocol, Dr. Richmond." He sounded more than sleepy. He sounded drunk.

"Protocol is important. The emergency room is not a dictatorship, and you don't call all the shots. Why are you giving this new doc such a hard time? Give it up, Jarvis."

Silence.

"Jarvis? What's—"

"Let me remind you, Dr….Richmond, that I am the director of Knolls's emergency room, not you. I will do what I…as I see fit to ensure…to see to the safety of the patients in this community, and if that means pulling a surprise drill to test the skills of a particular health care employee, I will do so with no lip from you, young woman."

"What?" Mercy snapped. "Jarvis, have you been drinking?"

There was a swift intake of breath at the other end. "What are you talking about?"

A long, indignant pause radiated tension so taut Mercy felt her own hand tighten on her cell.

"Aren't you confusing me with your father?" he snapped. "Why don't you take care of your own job and let me see to mine?"

Mercy's mouth fell open.

Behind her she heard the door swish open. She turned around, saw Dr. Bower standing there, and she waved a dismissing hand at him.

"This *is* part of my job, Dr. George," she said coldly. "You don't have the authority to call a drill just because you've been on staff since the Boston Tea Party. Dorothy should have known better than to make the arrangements on your word alone. I don't care if she does worship you. I'm ashamed of the way our new recruit is being treated by—"

There was a click. Jarvis had hung up.

In spite of his mood, Lukas walked out of the call room with a bemused smile on his face. He shouldn't be smiling. Dr. George had apparently pulled this on him out of spite and had also probably told every other physician in the area, including the physician backup, not to respond to the drill. But he certainly hadn't told Dr. Richmond about it, and she wasn't afraid to complain. That was especially comforting after seeing Jarvis sitting with Mercy's family at the funeral a little over two weeks ago. Maybe Jarvis wouldn't get his way about everything.

Mercy came out of the call room a moment later, and Lukas watched her march toward the exit. She had taken her long, dark hair out of its customary knot, and it hung loose around her shoulders. She didn't look his way, but stalked out of the E.R. with long strides, pulling off her lab coat as she went.

"Dr. Bower." A frowning Dorothy Wild stepped in front of him, one arm around a clipboard, the other reaching up as if she wanted to point a finger in his face. "Can we please get on with the drill now? Do you realize these people are getting paid for this? It's costing the—"

Still thinking about Mercy's actions, Lukas made an about-face and walked back into the call room to get what he'd gone after the first time. He hadn't eaten anything since his late breakfast, and it would be a while before he could get away for dinner. He needed a Snickers.

Mercy parked at the side of her mother's house and spied her through the kitchen window, bent over her work at the sink, her hair falling out of its ponytail. Mom never closed her curtains at night, never locked her doors and always left her keys in the car.

Sure enough, not only was the front door unlocked, it was ajar. Mom always did that when she expected company, just so they'd know to come on in. Mercy pushed the door open and walked in.

"Mom?" She glanced at the clock on the living-room wall. It was eight already.

Ivy stepped into the threshold from the kitchen and for a moment stood looking at Mercy. Robert was right. Mom was in great shape for sixty-six, and she looked ten years younger. People were always remarking on how much Mercy looked like Ivy. She didn't mind. Mom was beautiful, except when she had that challenging glare in her eyes. Like now.

"No trip," Mercy said.

Ivy nodded. "So he told you. I figured he would. In fact, I thought you'd be calling a lot sooner than this. I can't believe the lack of patient confidentiality in this town. I've never had any privacy, being married to one doctor and being the mom of another."

"Dr. Simeon didn't call until tonight when I was making rounds at the hospital. You could've contacted me at work. I can't believe you're still planning that trip. There's no way—"

"I'm going."

"Don't be stupid. It's dangerous."

"Don't call be stupid. I'm your mother."

Mercy pulled off her fake leather jacket and threw it on the sofa. Without looking again at her mother, she went into the kitchen. "What're you cooking? I'm starved. We got hammered all day. I barely had time for breakfast. I had to fly a patient out on the chopper today, and then dear ol' Jarvis up and decides to pull a disaster drill on Dr. Bower. No warning, no time to prepare. I was so mad. Guess who tried to assist and got turned down?"

"You?"

"You betcha. Jarvis has it in for Lukas."

"Jarvis has his reasons."

Mercy glanced at the stir-fry on the stove, picked out a piece of water chestnut, and opened the fridge. "The way I see it, Jarvis has some problems of his own he'd better get worked out before he starts criticizing others. He's had a brain glitch the past few days. Got any milk?"

Ivy sighed heavily, her impatience giving way to sarcasm. "I'm fine. Thanks for asking, dear. Joints were a little stiff when I got up this morning, but I felt great by the time I hit the treadmill. Speaking of which, didn't Dr. Simeon tell you he got an appointment for me with a big-shot cardiologist in Springfield? I'm going to see him tomorrow. Why don't we let him decide about the trip."

Mercy put down the milk jug and turned to her mother. "I can't believe you agreed to an appointment for to-morrow. You should have known I'd want to go with you for this."

"Why? So the doctor can talk to you instead of me? I hate that, and I sure hope you don't do it to your own patients. I don't have Alzheimer's, I'm not that forgetful yet, and I've got my own life to live, just as you have yours."

"But this is important. I want to hear—"

"I'll take notes and let your secretary transcribe them for—"

"Cut the sarcasm, Mom. Is there something wrong with caring about your own—"

"Caring? A little kindness, a little concern for how I'm feeling about all this, would—"

"Maybe I can get Jarvis to cover for—"

"Don't even think about it!" Ivy's voice hit a few more decibels than necessary.

"No, you're right. The way Jarvis has been acting, he may feed my patients to the wolves."

"Would you at least listen to me a minute?"

Mercy closed her mouth and watched her mother in silence for a full five seconds. "I promised myself I wouldn't do this. I wanted to be strong and supportive for you, I really did, and here I am jumping down your throat. Sorry, Mom. But really, the trip to Colorado…"

"I need the break. It's been so long since I've gotten out like this. I need—"

"It's only been two and a half weeks since Grandma died. You want Tedi and me to lose you, too?"

"Mercy, stop it! Hiking in Colorado can't be as stressful as this."

"There's no oxygen out there on those mountains at fourteen thousand feet."

"Oh, sure, like our group is going mountain climbing. Get real. I'm the youngest one going, and as I've already told your Dr. Simeon, Doc Heagerty will be going, too."

"First of all, the whole state of Colorado is higher in elevation by far than the highest peak in Missouri. Second, Dr. Simeon is not mine and third, Doc Heagerty has earned his rest. The last thing he'll want is a needy patient following him into the wilderness."

"He'll want this patient."

"And how's he going to do you any good if you have a heart attack, or…" Mercy stopped and stared at Ivy. "What?"

Ivy held her gaze calmly. "Do you have a problem with that?"

"Uh, problem?"

Ivy nodded, as if satisfied she'd managed to cut off

Mercy's word flow, if even for a few seconds. She sauntered across the kitchen and opened the cupboard for
plates. "Close your mouth, or you'll catch a bee. There's
plenty of stir-fry for both of us. I have some fat-free garlic
bread ready to put in the oven. It'll only take a minute.
You could use some healthy food for a change instead of
that greasy hospital stuff." She held her daughter's glazed
stare for a moment, then continued with her preparations.

"How long has this been going on with Hugh?"
Mercy asked.

"This 'thing' is called friendship, simple as that. Hugh
and I have been friends for years."

"Yes, but when did you cross the threshold from
doctor-patient friends to…you know…*friends?*"

"Since Elizabeth Heagerty died with a heart attack
three years ago." Ivy placed the food on the bar and took
a stool beside Mercy. She bowed her head in silent grace
as she always did.

"I didn't know," Mercy said when Ivy raised her head.

Ivy picked up her fork. "There's nothing more to know.
We're friends. Your father has been gone for five years,
and some of the nightmare has faded."

"Which nightmare?" Mercy asked bitterly. "The marriage or the death?"

Ivy poured habanero sauce on her food. "A combination, I suppose."

Mercy remained silent for a few moments as she ate.

"Life goes on," Ivy said at last. "I was hoping you'd
be happy that I could build new relationships after…bad
experiences with a previous marriage."

"I am happy for you, really, Mom. I admire your
ability to recover. I can't imagine ever even considering
remarriage after the first disaster…and after Dad." Mercy

had experienced a triple whammy five years ago, and she didn't know if she would ever recover. Not only had her father died from alcoholic cirrhosis, but she had gone through a nasty divorce and had lost her daughter to Theo Zimmerman in a vengeful double cross.

Ivy placed a hand over Mercy's and squeezed. "I haven't said I'm getting married."

"That's a relief."

"As for the future…" Ivy shrugged. "So what's the difference between my friendship with Hugh and yours with Robert Simeon? You two spend some time together outside office hours. If you're so set against relationships—"

"We spend very little time together outside office hours, and we always talk shop."

"I think he would like more."

"I don't give—" She hesitated. "Mom, there's no relationship there. It would be a waste of my time and his. The only relationships I want are those with my daughter and my mother. Thanks to that maggot of an ex-husband, Tedi is more confused at ten than most sixteen-year-olds. She's certainty more worldly-wise."

"Get her back."

Mercy rolled her eyes and leaned back in her chair. "Fat chance. You know what happened the last time Theodore dragged me through the court system. It hurt Tedi too much. How do you think she felt about seeing her mother being involuntarily committed to a psych ward?" Mercy had been suffering from a great deal of depression during the divorce and her father's death, so much that she'd taken a couple of extra Valium one night just to blunt the pain. It hadn't helped, so she'd tried to check herself into the mental heath center voluntarily. A friend of Theo's, who just happened to be on duty that night, had called the police and forced a ninety-six-hour stay. Theo used it to his advantage in divorce court and won custody of Tedi.

"I can't put Tedi through another court battle," Mercy said quietly. She looked up and held Ivy's gaze. Tedi was five at the time, and when allowed in the court-room, she'd listened solemnly to every word. Ivy had paid for the child's counseling for three years while Mercy struggled to build up a ruined practice and pay Theo's bills.

"She's not happy living with her father," Ivy said.

"Who would be? There's nothing I can do. It would just dredge up old pain for all of us, and I would lose the case again. I can't risk it, not with Tedi."

"Don't let Theo pull another bluff on you, honey. You know how good he is at that."

Mercy held her mom's silent gaze for a moment. What would it be like to have Tedi back with her all the time, after five years? Dare she hope?

"The man is an abuser, Mercy. How do you know he's not playing the same mind games on Tedi he played on you?"

"He loves his daughter."

"He doesn't know how to love."

"Loving a daughter is different from loving a wife. Who wouldn't love Tedi?"

"Your father loved you." Ivy's voice held the pain of too many memories. "I know you haven't forgotten. Theo drinks, too."

"You're saying that Theo might be treating Tedi the way Dad—"

"I don't know what Theo might be doing," Ivy said.

"But remember that you had some protection because I was home with you most of the time."

"And I'm not home with Tedi." Mercy's jaw jutted out. "That's not my fault, Mom."

"It doesn't matter whose fault it is. Try to get Tedi back."

"We could lose a lot, Tedi and I."

"You won't lose Tedi's love. She needs you."

Mercy swallowed the rest of her milk and wiped her lips with a napkin. "Okay, I'll think about it."

"Wouldn't hurt to pray about it."

Mercy shot her mother a scowl. "Wouldn't help, either. How about a deal? I won't hassle you about your friendship with Doc Heagerty if you'll lay off the Jesus stuff. And I'll even shut up about Colorado if you'll listen to the cardiologist. But if he tells you not to go to Colorado, forget the trip, okay?"

"Never hurts to listen."

"And do what he says."

"You act as if I have a death wish. I'm not what you docs call a 'noncompliant' patient, but I'm not going to panic and curtail all my activities. You're being overprotective."

Mercy grinned and picked up an apple from the fruit bowl on the counter. "Now, where did I learn that?"

"Speaking of docs, how has the new one been working out lately?" Ivy didn't quite keep the thread of antagonism from her voice.

Mercy shot her a suspicious glance as she chewed her apple. "He's good, even if he is an uncertified osteopath. He's had some experience, obviously. And he's smart, a really good diagnostician. He's called me on a couple of my patients, and I've been impressed. So have his patients and the E.R. staff. Hate to disappoint you."

"So you get along well with him?"

"I'm not sure 'get along' is a fitting term, and I'm still not convinced we need him. His presence has cut my moonlighting hours and rearranged my schedule to the point that I have to choose between working two extra shifts a month and keeping Tedi for my regular visitation, so my income is down. But you can't fight administration."

"You can if you are administration."

"No, Mom. Don't use your contributions as a source of blackmail just because you're mad at someone. I thought Christians were supposed to be above that stuff."

"I'm not using blackmail when it's my money in the first place, and I control the distribution. I can just as easily donate to Cox South in Springfield."

"Okay, then, call it bribery. Same thing."

"Not when I feel I'm following my conscience. Jarvis is still trying to find out why Dr. Bower was kicked out of his residency program in KC." Ivy bent to peer through the oven door.

"I doubt it had anything to do with clinical skills. He's going to be popular with the patients. He takes too much time with each one, but in their opinion, that's good."

Ivy glanced up at Mercy from her bent-over position. "So you like him?"

"I didn't say that."

Ivy sighed and straightened. "If this were a female doc, would it make a difference?"

"That's not fair."

"It's not fair to judge someone by gender."

"Why should you care? You want to get rid of him because you think he killed Grandma."

"No, I don't!" Ivy's words came with extra velocity.

Mercy heard the force of continued grief. Maybe Mom did need to get away. But to Colorado?

Mercy chewed and swallowed a third bite. "Yes, I would like him if he weren't a man. He's not as obnoxious as some. If Jarvis George has his way, though, Dr. Bower will be out by the time the next schedule goes up. And speaking of Jarvis, have you ever known him to drink?"

"Drink? You mean, alcohol?"

"No, Mom, I'm talking cream soda." Mercy made a face. "Of course, alcohol. He sounded drunk to me when I called him tonight. I've never heard him talk like that. He was insulting and rude, to boot. I don't know what's gotten into him."

Ivy shook her head. "I haven't spoken with him for a few days, but I've never known him to drink. Remember how he used to disapprove of your father's drinking? Did you wake him?"

"If that's all it was, he'd better not take night call anymore. He acted really weird. He even hung up on me." Mercy took another bite of apple, got up and hugged Ivy, and went into the living room for her coat. "Thanks for dinner. It's the best I've had in a while, but now it's past my bedtime and I'm tired. See you later."

"What? No dessert? I've baked some apples with honey and oats. They're delicious."

"Thanks, but I had a stale doughnut tonight while I was doing dictation. I'm stuf—" She gasped, glanced at her watch, and groaned. "Oh, no."

"What? Did you forget a chart?"

Mercy jerked on her jacket with sudden irritability. "Of course not. Just a man. See ya!"

She almost didn't stop at Robert Simeon's on the way home, but at the last moment she felt guilty. The guilt fostered a growing irritation. Robert had been trying to convince her to go out on a real date with him for the past several weeks, and she'd turned him down. Tonight had not been her idea. She'd only agreed to dinner to get him off the phone. She should probably be just as irritated with herself for allowing him to talk her into it.

This friendship had become a little too confining.

She knocked on the door hard enough to hurt her knuckles, then spied a lighted button to the right of the door. She rang it. She'd only been here once before, and that was to bring Robert home when his car had broken down three months ago. His new Porsche Carrera would prevent future episodes. Robert enjoyed many of the finer things money could buy. He enjoyed them a little too much for Mercy's taste, and lately when she was with him, she had become aware of the basic differences in their thought processes. He was a little too involved in himself. But then, maybe she was, too.

Mercy could tell the moment Robert opened the door that he was disappointed, even a little upset, about her extreme tardiness.

He smiled at her, a tight smile that did not reach his eyes.

"I'm sorry, Robert, I blew it."

He shrugged and turned to walk back toward what Mercy supposed was the dining room. The decor of the rooms was exquisite, all polished wood and brass and crystal, as she would have expected. He wore a burgundy silk shirt and tie. He looked meticulous. Mercy felt scruffy in comparison.

"You had a busy day," he said. "I know how that can be."

She followed him and saw the formal dining table set

with fine china, silver and crystal wineglasses filled with amber liquid. Fresh-cut purple orchids graced a glass dish and ivory candles had burned halfway down before being extinguished. This was no casual dinner invitation.

"I waited for your call for the first hour," he said. "I'm not used to being stood up. Most women would come early for *duck à l'orange*." He helped her with her coat and laid it on the back of a dining-room chair.

"I'm sorry," she said again. "We had a disaster drill and I forgot."

He stared at her for a moment. "You forgot?"

"I went to talk to my mother about her trip to Colorado."

He picked up a green crystal goblet and sipped at it. "Well, now you must be starving."

"I ate at Mom's."

He put the goblet down harder than necessary. "You already ate? So I kept everything hot for nothing? Dessert? Wine?"

"Sorry, Robert, I don't drink. What kind of dessert?"

"Bread pudding with rum sauce. It's an old family recipe, and there surely won't be enough rum to affect you. Religious beliefs? Your mother's influence? I didn't think you bought into that mind-set."

"'Bought into'?" Mercy snapped. "Actually, Robert, it's none of your business why I don't drink, but just for the record, my mother's personal beliefs have nothing to do with it." She pulled out a chair and sat down at one of the place settings. "I know firsthand what too much alcohol can do to the human body. You know," she said drily, "things like alcoholism, cirrhosis. My father was an alcoholic and I don't want to chance a hereditary resemblance."

Robert went into the kitchen and came back with two

delicate china dishes of bread pudding. "Believe it or not, I kept these warm in the oven, too." He set them on the table with a flourish and took his seat. "You missed a good meal." He patted his stomach. "So did I."

She scowled at him. "You could have eaten. I said I was sorry, okay?"

He poured rum sauce from a small ceramic jug and coated both servings of the dessert with it. "You don't sound sorry. You sound defensive."

"I didn't come here for a romantic tête-à-tête. I came to discuss my mother."

Even in the candlelight, she could see a flush creep up his neck and face, and she instantly cursed her predilection for speaking before she engaged her brain, especially when she was irritable already.

"I'm sorry, that was unkind," she said quietly. "As I said, I just came from Mom's, and I'm in argument mode. I went by to debate the issue of Colorado, and she took the wind out of my sails by leaving the decision up to the cardiologist. It seemed fair enough."

He shrugged and picked up his fork. "Works for me."

Mercy stared at him for a moment while he ate. "That's it? That's all you have to say?"

He stopped chewing and looked at her for a moment, then swallowed. "What do you want me to say, Mercy? She's at least willing to listen to the cardiologist. He's a specialist in electrophysiology. Why should I bust my rear with it when a specialist will do it for me?"

"I don't know." Mercy's voice was clipped. She knew that her temper, always on edge lately, was slipping past control. "It sounded acceptable when you suggested over the phone tonight that we should get together to discuss

Mom's case. Maybe I really thought you meant it, not just as a ruse to show off your cooking skills, but because you cared about a patient of yours who just happens to be my mother. Why on earth I should take your word at face value is beyond me. Esoteric ideas like integrity and human compassion shouldn't enter into the discussion where dating and prospective sex partners are concerned." She shouldn't have come. She'd been spoiling for a fight all day.

His fork clattered to the table as he spat a curse and glared at her. "What's gotten into you, Mercy? This is a simple dinner, not a seduction scene. I thought you might enjoy a little attention after a hard day at work."

Mercy glared back. "This is no simple dinner, and I've had all the attention I can handle today." How dare he put the blame on her? Typical jerk attitude.

Or maybe she really was blowing this whole thing out of proportion. At any rate, she wasn't up for another confrontation tonight. Relationships like this she did not need, had not asked for, and she thought she'd made that very clear to Robert several times in the past.

She pushed her dessert back and stood. "Smells delicious, Robert, but I'm out of the mood for some reason."

He threw his napkin on the table and stood with her. "I can't imagine why. My appetite seems to have died an unnatural death, as well."

She'd never noticed how well his voice carried sarcasm. Had to admire that in a man, especially since there were so few things in men to admire.

She reached for her coat.

Robert put a hand on her shoulder. "Hold it." He sighed and shook his head, the anger gone. "Listen to us. We're doctors. Colleagues. I'd like to say we're friends."

She did not reply. To do so would have continued the

fight, and she did not want to hurt Robert's feelings any more than she already had.

"Because I *am* your friend," he continued, "I know you have a chip on your shoulder the size of Missouri, and I know why. But, Mercy, you're turning into a real misanthrope."

"No, I get along fine with women and children. It's just the men I have problems with."

"See what I mean? You're suspicious of every male you meet over the age of ten, and even the hint of a relationship sends you into combat readiness."

"I like it that way." She gently stepped from his touch and pulled on her coat.

"You know enough about psychology to know your reactions aren't healthy. For your own sake, may I suggest you do something about the real source of your anger?"

"Funny you should mention it. Mom suggested that very thing tonight."

"And?"

"I told her I'd think about it. Good night, Robert." She let herself out of the house.

Chapter Ten

Tedi Zimmerman glanced from the television screen to the front bay window and shivered. The sun was gone. Shadows deepened around the set until Little Joe Cartwright seemed to be the only figure in the room. This was a third rerun.

Instead of channel surfing the way Dad always did, Tedi used the remote to turn off the set, then realized she didn't have a light on. She scrambled to the lamp and switched it on before anything that thrived in the dark could grab her.

A sudden, reassuring glow chased the shadows back behind the furniture and into the other rooms. Dad was late again. Wasn't there some kind of law against parents leaving their ten-year-olds home alone after dark?

Tedi hated the dark, but the last time Dad had come home this late she'd wished he hadn't come home at all. She picked up a burgundy-and-gold decorative pillow and hugged it to her chest. She buried her face into it. Her stomach was starting to hurt the way it did in school lately when she had a test, or when Mrs. Watson asked her a question in front of the whole class.

What would it be like to just disappear? Probably

nobody would care except Mom and Grandma Ivy. Dad wouldn't care, but he would blame Mom anyway.

Dad hated Mom. He never said anything good about her.

No matter how nasty Dad was to Mom, she always sent the child support checks. Tedi got the mail, so she knew. She knew a lot of stuff a ten-year-old shouldn't have to know. If Dad would keep his big mouth shut about Mom, maybe all that knowledge wouldn't be so painful.

The phone on the end table rang, and Tedi jerked, squeezing her pillow tighter for a moment. It rang again. And again.

On the fourth ring, she answered, trying to make her voice sound deeper, older.

"Hello?"

"Where were you? What took you so long to answer?" Dad's voice had a slight slur, which Tedi had long ago learned to recognize.

Her stomach hurt a little more. "Sorry, Dad. I didn't know if I should answer."

"I'll be a while longer."

Tedi tried not to whine. "Do you have to work late? Should I get a taxi to Grandma's?"

"No! You don't need your grandma. You're a big girl. Just stay there and do your homework." He paused, and voices and laughter could be heard in the background. "I'll only be another hour or so. I've got a couple of hot clients looking at the Polsner building."

Tedi wondered if the clients were drinking, too. "D-Dad, it's dark. Can't I just go next door and spend the night with Tasha?"

"You'll be okay for another hour. See you soon." He hung up.

Tedi's face scrunched up as she fought tears. She replaced the receiver and buried her face once more into the pillow. Her stomach hurt even worse, and her whole body trembled.

She wished she could go to Grandma's. Grandma Ivy didn't drink, and she told Bible stories and tucked Tedi into bed and prayed with her. Tedi loved her. It was easier to talk with Grandma than with Mom, because Grandma didn't get mad about everything Dad did.

"Grandma."

Tedi picked up the receiver and dialed the number she knew as well as her own. Good thing it wasn't long distance. Dad didn't know how much Tedi called her. He didn't hate her as he did Mom, but he didn't really like her, either. He talked about her as if she were a stupid old woman. Dad didn't know much.

"Hello." The voice wrapped a blanket of comfort, warmth and acceptance around Tedi.

"Grandma." Tedi's throat closed in a sob. She couldn't help it. She couldn't talk.

"Tedi? Honey, what's wrong? Are you okay?"

"Uh-huh." Tedi's sobs came harder. She sniffed and grabbed some tissues from the table beside the sofa.

Grandma waited for a moment, then gently asked, "Is your father there?"

"Uh-uh." Tedi dabbed her face and blew her nose. She swallowed a couple of times and cleared her throat. "It's dark." She knew ten-year-olds weren't supposed to be afraid of the dark, but Grandma would understand.

"Why don't I come over and—"

"No! Dad said I couldn't see you."

"Did he say how long he was going to be?"

"He said an hour, but…I think he'll be later."

"Is he…?" Grandma hesitated.

Tedi guessed what she wanted to ask. "I think he was drinking." She felt like a tattletale.

There was silence, and Tedi knew Grandma was trying hard not to say anything bad about Dad. She knew that because she'd overheard Mom and Grandma talking about him one time. "Mercy," Grandma had said, "the child doesn't need us confusing her anymore. We've got to hold our tongues and be forgiving for Tedi's sake. But sometimes I'd like to string him up by his…little toes."

Tedi frowned when she thought about Dad hanging from his little toes. He was pretty big. Wouldn't his toes come off? Maybe if they just hung him by his arms or something….

"Honey, has he been drinking more lately?"

"I…think so." She still felt like a tattletale, but she was just tattling the truth. "I don't think Julie likes his drinking so much, but when she's with him she drinks, too."

"Maybe Julie can convince him to slow it down a little."

"She tried. It didn't work. I don't know if she really likes him that much anyway. I think she thinks we're rich, because of our house and the BMW. She said something about it one time." Tedi smiled. "She told me my father must be pretty good if he could afford all this."

"Oh? Dare I ask what you told her?"

"I told her the truth, Grandma. You always tell me to tell the truth."

"Uh-oh. How much of the truth did you tell her, Tedi?"

"Everything. I told her Mom was still paying on the house and car and sending big child support payments. I also told her that Dad said Mom was crazy, and that he got her committed once. I said that it probably ran in families and that I was probably going to be crazy, too."

"Where on earth did you hear that?"

"I read it in a book. It said depression is haired… um…hired…"

"Hereditary. Babe, you're too smart for your own good, but being depressed does not mean a person is crazy."

Tedi didn't want to think about that right now. "You really think I'm smart?" It felt good just talking with Grandma.

"Smartest kid in school. Don't settle for my opinion. Tests have proven it."

"Mrs. Watson doesn't think so."

"I'm sure she does. Do you think Julie told your father what you told her?"

"I don't know. He never said anything."

"She probably didn't want your father to know she's been feeling you out about his financial status. And the fact that she's still seeing him means she's either not that greedy after all, or you've convinced her you're just a cheeky kid."

"A cheeky kid!"

"Yup. You take after your grandmother."

"And Mom. You told me I'm like Mom."

"Spitting image."

"Yuck. I don't spit."

"Not even when you brush your teeth or catch a bug in your mouth?"

Tedi laughed. "Oh, Grandma."

"I love you, kid."

"I love you, too."

"You sure you don't want me to come over and stay with you?"

"Yeah, I'm sure. I don't want to make Dad mad. He gets mad so easy lately."

"Okay, then, we'll keep a low profile. Are you feeling better?"

"Lots."

"Good. I bet you haven't eaten, have you?"

"No. I'm not supposed to cook when Dad's not home. I had an apple when I got home."

"Fix yourself a bowl of cereal. You don't have to cook Cheerios."

"I think I'll be okay now, Grandma."

"That's my gal. You'll call me again if you need me, or if your dad doesn't come home?"

"Yeah."

"Bye-bye, honey."

"Bye, Grandma."

Dad didn't come home. Tedi didn't call Grandma.

By eleven-thirty the disaster drill was long past, though not without a few more disgruntled comments from Dorothy when more real patients came in, and Lukas insisted on treating them first.

Lukas didn't care. He was tired. He hadn't asked for this twenty-four-hour shift. In fact, during his preliminary interview, he'd told Mrs. Pinkley that he heartily disapproved of long shifts. She'd seemed agreeable at the time. Was she aware of tonight?

Lukas didn't intend to run and whine to her about everything, but he didn't want to be mistreated by an antagonistic director, either.

He shook his head, turned out the bedside lamp, and stretched out on top of the covers. Maybe he was imagining things, but it had been his experience that whenever one crawled under the blankets and got too comfortable during a night shift, one got called out sooner. Right now all was quiet in the emergency department.

He smiled as he remembered Mercy Richmond dressing-down Dr. George over the phone about the drill. She had a way with words. She had guts…and she was an attractive person. He liked what he knew of her, which he had to admit to himself wasn't much. It occurred to him that his initial response had not been what it was with most other single women: mistrust. She seemed to be the type of person who would have integrity, though there was no way for him to know something like that about someone he'd only met a few brief times. Funny that he should feel that way about someone who had a reputation as a man-hater and who wasn't necessarily always friendly with everyone.

But what about Lauren? He didn't think she was un-trustworthy. She was open and friendly, maybe a little bit of a chatterbox, but she was good with patients. And she was certainly not ugly. Several male patients and staff members had indicated that they found her very attractive. And she had shown quite a bit of kindhearted interest in Lukas; besides that, she was a churchgoer and quite possibly a Christian. If Dad knew about her, he would nag Lukas constantly to get to know her better. Lukas didn't want to. Their working relationship was fine.

So was he feeling plain old male-female attraction to Mercy? Or was it just a sense of kinship or identification, perhaps because she was a doctor and because she'd also suffered at the hands of the opposite sex?

He shook his head and sighed. He hated analyzing emotions to death…especially in the middle of the night when he needed sleep….

The phone shrilled sometime later, startling Lukas

awake. He picked up the receiver and peered at the bedside clock. Oh, wow, he'd slept a whole twenty minutes.

"Yes."

"Ambulances coming in, Dr. Bower. Plural."

"Okay. Thanks, Beverly. I'll be right in." Lukas groaned as he hung up. "A disaster drill with no medical backup, and possibly no sleep during a twenty-four-hour shift," he muttered as he left his call room. "Jarvis really does have it in for me."

A few moments later he sauntered toward the central desk, where Beverly stood talking softly to Rita, the night secretary. He heard his name mentioned, then Dr. George's; then they saw him and stopped talking. Beverly avoided looking at him.

"Dr. Bower, the first call came in about an elderly man who is unresponsive," Rita said.

"What's the ETA?"

"He'll be here in about four minutes."

"Vitals?"

The phone rang again. Rita reached over to answer. "I wrote them down. His neighbor found him in the grass out in his front yard."

Lukas stepped toward the central desk and glanced at her note while she spoke with an apparently distraught mother with a sick baby.

The incoming patient was an elderly man with a blood pressure of 109 over 68, a heart rate of 114, respirations of 14, pulse ox of 92 percent.

"Did they mention any signs of injury?" Lukas asked when Rita disconnected from her call.

"No, they didn't say anything about it," Rita said. "But they do have him fully immobilized and an IV established, and his pulse ox is 100 percent on a nonrebreather."

"What about the other ambulance?"

"It's BLS, and they're worried that this patient might be cardiac."

Lukas grimaced. A BLS ambulance—basic life support—was not set up for cardiac under the service here, but the area only ran one BLS and one ALS—advanced life support—per shift.

"The ETA for the BLS is probably about six minutes now," Rita continued. "They had some trouble understanding him. He doesn't speak English, and they couldn't find a Spanish-speaking interpreter at this time of night."

"So what have they done?"

"They've got an eight-year-old boy translating right now. The patient is about forty-five years old with chest pain, severe headache and nausea. He was fine until he went to work—" The phone rang again, and she pushed another note with vitals toward Lukas while she answered.

Lukas read the note, then motioned to Beverly. "Looks like we have a couple of serious ones. Let's call another nurse down from the floor."

"Okay." She still avoided looking at him. "I have room four ready for the first arrival and five for the second."

"Good." He turned to see Connie, the paramedic, and a male EMT wheel the first patient in on an ambulance cot with an IV pole. A young woman followed directly behind them.

Lukas recognized the woman and glanced with concern at the patient. He was still unresponsive. The man's features showed clearly, even through the nonrebreather mask. It was Frankie Verris. Disappointment overwhelmed Lukas. Had Frankie taken another overdose?

"Hi, Shelly." Lukas reached out and took her hand.

Again, as before, she had been crying. In her hand she carried a damp, wadded tissue.

Lukas turned to Beverly. "Are we getting another nurse?"

"No. The floor supervisor said she wouldn't send one down unless it was a real emergency."

"Did you tell her this was an emergency?"

"Yes."

"Who is the supervisor?"

"Rachel Simmons tonight."

Lukas nodded. He was becoming aware of some serious attitude problems among the staff, especially between the E.R. staff and the nurses on the floor, at least while he was on duty. Rachel Simmons was especially bad about refusing to send the float nurse down when they needed one. According to the grapevine, Rachel was having marriage problems and was difficult for everyone to get along with. She was also close to Dr. George. Bingo.

Lukas picked up the phone and dialed Rachel's number. He told her as kindly as possible that they were having an emergency and that he expected to see another nurse in the E.R. by the time the next ambulance arrived. She hung up on him.

The entrance door opened, and ambulance attendants brought in the next patient.

Lukas motioned to Connie, the paramedic with Frankie Verris. "We're ready for you in room four. Have you done a bedside glucose test?" He turned to walk beside them into the exam room.

"Yes, Doctor, it was 122. Nothing there. The patient has also received one amp of Narcan, IV push and 100 milligrams of thiamine." She pushed the cot up beside the bed and raised the bed up even with the cot.

"Any response?"

"None noted. The patient also received an IV fluid bolus of 250 CCs."

"I noticed the BP was a little low on report. Do you have a current BP?"

"It's 130 over 85."

Lukas stepped to the other side of the bed and reached across to help with the transfer.

Connie grasped the edge of the backboard from above Frankie's head. "On three. One. Two. Three."

They transferred the patient to the bed, and Connie snapped off her monitor leads.

Lukas bent over him. "What about the monitor?" He snapped his own leads onto Frankie's chest and checked the rhythm.

"Occasional PVCs and mild sinus tach," Connie replied.

He nodded with approval. She seemed to know her stuff. Nevertheless, the PVCs worried Lukas. They could be a signal for cardiac irritability.

While Lukas checked Frankie's pupils, listened to his chest and searched for signs of injury, the neighbor, Shelly, explained that, once again, she had not seen the elderly man fall.

"Did he flush his pills when he got home from his last trip to the hospital?" Lukas asked.

"You'd better believe they got flushed. I cleaned out his medicine chest when I took him home, all except for his aspirin. I nag him to take one every day."

"Good for you." Lukas looked up at her with a relieved smile. "I don't think it's an OD this time. Could be his heart."

Beverly entered the exam room. "Dr. Bower, another nurse just arrived from upstairs, and she says Rachel is having a fit. Too bad, huh? Need some help?"

"Thanks, Beverly. I need you to assist with Mr. Verris while we try to figure out what's going on. Get me an EKG. He's already on a monitor and an IV. I want the new nurse to help with the next one. Does anyone here speak Spanish?"

"Uh, I do, a little," the EMT who had helped bring Frankie in spoke up. The technician was a big guy with big ears and short hair.

"I know you," Lukas said. "Buck Oppenheimer. You're supposed to be in a class-two trauma center recovering from a fake tension pneumothorax from the drill. Quick recovery time. I'm impressed."

The man grinned. "Yeah, I'm feeling better so I opted to work tonight. I'm usually first responder for the fire department, so I don't get in here much. Right now I'm moonlighting."

"We may need your services with the other patient. He doesn't speak English."

"Sure, Doc."

"Hey," Beverly said, looking with dismay at the spider straps that secured Frankie to the backboard. "Dr. Bower, how can I get an EKG with him strapped down?"

"You may remove the spider straps, but leave the c-spine immobilized," Lukas said. "We still can't rule out a neck injury." He turned to Rita and gave instructions for blood tests and X-rays. "That's enough for now."

He led the way into the next room, where the nurse from upstairs was helping transfer an overweight man, Mr. Mancillas, onto the bed. Through Buck's halting translation, Lukas explained what he was doing as he auscultated the man's chest. Information from the ambulance team revealed that Mr. Mancillas had felt fine until he had been at work for about an hour; then he began having trouble with confusion and blurred vision, as well as the chest pain.

"Where does he work?" Lukas asked.

"We picked him up at the school bus garage," the tech told him. "We thought it sounded like his heart."

Lukas frowned. The patient's skin was very red. "Buck, ask him if he has ever had any problem with his heart before."

Buck grimaced. "I'll try. Like I told you, I just speak a little Spanish."

"Understood. Just do the best you can. Nurse, we need to hook up a cardiac monitor." He ordered an IV, EKG, X-rays and blood work. "Keep him on his O_2."

Beverly came in with the printout of the EKG for Frankie.

Lukas read the lines depicting the intricate rhythm of the elderly man's heart. He was having a heart attack. "Okay, Beverly." He gave orders for the meds needed.

Still without eye contact, Beverly nodded and left to prepare for another IV. Lukas frowned as he watched her walk away. Was it something he'd said? His breath, maybe? Whatever it was, he had no time to worry about it now.

"Rita, get me a chopper," he called along the hallway as he stepped over to exam room four. He walked in to find Frankie waking up and blinking. As before, the man looked helpless and vulnerable, and Lukas felt a wave of compassion.

"What's going on?" Frankie asked, his voice weak and shaky. He winced and grabbed at his chest. "Why am I here?" His thin, pale fingers played at the leads of the EKG machine.

Lukas gently moved the man's hands away. "Shelly found you unconscious. Now we know why."

Mr. Verris groaned. "It hurt so badly."

"Your chest?" Lukas asked.

Frankie nodded.

Lukas squeezed his arm reassuringly. "On a scale of one to ten, how badly does it hurt now?"

Frankie frowned and thought about it. "Maybe a five or six. Not as much as it did."

"Okay, we'll take care of your pain. I'm sorry, Frankie, but you're having a heart attack." He turned to find the nurse coming back into the room. "Beverly, I need morphine. Start at two milligrams, slow IV push; then we'll see how much more we need to relieve his pain. I'll contact Dr. Simeon to see which cardiologist he wants me to call. Frankie, do you remember what you were doing when the pain started? What time was it?"

"About ten o'clock tonight. I was watching the stars, just getting ready to go to bed, when it started. I tried to get over to Shelly's house, but I didn't make it."

Ten o'clock. If they got him to the cardiac cathlab as soon as possible, they might be able to save a lot of muscle.

Frankie reached out and touched Lukas's arm. "Can you do it again, Doctor? Can you save me?"

Lukas patted the man's hand and leaned forward. "We're going to take good care of you, but it's never up to me."

Frankie nodded. "You're going to preach again, aren't you?"

Lukas grinned, once again feeling a rush of tenderness for this gentleman. "I'll spare you if you'll just keep in mind what I said last time."

"Maybe you shouldn't spare me. Maybe—" Frankie winced. "Really hurts."

"Just hang in there, and we'll try to get rid of that

pain," Lukas said as Beverly came back into the room with her supplies. He hesitated. "Frankie, do you want me to pray with you?"

The man held his gaze for a moment, then nodded. "Maybe just a short one. I know you've got other patients." He grimaced as Beverly stuck him for an IV, then relaxed when Lukas laid a hand on his shoulder and bowed his head.

"Lord, we know You're the Great Physician and that You're all-powerful. No healing comes about except through You, and that healing begins when our spirits come into contact with Yours. Please touch Frankie's heart physically, Lord. Ease his pain, both in his body and in his soul, and draw him to You. Show him Your love, and give me Your guidance as I treat him. Help us to work together as a team as we seek Your will. Lord, please help Frankie to understand that he really does matter to You, and that his next home can be with Doris if he will only accept Your gift of love."

After Lukas closed his short prayer, he raised his eyes to see Frankie watching him. "You can sneak a sermon in as well as Doris used to."

Lukas returned to his other patient, who seemed better. His face wasn't as red, and the vitals didn't look bad. This probably wasn't even a cardiac.

"Did you notice if there was a motor running in the bus garage when you picked him up?" Lukas asked the ambulance tech.

The man looked surprised. "Yes, there was. He was working on it."

Lukas nodded. Of course. Carbon monoxide poisoning.

Dr. Simeon called about Frankie, and they arranged for helicopter transport for the elderly man to Cox South.

Since Simeon was the physician on call for the night, he also admitted Mr. Mancillas to his service at Knolls since the carboxy-hemoglobin level could be managed here. As Lukas made the arrangements, he heard voices in the waiting room, both in Spanish and English.

Beverly saw Frankie off on the helicopter, then came back inside.

"Got any more patients?" Lukas asked.

She sighed wearily. "We have three darling little children bouncing off the walls over in three, another elderly gentleman being checked in, and while I was seeing Frankie off, another car drove up and parked in a patient parking slot. We're in for a long night."

"Just what I always wanted."

Chapter Eleven

Theodore Zimmerman awakened in the gray morning darkness with a heaving stomach and a skull that threatened to scatter against the four walls of his room. After three attempts he managed to force open sleep-encrusted eyes to peer toward the digital alarm clock.

No illuminated numbers presented themselves. No night-light glowed from the hallway. Electricity must be out. Had there been a storm?

He forced himself to sit up and swing his legs out of the bed. His left foot hit something hard and sharp, and sudden pain on the inside ankle bone rivaled his headache for a moment.

With a blast of cursing he reached out, disoriented, and felt the hard top of a table. A coffee table. He'd kicked the corner.

He wasn't at home. He was on the lounge sofa at the agency. It was Tuesday morning.

He groaned and laid his head back against a cushion. He'd left Tedi alone last night. He'd failed her. Again. Failed himself, too. He'd tried to sell that albatross for two years, and it just wouldn't sell. Last night he'd been so sure those men would buy, but after their second walk through the building, they'd found more rotted floor-boards, and in spite of all his fast talking, they'd balked, then left. And Tedi…

What if Mercy found out about last night? She could take him back to court, take Tedi away, stop child support. She could even have him evicted….

With difficulty, he slowed his panicked imagination. "She wouldn't." He allowed himself a tentative smile. She had too much to lose, and she knew it.

Twice he'd requested more money for child support, and both times Mercy had complied without court inter-vention. Unfortunately, her resentment was becoming more and more obvious, and her sharp tongue had always cut deep. Recently it had been rubbing off on Tedi, who always made such a big deal about the money Mercy sent him. Good grief, didn't the kid even think he had a right to child support? Mercy was the big, im-portant doctor with the big bucks. Sometimes lately, with that long, dark hair and dark brown eyes, Tedi looked too much like her mother. Mercy had always been capable of infuriating him. She always had to prove she was better than him, so much smarter than a lowly real estate agent.

Sometimes the real estate agent called the shots.

Theo pulled himself up from the sofa and felt his way toward his office cubicle. The lighted display on the desk read 6:15 a.m.

In the bathroom he swallowed some Tylenol and splashed his face with cold water. He didn't remember much about last night after the sale fell through, but what he did remember worried him. He'd called Julie to meet him at the Golden Lion for a drink, and she'd refused, accusing him of being drunk already. She'd hung up on him. All he'd wanted was a little companionship after his disappointment about the building, and she'd hardly ever complained about his drinking before. In fact, she drank with him a lot, so why come across as some perfect Miss Priss when he was already down?

He really needed to sell the Polsner building. Sales were down all over this year. Prices continued to drop, and profits from that handy little land investment he'd made two months ago looked as though they might slip through his fingers. With the cost of improvements, it was a good thing he hadn't gone into it alone. His other investors, however, could become a problem.

Theo looked at himself in the mirror and nearly gagged. Bags puffed out from beneath his eyes, and his face looked as if he'd been drained of blood. He always took pride in his appearance because he knew it helped him sell property, especially to female buyers. But lately the dark circles under his eyes from lack of sleep might even be hindering sales. Who wanted to buy a house from a zombie? He had to figure out how to cut his stress level.

Maybe it was a good thing he hadn't gone home last night, even though Tedi had probably been afraid. It was better to be afraid of the dark than of your own father. That day a couple of weeks ago... That had been too close. Must've gotten ahold of some bad booze. He didn't usually get that mad, especially not at his own daughter.

And since Tedi was on his mind, he'd better take care of a situation he should have dealt with earlier. Mercy was due a telephone call. He punched the speed dial on his speakerphone.

* * *

Mercy stood in the trickle of lukewarm water that passed as a shower in her rental house, hoping the warmth wouldn't dissipate before she rinsed again. Last time, she'd gotten carried away and stood under the showerhead for a full five minutes. Had to rinse her hair bent over the faucet to keep from freezing in the cold water.

She was washing shampoo out of her eyes when the telephone rang. She finished rinsing, grabbed a towel, and turned off the water as she plunged out to catch the phone. Her answering machine had broken three weeks ago, and she didn't want to miss any possible patient calls.

She dripped water all over the kitchen counter as she grabbed up the receiver. "Hello?"

"Good morning, Dr. Richmond."

The too-familiar male voice dripped sarcasm, and Mercy almost dropped the telephone. Old anger surfaced in her like hot lava.

She held the line without replying. He hated it when she did that. It scared him, made him wonder what she was thinking. He was intimidated by people who thought for themselves.

"I wanted to catch you before you left for work, Mercy," Theo said at last.

Mercy smiled darkly to herself. The ploy of silence had worked again, and his tone had gone from hateful to conciliatory. It wouldn't last, but Mercy would milk it. She still didn't say anything.

"Tedi tells me Ivy's having some problems," he said. "Is she going to be okay?"

Continued silence.

"Mercy?"

"Look, Theo, I've got a job to get to. Cut the garbage and tell me what you want."

It was his turn for silence, and Mercy could imagine him fighting to control his own temper now. Ever since the day of their wedding, they had brought out the worst in each other, and it had escalated during the divorce. Mercy couldn't remember a single space of time when they'd actually been happy with each other, and for a long time she'd blamed herself. No more.

"I would have thought your daughter would be of more interest to you than your job," Theo said in a deceptively soft voice.

"Don't start with me this morning, Theodore. I'm not in the mood. Let me talk to Tedi."

There was a pause. "What, and wake her up?"

"She'll have to get up for school soon, anyway."

"Well, school was what I wanted to discuss, Mercy. Seems we're going to be out a little more money."

"*We?* For what?"

"A special tutor. Her grades aren't meeting the expectations of her teacher, Mrs. Watson. The old cow has sent three notes home with Tedi in the past month, and a couple of weeks ago she called me out of an important luncheon to pick Tedi up and take her home."

"Why didn't you tell me about it when it happened?"

He ignored the question. "Tedi is not paying attention, she disrupts class and she doesn't get along with her peers."

"Sounds to me as if she needs more counseling, not tutoring."

"You're not making the decision, I am. I'm the legal guardian, remember?"

"I'm still her mother, and guardianship can change."

Mercy heard a soft intake of breath.

"We don't need a shrink to tell us what's wrong with Tedi, do we?" His voice grew rougher. "We both know that a mother with a history of mental illness—"

"When did you graduate with a degree in psychology?"

"I don't need a degree to tell me—"

"I think this time we'll let a judge decide," Mercy snapped, surprising herself. He didn't reply, and she continued. "I'm fed up to here with your threats and your attitude and your insults, and if it's getting to me, it must be getting to my daughter, too."

"Don't try to blame me for—"

"I've let you bully me for ten years, Theodore Zimmerman, from the day we got married. You're not going to do it anymore, and you're not going to do it to Tedi, either. Furthermore, if you want more money, you're going to have to take me to court." She paused for breath, then amazed herself. "While we're there, we might as well cover everything at once. I'm going to sue you for damages to my reputation." Was she actually saying these things? "As you know, a doctor's reputation is her livelihood. You've already damaged that livelihood once. You won't do it so easily again, unless you have a couple of million lying around to donate to the cause."

She heard Theo gasp, and she shook her head in shock at what she'd just said. What had gotten into her? She'd never spoken so boldly before.

"Hey, hold it, there," he said in a voice that betrayed his instinct to backpedal fast. "What's going on? What's upsetting you so much, Mercy? We don't want to air our dirty laundry in the public court system. Half the population of Knolls will come for the show."

"That didn't bother you five years ago. You got a kick out of broadcasting my problems."

Theo inhaled slowly and deeply. "Look, I know a lot of people found out about things, and I feel bad about that."

What a liar! He was the one who spread the story.

"I'm willing to shoulder my share of the blame for that," he continued, his voice shaking more obviously now. "Right now we have a ten-year-old daughter to consider."

"I'm sick of hearing you use Tedi as a shield. I want her to see a counselor."

"I'll talk to her about it."

"Fine, you talk to her. I'm going to do some talking, too. If you can't find help for her, I will—on my terms. I expect to receive word of an appointment by the end of the week." Mercy slammed the receiver down.

The bedside phone shrilled its alert through the call room four times before Lukas could awaken enough to reach out and stop it. He glanced at the lighted dials of the alarm clock beside the phone as he brought the receiver to his mouth. It was ten-thirty Tuesday morning. He'd had three and a half hours of sleep. Must be a wrong number.

"This is Dr. Bower. My twenty-four-hour shift was over at seven. Try the other call room."

He took the receiver from his ear but heard someone say, "Dr. Bower, please!"

He stayed in position for a moment, trying to recognize the voice of the kamikaze caller. No use. His brain was still numb.

He brought the receiver back to his ear. "I'm sleeping. Leave a message."

"I'm sorry for bothering you, Dr. Bower." It was Carol, the courteous, perky E.R. secretary. "Someone you recently treated is begging to talk to you. She says there's an emergency with her brother, and she can't get him to the emergency room. She says he's too big, and he won't go."

Lukas groaned. He was too tired to figure this one out. Maybe it was a bad dream. Technically he wasn't here. After twenty-four hours without sleep, he had no business even talking on this phone, much less discussing a patient.

"What's his problem? Who are these people?"

"Her name's Darlene Knight. Her brother is Clarence Knight. She says you treated her for asthma a couple of weeks ago. I told her you were off duty, but she's begging for you to go see Clarence."

"But I don't treat patients outside the emergency room. My hospital credentials are specifically set up so that—"

"She's on the other line, Doctor. Would you tell her? We're getting piled up out here."

"Wait, Carol, I don't—"

"Thanks, Dr. Bower. Here she is."

Lukas groaned again. He needed sleep desperately.

"Hello? Is this the doctor? Hello?"

At the timid sound of the woman's voice, Lukas remembered the asthma patient. She had refused to stay in the hospital because her obese brother had no one to care for him at home. The poor woman was caught in a tragic situation.

Lukas hesitated a moment more. He tried to speak, but it came out in a croak. Even his vocal cords were asleep. He cleared his throat. "Darlene? This is Dr. Bower."

"Thank goodness." She sniffed as if she'd been crying, and her voice had a slight wheezing sound. "I don't know what to do, who to turn to. You probably don't remember me, but—"

"I remember you, Darlene. How is your asthma doing? Are you taking your medication?" Stall for time. How was he going to tell her he couldn't treat her brother at home? When he'd told Darlene she could call and talk to him, he only meant he would listen.

"It's not me, Doctor. It's my brother. He's really sick, worse than ever, and I can't get him out of his room. He won't let me call an ambulance. I told him about how you helped me and seemed to care, and he finally said he would be willing to see you if you would come here."

"Why don't you tell me some of his symptoms." Lukas could at least write them down, then try to convince her that Clarence must come to the emergency room.

"I've caught him clutching his chest, but he won't admit to chest pains. He's been sweating a lot. He's having trouble breathing and he's admitted that his stomach hurts badly."

"Has he been urinating normally?"

"More than usual, but I don't think he's…you know… done anything else in about a week. His legs are swollen and he's really thirsty."

"How is his breath?"

There was a pause. "Awful. How did you know?"

Lukas shook his head, awake in spite of his fatigue. The man was in trouble, and a house call wouldn't take care of it.

"Darlene, does diabetes run in your family?"

"Yes, our uncle had it. He was heavy, too."

"I want you to call an ambulance, tell them they need a double crew, explain why and get your brother to the emergency room any way you can. It'll take some manpower, but they can get him there. He needs much more help than—"

"He won't." Her voice held a note of despair. "You don't know how hard I've tried. He's given up. You're my only hope, Dr. Bower." Her voice faltered. "I can't just let him die, Doctor, and I think that's what he wants to do. Please help me."

Lukas took a slow, deep breath. "Okay, let me see what I can do."

Chapter Twelve

"Here you go, Doc. Guess you know you're running thirty minutes behind." Josie Collins tossed the chart on Mercy's cluttered desk and stood with her arms crossed.

Mercy looked up at her black-haired, disgustingly cheerful nurse. "Yeah. So?"

Josie grinned. "Feels good, huh? You're in demand. You've received your third transfer patient of the morning."

"Flu epidemic is good for business, especially when the other docs are in Hawaii for a conference."

"Being female and having a gentle touch has something to do with it. It's all I've heard this morning from all those patients eagerly awaiting your arrival."

Mercy scowled at Josie. "Don't nag."

Josie made a face at her and turned to leave, her short hair shining beneath the fluorescent lights. "I've got patients to placate."

Josie was Mercy's most avid cheerleader. She was a newlywed who had been gloriously happy and in love for five long, boring years. In spite of that serious failing, Mercy kept her on. She was good with the patients, and not everyone gagged when they heard her lapse into sighs of ecstasy at the mention of her husband's name.

To Mercy's surprise, Josie poked her head back in a few moments later. "Phone call, line three. It's your mom, or I wouldn't have bothered you."

Mercy picked up the phone. "Hi, Mom. I hope you're calling to say you've canceled your trip."

"You know better," Ivy said. "I'm calling about Tedi. Have you heard from her?"

"Since when? I saw her at my regular visitation time last weekend, and—"

"She didn't call you last night?"

"No, why?" Mercy frowned. "What's wrong? Did she call you?"

"Yes, and she was crying. It was getting dark, and her father wasn't home yet. He'd called to tell her he'd be late, and he was drinking."

"Why didn't you tell me last night?"

"You know how Theo reacts to you, and I didn't want him to take it out on Tedi later. I told her to call me again if he didn't come home, but you know how reluctant—"

"Are you telling me she might have stayed at home alone all night long?"

"It's possible. I can't prove it, and Theo would never admit to it."

"Of course not."

"Now don't you think it's time you did something to get Tedi back?"

"Yes."

There was a moment of surprised silence.

"Took the wind out of your sails, huh, Mom?"

"It's a nice surprise."

"There'll be nothing nice about it. It'll be a dirty court

battle." Mercy grimaced at the very thought of it. The whole idea scared her. "I just don't want Tedi hurt any more than she has been. But if I find out she stayed home alone last night…"

"Do you need the name of a good attorney?"

"I'll use Bailey Little. He's president of the hospital board."

"He plays dirty," Ivy warned.

"He works for his clients."

"He's dishonest, and you won't stand for it, and you know it."

"I'll do what it takes to get Tedi back. I have to go, Mom."

"Hang in there, babe. I'll be praying for you both."

"Yeah, sure." No sooner had Mercy replaced the receiver than the intercom buzzed.

"Dr. Mercy, we've got another call for you on two," came Josie's voice over the speaker. "You may want to take this one, too."

"Another one? Josie, you know I'm busy." It was well understood throughout the office that Mercy took only emergency calls when busy with patients.

"It's Dr. Bower."

"What does he want?"

"He wants to discuss a patient with you. I figured since you were between patients at the moment—"

"And thirty minutes behind, as you have reminded me twice—"

"Thirty-five minutes now. But since he sounds almost desperate—"

"And he has yet to learn our office rules around here—"

"And he's single and eligible, and from what I hear, he's really nice—"

"About which you will hold your tongue if you want to keep your job."

"Come on, Dr. Mercy. This sounds serious."

Against her better judgment, Mercy switched off the intercom button and picked up the phone. "Dr. Bower, may I help you?"

"Yes, I've got a problem."

He sounded relieved that she'd actually answered. He also sounded groggy, not that she cared.

"Do you ever make house calls?" he asked.

"Excuse me?"

"You know, house calls, where the doctor actually visits the home to—"

"I don't ordinarily make them, no." Mercy tapped her fingers on her desk impatiently. "Is this an emergency, Doctor? I'm behind with my patient load, and I don't usually take calls when I'm working."

"I think it's urgent. We have a morbidly obese patient with possibly advanced type-two diabetes, heart failure, a probable intestinal blockage—"

"Get him to the emergency room. What are they waiting for?"

"He won't go. His sister has tried to get him to go, and he apparently is also suffering from severe depression. They have no money, no way to pay, and he doesn't want to be a burden on his sister. They come from a welfare background and have sworn never to go back. I treated his sister in the E.R. and he has agreed to see me, but they want me to go there. The problem is that I'm only credentialed to work in the Knolls emergency room. I have no professional liability coverage for any other setting. So what are you doing for lunch?"

Mercy looked up as Josie came in and dropped another chart on her desk. "For lunch?"

Josie froze, and her eyes widened. She nodded wildly.

Mercy shook her head. "I'll be working through lunch at this rate."

"Which means you're dedicated to your patients. You were the only one dedicated enough to show up for the drill last night. You care about patients."

"What if I don't take this house call?"

"I'll go by myself and risk losing my job, everything I've worked for my whole life."

"Oh." If it weren't this one particular man— "I thought you told me this guy agreed to see you, not me." She glared at Josie, waving her out of the room.

"I'll go with you," Dr. Bower said. "Curb your tongue more than you did with Jarvis last night and you might be able to cajole this patient into letting you examine him."

"If what you say about him is true, he'll need much more than a house call to save him."

"I'm hoping we can convince him to go to the hospital once we've spoken to him in person. Remember that this guy doesn't have a job, no insurance, no Medicaid. We won't be reimbursed for our time or any expense we incur."

"Sounds like a sweet deal to me," Mercy said drily.

"So you'll bail me out?"

"Let me get this straight. I'll miss my lunch, I'll risk losing patients and I won't be reimbursed a dime for my trouble. I'd say that's a great incentive plan."

"What if you save this guy's life?"

She sighed. "What's the address?"

"If you'll give me a lift, I'll show you. Oh, and would you please bring some supplies with you?"

"Who do you think I am, the Salvation Army?"

"The sister was wheezing when I talked to her this morning. She's already been hit with an E.R. bill, and I don't think she can afford her medicine. I think she needs a treatment."

"Fine. I'll meet you outside the emergency room at about twelve-thirty."

When Mercy said goodbye she looked up to find Josie standing in the doorway, beaming at her.

"You're fired."

Josie walked out of the room sporting a stupid grin.

Lukas sat on the bed in his call room for a long moment, relieved that Mercy had agreed to go with him to see Clarence Knight and wishing he could go back to bed. He stood up, pulled the covers up over the pillows to lessen temptation, then walked into the bathroom and splashed his face with water. He took his street clothes out of his designated locker and changed. They weren't quite as wrinkled as the scrubs he'd worn and slept in for the past twenty-four hours, but he still needed to find some hangers and start using them. He also needed to find some gum or something before he opened his mouth and committed involuntary manslaughter.

Just as he was about to leave the bathroom, he heard the call room door squeak open. He hesitated with a frown, expecting to see a representative from housekeeping coming in to clean the room and change the bed. He should have locked the door. What if he'd been undressed? They should at least knock. Of course, they probably didn't realize he was still here.

To his surprise, he saw the short, gray hair and army-straight shoulders of Dr. Jarvis George as the older doctor crossed his field of vision and approached the beside desk. The man pressed his knuckles against his upper right temple, and Lukas could see a grimace of pain from a side view of his face. He also saw a shaking hand reach up to a shelf above the desk and take down a box of pre-scription drug samples. Ultram. Lukas watched as Jarvis ripped the sample packet open and turned toward the bathroom. He then stopped, obviously shocked to see Lukas standing there.

"Morning, Dr. George."

Jarvis jerked as if guilty. "Morning."

"Don't mind me, I'm just getting ready to leave." Lukas stepped across the small space and checked the desk, picked up his bag and turned back to Jarvis.

Jarvis stared at him, his face grimacing with irritation and probably pain. He flexed his left hand, then looked down at it.

"Are you feeling okay, Dr. George?" Lukas asked.

"I'm fine," Jarvis snapped.

"Isn't that the hand—"

"Don't you have to be somewhere?"

Lukas raised his brows and shrugged. "I'll be leaving shortly. Are you sure you're okay? I saw you holding your head. If you need—"

"Why do you have to hang around here after hours?"

Lukas controlled his irritation. The man was obvi-ously in distress. His hands clenched as if in a sudden spasm, and perspiration moistened his lined forehead. He was on duty today and would be until seven tonight.

Lukas turned to leave.

"News about your lack of cooperation has certainly made the rounds."

Lukas stopped and turned back. "Excuse me?"

"You think you're too good to take part in our disaster drill?"

"Of course not. I cooperated fully with the drill right after I saw to my patients."

Jarvis shook his head and winced. "Don't forget you're in your trial period here."

"Really? I didn't realize the hospital had a policy about probationary time." And he also hadn't realized just how irritable he could be after a long shift.

Jarvis took a step toward him. "You blatantly wrote me up about that stupid needlestick. That's strike one against you in my opinion, Bower."

Lukas spread his hands. "I followed hospital protocol, as was required of me. I had no ulterior motive, I assure you."

"You have also managed to offend and incur the suspicion of Mrs. Ivy Richmond by your poor handling of her mother's case. Mrs. Richmond just happens to be one of the sweetest and most generous benefactors of our hospital, at least until now. She has her doubts about a hospital that will hire someone who so easily disregards human life. That's strike two."

Lukas felt his spirits plummet as his temper rose. So that was how it was going to be. More politics. He had hoped to leave this behind in Kansas City. "I have a high regard for human life."

"We are awaiting info from Cunningham in Kansas City about a certain incomplete residency of a certain Dr. Lukas Bower. When we receive that info, it could be strike three for you, Bower."

Lukas had never been able to conceal his emotions, but he tried to keep his expression blank as he met and held Jarvis's hard stare. "May I remind you, Dr. George, that administration is aware of your ambivalence to my presence here." He kept his voice calm, even gentle, as if handling a testy patient. "I was even warned to expect it. The needlestick protocol is a good hospital practice. I reported the incident in obedience to the rule which states that anyone who refuses to follow proper protocol is to be written up. This is to protect the victim of the needle-stick from incurring any lasting effects from the incident, and also to protect the hospital in the case of possible contagion or litigation."

"That woman was suffering from Alzheimer's! She wasn't contagious!"

"So why is your hand bothering you? Have you had it checked out? Have you done any follow-up on the patient?"

"That has nothing to do with you!"

"Speaking of protocol…" Lukas heard his voice rising. He was weary and grumpy, and he paused to get control. "I followed it to the letter with Jane Conn's case, and I made excellent documentation. If Mrs. Richmond possesses the sweet and generous nature you describe, I'm sure she also has the common sense, once her grief has abated, to consider all circumstances surrounding her mother's death. I'm sure, also, that her daughter has the wisdom to help her see reason."

"We'll see what Ivy has to say when we hear from Cunningham."

"Also well documented and fully disclosed in detail to this hospital's administrator is my residency termination and subsequent trial to gain my permanent licensure and to reinstate my reputation in the medical profession. She has checked my references and read all the legal reports." Lukas needed to leave, but anger held him there.

Jarvis's face reddened. "Administration has passed along

a patient complaint against you for the indiscreet attempt to use Narcan with morphine for the relief of headache pain."

"That's within the FDA approved guidelines. There are no contraindications to using the two drugs together except with an addict."

"In which case you could have killed him."

"Are you admitting Dwayne Little is a drug addict?" Lukas demanded.

"Of course not."

"Since you're doing such a thorough job checking my background, you will find that I have never used the two drugs together. I specifically listed the dangers the drugs presented for an addict, and I offered to help him into rehab if he needed it. Mr. Little got mad and left. Where's the medical error?"

"You'll find out when Dwayne's father contacts you. Don't forget Bailey's the president of the board of directors for this hospital." Jarvis raised his hand to point at Lukas, but the hand shook and he lowered it. "That could put you out of the game."

"Dwayne Little attempted to coerce me into giving him a narcotic, as he has done in several emergency departments in the area recently. I believe the law still states that the physician is the only one with the authority to decide which drugs to use with which cases, especially with controlled substances. If you are questioning my judgment, perhaps you should discuss it with the QA committee." Lukas pivoted and stalked from the room.

By the time he reached the E.R entrance, he realized that he was shaking almost as badly as Jarvis had been. He marched out across the ambulance bay to the parking lot, breathing deeply, frustrated and furious. That man was an obnoxious jerk! How had he lasted in practice this long, worked with staff this long, without being run out of the hospital, or out of town? One might even question the intelligence of a hospital administration that kept an irrational, verbally abusive, obstructionary person like that on medical staff.

Lukas took a brisk walk around the lot, his temper unrelenting as he continued the argument in his head. As he did so his thoughts churned deeper, grew darker, until a little warning system from the past alerted him. *Pray.* He needed to pray now, when he least felt like it. The warning came through his Dad's remembered voice, when Lukas was little and his brothers ganged up and picked on him unmercifully about his glasses or his size or his inability to carry a tune during hymns in church. Then he would lose his temper and attempt to punch one of his bigger, stronger brothers. He'd never succeeded, but Dad had seen it and chided him for it. *"Lukas, if you can't control your temper, let God do it for you. Just pray. Ask Him to take control of your emotions immediately. It's an SOS. You don't have to feel all pious and worshipy. Just open your mouth and tell Him how you feel. He's big. He can handle it."*

Lukas had used that method a lot when he was growing up, and he did so now. "God, help me! I'm so mad right now I could hit Jarvis George! I can't think straight, I can barely walk straight, and I don't know why this had to happen this morning when I'm sleep deprived. Did he plan it that way?" A thought occurred to him. "Did *You* plan it that way? Because if You did—" he broke off, then continued "—I don't appreciate it!"

Long ago he'd learned not to fear a sudden lightning bolt from the sky when he confronted his Lord like this.

What he'd learned to expect was an immediate answer to this particular type of prayer.

And he received it. Already he was concentrating on God instead of Jarvis George. God did not stay meekly in the background when He was addressed honestly and passionately at times of stress. There was always an answer of some kind, a way out of the temptation.

For a few more moments Lukas walked and prayed, until finally he realized that he had stopped shaking. His breathing came more normally. His heart felt better. He still felt singed and abused by the confrontation, but he wasn't mad at God anymore.

"Lord, forgive me," he whispered. "And help me to forgive. Help me to remember that Jarvis George is—at least in my opinion—a lost soul who needs to see me serve as a loving Christian example to him." He snorted at himself in derision as he turned for another round across the paved lot. *Oh, yeah, I'm some great example, all right.* "Control my actions, Lord, because I don't seem to be doing a good job of controlling them myself. And please, Lord, give me a chance for some sleep before I have to return to work tonight."

"Dr. Bower?"

The voice startled him. He stopped walking and turned to find Lauren stepping up behind him, her purse slung over her shoulder, and her long, blond hair loose and ruffling in the breeze. She bit her lower lip and watched him with pensive eyes. *Oh, great. How long has she been standing there?* Did she think he was talking to himself?

"I was in picking up my paycheck today when I heard the…uh…raised voices." She glanced toward the emergency room entrance, then looked back at Lukas. "Don't take Dr. George's words too personally."

"I'm trying not to, but if you heard him, you probably realize that the words were pretty personalized." His sudden openness with her surprised him. But then, her sudden appearance surprised him, too, especially after praying to God for help. Surely God wasn't using *her*.

"He would find something to complain about no matter who the new doctor was." She took a step closer and lowered her voice. "The problem is that he's buddies with Bailey Little, and everybody knows by now what happened between you and Dwayne. I've been praying for you, Dr. Bower. You're great and I hope you stay, but I don't know what those two will…" She stopped and rolled her eyes. "There I go again, gossiping. Sorry. Just be careful, okay?" She glanced around the parking lot. "Did you need a ride home? I don't see your Jeep. I'd be glad to clear out the junk in my passenger seat and squeeze you in."

"I appreciate that, but I'm parked in the other lot, and besides—"

A car horn blared suddenly from a few yards away, and they both turned to find Mercy pulling up to the curb along the street in her ten-year-old Pontiac. She waved at Lukas and he waved back.

"My ride's here."

Lauren glanced at the car, her face turning red. "Good. Have fun. See you at work, Dr. Bower." She waved at Mercy, then turned and walked away.

Chapter Thirteen

Tedi lay on her bed with the curtains drawn, staring at the ceiling, her door locked. She wished she'd put a chair under the knob, but she'd been too scared to get up once she got into bed last night. The house had made scary sounds all night, and Tedi had cried so much her wet pillow still cooled her cheek. Even after morning light filtered through the curtain, highlighting tiny rays of floating dust, Tedi lay there, scared. Her eyelids drooped, and she forced them back open. She was still alone. It was so hard to stay awake after a whole night of crying. Her lids drooped again.

A slight sound reached her from the distance, and for a moment she froze. Was someone inside the house? Was it Dad?

When she strained to hear more, the sound of laughter reached her…a woman's laughter, coming from downstairs. Was Julie here?

Other voices joined in, men's voices. She lay listening. Was that Dad?

Still scared of the lingering dark shadows in the room,

she pushed her covers back and forced herself to get up. She cringed when her feet touched the floor; she expected something to grab her legs and drag her beneath the bed.

The voices grew louder now, several at once. Tedi couldn't hear what they said, but they were there. Nothing could reach her from the darkness with someone else in the house.

She crept across the room and pulled open her bedroom door. It made no noise, but the voices increased. She heard Dad's voice for sure now, and Julie's. She crept down the hallway to the balcony and looked down into the parlor. What she saw made her gasp.

Mom stood there by the flower arrangement, telling Julie to stay away from her daughter. Grandma Ivy stood over in the corner shouting at Dad about the way he'd been treating Tedi. Mrs. Watson sat on the love seat talking to Jarvis about how Tedi behaved in school.

Tedi started down the stairs toward them, but the steps were buried in shadow, dark and menacing. She froze on the top step and could not move.

"Mom?" she called. "Can you come up here and get me?"

Her mother did not look up.

"Mom! I'm scared! Come here!"

No reply.

"Grandma?" Tedi called more loudly, but Dad shouted at Grandma to mind her own business and not to interfere in his family's problems. No one heard Tedi.

She held tightly to the banister and felt with her foot for the second step. Her feet landed on solid support. She could do this. She could get down to everyone if she took one step at a time.

She took another step, then another. The darkness

grew deeper. She couldn't even see the banister, but she could still feel it. She held tightly and stepped down again.

Something grabbed her leg, and slithering tendrils wrapped around it. She screamed.

"Mom! Grandma!"

The voices grew louder, and she looked down to find Dad standing in front of Mom, shouting at her. Now Julie shouted at Grandma. Even Mrs. Watson and Jarvis shouted at each other. No one heard Tedi, but they were all arguing about her.

She tried to jerk free. "Dad!" she screamed.

The monster clung more tightly to her, inching up her leg. It reached her waist, coiling tightly around her torso. She tried to wrench free, but it just squeezed harder. She tried to take another step down, but it blocked her way. It was as if the darkness itself had taken form and held her as its prisoner.

"It's your fault!" Dad yelled at Mom. "You're the crazy person, and you're not making enough money."

The darkness wrapped around Tedi's arm and tugged.

She pulled back, hitting at it.

It grabbed her other arm, too.

"Mom!" She screamed the word as loudly as she could, but her voice didn't carry. "Mom! Mommy!"

It hovered close, its blackness swallowing her into the deepening shadows. She screamed again, and the monster absorbed her scream, cutting her off from help. It came closer, inching up her shoulders. It shook her and opened its mouth as if it would take her completely.

It shook her again. "Tedi! Wake up!" Dad's voice shocked her awake.

She opened her eyes to find light streaming in through

her open curtains and Dad looking down at her from his perch on the side of her bed. He held her by the shoulders.

"Tedi? Wake up. It's okay. You were dreaming."

Tedi hovered in that moment between nightmare and reality, letting the relief soak in. Fear still hovered over her, but it didn't cling to her like before. She wasn't alone.

"Dad?" Her face crumpled with tears.

Dad put his arms around her and held her tightly. "I'm sorry, Tedi." He sounded awful, his voice all crackly and dry. "I really blew it last night. Didn't your grandmother come over to stay with you?"

Tedi stifled her sobs for a moment and pulled back. She looked up at Dad accusingly. "You know you told me not to call Grandma. You said I didn't need her. I was afraid you'd get mad if I had her come over, so I spent the night alone." Tears regrouped in her eyes. "I was alone, Dad."

He sighed, head lowered, the same expression he always used when he sobered up after a night of drinking. But Tedi wasn't going to let him get away with it so easily this time.

"I wish I'd called the police," she muttered.

He stiffened, staring at her.

"I was scared." She hesitated. Don't push him too far. "A ten-year-old kid shouldn't have to stay at home all by herself while her dad's out partying with his friends. A ten-year-old kid should be at home with her mother."

His head shot up, and his eyes narrowed as his fingers dug into the flesh of her shoulders.

"Ow! Dad, stop it. Let go. That hurts." She tried to pull free, but he wrenched her closer.

"Look," he snapped, "I wasn't partying, I was working! I told you I was sorry. Can't you ever settle for that?"

Angry tears formed again in Tedi's eyes. He wasn't sorry for her. He was sorry for himself. She'd heard Mom tell Grandma that before.

With a more forceful jerk she pulled from his grasp and rubbed the sore spots on her shoulders. The pain made her madder. "I think I'm just in your way here. Why don't you send me back to live with Mom?"

He watched her in silence for a moment. "Your mother wants you to see a shrink."

Her eyes widened. She felt as if she'd been punched. "What? Why?"

"Isn't it obvious? She thinks you're crazy just like she is."

"I don't believe you!"

"She told me so this morning when I told her about your little run-in with your teacher."

"That was over two weeks ago," Tedi said between clenched teeth. "And I didn't have a run-in with my teacher. I fell asleep in class because of you and Julie. I bet you didn't tell Mom about that, did you?"

He held her angry gaze. "I told her you're having trouble in school and need a tutor for some of your classes. She's the one who wants you to see a shrink, not me."

"I don't believe you."

He shrugged and got up from his perch on the bed. "Fine. Wait and see. If I don't have an appointment for you by the end of the week, she's going to do it herself. That's what she told me this morning. Just ask her. Better get ready for school, or we'll both be in trouble again."

Mercy had to struggle to hide her amazement as she stepped into Clarence Knight's bedroom behind Lukas and Darlene. The huge man made his standard, dilapidated double bed look like a doll's crib. The center of the mattress formed a deep well that strained beneath the weight of his enormous, sleeping bulk. The sound of snoring reached all along the length of the dimly lit hallway leading to the room. He slept propped up on shabby, worn pillows, with nothing but a huge pair of shorts to cover him.

Clarence had a full head of dark, nearly black hair that grew below his ears. A full beard and mustache disguised much of his face, but they did not hide the great slope of flesh that bulged from chin to chest. Without the fat, some women might have called him attractive. To Mercy he was just another man who didn't know how to handle his physical appetites.

Immediately she felt guilty for the tenor of her thoughts. What if it were a woman lying here encased in this prison of flesh instead of a man? What did it matter? Clarence was in trouble. Even in the dimness of the room, Mercy detected superficial ulcers on the man's grotesquely swollen legs. Why hadn't he been to the doctor long ago?

Darlene clicked on the bedside lamp and leaned over, her own wheezing drowned out by the sound of her brother's troubled sleep.

"Clarence," she called softly, shaking his arm.

No reaction.

She glanced up at Lukas and Mercy with an apologetic shrug. "He's hard to wake. He doesn't sleep well at night because he stops breathing so many times. I'm always afraid he'll stop breathing for good."

"You probably don't sleep too well, yourself," Mercy said. She couldn't keep the cynical tone from her voice. Had it ever occurred to this man that his sister might be sacrificing her life just to keep an eye on him? Her breathing sounded awful. Darlene was the one Mercy wanted to check out.

Lukas squeezed his way around Mercy in the crowded room. He leaned forward and grasped the giant by the arm. "Clarence," he called loudly. "I'm Dr. Bower, the person your sister told you about. Clarence? Try to wake up now, please. Dr. Richmond and I need to talk to you."

Clarence's eyes opened slightly, and he growled and shifted in the bed. The bedframe shook as if an earthquake had hit. His eyes came open more, and he glanced at his sister.

"You're wheezing again." The deep, grating bass of his voice betrayed concern. "Where's your stuff?"

"I'll get more," she said. "But first, I want you to talk to these doctors. They came here to help us."

Clarence's chocolate-brown eyes came open wider. "Doctors?" He looked up at Lukas, then at Mercy standing slightly behind him. As if suddenly embarrassed by his state of undress, he reached and pulled a sheet over his bare torso. The sheet didn't quite fit across his huge abdomen. His attention focused back onto Mercy, and he frowned.

"Mr. Knight," Lukas interjected, "I'm Dr. Bower, the emergency room physician Darlene told you about. This is Dr. Richmond, a friend of mine. We're here to help you."

"Help me what?" Clarence growled. "Darlene needs the help. Can't you hear her? Take care of her and leave me alone." He pulled the sheet up higher on his chest.

"That's exactly what I intend to do," Mercy snapped. "But she wants you to be treated first. For once why don't you consider her feelings?"

Lukas shot her a warning glance, and she looked away. She shouldn't have come on this wild-goose chase. The man wasn't going to accept their help anyway. She could see it in his eyes. And she certainly wasn't in the mood today to deal with the male species. They should exist on another planet. Maybe in another universe.

"I'm in good health," Clarence Knight growled. "Can't you see how healthy I am? Get out. I can't afford your medicine."

"I'm not after your money," Mercy shot back.

He leaned back and grunted, studying her expression more closely. "You'd be the first doctor who wasn't."

Mercy opened her mouth to argue, but Lukas reached out and gently squeezed her arm.

"When Clarence lost his insurance," Darlene explained to Lukas and Mercy, "the family doctor refused to see him anymore."

"I'm sorry you had so much trouble, Mr. Knight," Lukas said. "We aren't charging you for the medication we brought you today, and we aren't charging you for our help."

"I didn't ask for your help."

"You told Darlene you would see me," Lukas said. "But you wouldn't come to the emergency room."

"Those places cost money," Clarence said. "I know. I got hit with a bill from Knolls three years ago. Darlene had to help me pay it off."

"You know I wanted to do it," Darlene told him. "Clarence, please just talk to them for a little while." She stopped and took several breaths. "You told me you would. They really care."

"If they really care, they should know you're in trouble, sis."

"More than you realize, and you're part of the reason," Mercy snapped, ignoring Lukas and his warning glance. "We brought medicine for her."

"Then help her and leave me alone."

Mercy clamped her teeth down on her tongue to keep from making another angry retort. She raised a brow at Lukas, then looked at the sister, who continued to struggle with her breathing. "Come on, Darlene, let's leave these...gentlemen alone for a few minutes and see if we can get rid of that wheeze."

Darlene hesitated, looking at her brother.

"Go on, sis. I'll be fine."

Mercy led the way out of the room and waited for Darlene to follow. The only redeeming quality that man had, in her opinion at the moment, was the fact that he did seem to love his sister very much. That might save him in the end if he listened to Dr. Bower, which he was probably too bullheaded to do.

Lukas closed the door.

"Lock it," Clarence growled.

Lukas did so.

The big man visibly relaxed. "Thanks. Okay, Doc, let's get some stuff straight." He tossed off the sheet and struggled to move his bulk to the side of the bed. He swung his legs over to the floor, then sat there for a moment huffing. "I don't want a doctor here."

"You told your sister you would see me."

Once Clarence caught his breath sufficiently, he inched closer to the side of the bed and anchored his hands on the edge of the mattress. "I only said that to stop her crying. Can't stand to see a lady cry."

"Then you'd better go through with this, Clarence, because if you don't, she'll be crying again. You're in trouble and you know it. What's worse, she knows it."

"I told you I can't pay, and you and I both know this one trip ain't gonna cut it. I'll have to go in for all kinds of tests, maybe even surgery. I'm not gonna saddle Darlene with all those bills."

"You won't have to."

"How can you say that? They told me three years ago how much it would cost to fix me up, and I'm a lot worse now."

Lukas took a deep breath. "You obviously qualify for aid."

"No. No handouts." He leaned forward and tried to push himself off the bed. He fell back, gasping.

Lukas stepped forward to help him.

Clarence held a hand up to ward him off. "I'll do it myself or I won't do it at all." He leaned forward again, and this time made it to his feet. "Gotta go to the john. At least I can still do that for myself. Don't know how long it'll last."

Lukas heard the man's labored breathing and itched to use a stethoscope on him. But first things first. "Have you been urinating more often lately?" he asked.

Clarence's sour breath filled the room as he puffed his way to the attached bathroom. "About twice as much, seems like. Maybe even more."

"Thirsty a lot?" Lukas listened to the floorboards groan.

"Lots." Clarence squeezed into the bathroom and closed the door.

Lukas reached into his medical bag and pulled out his stethoscope and his sphygmomanometer with a thigh cuff. He might as well be prepared.

The toilet flushed and the door opened. Clarence extricated himself from the bathroom and lumbered back toward the bed. Lukas could have heard him breathing from the far end of the house.

Clarence clutched his chest as he lowered himself to the mattress once more.

"Feels like someone is sitting on your chest, doesn't it?" Lukas observed.

Clarence continued to catch his breath. He nodded. "How'd you know?"

"I'm a doctor. You also seem to have a lot of difficulty breathing." That was the understatement of the week.

"Some. I'm okay after I rest. You try carrying all this weight around for a while. You'd be out of breath, too."

"Of course I would. Especially if I were in heart failure, had diabetes and a possible bowel obstruction. Your heart is straining to keep up with your body, and the angina pain indicates your coronary vessels are clogging up, probably due to high cholesterol and triglycerides."

"Use English, Doc."

"I'm saying you could have a heart attack at any time. All of it's treatable, Clarence, but time is your enemy right now."

"How's that?"

Lukas stared at the man. Was he in denial? "We're talking life and death here, Clarence."

"We all have to die sometime."

Lukas felt a chill as he looked into the big man's eyes. They were not cold, hard eyes. They were a deep, warm brown. But he wanted to die. Darlene was right.

Clarence leaned forward. "Let me tell you something, Doc." He kept his voice low. "Darlene's going to be okay once I'm gone. I made sure of it."

"How can you say that?"

"Insurance." He sat back with a nod of satisfaction. "They wouldn't carry me for medical, but they couldn't dump my death benefits. I paid them off before all this happened."

"Do you really believe your sister would rather have your money than you?"

"She doesn't know what she really needs right now. I'm just a dead weight to her." His face contorted in a humorless grin. "No pun intended."

"Why don't you treat your sister like an adult and let her make her own decision about this?"

"I've always taken care of Darlene. I can't do this." He gestured around him helplessly. "I can't live like this. It'll drain her dry, and then she'll die, too."

"Not if you'll swallow some of that pride and let us help you. Clarence, what you're planning will destroy your sister."

"No, it won't. She'll miss me for a while, but she'll be fine. She's a lot tougher than she looks."

"Doesn't love count for anything with you?"

"Why do you think I'm doing this? Do you really think I look forward to dying? There's no other way."

"Yes, there is. You have someone who wants to help you right here, right now, with no strings attached. I think you're worth it and I think your sister is worth it."

"How can you think that? You don't know us."

"You're a human being, and I hold human life sacred. Call it a sacred trust." *Lord, show me how to reach this man. He's not listening to me. Will You speak to him Yourself, please? I'm not good at this kind of thing.*

Clarence grunted.

Lukas sighed. "Look, Clarence, I risk losing my job by treating you, and Dr. Richmond is at risk of losing patients today because we care about what happens to you."

"I didn't ask you to come here."

"But we're here. Dr. Richmond is proving right now that she cares about your sister. What can it hurt? If you're planning to die anyway, what's a little needle prick to find out what's going on in your body? It won't hurt nearly as much as a heart attack. What've you got to lose? We can't call out the national guard to drag you into the hospital if you don't want to go."

For a moment Clarence seemed to waver.

"Won't you at least let me check you out?" Lukas asked. "Let me take some blood, a urine sample, listen to your chest and back, take your blood pressure. The tests won't cost you or your sister anything. I promise. Let me make up for some of the mistreatment you feel you've received from the medical profession before."

Clarence looked at Lukas for a long moment. "No strings?"

"None."

"I won't leave this house."

"I wish you would, but we'll do what we can here for now."

"What's in it for you and the lady doc?"

"Glory," Lukas said drily, grinning. Then he sobered. "I can't just sit by and let someone die if there's something I can do to help. I think Dr. Mercy feels the same way in spite of her outward attitude."

Clarence hesitated for another moment, then shrugged. "Okay, Doc, slap that cuff on and let's see what happens." He held up a finger. "But I'm staying here."

Chapter Fourteen

Mercy checked Darlene's pulse oximetry after one breathing treatment with a portable Pulmo-Aide nebulizer unit. Ninety-four. Not perfect, but a little better. She only had a little expiratory wheeze now.

"Darlene, I wish you were breathing a little better, but I can leave you a Proventil metered dose inhaler. I want you to use two puffs every six hours, as needed. You're probably familiar with it, aren't you?"

Darlene nodded, her face set as it had been ever since they had left Clarence's room.

Mercy sat down beside her new patient. "I know you're worried about your brother, but you need to start thinking a little about yourself right now. He's responsible for his own health. You can't—"

"I realize I can't force him to take care of himself, Doctor," Darlene said. "But I can't help trying." She glanced at Mercy, then away. "You're acting just like all the rest. You don't understand Clarence. You don't know what he's been through—what we've both been through. Everyone's so quick to judge someone just because he's heavy. They just see the outside, not the heart. You don't know why he is the way he is."

"Why is any man—" Mercy caught herself and glanced at Darlene, chagrined. "Sorry, I didn't intend to bring my prejudices to work with me. Dr. Bower told me a little about your situation on the way here, and I understand...even admire the fact that you want to make your own way without state aid. I can't, however, agree to the extent Clarence has taken it. Doesn't he see what he's doing to you?"

"He thinks that if he dies I'll be free to live my own life again. He thinks he's going to die." Darlene's eyes filled with tears. "So do I."

"Maybe not if you'll let us help. I wonder how Dr. Bower is doing with him right now."

Darlene shook her head. "Clarence is very stubborn."

Mercy put a hand on Darlene's shoulder and squeezed. "They've been in there for quite some time, and I haven't heard any raised voices. I've found that Dr. Bower can be very good with patients."

The door to Clarence's room opened and Lukas stepped out. "Dr. Mercy, may I have the venipuncture kit and blood tubes? I'll also need a specimen container for a UA."

Mercy stood up and grinned at Darlene. "See what I mean?"

Jarvis George sat in his darkened office and hoped his phone would not ring. At two o'clock on Tuesday afternoon, it might not get too bad in the emergency room. With a little luck maybe no one would get sick or have a wreck or try to saw off a finger before someone took over at seven...whoever it was. Jarvis frowned. He didn't even remember who was coming.... Oh, yeah, it was Bower again.

He muttered an oath and opened the top drawer of his desk. He felt through the shadows for the little blister packages of Ultram. But did he really need them? The pain wasn't as steady as before, but the confusion was worse. For the first time in his life, he understood what patients meant when they said their symptoms fluctuated. Sometimes he felt almost normal, then another headache would attack, like an invisible monster stalking him. He felt so frustrated. He got so angry at the littlest things lately.

With the bare amount of light that seeped in past the heavy gold drapes at his plate-glass window, he glanced at the sheet of paper on the corner of his expansive desk. June had followed through on her promise to find out more about Lukas Bower at Cunningham. The unsatisfactory results caused more confusion, and Jarvis buried his face in his hands. Why keep pushing this? Why did he feel so much antipathy and fear over the new doctor? Just let it go.

But he couldn't let it go. Not only was Bower uncertified and undisciplined, his presence here posed a problem for the hospital, a change this community wasn't ready to make. Didn't they understand how much money it would cost them if Pinkley decided to hire more full-time physicians for the E.R.? The docs would all expect more money, raises every year. Knolls wouldn't be able to afford it, and then what? They'd be taken over, bought out by the big boys in Springfield or St. Louis, some moneygrubbing HMO that didn't give a rip about human lives. He hated that! He slammed his fist against the desk, then grimaced and grabbed his hand.

A sudden, soft knock at his door startled him and shot another wave of pain through his head. "Go away."

He mouthed the words without sound, making no attempt to rise.

The knock came again. "Jarvis? You in there?"

Ivy.

Slowly Jarvis pushed his chair back and stood. He walked to the door and unlocked it, then turned on the light. The brightness made him wince, but he must not let Ivy see.

He pulled the door open and forced a smile. "My dear, you look wonderful." She didn't. She looked haggard and worried. Dark circles still underlined her eyes, and her mouth came together in an uncharacteristic frown.

"Liar. Mind if I come in for a minute?" She stepped in without waiting for an invitation, as she had done for years. For the first time Jarvis felt a rush of irritation with Ivy, which he quickly covered. Everything irritated him lately.

She stepped over to the love seat that faced the long leather sofa. "You're going to be mad at me in a few minutes, so I'll say what I have to say and get it over with."

He sat down on the sofa. "How could I possibly be mad at you?"

"Because you'll try to talk me out of going to Colorado, just like everyone else has done, and I'm going."

"Then I won't even try. What did Dr. Walker say about your ticker?"

"It isn't angina. I don't have any artery blockage. It's a bundle branch block, just like Dr. Simeon told Mercy. I could've saved the insurance company a bunch of money."

"What did he say about your backpacking expedition?"

"Not a thing."

"He said you should go?"

"Nope."

Jarvis turned his head and stretched his neck. He

wasn't up to these word games. He was tired. Why couldn't she just say what she'd come to say?

"Jarvis? You okay?"

"I'm fine. Ivy, you didn't tell him about your trip, did you?"

"No need. He said we can manage this with medicine, and I should be able to resume my regular exercise in a few days. Hiking is one of my regular exercises."

"Not in high altitudes."

"We're not going to be climbing that high."

"You'll be in Colorado. It's all high altitude."

"I'll get used to it."

Jarvis shrugged, and the motion made him feel slightly nauseated. Could be the flu, but he'd felt this way a couple of times before and nothing had come of it.

"Jarvis? You don't look too great."

"I'm fine. If you want to go on the trip, it's up to you." He remembered the letter on his desk. "I have some information for you to think about while you're gone. Remember my friend June? She was going to get us something on Bower."

"The nurse from Cunningham?"

"That's her. Great gal. She says administration there suspected Bower not only of endangering patient lives, but the reason they felt he was dangerous was because he was showing signs of bipolar disorder. Scary stuff if not treated, especially for a doc, so they had a meeting with him and he told them he was grieving over a death in the family. They instructed him to be seen by a psychiatrist. He made an appointment, then didn't show up. When his trainer asked why, Bower gave the excuse that no one would cover him for the appointment."

"You mean he didn't get treatment?"

"Apparently not. About the same time Bower was accused of fathering the child of a certain nurse on staff, whose father just happened to be the head of the internal medicine department. Really stupid of Bower. He denied everything, of course."

"He's manic depressive?"

"That was the accusation."

"But did they prove it? Jarvis, these are serious charges. Did they prove these things about Dr. Bower?"

"Would they accuse him of all this stuff if it didn't have some basis in fact?" His head pounded, probably caused by guilt. "Would they have fired him if they couldn't prove it? They could get sued."

"You're forgetting this is Missouri, a right-to-fire state. If they didn't directly list these things as a reason for his termination, he couldn't sue. Remember what Sal told you when we called him. He said Dr. Bower was not really popular with his colleagues because he was not a politician. Maybe he made some powerful enemies."

Jarvis glared at Ivy. "Why are you defending him all of a sudden? You're the one who asked me to investigate him, remember?"

"Yes, but—"

"He comes in late, he is uncooperative and he's already endangered a life in our E.R."

"How?"

"He chased off a pain patient, accusing him of drug abuse. The patient didn't get any help here. Do you know who that patient is? Just the son of one of our hospital board members, that's all."

"Really? Who?"

"Now, Ivy, you know I can't—"

"Just tell me, Jarvis. You know I'll find out soon enough. Who?"

"Dwayne Little was the patient."

Ivy gasped. "Bailey's son?"

"That's right. Bailey will have our hides over this, thanks to Bower."

"How do you know Dwayne isn't into drugs? He's been arrested for drunk driving before. Alcohol's a drug, isn't it?"

Jarvis stiffened. "Alcohol is not illegal. Don't go dragging your husband's personal problems into this."

Ivy jerked up and stared at Jarvis as if he'd slapped her. "How can you say that?"

Jarvis shrugged. That was a wrong move, but he didn't care. Why didn't she just leave?

"My husband was your best friend, Jarvis George. He made you an equal partner in his practice. How could you say that?"

Jarvis avoided her eyes. "Bailey Little and I have hunted together for twenty years. He didn't raise his son to do drugs."

"How do you know? Dwayne didn't live with his father. He lived with his mother. I didn't raise Mercy to marry a no-good jerk like Theodore Zimmerman, but that didn't stop her."

Jarvis glared at Ivy. "Life isn't always about you and your family, Ivy." The force of his anger lifted him to his feet. "I'm talking about the future of this hospital with Bower on board. If you want to crack jokes about something this serious, you can do it somewhere else."

For a moment Ivy didn't react, but stood staring at him as if she were stunned. "Jarvis, what are you talking about? I'm not joking."

He stumbled and grabbed the back of the sofa. "You

said yourself that Lukas Bower is a dangerous man. He obviously has no moral integrity. I…I d-don't need your help to see justice done, but I did think I could count on you, of all people."

Ivy's eyes narrowed. "Jarvis, what's wrong with you?"

"Nothing. What's wrong with you? You can't even see the truth when it slaps you in the face. When it kills your own mother." He heard her swift intake of breath and was immediately sorry.

"Cancer killed my mother," she said quietly. She stood up and took a step toward him. "You're sick." She reached out and laid a hand on his arm.

He jerked away. "I'm the doctor, remember? I'm f-fine. You're the one who's sick and won't listen to your cardiologist. Go ahead and…t-take your stupid hike, but don't come crying to me if you wind up in some hospital in Colorado."

Chapter Fifteen

At five forty-five Mercy leaned back in her desk chair and stared at the pile of charts stacked in her in-tray. She'd barely had time for half a sandwich on the way back from her house call, and she was starving. The least Lukas Bower could have done was offer her dinner—not that she'd have accepted, but he could have.

Her office door opened, and Josie stuck her head in. "It's him again, Dr. Mercy."

"Him who?"

"Dr. Bower. I told him you were buried beneath a pile of work, but he's holding on line three. He wants to know about the results of some tests."

"Fine, I'll take it." At the pleased smile on Josie's face, she scowled. "Out." She pointed at the door, punched the button and picked up the receiver. "Yes, Dr. Bower."

"Good, you're still there."

"Of course I'm still here. I'll be here until midnight at this rate."

"Business booming?"

"Not if I keep doing house calls. Some of my patients waited two hours this afternoon."

"Sorry."

She relented. "I'm glad I went, especially after I saw the results of the tests." She picked up the sheets she had received from the lab this afternoon. She read him the report, which confirmed that Clarence was dangerously diabetic and probably had chronic heart failure.

"We need to get to work on this guy right away," Mercy said. "I still don't think he'll accept my help." She looked up as Josie walked back in with another chart.

"I'll accept your help," Lukas said. "He obviously needs another house call."

"Thursday's my day off. Want to set a time?" A clipboard clattered to the desk. Mercy looked up to find Josie staring at her, eyes wide in eager anticipation.

Mercy pointed to the door. "Out, I said! And if you come in here again, you'll be fired for the second time today."

"Uh, excuse me?" Lukas asked tentatively.

"Nothing. What time Thursday?"

"How about noon. I owe you lunch for today, and maybe I'll get some sleep between patients tonight."

"How about one o'clock, so you can sleep at least one extra hour after morning shift takes over? And I think you owe me more than that—at least a dinner. I'm starving." Mercy bit her tongue. What was she saying? Had she suddenly lost her mind? Good thing she'd chased Josie out of the room.

"Okay, I'll see that you get fed. Unfortunately, I can't share it with you because I have to be back to work at seven, and I just got up."

"That's a tight schedule. Did you get any sleep this afternoon?"

"About four hours. At least it's only a twelve-hour shift tonight."

"Still too much. See you Thursday." Mercy hung up, glanced toward the door, and noted that it was ajar. "Josie, you'd better not be out there!"

She heard feet scurrying away, but before she could pursue it, her intercom buzzed. "Dr. Mercy, line one is for you," came her secretary's voice. "It's your daughter."

Mercy glanced at her clock as she pressed the intercom button. "Loretta, what are you still doing here? It's after quitting time. Go home. You can finish your work tomorrow." She pressed the phone button. "Tedi? Hi, sweetie. What's up?"

"Hi, Mom. Can you meet with my teacher at school Thursday? That's the day after tomorrow. Your day off."

"Of course I will…. Tedi, did you stay at home alone last night?"

There was silence.

It was all the answer Mercy needed. Theo would put up a big fight if she fought him for custody, but she was going to take him on this time. "Honey, try to get some sleep. I'll call your teacher and make an appointment for Thursday."

"Okay. Mom? What if she won't talk to you because you're not my legal guardian?"

"I will explain to her that guardianship is in the process of changing."

Tedi gasped. "Mom! You mean it?"

"There'll be a fight. You'll most likely get dragged into the middle."

"I don't care! Do it, Mom!"

"Are you sure this is what you want?"

"Isn't it what you want?"

"I never wanted it any other way."

"Won't Dad cause you a lot of trouble?"

"Don't worry about that."

"Mom, do I have to see a shrink Thursday morning?"

"A what?"

"Dad made me an appointment with this guy he knows."

Mercy bit her lip. Theo was using his mind games again. "I did not request a 'shrink,' Tedi. I told your father I wanted you to see a counselor." And the jerk had set Tedi up with one of his friends in the "good old boy" system, but it wouldn't do to complain about something like that now.

"Why did you tell Dad I had to see a counselor?"

"Because I want you to be able to talk about anything that is bothering you right now without having to worry if you'll start a fight between your mom and dad. I want you to be able to trust someone who will listen and not cause trouble."

"Okay."

"I love you, Tedi."

"I love you, too, Mom. Bye."

Thirty minutes later, a pizza supreme arrived at the door.

Lukas had discovered, to his relief, that weeknight shifts at the Knolls E.R. were about as different from those in KC as the Mark Twain Forest was from Swope Park. He hadn't seen a gang shooting since he'd arrived, and the few knife wounds he'd treated had been from the local poultry processing plant over in Summit. The only enemy most patients had was the specter of infection if they didn't properly care for their wounds.

What amazed Lukas even more was that some nights he even had a chance to sleep a few hours, which freed up his daytime hours to read through his junk mail. If he had lived closer to his dad and stepmom, he would have visited them on his days off. As it was, free time found him depending too much on television or hanging around the hospital to keep loneliness at bay.

By Wednesday night he was too tired to think about being lonely, and he had little chance to sleep. He dozed off about three o'clock Thursday morning, but barely an hour later a loud screech from somewhere in the emergency room shot him up in bed with all the subtlety of an explosion.

"Leggo of me, Emmett!" came a woman's shrill voice. "I ain't drunk! I din't ev'n have a full jar!"

It was Ruby Taylor's voice, one well recognized here in the hospital. Lukas had treated her when she'd sprained an ankle at a country dance and had continued dancing with all the vigor a drinking binge could give her. Her family had dragged her in kicking and screaming that time, too. She didn't like doctors. Great. Lukas threw off his blanket and sat up. From the other room he heard a tired male voice clearly.

"I didn't think she'd had time to drink too much this time, Nurse."

Lukas recognized Emmett Taylor's longsuffering tone. Why did the hospital designers put the call rooms right here in the emergency department? Every single sound penetrated the door.

Lukas braced himself to go out and face Ruby and her worried family—tradition had it that they always came as a group: the husband, drunk wife and two teenaged sons. From what Lukas had heard around the hospital, the Taylors drove an old '76 model Ford truck held together by rust.

"Did you see how much she drank?" the night nurse,

Claudia, was asking the family as Lukas joined them in exam room two.

"Prob'ly more'n she's admittin' to," the fourteen-year-old piped up. "Ma can really put it away."

"Shut up, boy!" Ruby snapped. "I'm the patient here, Nurse. T-talk to me."

"Okay, I'm only trying to help you," Claudia said patiently. "I need to check you out and see how your heart's beating, how well you're breathing, and—"

"I don't need checkin' out! Emmett, get me outa here!"

"Stop it, Ruby," the husband said. "You're sick, you're throwin' up, and I know you have another bad headache." He glanced at Claudia, then Lukas. "She's been awfully moody lately, Doc. She can't even walk straight across the front porch."

"Yeah," the sixteen-year-old said. "I had to catch her once tonight, or she'd've fallen."

Ruby, a middle-aged woman with premature gray hair and a permanent frown, turned to glare at Lukas. "You're the doc that treated me last time. Tell 'em they're crazy. I ain't drunk."

Lukas stepped forward with his stethoscope. "Okay, if you don't need to be here, I'll tell them to take you home. Since you're already here, though, and you obviously don't feel well, let's see if we can help you feel a little better before you leave."

She held a hand up to ward him off. "I ain't sick! Get away from me, all of you!"

Lukas was close enough that the fumes from her breath nearly choked him. He glanced at the husband. "May I speak with you a moment outside, Mr. Taylor?" He turned to Claudia, a competent, no-nonsense nurse in her fifties. "Please get Mrs. Taylor's blood pressure and pulse if you can. Temp, too, if possible." He turned to lead the husband out into the hallway.

"What is it, Doc?" Emmett Taylor looked ten years younger than his wife, even with the frown and defeated expression that seemed to be a part of him. "You can treat her, can't you?"

The shrill sound of Ruby's voice reached them from the other room. "Get that thing off me! Help me, somebody, they're takin' my arm off!"

"Ruby, hold still," Claudia soothed. "It won't read your pressure right if you don't—no, don't pull it off!"

Mr. Taylor shook his head and grimaced. "She's worse than ever. I can't even get her to see reason anymore."

"When did she start drinking today?" Lukas asked.

"About dinnertime. You're not gonna send me back home with her like this, are you? We don't know what to do with her there."

Lukas suppressed a weary sigh. Alcohol use seemed widespread in this town, but then, that was the case in every town. He got most of his drunks late at night, especially on weekends. "I need you to sign a consent for us to treat her," he said. "She's obviously incapable of making that decision."

"Yeah, show me the paper. I'll sign anything you need, Dr. Bower. She seems to be gettin' worse, especially when she drinks."

"What do you man 'especially'? Does she do this when she hasn't been drinking?"

Emmett frowned thoughtfully. "Seems like it. Sometimes she just starts getting bad while she's drinking and stays that way awhile after. She doesn't get over her hangovers as well as she used to, either." He sidled closer and lowered his voice. "Doc, you think it's the change?"

"The change?"

"Yeah, you know, the midlife thing. I hear women go out of their heads when that happens. A couple of times last night she doubled over and grabbed at her stomach and screamed like she did when she was givin' birth."

"Since we haven't been able to get close enough to examine her, I don't know what it is yet. Has she been drinking more than usual lately? Does she drink every day?"

"I don't see her drink every day, no."

"She hasn't hit her head lately, has she? Maybe it's something besides the alcohol."

"She never told me about it if she did." Emmett shook his head. "I don't know, Doc."

"Has she been taking any new medications in the past few weeks?"

Emmett raised his eyebrows at Lukas. "Only time she ever sees a doc is here. She calls the stuff she drinks her medicine. Dr. George gave us something for her stomach a few months ago when she came in, but I don't think she ever took it."

"So she doesn't have a family doctor?"

"I guess we've got Dr. George for a family doc. That's who we put on her check-in papers. He's the one who admits her when she comes in drunk."

Lukas suppressed a grimace. He was not in the mood to face Jarvis, even over the telephone. "Okay, Mr. Taylor. I'll have Rita get a form for you to sign. We may call Dr. George in a little bit."

Emmett followed him to the central desk, where Rita sat studying the computer screen. "Doc, do you think the boys and I could go back home for a while?" Emmett asked. "We left before we could do our morning chores, and if those cows don't get milked, they'll go dry for sure. We could come back later on in the morning after we're done."

"Do you have a telephone at home so we can call you if we need to?" Lukas asked.

"Nope, the line doesn't come that far out. We've always kinda liked it that way."

After the form was signed and Emmett and the boys left, Lukas returned to the exam room in time to see Ruby burst into tears. "They left me here to die."

"Why do you think you're going to die, Ruby?" Claudia asked gently, stroking the woman's hair. "We've always taken good care of you before. We're not going to let anything happen to you."

"But I'm not drunk. I told you, I didn't even drink a whole jar."

Lukas frowned. Drinking from a jar? She had stomach cramps that made her scream as if she were in labor. She displayed irrational behavior, possibly even when there was very little alcohol in her system. Emmett had mentioned headaches. It didn't add up to simple alcoholism.

But what? Lukas walked out to the desk to check for old records on Ruby that might show him something, but he didn't make it.

"Dr. Bower," Claudia called from the exam room door. "Our patient just passed out."

Lukas turned and headed back for the room. "Put her on the monitor, then get her vitals. Rita, call lab. CBC, chemistry panel, amylase and alcohol level." He stepped into the room and bent over Ruby with his stethoscope. Good heart tones. Breathing fine. Strong pulse.

He straightened, pulled the penlight out of his pocket, and checked her pupils. They were somewhat dilated, but equal and reactive. A quick look at the monitor showed normal sinus rhythm, no acute changes. Claudia reported good vitals.

A sleepy-looking lab tech came in with her tray. "This the patient?" She looked down at the requisition sheet she'd just picked up at the desk. "Ruby Taylor?"

"This is her," Lukas said. He did a sternal rub, with his knuckles over Ruby's breastbone, but the pain only brought a slight moan in response. "Let's get a heplock started," he told Claudia. "Then give her thiamine 100 milligrams. IV." He turned to the lab tech. "I need her blood glucose level as soon as possible."

"Yes, Doctor. It'll all be back quickly, except the alcohol."

Lukas stepped over to a window that overlooked a parklike garden outside the emergency department. The sun didn't even hint at an appearance, and stars still filled a cloudless sky. There would probably be no more rest tonight, and he had a date with Mercy Richmond at one. Maybe he could use his earplugs and catch a few more hours of sleep in the call room.

The word *date* made him uneasy. He hadn't been out with anyone since last year when his father and stepmom had set him up on a blind date with an acquaintance of theirs. It turned out she was ten years younger than Lukas, and she'd complained all evening about the movie they saw, the restaurant where they ate, even the clothes Lukas wore. It made him appreciate his solitary existence for several months. But this date with Mercy was work related. Business. That was it.

For some reason his mind switched to Lauren. She'd seemed sincere yesterday when she told him she was praying for him. Her words had actually comforted him, although her warning had disturbed him. Lauren chattered a lot, but what she talked about had always turned out to be true. Sometimes at work she caught her word flow and apologized for gossiping, but she was never vicious about the things she said, just painfully honest.

Could Lauren's appearance and words yesterday have actually been part of God's answer to his prayer?

He shook his head and turned away from the window. He'd learned long ago to accept comfort where God gave it, but not to read some significant message from God in every passing word spoken or action taken.

He heard the outside door open and turned to see the fireman, Buck Oppenheimer, enter the emergency room alongside a smaller man who held a towel over the front of his face. Blood stained the front of the smaller man's gray sweat suit.

"I told you to put ice on that," Buck muttered to his friend. "You're going to make me look bad, like I don't even know how to take care of a patient." He caught sight of Lukas and smiled. "Oh, it's Dr. Bower. You're in good hands, Reese."

"Hi, Buck," Lukas greeted. "Did you come by ambulance? I didn't hear a report."

"No, this is my cousin," Buck said. "Name's Reese Oppenheimer. A drunk landed his car in Reese's front yard about three this morning, and being a Good Samaritan, Reese tried to help out—I think he's got a broken nose." He shot his cousin a sleepy glance. "Of course his first thought was go call good ol' Cousin Buck and get him out of bed."

"So you've already reported this to the police?" Lukas reached over to a tray and picked up a pair of latex exam gloves.

"Sure have," Buck said. "They'll need a report from you after you fix the damage."

Lukas gently removed the towel from Reese's nose. Both eyes had begun to swell. "Were you hit by the car?" he asked Reese, gently touching the center part of the nose, which was swollen and already turning blue.

"Ouch!" Reese jerked back. "No, the drunk hit me. He missed the curve in front of my house and just plowed out the front fence. Didn't hurt him none, I don't think. Didn't act like it, anyways."

"Why did he hit you?"

"I don't think he wanted me calling the police. I helped him get his car loose from the fence, then told him to come on inside while I called the sheriff."

"And he hit you for that?" Lukas asked, reaching for a chemical ice pack from a shelf. He popped the pack, shook it, and gently placed it over Reese's nose. "This is cold."

"Sure is!" Reese complained. "Ever had one of these things on your nose?"

"Nope. I've never been hit by a drunk. Yet. If it's too cold, we can insulate it with a washcloth, but it's best to take it straight if you can. I'm going to have our secretary check you in; then we'll get an X-ray and I'll finish looking you over. Did he hit you anywhere else? Any other damage you know about?"

"No, Doc, this is it." Reese slumped down in front of Rita's desk. "I hate drunks."

"That's what you get for being a Good Samaritan," Buck said. "You'll think twice next time someone plows into your fence and tears up eighteen feet of sod and three rose bushes."

"No, I won't," Reese said. "What if they were seriously injured? I couldn't live with myself. Don't give me a hard time. You're the fireman who wanted to be an EMT."

"Doc, can I go with him to X-ray?" Buck asked.

"As long as there's no chance you're pregnant," Lukas said with a straight face.

Buck scowled at him. "You're doing too many night shifts."

Lukas turned back toward Ruby's room and found the lab tech approaching him.

"Here's your report, Doctor. It all looks pretty normal, except she's anemic."

"Thanks. I'll want that alcohol level as soon as you get it."

As the tech turned to leave, Claudia stepped out of Ruby's room. "She's coming around just a little, Dr. Bower."

"Good, the thiamine's working. Let's see if we can't get a Breathalyzer test as soon as possible. I don't want to wait on the blood alcohol level."

"I'll see what I can do."

She came back just a few moments later with a smile of triumph. "Got it. It's 2.86."

"Okay, thanks. We have enough to admit her. Have Rita call the family physician."

Claudia grimaced. "It's Dr. George."

"I know. We have to call him. I'm going to talk to Ruby for a few minutes. Let me know when we have Dr. George on the phone."

Claudia shrugged. "Whatever you say."

Lukas entered the room to find Ruby groaning softly with her hands over her abdomen.

"Does your stomach still cramp, Ruby?" he asked.

She frowned up at him. "Some," she admitted. "When do I get outa here?"

"As soon as we make you feel better." He sat down on the exam stool. "How much did you really have to drink last night?"

"I...I don't know."

"You told us earlier you hadn't had a whole jar. What kind of jar do you use?"

"Jelly," she said irritably. "You know." She held her hands out about the length of a pint canning jar.

"Do you make your own wine?"

She glared at him. "I'm no wino! That stuff's for little old ladies."

"Where do you buy your liquor?"

"Buy? Whad'ya mean, buy? I don't buy no booze."

"I see." He tried to keep the sarcasm out of his voice. "You make your own, then?"

She narrowed her eyes in suspicion. "What'd Emmett tell you? He's got no right givin' out fam'ly secrets."

Lukas stared at her in surprise. He leaned forward. "Ruby, do you have a still?"

Her face contorted once again in pain. She put her hands over her abdomen and curled up in a fetal position.

Claudia came back in. "Dr. Bower, we have Dr. George on the phone."

"Good. Send it back to the wall phone, then come back in here. I don't want her left alone." He stepped outside the room and picked up the receiver as soon as it rang.

"Dr. George, this is Dr. Bower. We have a forty-nine-year-old Caucasian female with complaints of nausea and vomiting, severe headache, mental status change—"

"Who's the patient?" Jarvis snapped.

"Ruby Taylor."

"What's the ethanol level?"

"We don't have a blood alcohol level yet, but the Breathalyzer is 2.86."

"Like usual. Admit her to my service for short stay only."

"But there could be more than that going on this time,"

Lukas said. "I think the Taylors have a still. Depending on how the still is made, it's possible she could be suffering from—"

"Do you always believe what every drunk tells you?"

"But this could mean possible lead poisoning, and we may need to transfer her. Is it possible to get a stat lead level in our lab?"

"Can't you even take a simple order?" Jarvis growled. "You have my instructions. Follow them!" The line went dead.

"Doctor," Claudia called from exam room two, "Ruby's pain is getting worse. Can't we give her something for it?"

In frustration, Lukas hung up the phone and rushed back into the room.

Ruby cried out, still in her fetal position, holding her abdomen with both hands.

"Where does it hurt, Ruby?" Lukas bent over her. "Is it your stomach? Lower? Can you point it out exactly?"

Ruby didn't acknowledge him.

Lukas turned to Claudia. "Let's give Nubain, 10 milligrams, slow IV push." He put a hand on Ruby's arm. "The nurse is going to give you a shot for pain."

Ruby grew still. Her eyes widened as she stared at Lukas's hand on her arm. She bolted up. "No! Get those needles away from me! Help! Emmett, they're killing me! They're killing me!" Her lips drew back in a feral snarl, and she caught sight of the IV needle in her right arm. "What's this?" Get this thing outa me!" She groped for the IV needle with her left hand.

"No, Ruby, here, don't do—" Lukas reached for her left arm.

She drew back and swung at him. Her fist jabbed his

right eye, and pain shot across his face. As he stood there, stunned, she drew back and punched at him again. He blocked the blow, and her fist connected with his chest.

"Ruby, we're not going to—"

She bared her teeth and tried to bite his arm.

He jerked his arm back and grabbed both of hers, stepping around behind her. "Claudia, get Rita in here now! And get Buck in here, too. He's with Reese in radiology. Forget the Nubain. Get me Haldol, 2 milligrams IV push, and hurry, or she's going to pull out the IV."

Ruby screamed like a raging tiger, jerking and pulling him with surprising strength.

Claudia rushed forward, shouting over her shoulder, "Rita, get Buck and get in here! We've got a wild one!"

Lukas tried to hold Ruby still while Claudia tried to connect her needle to the IV hub. Every time she came close, Ruby jerked.

Buck rushed in behind Rita. "What's the matter, Doc, can't you even handle a little old—" He caught sight of the thrashing patient. "Uh-oh, it's Ruby." He rushed forward and grabbed the patient's right arm. "Okay, Claudia, I'll hold the arm still. Get the shot in fast."

While Claudia worked, Buck frowned at Lukas. "Looks like you're going to have a shiner, Doc. How many times did she hit you?"

"One more time than I expected."

Buck grinned. "Don't you hate getting the drunks?"

Some of the tension began to ease from Ruby's arms.

Lukas didn't dare release her yet. "This one isn't a drunk." He watched her face as it slowly relaxed with the influence of Haldol. "There's something else going on here."

Ruby's eyes gradually lost their wild look and closed.

"Whew!" Rita helped Ruby lie back on the bed. "She's never done that before. What's gotten into her?"

"I have an idea." Lukas reached down and gently pulled back the patient's lower lip. She obviously disliked dentists, as well as doctors.

"Dr. Bower, what are you doing?" Claudia asked.

"Playing a hunch. See this thin, blue-black streak at the gum line? That's the hallmark of lead poisoning. Get lab again. I want a stat lead level. Rita, call an ALS ambulance. Tell them to be here in ten minutes."

"An ambulance?" Claudia exclaimed. "Don't you want to see what the level is first? We need to call Dr. George back."

"Her level is obviously high enough to be symptomatic, and I know we don't have any of the antidotes for treatment here. Dr. George didn't want to discuss the possibility of lead poisoning. He hung up on me. I'm not wasting time on this one."

"Here, Doc," Buck said from behind him. He held out a chemical ice pack, already cold. "You'll need this on that eye. Want me to check it for you? I know about black eyes."

"Thanks, Buck." Lukas took the pack. He almost reached for a cloth to place beneath it, but just then Reese walked in from radiology.

"Hey, what happened to you?" Reese asked.

Lukas placed the ice pack on his eye. The cold stung, but he didn't let on.

"Drunk got him," Buck said.

Reese shook his head. "Don't you just hate drunks?"

Tedi sat in a chair that was too little for her and faced the red-headed, freckle-faced man who was supposed to be helping her. He hadn't helped her yet, and she'd already been here for twenty minutes according to the big clock on the wall behind him. Her appointment was for eight o'clock Thursday morning, and he'd been ten minutes late, which would make her later for school. She'd already missed too much school. But she was supposed to talk to this man as if he were her best friend or something.

"I had a nightmare one night that a monster was trying to kill me." Tedi frowned at her interrogator. "You have to keep this confidential, don't you? You can't tell anybody." She watched him for a moment. "You're a friend of Dad's. How can I trust you?"

"Do you feel you can't trust me because you don't trust your dad?"

"I asked you the question." She glared at him. "Mom said she wants me to be able to talk about anything to my counselor. Does that mean you can't tell anybody what I say?"

"You're a minor, Tedi. Your legal guardian has a right to know what's going on."

"Even if he kills me?"

"Why do you think your dad would kill you?"

"He gets drunk and loses his temper, and if you tell him I told you this, he'll remember it next time he drinks." Tedi stared silently at Dr. Carpenter. The man had pale red hair and light green eyes. He wouldn't hold her gaze. She didn't like him, and she'd already decided she wasn't going to come back. "Mom's paying for this. You can tell her anything I tell you."

"She's not your legal guardian."

"You're just talking like that because Dad's a friend of yours, Dr. Carpenter. Are you going to help him gang up on my mom?"

"I told you to call me Nick." He leaned forward and

formed a little steeple with his hands. He met her gaze then. "Tedi, this is my job. It's what I do for a living, and I love my job. I don't mix business with pleasure, and I don't play favorites with friends. I'll do what I feel is best for you no matter what my friendship is with your father."

"Good. Will you testify for me in court so I can go live with Mom?"

He raised a nearly invisible eyebrow. "For now the court has decided that it is in your best interests for you to live with your father."

Tedi gritted her teeth. "My mom was set up. She's not mentally ill. She's a doctor with a bunch of happy patients. Crazy people can't do what she does. Besides, isn't alcoholism an illness?" She stood up, grabbed her book bag. "I've got to get to school."

"Not yet. Your teacher knows where you are. Have a seat, please."

Tedi turned to frown at him. Could he get her into worse trouble? Yes, and she was in enough already. Reluctantly, she sat back down.

"Now, Tedi, an occasional drink does not make someone an alcoholic. I have a beer sometimes when I get home at night."

"Do you hit your kids?"

"Of course not."

"Do you get drunk and fight with your girlfriend all night?"

"I'm married."

"Well, your wife, then."

"No, Tedi."

"Do you stay out drinking all night and leave your kids home alone?"

He frowned. "Has your father done that to you?"

"Yes, he has. Then he made me go to school the next day, and I fell asleep in class again and got in trouble again, and he chewed out my teacher for bugging him. Everyone makes fun of me at school, and my best friend doesn't even like me anymore." She sat kicking the leg of her chair with the back of her heel. She glanced at the clock again. "Are you going to tell my father I told you this?"

"No. Tedi, does your dad hit you?"

"Not yet."

"Do you think he's going to?"

"Yes. He might even kill me someday."

The counselor frowned. "You really think he will? Or are you telling me this so you can go live with your mother?"

Tedi stood up again. "Why should I tell you? You're not going to believe me anyway. I'm already behind in math, and that's the first class of the day. Can I go now?"

"Your mother wants you to talk to me for an hour."

"She won't when I tell her you're taking Dad's side. And you don't believe me. Why should I talk to you?" She could tell he was getting mad, because his face was turning red.

"I didn't say I didn't believe you. I asked a simple question. Why are you so defensive if you're telling me the truth?"

Tedi picked up her book bag, slung it over her shoulder and walked out.

Chapter Sixteen

Mercy sat on her secondhand sofa and stared out the large bay window of her living room. That window was the one thing about this rental house that she had always liked. Now if only it were out in the country somewhere, with about twenty acres surrounding it and a duck pond out front with a rowboat that Tedi could paddle around the shoreline while she daydreamed….

Lunchtime traffic returning to work clogged the main thoroughfare two blocks away. Mercy had always hated living in town, even a small town like Knolls where the people were mostly friendly and everyone knew everyone else. So many times it felt confining, as if she were living in a fishbowl, and it had become especially that way when word leaked out about Dad's alcoholism. Then when Dad died and the messy divorce hit, all people could talk about was Mercy's stint in the hospital. She'd had to struggle to rebuild her practice, pay off all the bills Theo had incurred during their marriage and continue payments on the car and house that Theo had retained out on the edge of town in an excellent neighborhood. For Tedi's sake, she'd done it. Was she crazy now to consider taking Theo back to court to get custody of Tedi? Would he throw a fit? Of course he would. And how would that affect Tedi? She was five years old during the divorce trial, and it had wounded her deeply. What would happen to her this time?

Mercy glanced at her watch for the third time in ten minutes. A date. Why'd she have to open her big mouth? She and Lukas could have made this house call without sharing a meal together. And to make things worse, he was already fifteen minutes late and her stomach was growling.

Maybe she was getting the tables turned on her. Monday night she'd stood up Robert Simeon, so today was her turn. She didn't think Lukas was the type to stand up a date, especially when a patient was involved, but what did she really know about Lukas Bower? How would she know how he treated women? This wasn't a romantic thing anyway. How could it be? She was nearly forty, and he didn't look old enough to have been out of med school very long. That meant there could be as much as ten years' difference in their ages. So this would be just a friendly get-together between colleagues. Nothing else. She liked the way he handled patients, and she enjoyed talking with him. She definitely was not interested in a relationship with a man.

She frowned. The same blue Mercury Sable had slowly passed in front of her house twice now. Someone was lost, but it couldn't be Lukas. He had an old rattle-trap Jeep. The staff joked about it in the E.R.

She glanced at the clock again. Five minutes later than last time.

Her day off was not turning out to be as relaxed and laid-back as she'd hoped. The talk with Mrs. Watson had gone well this morning, though.

Mercy smiled to herself. Theo had hurt his reputation with the teacher when he'd referred to her "airheaded" ideas about handing children and refused to come and get Tedi the other day when she'd fallen asleep in class again. The lady had been full of information about Tedi's recent difficulties and had blamed Theo. True, she seemed somewhat emotional, but she obviously loved her students and believed Tedi just needed more attention at home. Nice teacher. But would she be willing to testify against Theo in court? Mercy hadn't asked her this morning, but she probably would.

The blue Sable slowed again in front of her drive, then braked and turned in. Oh, no, all she needed was company right now. She didn't have time…

The door opened and out stepped Lukas.

Her dismay turned to a strange combination of anticipation and trepidation. A date. And she'd been the one to suggest it. Was she out of her mind? Josie wouldn't think so. Josie would be hyperventilating right now. Best not to tell her.

Mercy opened the door just when Lukas raised his hand to ring the doorbell. He jumped as if startled.

"You're late," she said with a smile as she opened the storm door. She caught sight of his face, and her smile died. He looked as though he'd been in a bar fight. Deep purple and black underscored his right eye, which was partially swollen shut. "What happened to you? Did you and Jarvis finally have it out?"

He shrugged sheepishly. "He sent one of his patients to beat me up."

At Mercy's raised brow, he explained. "A drunk came in who didn't like needles. It was an interesting visit because it turned out to be a case of lead poisoning. When

Dr. George finds out I sent one of his patients to Cox South against his orders, he'll do worse to me than she did. He probably already knows. I've had my phone turned off this morning so I could sleep. I don't know if he's tried calling me at home."

"Well, let's make sure your last meal is a good one." She reached down beside the threshold and picked up her medical bag. "Ready?"

"Yes." He turned and walked with her to the car. "Sorry I'm late. I couldn't remember if I'd closed my garage door, and I'm storing some things there for my oldest brother, so I had to turn around and go back. Then I realized I was nearly out of gasoline." He looked tired.

"Get any sleep last night?" she asked.

At the last moment he changed directions and stepped over to open the car door for her. "A few hours. I slept from about eight until noon, though."

Mercy settled herself into the soft, cushioned seat and watched him walk around. He'd obviously just had a shower and shaved, because his hair was still damp, and there was a tiny nick on his chin where he'd cut himself shaving. He wore new blue jeans and a short-sleeved, button-up blue plaid shirt that needed ironing. As he backed out into the street, she automatically glanced down to see if his shoes matched. Yes, they did, but his socks didn't. He probably had a navy and black pair just like them at home.

"Nice car," she said. "But I thought you drove a Jeep."

"I do. This is my car. It's been in the repair shop for the past couple of weeks. I had a fender bender in the grocery store parking lot. I thought this would be more comfortable for today. Besides, the Jeep was almost out of gas, too."

Mercy glanced sideways at him as he turned into the left lane of traffic. "You realize, of course, that this is a business date only. I'm probably ten years older than you."

His foot eased slightly from the accelerator. "You're forty-five?" he exclaimed, glancing at her. "Wow. You sure don't look it." He turned his attention back to the road. "Do you like Italian? I've eaten at Angelino's, and the food's good."

"Italian is perfect."

"Good. I'm starved."

"I'm not forty-five," Mercy said. "I'm thirty-nine."

"You don't look thirty-nine, either. You thought I was twenty-nine?"

"I suppose I should have known you weren't fresh out of med school. You're too good with patients." She grinned at him. "I hear you're also good with staff, especially those of the female persuasion."

Lukas glanced at her with raised eyebrows. "Uh, I don't think so."

"I hear comments like polite, easygoing, hunky and single." She enjoyed watching his face turn red. "I heard that single bit a lot. What ever happened between you and Lauren? I heard the two of you really hit it off."

His eyes widened, and his foot slipped from the accelerator altogether. "There's nothing going on between us, if that's what you mean. Is this where I turn?"

"Not yet." He was fun to tease. "Lauren's adorable. She's also available, and I don't think she makes any secret about the fact that she likes you."

"I like her, too. She's a good nurse, and she's easy to work with."

"And that's it?"

He gave a firm, no-nonsense nod that put Mercy in her

place. She grinned again, but respected his wishes. "How did you convince Clarence to accept our help Tuesday?"

The tension seemed to relax in his hands and shoulders. "About the same way I convinced you to make the house call with me. Manipulation by guilt. It's sneaky and underhanded, but it works."

"Do all men learn the same tactics in the womb?"

He paused for a moment, as if thinking seriously about her question. "I don't think so. My mom taught me. You know, 'Lukas, I can't believe your grades this semester. Your father worked long hours to help you go to a good school, and I think he deserves better than this.'" He smiled. "Mothers are the best at it."

Mercy shook her head. Ex-husbands were the best at it. "Is that the way you're planning to handle Clarence again today? Guilt trip?"

"Why not? He obviously feels very protective of Darlene. We might as well make the most of it."

"What do you men 'we'? That man won't listen to me. He doesn't even like me."

"Don't be too sure about that, but I think it's best if I do the talking today." Lukas grimaced. "I never liked mean doctors, but I can be pretty convincing when a patient's life depends on it." He touched the brake and flipped on the signal. "I think this is the turn. I still don't know my way around town very well."

"Imagine that," Mercy said drily. "You're always at the hospital. It's almost as if they keep you on an invisible leash." When they pulled into the restaurant parking lot, she said, "I brought several drug samples to give to Darlene and Clarence today. I'll leave my bag in the car if you'll lock up."

"Thanks. Give me the bill for the lab tests, and I'll pay

it, then I'll contact the hospital pharmacy and put Clarence's account in my name." He pulled into a spot and parked. "You won't be able to give samples for everything he needs."

"Tell you what. I'll pay for this round of lab tests if you'll promise to talk Clarence into checking into the E.R." Mercy opened her door and got out. "I guess you know we've committed ourselves and this could turn out to be expensive if we keep paying his tab." And she couldn't afford it. "Maybe we can convince him to accept state aid."

Lukas hit the locks and shut his door, then walked around to join Mercy. "Don't count on it. He's very independent."

"What's the difference between accepting our help and accepting the state's?"

"I think I've convinced him we're making up for the treatment he's received from former medical people. It won't last." He reached out to close her door, and she grabbed his arm.

"Do you have an extra set of keys with you?" she asked, gesturing toward the set still dangling from the ignition.

Lukas groaned and rolled his eyes. He reached in through her open door, removed the keys and put them in his front pocket. "I guess you can tell I don't date much," he said as he closed the door.

"Neither do I. It's a bad habit to get into."

Mercy couldn't tell exactly when it took place, but something in Lukas's demeanor changed between the time they ordered and the time their drinks arrived. He suddenly grew tense, then picked up the menu the waiter had left and studied it again.

"Excuse me," he said, putting down the menu. "I'll be right back."

She watched him walk toward the kitchen and disappear, then shrugged and took a drink of her pink lemonade.

When he came back, he sat down without saying a word.

"Everything okay?" she asked.

"Hmm? Yes, fine. How's your lemonade?"

"Delicious. Not too sweet."

The bread arrived, for which Angelino's was famous, and with it came Mercy's salad. She glanced at the waiter, then at Lukas.

"Didn't you order a house salad?" she asked.

He took a piece of bread. "Changed my mind."

Before she could ask more, he bowed his head, just the way Mom did when she was praying. *Oh, great, another Christian.*

When he raised his head, she said, "So you don't date much?"

"I don't seem to have much of an aptitude for it. I'm always saying or doing the wrong thing at the wrong time. I've insulted more than one blind date without even realizing it."

"Blind dates?" she asked. "Who sets you up with blind dates?"

"My family whenever I visit. They've despaired of ever seeing me married. My two older brothers used to really nag me, especially since they both got married in their twenties, and they've always encouraged their wives to introduce me to as many girlfriends as possible." He grimaced and shook his head. "You'd be surprised at how desperate they've become. My oldest brother's wife once set me up with a widowed lady with four kids, because they felt I'd waited too long to start a family and needed a boost in the right direction."

Mercy frowned. "You didn't like the kids?"

"Yeah, a lot better than the mother." He shrugged. "We didn't hit it off. I think she was looking for someone who behaved more like a 'distinguished doctor,' and less like another kid."

"What do your brothers do for a living?"

"They're computer programmers for the state, and they work in Jefferson City. It's good for them because they live close to each other and their families are close."

"Do you ever feel left out?"

"Not since I was a kid. They're four and five years older than me, so I was always just the bratty little brother to them." He shrugged. "I got used to it. We're close and I visit them, but I don't think they'll ever be able to take me seriously."

Mercy wasn't sure she would like his brothers. She did find, to her surprise, that she liked Lukas. He was talking more openly than she'd ever heard him talk, and there was some quality she couldn't quite put her finger on—unless maybe it was innocence—that tragically few men had.

Though she hated to admit it, she was very much enjoying this date.

Her biggest surprise came, however, when the meals arrived. She received a large plate of seven-layer lasagna. The waiter placed a bowl of plain spaghetti in front of Lukas.

Mercy gaped at the bowl. "I thought you ordered lasagna."

"Changed my mind." He picked up his fork, then perused the sauces in bottles beside the salt and pepper shakers. He picked up a hot sauce, sniffed it, put it back, then picked up the bottle of horseradish and shook it over his noodles. Liberally. Next he picked up the Parmesan cheese and sprinkled some of it over the horseradish. He picked up his spoon and fork and swirled some of the spaghetti onto the fork.

"You like it hot, do you?" Mercy observed as he put the forkful of spaghetti into his mouth.

He blinked at her in surprise and shook his head; then his eyes widened behind the gray frames of his glasses. He coughed, sputtered, dropped his fork into the bowl and grabbed his napkin and drew it over his mouth.

Mercy watched him in growing alarm. "Drink some lemonade, quick."

He shook his head, eyes watering in misery as he choked. He slid from the booth and stumbled, nearly blind, toward the restrooms ten feet away. And when he chose the wrong door, Mercy could no longer contain herself. She burst into laughter.

A woman came rushing out of the ladies' restroom, followed closely by Lukas, who finally found the right door and rushed through it.

Mercy shook her head and picked up her fork, still chuckling. "I sure know how to pick 'em, don't I?"

Lukas lay on his stomach across the car seat. The glove compartment had been no help at all. So far he'd found three quarters and a penny in the back floorboard, not enough to cover the triple death chocolate dessert Mercy had ordered. Why, oh, why had he switched to the car? And why, if he had to show off the fact that he had two automobiles, couldn't he remember to take his wallet out of the Jeep's glove compartment?

At first, after discovering he didn't have his wallet, he'd thought he could get away with it by changing his order from a seven-layer lasagna to a plain bowl of noodles. He always carried an emergency twenty in his shirt pocket. But he hadn't counted on dessert. And he was still hungry even after consuming an extra basket of rolls and asking for a new bowl of spaghetti.

He didn't even want to think about the horseradish. He hadn't known it was horseradish when he dumped it on the noodles. For all he knew it could have been Alfredo sauce. And as if it wasn't embarrassing enough that he had to jump up and run to the bathroom with a flaming mouth, he somehow ended up in the ladies' room—with a lady already in it. His first date in almost a year—it would probably be as long before he had the nerve to go out with anyone again.

Oh, well, nothing else could go wrong today. Ah! A dollar bill stuffed behind the seat. Now if he could only find another couple of bills.

"Did you lose something?"

He froze. Mercy.

He groaned aloud and turned over in the seat to look at her. Time to come clean. "Uh, well, when I switched from the Jeep to the car, I forgot and left my wallet…"

"In the Jeep." She grinned and shook her head. "I paid the waiter already. I figured it was the least I could do for today's entertainment."

He smiled, relieved, and watched the lines of humor play across her face. She was pretty. Really pretty. Why hadn't he noticed that before? Probably because he hadn't seen her like this very often. She'd laughed more today than he'd ever heard her laugh. It looked so natural on her. So good.

He sat up and slid out of the car. "I'm sorry. I didn't mean for you to have to pay." He opened the front passenger door for her.

"You can pay next time."

He raised a brow at her. Next time? There would be a next time? "Sounds good to me. Ready to go see the Knights?"

Estelle Pinkley loved being the Knolls Community Hospital administrator. She'd held the job for five years, well into retirement age, and had no plans to retire until she was forced. And then she'd fight it.

What she didn't like was the particular job she was doing now, as she faced Bailey Little, president of the hospital board, across the broad expanse of her mahogany desk. She and Bailey had a shared history together—not a good one. She had represented Bailey's wife against him during divorce proceedings ten years ago. She and Mrs. Little had won big-time after an ugly fight. Dwayne, their son, had lost the most. The poor boy had been in trouble at school ever since, and his good grades had dropped until he barely graduated.

"Let me get this straight, Bailey," Estelle said slowly. "You think I'd fire Dr. Bower on your word alone, no questions asked, just because he insulted Dwayne the other day?"

Bailey leaned forward in his cushioned, straight-back chair and watched Estelle over the top rim of his silver-framed glasses. "I think it would be a very wise move on your part. Unprofessional behavior is always grounds for termination in my opinion. And Missouri is—"

"A right-to-fire state," Estelle said drily. "I'm well aware of the laws of this state. Don't forget that I, too, was an attorney."

"Do you take exception to Missouri law?"

"I have no intention of firing a man without just cause, whether or not state law backs me up." She also had no intention of firing the first emergency room physician this hospital had ever had. She'd been the one to push this, and she wasn't about to back down now. "What, exactly, did Dr. Bower do to your son?"

"I told you, he implied that Dwayne was a drug addict. He sent him out of the emergency room without treatment for his headache."

"So you're telling me that Dr. Bower did not offer Dwayne any treatment?"

"He did not offer him sufficient treatment."

"What do you call sufficient treatment? I thought the physician was supposed to make that decision. I wasn't aware you had a medical degree, Bailey."

His face remained stony. "He refused to give the treatment Dwayne has received before from qualified physicians. Further, Bower had the secretary inform other area EDs that he felt my son was a drug seeker. In my opinion, that is defamation of character and directly affects my name, as well. It will not be tolerated." He sat back, holding eye contact.

Estelle couldn't shake the image of an eagle seeking prey. His stern demeanor and strong, well-defined nose fostered that impression, and he used it to his benefit when cross-examining a witness on the stand. She would not let him intimidate her the way he did others. She never had.

Estelle raised an eyebrow. "You plan to take it further, then, if I don't fire Dr. Bower?"

"I do indeed, especially after speaking with Dr. George about Dr. Bower's background. Jarvis is, after all, still the E.R. director, and he agrees with me."

Ah, yes, Dr. George. Why wasn't she surprised? Not only had he opposed a full-time physician, he had opposed computerizing the hospital office system and the addition of the new outpatient clinic. If it were up to him, this hospital would still be using lanterns and leeches. She'd seen to it that he didn't get his way, and she could do it again.

"I'm well aware of Dr. George's opinion of Dr. Bower," she said. "I also know that Dr. Bower has the lowest patient complaint rate in our hospital." She had decided not to count Dr. George's patients, whom she felt had been brainwashed.

"Are you also aware that Dr. Bower was terminated from his residency program at Cunningham in Kansas City?"

"Yes, and the physician credentials committee is also aware of it."

Bailey paused, obviously struggling to control his surprise. "And you withheld this information from me?"

Estelle bristled. "Is the hospital administrator now required to go running to the hospital board for approval every time she makes a decision? My judgment has always proved to be sound, as can be attested to by the fact that we are still operating as a hospital, have not been bought out by the big boys, and are in the black for the first time in years. Our census continues to increase, and no one on the board has seen fit to criticize my actions in any way, except for you and Dr. George. Are you speaking as the president of the board in this case, or as an angry father who is using his position to try to intimidate me?"

"The only reason I'm here is to stop this thing from getting out of hand," Bailey snapped. "You can take care of it quickly, with little outside involvement, and protect the name of the hospital. It's your call."

Estelle held Bailey Little's steely gaze. "Oh? So now the reputation of the hospital is at stake? I'm not buying it, Bailey. The hospital board president is threatening the hospital?"

"I warn you, Mrs. Pinkley, I'm a father before I'm the hospital board president."

"Oh, come on, Bailey. The only time you ever put your son ahead of your career was when it was convenient and beneficial to you." Estelle knew she was striking below the belt, and she saw that she'd hit her mark.

Color suffused his face. "I think the public will listen to a well-respected family physician and an attorney-at-law." He paused, a nasty half-smile touching his lips. "I also think a COBRA violation, if worded correctly, could shut the hospital down."

Estelle went cold. COBRA was the federal watchdog of hospital operations. If they investigated a hospital and found a problem, they could issue a huge fine, or even withhold Medicare and Medicaid payments, which would effectively shut down a hospital—a large percentage of medical income came from those sources, and hospital emergency rooms were required to accept any and all emergency cases.

Bailey nodded with satisfaction at her silence. "Refusing to give the proper treatment for pain is considered a violation. But of course, as an attorney, you're already aware of that."

Estelle raised a brow. "I'm also aware that under COBRA law the hospital cannot be held liable if the patient refuses the treatment offered. You don't have a case, Bailey."

He stood up. "I strongly suggest you review the chart in question. In order for the hospital to be held harmless, the patient must sign an AMA form, which my son did not." An AMA form simply stated that the patient checked out of the hospital against medical advice.

"I find it hard to believe there was nothing signed to that effect, whether by the patient or the staff."

"Check for yourself. It's not in his file."

"Where did you get permission to go digging through the hospital files?"

"From the patient in question, or have you suddenly made a rule to disallow release of patient information to the patient himself? If you like your job so much, you'd be wise to think about this for a few days before you make you final decision."

"I've done all the thinking I'm going to do. If I have to, I'll go public with this thing. Bailey, you have to answer to the taxpayers just as the rest of us do. It's a county hospital, and they won't take kindly to a COBRA call by the president of the hospital board, especially if the hospital shuts down. Maybe you'd better consider your own job."

Bailey glared at Estelle for a moment. "The next board meeting is two weeks from next Monday. Be there. I would suggest you bring Bower with you. Both of you may be without jobs by the end of the month." He turned and walked out.

Chapter Seventeen

Clarence was awake this time, and he looked worse than he did two days ago. As before, however, the preliminary sparks flew between the patient and Mercy before she carted Darlene off into another room for a breathing treatment.

"What're you back here for?" Clarence asked Lukas after the two women had left. His gruff voice sounded weaker than before, and his eyes looked more listless.

"We have the results of your tests, and I wanted to come and talk to you about them and give you some medications that will help."

Clarence laid his head back on his pillow and closed his eyes. "I can't pay."

"We've already been through that." Lukas stepped forward with his stethoscope. "Mind if I listen to your chest?"

The man didn't answer, but made a vague motion with his hand. Lukas decided to take that as permission. He leaned over and pressed the bell of the stethoscope to Clarence's massive chest. As before, heart sounds were very muffled due to the thickness of the fat layer, but

Lukas thought he could hear a lub-da-dub of a diastolic murmur. Could be heart failure. It wasn't conclusive.

"Clarence, can I get you to sit up?"

The big man's eyes opened. "Why? What d'you hear, Doc?"

"I can't be sure. That's why I need to listen to your lungs. Then I'll tell you."

For a moment Lukas thought Clarence was going to refuse, but instead he heaved a sigh of resignation and struggled to force his body forward. Lukas knew better than to try to help.

As soon as the patient sat up enough, Lukas auscultated the thick flesh of the back for breath sounds. These came through more clearly than the heart tones. The diffuse nature of the coarse, crackling breath sounds, and the labored breathing, confirmed the preliminary diagnosis Lukas and Mercy had discussed two days ago.

Lukas straightened and wrapped the stethoscope around his neck. "Okay, you can lie back, Clarence."

The big man obeyed with relief. "Well?" he growled.

"Pretty much what I expected to hear. You're definitely in heart failure. Tests have also confirmed that your blood sugar is high."

Lukas thought he detected a fleeting expression of fear cross Clarence's face. "So I'm dying." It was not a question. It was a statement of acceptance.

"Your heart is being overworked due to your size," Lukas said. "The condition can be treated and even reversed, but only if we start treatment now."

Clarence sighed as if he hadn't heard Lukas. "How long do I have?"

"Could be years."

Clarence's eyes widened in shock.

"It'll keep getting worse, of course." Lukas steeled himself against the harshness of his own words. "Your condition could deteriorate until you have to be on oxygen all the time. You won't be able to walk, and your kidneys could eventually fail. We didn't pick up on any intestinal obstruction, which is a relief, but it is a future possibility. We've brought drugs to help get some of the excess fluid out of your body and to bring your blood sugar down closer to normal."

"Why drag it out?" Clarence asked bitterly.

"Death is not inevitable. At this rate, Darlene could die before you do." Lukas paused to let that sink in. "Her asthma is already bad, and one serious attack could kill her." He sat down on a bedside chair. "She needs your help, Clarence, and you're in no shape to be there for her the way you are now. The way I see it you only have one recourse."

"What's that?"

"State aid."

"No."

"Do you have a better suggestion?"

Clarence winced as if in pain. He closed his eyes and shook his head.

"Clarence, you don't want to die. I know you're desperate not to be a burden on Darlene, but death is not the answer."

"Neither is taking handouts."

"Then don't consider state aid a handout. Consider it a loan that you'll pay back when you get well. That's what I'm doing."

Clarence's bushy brows rose in surprise.

"I don't come from a wealthy family," Lukas said. "We had a dairy farm outside of Mount Vernon, Missouri, and we sure didn't make enough money for all my education, or that of my brothers. We got school loans backed by the government. I'm still paying on the loans."

"That's not welfare." Clarence shook his head, glowering at Lukas. "Don't you even compare 'em!" His face flushed with anger.

For a moment Lukas wondered if he'd done the right thing.

"You didn't have to use food stamps at the grocery store and have to listen to the whispers and feel the disgust from other shoppers." Clarence jammed his thumb at his chest. "I did. Darlene and I grew up like that. The kids at school called us trash because we took welfare. Their parents said our parents were too lazy to work, so they shouldn't eat. You know what? They were right." He paused to catch his breath. Even the exertion of talking wore him out quickly. "When I got old enough, I got a job and moved out. That way my parents couldn't draw money on me. Darlene moved in with me as soon as she could, and we both worked our way through trade school." He stopped to breathe again. "We didn't draw a dime off the state, and when we moved to another town, no one even knew we'd been welfare kids." He huffed for a long moment. "We won't go back to that."

"Are you saying you think your parents were welfare abusers?"

"I don't think, I know. They just didn't want to work. My father was born into a welfare family, and he got good at milking the system. How could anybody respect someone like that?"

Lukas waited while the man's breathing returned to normal. "I understand now. It's not self-respect you're worried about. It's public respect."

"That's not it."

"You're going to let public opinion dictate your future…or lack of one," Lukas said.

"You don't know what you're talking about."

"Do you realize that if you accept help, you could relieve the burden from your sister practically overnight? I know some charitable organizations that would be willing to help you out until the state aid kicked in. Don't consider it charity. Consider it a loan. You don't have to end up like your parents."

Clarence held his huge arms out to his sides and looked down at his enormous bare torso. "Do you know how long it could take to lose this?"

"Not as long as it could take you to die. I believe you would qualify for stomach surgery to cut down on your consumption. You can be up and around long before you reach your target weight. You could even get a job, maybe get a loan to set up your own business."

Clarence shook his head. "You've never been fat, have you, Doc? I haven't been outside this house in months." He paused to catch his breath. "The only place I can walk to is the bathroom. Nobody'll give me a job or a loan. People hate a fatso. Doctors hate Medicaids. I know. We went through six doctors when Darlene and I were growing up. As soon as they could dump us they did."

Lukas sighed heavily and watched the big man's sad, dark eyes for a moment in silence. He thought about the drugs in the bag beside his feet. Maybe he could convince Clarence to take them, and maybe he couldn't. Maybe the man was planning to hasten his own death by refusing to do anything to help himself. *Oh, Lord, help me to convince him of his worth.*

"Our emergency room gets Medicaid patients all the time," Lukas said. "Some of them are abusers, some are legit." He leaned forward. "I don't like the abusers. They come into our department and smoke their cigarettes just outside the doors and let the smoke drift in and choke the rest of us despite the smoking ban on the hospital campus. They buy Coke and candy from the vending machines, then refuse to pay the four-dollar fee at the desk because they're 'broke.' Most of the time I'm civil to them and treat the sore throats they get from too many cigarettes and the stomachaches they get from drinking too much booze. For the most part, these are the rudest, most demanding patients I see. It really frustrates me."

"Why do you treat 'em?"

"State law says I have to. Sometimes I get brave and send the obvious abusers away. Others are young children who can't do anything about their situation. I treat them with as much care as I'd treat my own family, and I care what happens to you. I'm sorry you had such a bad experience when you were a kid, but if you decide to draw Medicaid, Clarence, you can come into the emergency room anytime, and I will take care of you gladly. I know you'll be legit."

Clarence jerked his head toward the door. "What about the other doc?"

"She's here now, isn't she? Ask her yourself."

Clarence thought about that for a moment, then laid his head back wearily on his pillows and closed his eyes.

"I'll help you sign up for help, Clarence."

"No."

Lukas bit back a protest and sighed in frustration. "Okay. Have it your way. Will you at least use the medications we brought with us today?"

Clarence opened one eye, as if too tired to open both. "You'll keep taking care of Darlene?"

"Of course."

"Then lay those drugs on me, Doc."

Tedi knew she was in trouble the moment Heather's mother dropped her off at home after school Thursday. Dad's car was in the drive, and he never came home early on Thursdays. It could only mean one thing—that counselor had told him what she'd said this morning. But how much had he told him? She almost didn't go inside, but the moment she took a step along the sidewalk in the direction of the neighbors, the front door opened and Dad stepped out.

Tedi stopped and looked at him for a moment. She didn't smile and didn't speak, and neither did he. He just stared back at her. For the first time the thought came to her that her own father was probably her worst enemy in the world, not Abby Cuendet or Alex Holmes, the class bully. In fact, she decided, Dad didn't deserve to be called a dad. From now on she would call him what Mom called him—Theo. If she had the guts.

"Come in the house, Tedi." His voice was quiet.

She stood watching him. She didn't want to go in the house. He could say what he wanted to say to her out here where the neighbors could see if they looked out their windows.

He frowned. His voice rose an octave. "I said come in."

She readjusted her book bag over her shoulder and glanced longingly toward the road, where Heather's mother's car had disappeared out of sight. She couldn't tell from here whether Dad—Theo—had been drinking or not.

"Tedi!" His voice had that warning in it again.

"Why do I have to come in?"

He pulled the door open farther and took a step out.

She relented and walked toward him slowly, glaring at him the way she glared at Alex when he picked on the little kids during recess.

When she reached him he stood back and held the door open. "How was school?"

"Fine." She let her voice sound the way it did when she talked to Abby—hateful. She stepped through the door. He didn't move, but she could feel him watching her. She still couldn't smell his breath.

"Was math class okay?"

She didn't react, didn't even turn around to look at him. She didn't want to look at him. "Fine."

"Really? I thought you weren't supposed to be in math class this morning."

"I was there."

"You left Nick's office early."

She shrugged as if it were no big deal, but her heart started beating harder, faster. "So?"

He shut the door behind her. Hard. She froze. Don't turn around. Don't act scared.

"Don't you sass me. You wasted good money and Nick's valuable time and just walked out on him."

She gritted her teeth. "Why should you care? Mom's paying."

There was a long silence; then she heard a step behind her. "I'm sick of hearing that!" He grabbed her left shoulder and jerked her around so hard she thought she heard bones popping. His fingers dug into her flesh.

"Ouch! You're hurting me!" She tried to pull away, but he just squeezed tighter and grabbed the other shoulder.

His face was flushed deep red, and his eyes glared at

her like blue lights. He looked like a devil as his face grew closer and closer to hers, and his hot breath touched her skin. Booze breath. "You'll know what pain is if you keep using that smart mouth of yours." His fingers tightened even more. Tedi felt so scared she didn't even try to pull away.

She started to tremble deep inside her body, and she couldn't stop it. Quick tears stung her eyes. "I'm sorry! I didn't want to talk to him anyway, b-but Mom said—"

"Mom said!" Dad mimicked. "Mom said! You hang on to every word she says like you think she's the only one that matters!" He shouted loudly enough for the neighbors to hear. "And now you're trying to get a psychologist to testify in court against me?"

Tedi cringed. "He told you what I said?"

"I'm the legal guardian, in case you can't remember that, and it's not going to change. I have every right to know what you tell him. If I hear one more time that you're going to go live with your mother, I'll see to it you never see her again." Another shake. "Do you hear me?"

Tedi's chin quivered. She tried to answer, but she couldn't find her voice.

"I'll put her in the mental ward again. It's where she belongs anyway. I'll ruin her name in this whole county. She'll never practice medicine again. And don't tell me I wouldn't do it. I can make a living for us on my own. I don't depend on your mother's money. Besides, if you go live with her, the money will stop anyway. What've I got to lose?"

Tedi shook her head. He couldn't do those things, could he?

He jerked her by the shoulders again, but this time she was too numb to feel it.

"What happened to your smart mouth?" he demanded.

"It was working fine a minute ago. It was working fine this morning when you spilled your guts to Nick, wasn't it?"

Tedi couldn't stop shaking, and she couldn't make her voice work.

He shook her harder. "Answer me!"

Sobs rose in her throat. She nodded.

"You told him everything, didn't you?"

"H-he d-didn't believe me," she managed at last.

Another jerk. "What didn't he believe?" This time he forced her to within three inches of his face.

Her face crumpled with sobs. "Stop it, Daddy! Please! I'm scared."

"You should be. What did you tell him?" He shook her again.

"D-didn't he tell you?"

"Refresh my memory."

"J-just that…I spent the night alone." She could barely hear her own voice.

"What? Speak up! I can't hear you." He shouted so loudly it made her ears ring.

She took a deep breath and tried to straighten her shoulders. He just held tighter.

"I told him that I spent the…the night alone."

"What else?"

"That I was afraid of you because…you might get d-drunk and hit me."

His hold loosened on her shoulders for a moment, as if in surprise. "What else?"

"I told him…"

His hands tightened again. It felt like he was ripping her shoulders off. "What?"

"That I thought…" She couldn't say it. Her voice just wouldn't come.

"You thought what?" He released her right shoulder, and his hand came up to poise threateningly above her face. "What?"

She glanced in fear at the hand. "That I thought you'd kill me, Daddy!"

He released her and straightened. The shock on his face told her that Nick hadn't told him that. He paled, then once again the color returned.

Tedi took a step back. Fury filled his expression again, and he lunged for her.

She screamed, threw her book bag at him and turned to run. She reached the stairs and started up them. Dad grabbed at her arm and caught her sleeve. It ripped as she jerked away, still screaming as loudly as she could. The neighbors would hear. They would call the police.

She darted into her bedroom and slammed the door, then locked it and pushed a chair in front of it.

A loud thump filled the room when Dad hit the door with his body. The wood of the door crackled but held.

"Let me in this door, or I'll break it down!"

"No! The neighbors'll call the police!" she shouted past chattering teeth.

"Oh, yeah? Who're they going to believe? A kid, or her dad?" The doorknob rattled; then his weight hit the door again.

Tedi screamed.

Dad's fists pounded the wood. "They won't believe your mother, either."

Tedi tried to take a deep breath, but she was shaking so badly she couldn't get much air. Could he really ruin

Mom? Could he put her in the hospital again? Tears flowed freely down Tedi's face, and she hiccuped with sobs.

Everything grew quiet for a moment except for Tedi's crying; then Dad pounded the door hard one last time. "Okay, stay in there. I don't care if you starve to death!" She heard him back away from the door. "But remember this, kid. If you say anything to your mother or grandmother about this, you'll never see them again. Do you hear me? And it will be your fault."

She couldn't answer. Her sobs came so fast she could barely breathe.

"And I don't want to go to court again. If I do, I'll tear your mother to shreds. She doesn't want you anyway. She's just worried about what people are saying because she lost custody of her child."

Tedi shook her head. It couldn't be true, could it? What could he do to Mom? Could he really put her back in the hospital? The way he was acting right now, he might hurt her, run her over with a car or something, or even hurt Grandma. He was the crazy one.

Finally she heard him go down the steps and out the front door. Still trembling, she went to the window and saw him get into the car and back out of the drive. He drove away.

Still fighting for breath past her crying, Tedi removed the chair and unlocked the door. On shaking legs she went downstairs and to the front door. She looked outside one last time, just to make sure Dad hadn't changed his mind and come back. The drive was empty. She walked into the family room, sat down on the couch, and picked up the telephone receiver. She dialed Mom's number by memory and waited.

"Hello."

"Mom?" Tedi couldn't help it. Sobs shook her again. She caught her breath and tried to stop it, but her body wouldn't cooperate.

"Yes, sweetheart, what is it? What's wrong?"

She had to stop crying. She couldn't let Mom guess what was happening. She sniffed again and wiped her nose on her sleeve.

"Tedi?" Mom's voice sounded so warm and secure and close. "Talk to me, honey. Are you okay? What's—"

"I'm okay, Mom. It's just… I just… Oh, Mom, don't do it. Don't take Dad to court. I've changed my mind. I want…" She couldn't say it. It was such a horrible lie. She wanted to live with Mom so badly.

"Tedi, tell me what's going on. Talk to me. Why are you crying? Why have you suddenly changed your mind? Has your father—"

"Please, Mom! I just…don't…want to hurt your feelings." Her throat closed up again. She was lying! But she had to. She had to protect Mom and Grandma…and herself. "That's all. I love you, and I don't want to hurt your feelings, but I want to stay here. It's…home."

There was a moment of silence, and Tedi felt a rush of fear. Did Mom guess she was lying? Did she know from Tedi's voice what was really happening?

"Tedi, are you sure about this?" Mercy's voice was quiet and sad.

Tedi felt so horrible. She hated Theo Zimmerman. Hated him! "Yeah, Mom. I just miss you, that's all. I want to stay here, but I wish I could see you more."

Then suddenly there was a tone of suspicion in Mom's voice. "Did the counselor talk you into this?"

"No. I got tired of talking to him and left early. I'm sorry. I wasted money."

"It's okay, honey. I just wanted you to be able to talk to someone you could trust. If you felt you couldn't trust this person, I don't blame you for leaving. We'll find someone else for you. Do you want me to try to get more visitation rights?"

Another pause. "No. Don't go back to court. It'll just drag things out."

Mercy sighed. "Are you sure?"

"Yeah." *No, Mom! I want to live with you forever! I hate him.* "I've got to go do my homework now. I'll see you soon."

"Okay, Tedi."

"Don't be too disappointed, Mom."

"I'll be okay. How about you?"

"I'm…fine. I've just got homework. Bye, Mom." Her voice shook. Her whole body shook, and she couldn't make it stop.

"Goodbye, Tedi. I love you. Never forget that. Nothing will change that, ever."

Tedi sniffed, then hiccuped, then hung up the phone and fell across the sofa with fresh sobs.

Late Thursday night a sober but hungover Theo unlocked the front door of his home and stepped inside. No lights had shone from Tedi's upstairs bedroom window, and he hadn't expected any. Was she even here? He didn't want to go up and check her room and possibly terrify her again. He'd done enough damage for one day.

He'd spent the whole afternoon sitting in his office cubicle, staring at the wall and listening to the phone ring over and over and over again, both his office and cell phone. He couldn't forget his own daughter's screams, or the fact that he'd been the one to cause them.

This time he had to lay off the booze. He had to.

He'd drunk three pots of coffee and forced down three Big Macs and waited for Mercy to walk through the office door and start blasting away at him with a sawed-off shotgun. Or maybe she would come at him with a knife—she had a more hands-on style. He'd picked up the phone to call her once and maybe initiate some damage control, but he hadn't even had the guts to dial.

Now he was tired of waiting and wondering. He went into the den, pulled out his keys, and opened the bottom drawer of his desk. Inside was a small gray recorder connected to the telephone system. He'd installed this thing months ago but had only activated it this morning after Nick warned him that Mercy might try to take him back to court for custody of Tedi. He pressed the button, sat back and listened.

Chapter Eighteen

A week passed in peaceful, though sad, busyness for Mercy. She told herself that she could understand why Tedi wanted to stay in the home she'd known most of her life, but the rejection still stung. Security was important to a child, but Mercy couldn't help feeling just a little sorry for herself when she watched her own mother prepare for a hiking trip to Colorado. Everybody else had a life, but Mercy still felt stuck on hold, unworthy to even care for her own child. There was only so far she could bury herself in her work without total burnout, and sometimes her free hours weighed heavily—not that she would ever put the burden of her own social needs onto Tedi. A nasty little voice reminded her several times throughout the week that she was the one who chose not to have a social life. She'd countered with the argument that she'd prefer boredom and loneliness over marriage. After all, how many happy marriages had she witnessed in her lifetime? Few.

Josie, her disgustingly in-love nurse, constantly preached about the joys of being married to "the right man." "Oh, yeah?" Mercy had said. "And what happens when the 'right man' turns out to be a jerk in disguise? They don't show their real colors until after marriage."

Josie had smiled and said, "If you both belong to Christ and put Him first, then He will guide your marriage. A long courtship also helps, so you can make sure the guy really does belong to Christ and he's not just faking. Take a year or two to get to know the guy."

Mercy thought again about those words as she drove into the Knolls Community Hospital doctors' parking lot Thursday morning. She'd gone to high school with Theo but hadn't married him until she was twenty-nine. She had just moved back home after residency training in Tulsa when they became reacquainted at a high school football homecoming. They were married the next spring. Neither of them "belonged" to Christ. Mercy wasn't even sure what that meant, although she was sure Mom or Josie or Lukas would be happy to tell her.

It was obvious to her now that she'd never really known Theodore Zimmerman. The problem was, how could she have? No chemical company had come out with a litmus test for potential marriage partners. She couldn't trust her own discernment. Therefore, it was best to learn from past mistakes and leave the choice of matrimony to wiser, or more foolhardy, women.

She sighed as she wrapped her stethoscope over her shoulders and picked up her bag from the seat. It did no good to think about the past and wonder what might have been if she'd met the right man. She hadn't. She'd tried and lost.

Still, she thought as she walked into the quiet E.R., she had to stop dismissing all men as worthless. Some even showed signs of integrity—Lukas, for instance. His transparency ran deep. He was awkward and clumsy on a date, and he obviously had little experience where women were concerned. That was probably because he'd spent all of his time studying and working and discovering how to be the best doctor he could be. There was an inner peace about him, a kind of joy that he radiated to his patients, even though he also betrayed loneliness at times. Every patient of Mercy's that he had seen in the E.R. had nothing but praise for him about his gentleness, his caring and the amount of time he spent with them. He was obviously a patient advocate.

Granted, one good man out of twenty was a pretty poor representation, but it was enough to give Mercy hope that they weren't all duds. Speak of the devil, Lukas was sitting at the main desk doing charts when Mercy entered. He looked sleepy.

"Got a patient for me?" she greeted.

"Just dismissing the last one. Strep." He looked up at her and smiled. "How're you doing?" he asked. "I haven't seen you for a week."

"Don't ask." Mercy set her bag down and took another chair beside Lukas. "What have you heard about the Knights? I trust you've called to check on them as you said you would."

"Yes, twice, in fact." Lukas slid his stack of charts toward Carol. "The first time I called on Saturday, Darlene told me she felt better and that Clarence was complaining because he was wearing out the floor to the bathroom."

"Good." Mercy leaned back in her chair and rested her feet on an open file drawer. "That probably means he's taking the Lasix and that it's working."

"She said he was."

"And the metformin?"

"Apparently he's being compliant."

Mercy whistled. "Amazing. Who'd'a thunk it?"

"There's more." Lukas's grin widened.

For the first time, Mercy noticed the cleft of his chin and the firm line of his jawbone. *Stop it, Mercy!* "More?"

"Yes, remember I told you I called twice. The second time I called on Monday, Darlene told me Clarence had reduced his own food rations, and so far he was sticking to it. She also caught him exercising his arms in cadence to the music coming from that ancient black-and-white television in his room. He stopped when he saw her, but she was encouraged. So am I."

"What do you think about drugs to suppress his appetite?" Mercy asked.

"If he had his stomach stapled, we wouldn't have to worry about drugs." Lukas shook his head. "Unfortunately, I don't think either of us can afford an expense like that, and he sure can't."

"No, but he's moving in the right direction."

The phone rang. Carol answered, then glanced at Lukas. "Yes, Mrs. Pinkley, he's right here." There was a pause, and she frowned. "Yes, I'll tell him." She hung up the phone. "Dr. Bower, Mrs. Pinkley wants to see you in her office before you leave."

Lukas groaned. "So much for sleep."

After Lukas left, Mercy changed into her scrubs and walked back out to find Lauren McCaffrey deep in conversation with Carol. They fell silent for just a moment when Mercy joined them, which surprised her, because the female staff usually spoke more freely with her than they did with the male doctors.

Lauren hesitated, then said, "Dr. Mercy, how do you feel about Dr. Bower?"

Mercy shot her a suspicious glance. Lauren had seen

her pick up Lukas the other day when they went to visit Clarence, and Mercy had seen the disappointment clearly on the woman's face. "Oh, no, don't you start, too. Josie's bad enough."

Lauren blushed, though she continued to watch Mercy's expression with more than casual interest. "I meant, professionally."

"Oh. Of course. I think Dr. Bower is a dedicated physician. I've heard a lot of good things about him from staff. How do you feel about him?"

The nurse and the secretary glanced at each other again.

"I like working with him," Carol volunteered. "He doesn't mind helping the nurses out when they're busy, and he makes sure we understand his orders."

"I hear the patients like him, too," Mercy said.

"We think Dr. Bower is going to lose his job," Lauren said despondently.

"Why would you think that?" Mercy exclaimed.

"Because of Dr. George," Lauren said.

"Do you think anyone's going to listen to him, knowing how he feels about Dr. Bower?"

Lauren raised a delicate blond eyebrow at her. "Every time I have a shift with Dr. Bower, Dr. George comes to me with the charts for that shift and nitpicks everything everyone did. He even blames me for following all of Dr. Bower's orders."

Mercy scowled. How unprofessional! "Do you think Dr. Bower uses poor medical judgment?"

"No, but Dr. George has clout, and he could get at Dr. Bower indirectly. He could get me fired if he wanted to."

"How?"

"He's friends with Fern Davis, the director of nursing. She can dismiss me for any reason she wants. One of the nurses on the floor got fired last week without any explanation. She thinks it's because she wouldn't go to work for Dr. George in his office practice."

Mercy rolled her eyes. Jarvis was becoming more and more obnoxious.

Lauren hesitated, bit her lip and grimaced. "I've had a couple of patients come in and when they found out the doctor on duty was Dr. Bower, they refused to be treated by him."

Mercy felt her irritation build. "Did they explain why?"

"No, but they were Dr. George's patients. I think Dr. Bower is being stabbed in the back, and I don't like it."

Right then the door opened, and a man walked in. His left hand was clumsily wrapped, and blood seeped through the bandage.

"Time to get to work," Mercy said.

Lauren leaned toward her. "I hope Mrs. Pinkley didn't call Dr. Bower up to fire—" She broke off, shaking her head. "Sorry, I'm not trying to spread rumors."

The third floor of Knolls Community Hospital did not look like a hospital. With its plush carpeting and decorated walls, it could have passed for a high-dollar attorney's office. It was the administration floor. In the three and a half weeks Lukas had been at Knolls, he'd had two occasions to visit there, and the atmosphere made him feel uncomfortable. The clerks, secretaries and department directors stared at him when he walked by. No one smiled.

Mrs. Pinkley's secretary, Charlotte, seemed to be the only one who knew how to move her lips, and the smile barely touched her eyes. "She's waiting for you, Dr. Bower," she said, studying him carefully.

For a moment he considered hunting for a mirror to see if he had blood on his face or if his hair was sticking up, but in uncomfortable situations he liked the old adage "Never let 'em see you sweat." He thanked her, straightened his shoulders and opened the door in front of him. It was a closet. He turned back around to see her pointing toward a second, wider door.

Without another word he walked through the door into an even plusher office decorated in tones of pale green, pink and taupe.

Mrs. Pinkley remained seated behind her broad desk and watched him enter. She must be nearing seventy. She had white hair that was cut short and feathered straight back. No nonsense. Intimidating, yet still, somehow, feminine. Lukas had liked her immediately upon meeting her for his first interview.

"Thank you for coming so quickly, Dr. Bower," she said in her deep, gravelly voice. She sounded like a smoker, but everyone knew she was not.

She did not offer a handshake, which was good because their hands probably wouldn't have reached each other across the broad expanse of the desk. She didn't smile, either. "I realize I'm cutting into your sleep time, so I'll do away with formalities and try to keep this meeting short. Please be seated."

Lukas had already done so.

She indicated a stack of file folders on her desk. "These are charts on some of the patients you've treated since you came to work for us." She pulled up the reading glasses from a chain around her neck and cradled them on her nose. She picked up a chart, opened it and read a sticky note that had been attached to the inside cover. "One of my least favorite jobs is handling patient complaints. I don't get as many of them as I did before we added improvements to the hospital three years ago. Census is up, and we're doing well." She patted the stack. "These are on you, Dr. Bower." She paused and looked at him over the top of her glasses.

He stared back at her. "They're patient complaints?"

"Specific patients, yes. One of them is Ruby Taylor. She complains every time she's in the hospital. It doesn't matter to her that if not for your quick action, she could be dead now. I also have a complaint that you did not follow proper transfer procedures when you sent her to Springfield."

"I tried."

"I know. I read the file. I'm ignoring the complaint." She picked up a sheet of paper. "Two of the complaints I received by telephone don't match charts because the patients never even checked in. These two women were very displeased that you chastised them for Medicaid abuse and forced them to buy their head lice shampoo without a script." She looked again over her glasses. "Let me point out that I have not worded the complaint with the colorful jargon they used." There was a hint of a smile that disappeared quickly. "Another report is from Dwayne Little." She stopped and settled back in luxurious leather.

"I'm not surprised," Lukas said.

"Nor I, but this one could turn into a great deal of trouble before his father finishes with us. Bailey Little is not a man with whom you would want to tangle."

Lukas liked the "us" bit. In KC it had been him against the hospital, from the administrator on down. "I hear Mr. Little's father is president of the hospital board."

Mrs. Pinkley held Lukas's gaze. "Too bad you weren't aware of that before you chased him out of the E.R."

"I was." Lukas took a deep breath and let it out slowly. It was happening again. "I warned you before I started that I wasn't very good at hospital politics."

"Yes, you did. That was one of the many qualities that attracted me to you as an excellent candidate for your position. I don't like drug pushers, be they working through legal or illegal channels. People who abuse drugs need help, not more drugs from political doctors. I despise Medicaid abuse, Medicare abuse, insurance abuse of any kind. We have a problem on our hands, however, because Dwayne Little's daddy is threatening to sue. What's worse, he's threatening to report us on a possible COBRA violation on this thing if I don't fire you."

Lukas sucked in his breath.

Mrs. Pinkley nodded. "If somebody investigates the report, it could be touchy for this hospital. Most people take Bailey Little seriously, and he has a lot of support in high places, even into state and federal offices."

Lukas suddenly felt defeated and very tired. "Maybe you should fire me. Or maybe I should quit."

Estelle gave an impatient sigh. "I didn't ask you up here to fire you. I called for you because I am going to need your help to fight this thing. Why wasn't an AMA form signed before Dwayne left?"

"He got mad and stormed out before we had a chance to get one, but I filled one out afterward and signed it and left it for the nurse to sign and file. Beverly and I were both witnesses that he refused the shot of Toradol I offered, and the shots of morphine with Narcan. He nearly knocked Beverly down on his way out."

"We will need Beverly to sign a statement to that effect, but as of now there is no AMA form with the file."

Lukas shook his head. "Then I don't know what

happened to it. I don't think Beverly would forget something like..." But Beverly had been acting strangely the past few days.

"We'll talk to Beverly about it. If we get the right answers from her, I believe we can beat this. I'm more worried about public opinion at this point. I have to answer to the taxpayers of Knolls community." She leaned forward again and indicated the stack of files. "Dr. Bower, these complaints all come from the patients of one physician. They're mostly about tests and medications that they considered to be too expensive or unnecessary. Nitpicking. Would you care to venture a guess as to who their physician is?"

"Dr. George."

"You have a great deal of insight," she said drily. "Unfortunately, Dr. George still wields power here at the hospital and, therefore, in this town. Do me a favor for the time being and try really, really hard to placate him." She frowned. "Believe it or not, he's not usually this hard to get along with. I don't know what's bothering him right now."

"He may still be upset about the disaster drill and the Ruby Taylor case."

Mrs. Pinkley nodded. "The needlestick report couldn't have been popular with him, either, even though it was the right thing for you to do. He never did follow protocol on that."

"I think he needs to. The other day he was obviously suffering from a bad headache, and his hand seemed to be bothering him. He grew very defensive when I asked him about it."

"I bet he did." She sighed. "All these things have been ill-timed events, but not enough to trigger the backlash we're getting. These people are out of line. I just want you to be forewarned." She stepped around her desk and offered him a hand.

He stood and took it gently. "Thank you, Mrs. Pinkley." She had a firm grip, showing no signs of the arthritis he knew she had. "I'll try to show more restraint in the future."

"I appreciate it. This could be a learning experience for both of us." She released his hand and stepped back behind her desk.

"Tell me something, Dr. Bower," she said before he reached the door.

He stopped and turned back around.

"How did it feel to chase a drug seeker out of our emergency department?"

He grinned at her. "It felt great."

Her smile was genuine as he turned around and walked out the door.

Chapter Nineteen

Mercy had just finished a twenty-one-suture closure in the E.R. when Lauren came into the exam room. "Dr. Mercy, you're not going to believe this one. There's a hysterical woman on the line who says her brother is having a heart attack, but he weighs too much for an ambulance."

Mercy knew before she asked. "What's the name?"

"Their name's Knight."

Mercy snapped off her gloves. "Is she still on the line?"

"Yes. She insisted she had to talk to you."

"Okay, I'm coming." She turned to the young man on the exam table. "Mark, I'll be back as soon as I can."

She ran to the telephone and picked up the receiver. Before she could even put it to her ear, she heard sobbing. "Darlene? This is Dr. Mercy. What's wrong?"

There was a deep, trembling breath; then Darlene's words came out in a rush. "It's Clarence, Dr. Mercy. He's really sick and I can't get him to wake up, and I don't know what's happened. He just knocked over a glass, and—"

"Darlene, slow down. Take a deep breath. Are you saying Clarence is not conscious now?"

"I...I don't know. He wasn't just before I came to call you. He's breathing, but he won't open his eyes or say anything."

"Okay. I want you to put the receiver down and go in and rub your knuckles really hard against the bony center of his chest. See if there's a reaction, and then come back and tell me."

"But can't we just call Dr. Bower to come out? I tried to get his home phone number to call him, but it's not listed, but I know he'd come—"

"Darlene, we're wasting precious time!" Mercy spoke sharply. "We can get Clarence here, but I need your help. Go check him."

She heard a clatter as the receiver hit the counter, then turned to the secretary. "Carol, call an ALS ambulance, ask for a double team, and also request first responders. Get them on the line for me and have them hold. Tell them their patient weighs at least five hundred pounds."

Carol's eyes widened. "Five hundred—"

"Probably a lot more. Just do it. And check to see if Dr. Bower is still in the hospital. Page him."

Darlene came back on the line. "Dr. Mercy?"

"I'm here."

"He's groaning. His chest hurts really bad." Her voice shook with sobs again. "He's dying."

"Stop it! I need you calm, Darlene. I'm going to send an ambulance with enough people to lift Clarence. Just keep him still until they get there, and don't leave him. He needs you there with him. Are you okay?"

There was a pause. "I'm bleeding quite a bit."

"Bleeding?"

"I cut my foot on the glass he broke when he had the attack."

"Okay. Get a thick washcloth and fold it into a big square. Place it directly over the cut, then tie a towel around it was tightly as you can. That'll hold you until help gets there."

"I'll be okay. I'm worried about Clarence."

"You can't do him any good if you pass out from blood loss. I want you to come in with the ambulance. We'll take a look at you when you get here. Okay?"

Darlene took a deep breath. "Okay. I can do it."

"Good. I'll see you soon. Hang in there, Darlene."

She disconnected and punched the second line. "Hello, this is Dr. Mercy."

"This is Connie, the paramedic. Where's the patient?"

Mercy gave her the address. "I want you to double team and call the first responders."

"Right. Carol told us."

"Get a heavy-duty Stryker cot. The patient's name is Clarence Knight. His sister will meet you, and she has a glass cut on her foot. Hurry. He could be having an MI." She hung up and rushed back to finish her present patient and prepare for Clarence's arrival. Darlene would need stitches. It would sure be nice if Lukas were here.

She was writing Mark a script for pain when she glanced up to find Lukas walking in and looking around the E.R. as if expecting at least more than one patient after being paged.

"Lukas, thank goodness! I may need your help. It's Clarence."

"What happened? Is he okay? He called?"

"Darlene called. Sounds like he's in trouble, could be

his heart. They're bringing him in, and Darlene, too. I know you wanted to get some sleep, but—"

"Not now." He sighed. "We were afraid this would happen. What's wrong with Darlene?" he asked, setting his bag down.

"She cut her foot. I don't know how bad it is."

"Okay, you're in charge, you call the shots," Lukas said. "If you want, I'll check the cardiac room and make sure everything is ready."

"Yes, please."

Mercy had just finished releasing her only patient when the ambulance radio spoke to her from the central desk. "Knolls Community Hospital, this is Knolls 830 requesting medical control." It was Connie's voice.

Mercy punched the button. "This is medical control. Go ahead."

"Medical control, we have reached the Knight residence. The patient is alert and oriented, complaining of severe chest pain rated at a nine. Requesting permission to give sublingual nitroglycerin per protocol."

"Is IV established at this time?"

"Negative. Attempts have been unsuccessful at this point."

"Do you have a current set of vitals on this patient?"

"Heart rate 120, respiration 22 and labored, oxygen saturation 93 percent on nonrebreather mask."

"What is his BP?"

Connie's voice sounded sheepish. "Unable to determine blood pressure at this time. We were able to auscultate a radial pulse."

Mercy shook her head. "Permission for sublingual nitroglycerin denied until IV access is obtained. I suggest you attempt an external jugular route. Keep us advised of any change in the patient's condition. What is your ETA?"

"About fifteen minutes. Full patient report will be given prior to arrival." There was a pause. "Request change to private channel."

Mercy switched the button.

"Doc, are you there?" Connie asked.

"I'm here."

"Dr. Mercy, we're doing the best we can, but this guy's big. I've never had anything like it before."

"I know. Do your best. Medical control clear." Mercy turned to find Lauren and Carol hovering behind her. "Hope these rescuers have been trained properly on safe weight-lifting techniques, or we could have more than two patients coming in with that ambulance."

"I've got everything set up in the cardiac room, Dr. Mercy," Lauren said. "Dr. Bower is checking it out just in case we might need extra of anything. Is this man really over five hundred pounds?"

"That's a very rough guess. We'll definitely have our hands full because our patient has a lot of other health problems. Oh, and, Lauren, make sure we have a suture tray ready. We'll get two patients."

Lauren went to recheck supplies, and Mercy got up to pace, waiting for a radio report. Would the teams even be able to convince Clarence to come in? He might decide this was the big one, take advantage of it and stay at home, waiting, once more, to die. After all, it was Darlene who had called.

Lukas came back a few moments later and watched Mercy wring her hands as she stared out at the street. "You look like a worried mother. They're a professional crew. I think they'll do a good job."

"Are we all set up for him?"

"The cardiac room is stocked, and we have a good, sturdy exam bed. Lauren also has the laceration room ready for Darlene."

"Thanks, Lukas." She glanced at him and stopped wringing her hands. "Did you have a good meeting with Mrs. Pinkley?"

He winced. "Do you have to bring that up?"

"I need something to keep my mind off Clarence. Was it that bad?"

"Patient complaints."

She waited.

He glanced around, then lowered his voice. "Ever hear of Dwayne Little?"

"Sure, he's Bailey Little's son."

"Have you ever had him as a patient?"

"A couple of times in the past year in the emergency room."

"I offended him by offering to set him up in a drug rehab program."

Mercy groaned. "You didn't."

"I refused to give him the drugs he wanted, and I called the area emergency departments to check on him. His father wants me fired."

"And?"

"And Jarvis George obviously wants me fired, as well."

"What does Estelle say?"

"She says no way."

Mercy nodded with satisfaction. "Estelle usually gets what she wants."

He shrugged. "I don't know. They're talking big guns, maybe even COBRA. This may be out of Mrs. Pinkley's hands."

"Wait. Just wait. She seldom loses a fight, and she was a trial lawyer and a prosecuting attorney for thirty years before she decided to become a hospital administrator."

"I hear Bailey Little seldom loses a fight, either. He apparently has strong political connections."

"True, and he fights dirty."

"Oh, great, I needed to hear that."

"You just need to be prepared to defend yourself, Lukas. Bailey is powerful, but he's not God."

Connie's voice came back over the radio. "This is Knolls 830 calling Knolls medical control. Over."

Mercy went back to her chair and flipped the switch. "This is medical control."

"We are currently inbound to your facility with two patients. Patient one is a class-two medical, a forty-two-year-old male complaining of chest pain. Be advised that we have established a jugular IV on patient one. Sublingual nitroglycerin times two has been given, pain has been reduced from a nine to a four. Patient's current vitals are BP 92 over 68, respirations 18 and mildly labored, heart rate 112. Patient is on a cardiac monitor, revealing sinus tachycardia. No ST segment elevation is noted at this time. We have an ETA of two minutes. Are you requesting any further orders on patient one?"

"Negative. Proceed with report on patient two."

"Second patient is a class-three trauma, a forty-year-old female who has sustained a deep laceration to the right foot, vitals are stable at this time and bleeding is controlled."

"Knolls 830, are you requesting lifting help upon your arrival?"

"Negative. There will be ten of us."

"Medical control out." Mercy turned to Lukas. "Let's

hope Clarence isn't totally pain free when he arrives, or he may make them turn around and take him right back home."

"I don't think so. Not this time."

"Oh, yeah?" Mercy crossed her arms. "What makes you the expert on Clarence all of a sudden? You're the one who couldn't convince him to come in last week."

"Fear is a great convincer."

Mercy shook her head slowly, frowning. "I think he needs a motivator. Darlene."

"She's always been a motivating factor. I think it just took him some time to realize he's been going about it the wrong way."

"So you've made him see the error of his ways," Mercy said drily.

"Nope. I already told you. When fear and pain talk, people listen."

When the ambulance arrived, Lukas followed Mercy out to meet it.

"Dr. Bower," Clarence called from his seemingly precarious perch on the Stryker cot.

Lukas leaned through the ambulance door. "How's the pain?"

Clarence nodded. "Still hurts, but not like it did. Take care of Darlene."

"A nurse is already helping her inside." Lukas shot him a mischievous grin. "Dr. Mercy's on duty, and she's going to take good care of you."

Clarence looked at Mercy and groaned.

Mercy glared at him. "I see you haven't lost your chauvinistic charm."

She and Lukas backed out of the way while eight men and two women surrounded Clarence and heaved his huge bulk out of the ambulance. There was a tense moment when the stretcher nearly tipped, but they righted it and turned to push Clarence toward the entrance.

Mercy descended on her patient. "How's the pain now?" she asked.

"Better than it was," Clarence muttered.

"Rate it for me on a scale of one to ten," she said.

"I don't know." Clarence glanced down at the cot that carried him. Thick folds of flesh hung over each side. "Maybe a three, but it'll get worse if I fall off this sawhorse."

"Then you'd better hold still and do what the doctor tells you," Mercy said as the team wheeled him toward the cardiac room.

Darlene sat inside the E.R. doors with both feet elevated in a wheelchair, refusing to be taken into an exam room until she knew Clarence was going to be okay.

"We gave him a third nitro on the way here," Connie told Mercy. "His pain has eased more each time."

At the count of three the group lifted in unison, and amid grunts and groans, they gently placed Clarence onto the slightly wider exam bed. They expertly handled oxygen, IV and monitoring equipment.

Mercy leaned over Clarence with her stethoscope and auscultated his massive chest. Heartbeat and breathing were muffled. No wonder the paramedics had trouble getting readings on him.

When she straightened, Clarence asked, "Is it a heart attack?"

"I don't know yet."

"What about my sister? How's her foot?"

Mercy turned around and saw Lukas standing at the exam room entrance. "Lukas, would you mind taking care of Darlene? Looks like I'm going to be here awhile." She motioned to Lauren. "Let's give Mr. Knight another nitro and put him on a Tridil drip. Put him at three CCs an hour."

"Yes, Dr. Mercy."

Mercy walked out to the desk. "Carol, we need a stat cardiac workup, EKG, CBC, chemistry panel, cardiac enzymes and PT, PTT. And get us another nurse down here. We're going to need her."

"What about a portable chest?" Carol asked.

"No. With someone his size it would be a complete waste of time."

She walked back into the cardiac room. "How's the pain now, Clarence?"

"Still a three in my chest," he muttered. "Six in my arm."

"Feel like a pin cushion yet?" Mercy asked, grinning wickedly.

Clarence laid his head back wearily. Mercy stepped up and patted his huge arm. "We need to run these tests." She paused, almost expecting him to refuse the tests and demand to be taken back home. "Lukas will take good care of Darlene."

Clarence looked up at Mercy. "I know."

"And I'll take good care of you."

"I can't afford it."

Mercy sighed heavily. "We've been over this before. You have no choice."

He watched her for a moment, his dark eyes filled with sorrow. "I know."

Mercy hid her surprise well. Aha! Wait until Lukas heard about this.

"Once you get to feeling better, I'll have social services come by and talk with you." She waited for an argument. None came.

Now was not the time to shout for joy. She patted his arm again. "Stop worrying so much, Clarence. That's one of the things that put you here in the first place."

Chapter Twenty

Julie was back, and Tedi was furious.

For nearly two weeks, ever since the day Dad had really lost his temper and scared Tedi almost to death, he'd been better. There'd been no booze, no bad temper, no nasty remarks about Mom. And no Julie. Coincidence? Tedi didn't think so. It sure had been good while it lasted, with Dad in make-up mode.

Late this afternoon, though, about two hours ago, Julie had come ringing their doorbell. The first thing she'd stuck through the door when Tedi opened it had been a bottle of wine. The next had been a stupid fake smile, a tearful apology for Dad, and a hug. For him.

Tedi wanted to puke. She also wanted to break the wine bottle over Julie's curly blond hair, but it was too late now. Dad had finished most of the bottle. Tedi knew that because she'd spent the past two hours eavesdropping while she pretended to watch television and do her homework.

She knew she shouldn't eavesdrop, but how else would she have known that Dad and Julie were talking about marriage? Actually, Julie was talking about marriage, with a big, fat diamond ring, at least a carat. Ugh!

And how else would Tedi know how much Dad drank? The amount of booze he drank had a direct effect on his meanness. Julie didn't know that yet, but it was never far from Tedi's thoughts.

Julie's voice reached the family room just loudly enough for Tedi to hear over the television.

"Sweetie," she said, "I'm concerned about Tedi. Is she still having trouble over the divorce?"

With a scowl, Tedi got up from her perch on the sofa arm and crept closer to the hallway so she could hear better.

"She's fine," came Dad's voice. "You don't have to worry about her. Kids recover better than adults. My parents got a divorce when I was Tedi's age, and I turned out okay."

A commercial blared suddenly, drowning out everything but Tedi's indignant thoughts.

"Butt out, Julie," she muttered.

"She thinks her mother is supporting both of you," came Julie's voice again.

"Oh, no," Tedi whispered to herself. "I'm dead." Julie would just make things worse. When she left tonight…

Julie's hateful voice continued. "Maybe she's just jealous of our relationship, but I don't know why she would—"

The Energizer Bunny thudded his drums. Tedi jumped, and for a couple of moments, she didn't hear anything.

Then came Dad's irritated voice. "You've been discussing family finances with my daughter? My finances aren't any of your business."

"But when we're married—"

A screaming car salesman tried hard to get Tedi's attention. She wanted to ram her fist through the screen. But she wouldn't be the one ramming fists tonight. Dad would be.

She couldn't let that happen.

Tedi knew she had to leave first, at least until Dad had time to cool down and sober up.

"Ouch!" Four-year-old Timmy Bradley tried to jerk his lacerated arm away from the anesthesia needle. His tiny face scrunched up into prescream.

Lukas Bower finished the injection and held his hands out so the little boy could see he was finished—for the moment. "I'm sorry, Tim. Remember, I told you that the first one would hurt just a little, like a bee sting. The next one won't hurt." He placed Dermalon 5.0 suture in the needle driver.

The nurse, Claudia Zebert, shifted her grip on the child and gave him a warm, grandmotherly pat on the leg. "Want some extra help, Dr. Bower?"

Lukas shook his head and grinned at his patient, who watched him suspiciously and held tightly to his mother's leg.

"Thanks, Claudia, but Tim's a big boy. Besides, we're going to play a game." Lukas waited until Timmy's face registered curiosity. "Tim, I have some Popsicles in our freezer in the other room. If you can feel me stick you again, I'll give you a Popsicle."

The child's eyes held Lukas with growing interest and a little less fear than when he'd first come into the emergency department.

"But you can't cheat," Lukas continued. "You have to look at Mom so you won't be able to see when I stick you. Is that okay with you?"

Timmy frowned and nodded his head.

"Okay, here we go. No fair peeking." Lukas moved closer to the wound.

"Ouch!"

Lukas suppressed a laugh. "Hey, I haven't even stuck you yet. You really want that Popsicle, don't you?" He glanced over at Mrs. Bradley's tense face and winked.

She tried to force a smile, but her chin quivered. She was a young mom, and this was her first child.

"Okay, Timmy, can you count to three?"

Before the child finished his count, Lukas gave him the final injections.

Timmy got his Popsicle anyway.

Tedi stuck a jacket, an apple and a peanut butter sandwich into her denim school backpack. She couldn't go to Mom's. Dad would just cause more trouble for her, maybe even have her committed again like he'd threatened. Grandma was hiking somewhere in Colorado.

Tedi stepped to the door of her bedroom and listened. Their voices barely carried up the stairs from the den. If she was really quiet…

She put on a sweater, pulled the pack over her shoulders and turned off the light as she slipped out the door. Maybe if Dad didn't see the light, he would think she was asleep and not bug her. Or maybe he would be too drunk. Or maybe he would be thinking murder.

Now she heard anger in both voices as they carried up the stairs. Even Julie wasn't as sweet and fakey as she had been.

Better get out of here before Julie left and Dad exploded.

The voices continued as Tedi crept down the stairs. She skipped the third step from the bottom because it always squeaked, but she landed too hard on the next one. It thumped.

The voices paused.

Tedi froze.

The phone rang. No one made a sound. It rang again.

"I'd better get that," Dad said. "It's probably work. We've been waiting the whole afternoon on a client to arrive from L.A."

"What?" Julie sounded shocked. "You'd interrupt—"

"Let go!" came Dad's irritated voice, then the sound of the telephone receiver being picked up. "Yeah?"

There was a pause, then, "They're here? Now?" More silence. "Yes, Gordon. I'll be down. Give me a few minutes." He hung up.

"How could you do this?" Julie's voice was suddenly cold and harsh.

"Do what? I'm trying to earn a living." He paused. "How am I supposed to buy that ring for you if I don't make a sale now and then?"

Tedi didn't wait to hear anything else. She slipped out the front door without another sound and hurried along the sidewalk to the street.

Three blocks away was an open field. Across that field was a farmhouse and a barn. Tedi knew about it because she'd gone there last fall on a field trip with her class to see a bunch of beehives. The beehives weren't in the barn, so it would be safe.

It was the only place she could think of to go and hide for a while. She didn't feel like thinking about what she would do when it got dark. That would be a while yet. Right now she just had to get away, at least until Dad had time to sober up.

Lukas stepped out of the curtained exam room and walked Mrs. Bradley and Timmy to the central desk, where Claudia waited with follow-up instructions. They arrived at the desk just as the radio crackled with the familiar voice of Buck Oppenheimer.

"Knolls Hospital, this is Knolls 832. Please come in."

Lukas answered. "This is Knolls medical control. Go ahead."

"Medical control, we are currently inbound with a twenty-five-year-old Caucasian female patient who is complaining of acute pain in her lower abdomen. Her BP is 100 over 60 with slightly increased respiration. Heart rate is 90. She is very agitated and has twice asked us to return her home. We've convinced her to get checked out. Do you have any questions or orders?"

"Yes, what is your ETA?"

"We'll be there in about two minutes."

"Thank you. Please advise us of further developments. This is medical control out."

"What developments can happen in two minutes?" Claudia muttered as she watched Timmy and his mom walk out the door. "Why does the ambulance crew wait until they're almost here to call us? And tonight's going to be a full moon. You can already see it out there, and it's not even dark yet."

Lukas grinned. "Come on, Claudia. You're not super-stitious, are you?"

"Everybody knows all the psych patients and Obs show up during a full moon. From the sound of it, this gal could be both crazy and pregnant."

Lukas shook his head. He had only worked with this fiftysomething nurse a few times, but he appreciated her manner with patients. Her maternal, no-nonsense atti-tude gave her an edge over the other nurses in spite of the fact that she was the most recently hired, and therefore worked the night and weekend shifts no one else wanted.

"Relax, she may not even get here," he told her. "Remember that the ambulance attendants had to convince her twice to continue the ride."

"As I said…" Claudia shrugged.

"I thought recalcitrant patients were your specialty."

"That and grouchy doctors. I'm thinking of changing my specialty."

"Too bad. The emergency department is filled with both. We'd miss you around here."

"Can't say the feeling's mutual, except for you, Dr. Bower. You're never grouchy. I guess you haven't been at it long enough."

"You just haven't been around at the right time."

"Oh, I'm not denying you have a temper, but grouchy and angry are different. Dr. George is a grouch. Listen, is that a siren?"

"Sounds like it."

"Has it been two minutes?"

"Nope, but they haven't unloaded her yet."

In barely over two minutes the emergency department doors opened to admit Buck and Connie pushing a gurney. On it lay an overweight young woman with long, unkempt blond hair and a tight grimace on her face.

She opened her eyes momentarily when Lukas greeted the attendants, and her face contorted as tears dripped down her cheeks.

"I don't want to be here," she moaned, then glared at Buck. "I told you to take me home!"

Claudia stepped forward and nudged Buck away from the gurney. "Nonsense, honey. You look like a sensible girl to me. I'm sure you realize how silly it would be to come all this way, pay that whopping ambulance bill and go back home in pain. Connie, let's put her in five. It's got stirrups, just in case."

Buck stood watching them move off, then shook his head and ambled up to the desk. "Whew! It's a good thing Claudia's here tonight, Dr. Bower. She can handle Tia Calvin. Shoot, Claudia could sweet-talk Cowboy's pet lion and not get chased out of the pen like I did. How humiliating. I'm beginning to think I'm no good with animals or people."

Lukas raised a brow. "Interesting patient?"

"If you call a whiny neurotic interesting. That female is nuts. One minute she's grabbing my arm and begging me to help her. The next minute she's shouting at me for taking her blood pressure. By the way, don't ask her if she's pregnant. Connie did and got screamed at. You can sure tell we'll have a full moon tonight."

"You say Tia asked to be taken home?"

"Twice, but she was hurting so badly we were able to change her mind."

Rita joined them at the central desk and sat down in front of the computer terminal. "Kind of makes you glad your regular job is just fighting fires, huh, Buck?"

"You got that right. These moonlighting shifts are opening my eyes to some whole new experiences. First Leonardo, now Tia. Maybe I don't need this much experience."

"Oh, come on, Buck," Rita teased, "you didn't have to help Beverly feed the lion."

"No, and I learned a valuable lesson. I escaped the lion, but I didn't escape my wife when she found out about it."

"Does our patient tonight deny pregnancy?" Lukas asked.

"She not only denies pregnancy, she denies ever even kissing a man and was outraged that Connie would accuse her of it."

Connie came out of the exam room with the gurney. "Okay, Dr. Bower, she's all yours. Come on, Buck, let's get out of here. You could've helped us transfer her to the bed, you know. She's not exactly a lightweight."

"I already told them once!" came a shriek from room five. "Why do people keep accusing me—"

"Now, now, settle down, Tia!" Claudia managed to outshout the patient. "Nobody's accusing you of doing anything, but we have to ask. You wouldn't want us endangering any little babies just to be polite." Her voice was soothing and firm all at once.

"I just don't understand why nobody believes me," Tia complained and once again started to cry.

Buck grinned at Lukas and waved. "Good luck, Doc. Tonight's gonna be wild."

The dog started barking before Tedi got across the field. She stopped midstride and stared toward the barn, which blocked the house from view. She remembered the dog. He was big and brown with black markings, like a German shepherd. He'd been tied up the day her class visited. The dog's nice grandparent-type owners had explained that he was their watchdog, and they didn't always keep him tied up, even though they were supposed to.

Now what was she going to do?

Tedi glanced toward the other side of the field, which was farther from the house and the barking dog, and closer to the barn.

That looked good, except the beehives gleamed white in the evening sun on that side of the field.

Tedi wasn't crazy about bees. She also wasn't crazy about getting attacked by a mean dog.

He kept barking.

She crossed the field, keeping a close watch on the white hives as she drew closer to them. Dogs were bigger than bees, but there were a lot more bees.

When she drew close enough to see some of the little buzzing workers, she stopped again. Maybe this wasn't such a good idea.

For a moment, the dog fell silent.

Tedi carefully crept past the hives. Nothing happened until she was several yards from the hives; then she heard a buzz close by. She froze, then jerked around. It was coming from her backpack. She unfastened the pack and threw it off. Great, she'd left the back unzipped a little. The bee buzzed for a moment, then fell silent, and once more the dog barked. Tedi grabbed her pack and ran, bee and all.

The barn door had a latch on the outside, so if she could just figure out how to work it...

The dog barked again, this time louder and closer.

Tedi ran the last few steps to the door, grabbed the latch, and fumbled with it. The dog came closer.

The latch snapped up loudly. Tedi pulled the door open, rushed inside, closed the door and held her breath.

The dog stopped barking for a moment, and Tedi thought she could hear him sniffing outside the large, wide doors across the barn from where she had entered.

Someone whistled from near the house. "Sampson! Dinner. Here, boy!"

The dog didn't bark again.

"But I can't pee!" Tia Calvin burst into tears again for at least the fifth time since arriving less than an hour ago.

Lukas couldn't tell if she was really in as much pain as she claimed, or if she was just so upset she couldn't stand to be touched. He laid a cautious hand on her arm, which he would not have done without Claudia in the room. "Tia, we're here to help you." He interjected the same gentleness into his voice that he had earlier with little Timmy Bradley. "We're going to try to find out what is hurting you so we can stop the pain. Are you willing to trust Claudia so she can get the urine sample for us?"

Tia nodded, obviously struggling to stifle her tears.

"Good for you," Lukas said. "I'll leave so you can have some privacy." He nodded to Claudia and returned to the central desk to wait.

Tonight promised to be another one of those nights when a steady stream of patients trickled in one by one.

"Ouch! That hurts!" The emergency department was so quiet that Tia's voice reached easily past the privacy curtain.

"It won't take long," came Claudia's reassurance. "We'll run a test on this, then—"

"But it's hurting bad! It's cramping! I can't take it!"

At the desk, Rita looked at Lukas and rolled her eyes as they listened to Claudia's calming voice assuring Tia that it was almost over.

"Ow! No!"

"Oh, my...Tia! I thought you said you couldn't be—" The curtain flew back and Claudia rushed out.

"Dr. Bower, I need you to come in here and tell me if I really see a baby crowning!"

Lukas stifled his irritation. One would think that after all these years, Claudia would know what a— "A baby!" Lukas wheeled around and rushed into the exam room. He peered beneath the sheet Claudia had spread over Tia.

"Yep, it's a baby crowning," he said.

"But I told you I'm not pregnant!" Tia wailed.

"You won't be for long, honey." Claudia patted the young woman's arm. "Just hold on."

"Claudia, set up for an emergency delivery," Lukas said. "Get me fetal heart tones, a precip tray, and make sure the baby warmer is ready to go."

"Yes, Doctor, except we don't have a precip tray. They used it already today, and it's still being sterilized in central supply."

He pivoted toward the central desk. "Rita, contact the ob-gyn on call ASAP. We're having a baby." He shook his head as the secretary picked up the phone. "I hate full moons," he muttered.

Tedi Zimmerman awoke disoriented in uncomfortable darkness on a bed that was too hard and blankets that scratched at the exposed skin of her neck.

Something tickled her chin. She reached up to swipe at it, and it jabbed her right palm, hard and deep.

"Ouch!" She jerked her hand back.

Suddenly, she realized she wasn't home in bed. She caught her breath and sat up from the bale of hay where she'd fallen asleep.

It was dark, and she hadn't brought a flashlight. Her hand hurt so badly it brought tears to her eyes.

Something buzzed beside her on the square hay bale. It buzzed fitfully and didn't fly around. A bee?

The bee in her pack!

A whimper escaped from Tedi's throat, even though she tried to be quiet. If the bees heard her, would they come and sting her again?

But only that one bee buzzed, and it didn't buzz long. Tedi remembered learning that a bee died after one sting.

Warm tears stung Tedi's eyes. Her hand really throbbed, and she couldn't even see if there was a stinger there because it was so dark. Really dark. The only light she saw came through a couple of cracks beside the far barn door, looking like gray mist, hardly there. She couldn't even see the streaks of light when she looked straight at them.

The pain in her hand got worse, making her forget, for a moment, that she was stuck out here in the scary barn in the dark with beehives outside and a watchdog, with a dad back home who was probably going to kill her if she lived through this.

Tears fell down her cheeks and a sob shook her.

"Mom." Her voice cracked. "Where are you now? I wish you'd just come and get me." Why couldn't she live with Mom? This would never have happened if she lived with Mom.

And why did Grandma have to be gone right now? Grandma.

When it was dark and Tedi felt afraid, Grandma always said to pray. Just the thought of Grandma made Tedi's face crumple with more tears.

"Jesus," Tedi called between sobs, "help me. I'm scared, and Dad's drunk again, and it's dark and my hand hurts really, really badly." For emphasis, she flexed the fingers of her right hand—or tried to. They felt stiff.

She gasped. She couldn't move her hand. Her whole arm felt stiff. She tried to clasp both hands together, but she discovered that her right hand was so swollen that her fingers wouldn't mesh together. Even her arm felt swollen all the way up to her shoulder.

A sound reached her from the far side of the barn, where the meager light filtered through. She held her breath and listened.

Something snuffled from outside the door. Then it scratched. Then it whined. The dog.

Tedi stared hard through the darkness, searching for some kind of light near the door she had entered earlier. It wasn't far, she knew, because she hadn't come very far into the barn before finding the bale of hay. Could she reach the door without tripping over something?

The dog scratched again from outside, then uttered a short bark.

The sound startled Tedi. Her heart thudded hard, the force of its pressure pounding in her ears, and it kept pounding so loudly that she couldn't hear the dog. The throbbing hurt her hand, but not as badly as it did just a moment earlier. In fact, she couldn't feel her arm very well now.

She stood from the bale of hay and absently reached up with her left hand to brush tears from her cheeks. Her face felt weird. If felt stiff and almost numb. Her lips were big and thick.

She gasped.

At the sound, the dog barked. Tedi couldn't get her breath very well. She gasped again. Her throat felt tight. What was wrong with her?

The bee sting. Last fall, the beekeeper had told them about allergies to bee stings. Some people died when they went into shock from a bad allergic reaction.

She was having an allergic reaction just like what the man had described. Was she going to die here in this barn all alone? "Jesus, please help me," she whispered through a tight throat.

She crept closer to the door, arms out in front of her, feeling her way, hoping the dog stayed on the other side of the building. She had to get out of here, had to get to help. If she hollered, would the beekeepers hear her and get to her before the dog ate her?

"Hello?" she said, testing her voice. She was hoarse.

The dog barked.

"Hello? Can someone help me?" she croaked, then, "Help! Please, someone, help me!"

But her voice wouldn't carry. Only the dog kept barking and digging at the door.

It got harder to breathe.

Tedi tripped on some hay, caught herself, and kept reaching out, searching for the barn wall. Her left hand touched rough wood. She felt for anything that resembled a door as the wheezes of her own breathing sounded more loudly in her ears.

She found a metal latch with her left hand, but now even that hand didn't work so well. She couldn't get the door open. She leaned into it.

She couldn't hear the dog now, but the pounding and ringing in her ears kept her from hearing much of anything.

Suddenly the latch clicked open with the pressure from her thumb. The door opened outward, and Tedi fell out with it. She tripped over the threshold and landed hard on her stomach. Her breaths came harder and the ringing in her ears grew louder, but it didn't drown out the dog's barking—he was only a few feet away.

Chapter Twenty-One

Theodore had a buzz, but it wasn't a nice one. The feel of the wine burning his stomach and drifting through his veins fueled the growing anger he'd felt when Julie began to whine about his meeting tonight, and when she'd admitted she was pumping Tedi for financial info.

And Tedi!

He stalked into the family room where the television blared. She wasn't there. Big surprise. She made a habit of leaving the TV on when Julie was here, as if allergic to the sound of her voice.

He found the remote on the floor beside the sofa and hit the power button.

"Tedi!" He was tired of his own kid giving him heat every time he turned around. "Tedi, come in here." He grabbed up her history textbook and gathered some scattered notebook papers. Did they contain important history notes? Only if tic-tac-toe was history.

"Tedi, I said come here!" He climbed the stairs two at a time and knocked hard. "Answer me!" No light shone from beneath the door, but it was only eight o'clock. She wouldn't be asleep yet. She'd probably been eavesdropping and knew she was in trouble.

He turned the handle and went in. At least she hadn't tried to lock him out like last time.

The moonlight cast shadows across the bed, outlining a ten-year-old–shaped lump beneath the comforter.

"No bluffing. I don't have time for this." He strode across the room and pulled the bedclothes back. Tedi's body took the puffy form of two fluffed pillows.

Theo clenched his teeth. "Theadra Zimmerman, that's enough! Get in this bedroom right…now." He frowned. Her denim backpack was missing from the dresser, where she always tossed it. Her jacket was gone, too. She never put it in the closet, but threw it on the bed.

Just in case, Theo checked the doorknob and closet. No jacket. No backpack.

He stomped downstairs to the family room phone and punched the neighbor's number. That was the only place Tedi ever went without having to ask permission. None of her other friends lived close.

On the fourth ring the answering machine picked up. They always answered when they were home. Theo hung up without leaving a message.

Was he forgetting something? Did Tedi have something going on at school tonight? Had he been so angry with Julie that he hadn't noticed his daughter when she left?

He entered the kitchen and checked the calendar. Today's date was not marked for anything special. Nothing was going on at school.

So where was Tedi?

The phone rang, and he snatched it up. "Yes."

"Where are you, Theo? Our guys have been here for fifteen minutes, and they're hungry." It was Gordon.

"I've got reservations at the Golden Lion in thirty minutes."

Theo glanced at his watch again. "Can I meet you there?"

"You're not drinking again, are you, Theo? I told you to watch that. These guys are teetotalers, and I don't want you barging in here with wino breath and blowing the deal."

"I'll meet you at the Lion. Promise."

There was a pause. "You'd better," Gordon warned. "This is your baby."

"Trust me. I'll be right there."

A dog's bark barely penetrated the dark fog in which Tedi floated. Something wet slapped her face, then something cold nudged her cheek hard.

A bark shrilled two inches from her ear. She could still hear her own wheezing as she struggled to breathe. She opened her eyes to the dark face of a big dog, his shadow outlined by the glow of moonlight.

He nudged her again with his wet nose; then he grabbed her shirt in his teeth and pulled so hard it tugged against her neck.

She gagged.

He released her and barked again, obviously frustrated because he couldn't peel her before he ate her.

Tedi couldn't do anything to protect herself. She had to concentrate hard just to breathe.

Voices reached her—human voices.

"Honey, be careful," said a woman. "I wish you'd've brought the rifle." They drew nearer. "Never can tell what—"

The dog barked again.

"Help me," Tedi croaked as loudly as she could.

"Sampson?" came a man's voice. "Sampson, what in the—" There was a gasp. "Goldy, it's a…a little girl!"

"Please," Tedi whispered between gasps. "Help me."

The dog nudged her again with his nose.

"Okay, boy, we see her. We see her," the man said, gently turning Tedi to her side.

A bright light shone in her eyes.

"Hey, little'un, what happened?" the man asked. "You're swollen up like a toad."

"Honey, listen to her," the woman said. Soft hands touched Tedi's face and gently explored down her neck. "She's not breathing right. I think she's in trouble. She's swollen. Honey, I think she's been—"

"Yep, stung by a bee. Having a reaction."

"We've got to get her to the emergency room fast!"

"Here, take the light," the man said. "I'll carry her." Big, gentle hands turned Tedi from her side to her back, then lifted her up on strong arms.

"Be careful, honey," the woman said. "Make sure she can keep breathing."

"I've got her. You drive. If they try to pull you over this time, we'll make 'em escort us on in."

The dog whined.

"Yes, Sampson," the woman said as the couple made their way through the darkness with Tedi. "Good boy. Good! We've got her now. I've got a steak for you when we come back. Hope you didn't scare this little gal half to death."

Lukas dried his hands and gave a silent sigh of relief. With mother and baby safely tucked away in obstetrics, peace once more reigned in the E.R. Despite all lack of prenatal care, the baby appeared healthy. Tia, with her continued denial, showed signs of mental instability. Maybe social services could help. Lukas shook his head.

"Whew!" Claudia walked back into the department. "Still doing fine up there. That Tia's a handful, isn't she? What'd I tell you about the full moon?"

"Would you look around you?" Lukas said. "We don't have anyone in right now. Come on, Claudia, one difficult patient cites a virgin birth and you blame the moon."

"Night's not over, Dr. Bower. Ever been in the eye of a hurricane?"

"Never, and I doubt you have, either, or you wouldn't be comparing it to this. I think I'm going to go back and try for some slee—"

The E.R. doors flew open and an elderly couple rushed in. The man carried a little girl in his arms. The girl's mouth worked silently as she fought for breath, her lack of oxygen apparent. Dirt smudged her face and arms, and straw clung to her clothing. It didn't hide her swollen features or panicking eyes.

"Help us!" the man called. "She's barely breathing!"

Lukas rushed forward and took the gasping child. "Rita, get me another nurse down here now." He carried the girl into exam room one and put a nonrebreather mask over her face. A quick assessment showed a markedly elevated heart rate and deep, rapid respirations with little air movement. Her cool, moist skin revealed no evidence of cyanosis yet. She looked slightly familiar to him, but he didn't have time to try to place her.

Claudia joined him, followed by the elderly couple.

"She might've been stung," the man said. "We're bee-keepers, and we've seen this kind of thing before. Our dog found her in front of our barn. She was barely breathing then."

"Anaphylactic shock," Lukas told Claudia. "Get me an amp of IV epi so I can do a sublingual injection, and get an IV started. I also need the intubation equipment." He turned to the couple. "How much does she weigh?"

"I can only guess," the man said. "Maybe eighty-five pounds. About as much as one of my well-packed hay bales."

"That sounds good to me." He took the syringe and injected under the swollen tongue. "Claudia, as soon as you have the IV, I want you to give her a half milligram of epi and 50 of Benadryl."

"Sure will." The nurse quickly removed the child's clothing from the waist up.

"Will she be all right?" the woman asked. "We thought about calling an ambulance, but thought we'd get her here faster."

"We'll be doing our best," Lukas said, reaching for the intubation kit. "Would you please go to the waiting room? We'll let you know how she's doing as soon as we can."

"Sure, Doc," the man said. "Come on, darlin'. We've done all we can for now."

"Oh, no, we haven't," the woman said as they walked out. "We can pray."

Rita passed them at the doorway. "I'm sorry, Dr. Bower, but when I told the supervisor upstairs what you wanted, she said she couldn't spare an extra nurse right now. She'll send one down when she can. Wouldn't you know it would be Rachel Simmons tonight." She caught sight of the patient, and her eyes widened. "Dr. Bower, that's Tedi. It's Dr. Mercy's little girl."

"Then call Dr. Mercy, but first get another nurse down here. Stat." Surely Rachel Simmons wouldn't refuse a stat order. He turned back to Claudia. "Good, you got the IV started. Push the epi, then the Benadryl. After that she needs 250 of Solu-Medrol, IV push." If he could intubate, he could buy some time.

He opened the kit and pulled out a pediatric straight blade. He attached it to the laryngoscope handle and checked the light. It worked. He grabbed a 5.0 endo-tracheal tube and did a quick check of the cuff. It inflated. Good. He lubricated the tube and positioned Tedi's head for intubation. She didn't fight him. That could mean she was getting worse or that the Benadryl was beginning to work. Lukas wished he knew. He needed assistance, but Claudia couldn't help him while she pushed drugs.

"She's turning blue," he said. "We've got to have another nurse." He called over his shoulder. "Rita, are we getting help?"

"No," she called back. "Rachel said she's too busy to send anyone yet."

"I gave a stat order!"

"I told her that."

"Sorry, Doctor," Claudia said, "but if you'll just give me a little more time, I can—"

"We don't have any more time." Lukas opened Tedi's mouth and inserted the laryngoscope blade. The light revealed what he had feared—a hypopharynx so swollen he could barely see the vocal cords. He slid the ET tube down to them. Too tight. He pulled it out and grabbed the 3.0 tube. This time he used a stylette to force it. Nothing.

"It won't work," he said. "We'll have to do a cricothy-roidotomy." They had to cut. "We need help."

"I want to talk to Tedi," Theo demanded.

Mercy sat holding the phone, not sure she'd heard cor-rectly. "Is this some kind of practical joke?"

"Look, just let me talk to her. I know she's there."

Mercy held the telephone receiver out from her ear. The man had lost his mind at last. She knew the booze would get him someday. "What are you talking about?" she asked, keeping her voice quiet and in control.

Silence.

"Theodore Zimmerman, where is my daughter?" Still calm, but he would know she meant business.

"Uh…sorry, Mercy. I must have dialed the wrong number. She's spending the night with some friends, and—"

"What number were you trying to dial?" This time she couldn't control her voice so well. "What's going on? Why don't you know where Tedi is?"

"Like I said, I dialed the wrong number," he snapped. "Stop jumping to conclusions. Why do you have to be so defensive—"

"What's the number?"

Again, silence.

"Who's she staying with?" Mercy was finding it increasingly easy to mistrust every single word that came from Theo's mouth. Something was wrong with Tedi, and he was making a bad attempt at covering. "What's the name?"

The line went dead.

Mercy's grip tightened on the receiver until she felt sure it would implode with the pressure. These things were cheap….

She hung up the phone and paced the room to control herself. *Take deep breaths, in through the nose, out through the mouth.* "I've got to get Tedi back," she muttered.

The phone shrilled again.

She crossed the room and jerked up the receiver. "Okay, try your story on me. And it had better be a good one."

Silence.

"Don't pull this with me again, you—"

"Dr. Mercy?" It wasn't Theo. It sounded like…

"Rita?"

"Yes, Dr. Mercy. Would you please come down to the emergency room immediately?"

In the ensuing pause, Mercy overhead the distant sound of the hospital speakers. "Code blue, E.R. Code blue, E.R." It was a man's voice. It sounded almost like Lukas.

"Sure, Rita," Mercy said. "Sounds like you're busy. If you need help I'll come down. Just give me ten minutes."

"Dr. Mercy, you don't understand. It's Tedi."

Mercy went cold. "The code? I heard a code."

"Doctor, it's Tedi."

Tedi had stopped breathing. She lay unconscious on the exam table.

"Claudia, bag her." Lukas prepped her neck with an alcohol swab, then turned and pulled on sterile gloves as the code team assembled in the room.

Rachel Simmons, the team leader, came bustling in last, scowling. "What's going on?"

Lukas ignored her. "Randy, get another IV line for us. Rachel, get me some vitals. Millie, get her on a monitor."

Rachel hesitated, staring at the patient. "You mean you haven't even gotten her vitals yet?" She placed her stethoscope over Tedi's chest. "Who called the code? This patient is not coding."

"She's not breathing and she's unconscious," Claudia snapped, still bagging Tedi. "Dr. Bower told you to get vitals." Her voice grew louder and sharper. "That was an order!"

Lukas extended Tedi's neck and identified his landmarks, palpating the throat. There. The cricothyroid membrane. He reached for the scalpel and prepared to incise.

"BP's 50 by palp," Rachel said. "I can't get the diastolic."

Lukas nodded, hoping no one noticed the sheen of perspiration on his upper lip, his quickened breathing. He never liked invasive procedures, but it went with the job, and he knew his strengths and limitations. He also knew who was in control. *Lord! Help! I can't do this alone.*

He lowered the scalpel and placed the point of the blade against the tender flesh of Tedi's neck. He drew a fine line of red, an initial surface cut. The body jerked in reaction to the pain. She gasped. Aha! She was still unconscious, but the drug was working to reverse the anaphylactic shock.

Lukas pulled the scalpel back and checked her throat with the stethoscope.

"We have some promising air movement here," he said with relief. "Claudia, assist her breathing." He listened to the lungs. Good. He checked her heart. It sounded stronger and not as fast as before. The cyanosis was disappearing. *Thank You, Lord! Thank You!* "What's her BP now, Rachel?" Tedi may still need dopamine.

He turned to find Rita standing at the threshold. "Let's make sure we have a bed open in ICU," he told the secretary. "Have you called her family yet?"

"Yes. Dr. Mercy is on her way. She should be here any minute."

"Good. Tell that nice couple in the waiting room that she's doing better." He turned to Rachel. "Do you have her pressure yet?"

"Yes, it's 82 over 53."

Okay, it was slowly coming up. The child's color looked better. If she kept improving she would be okay.

For the first time he had opportunity for a more thorough assessment, and he frowned at some bruising on her shoulders. He checked it more closely. The marks were faded, slightly yellow in color, so they were fairly old. They couldn't have anything to do with her present condition. He would ask her about them later.

Chapter Twenty-Two

Mercy raced down the hospital hallway and into the emergency room without slowing down. "Where's Tedi?" she called as she continued past Rita.

"In here, Mercy," Lukas called from the open doorway of trauma room one. "It's okay. She's doing better."

The code team stepped away from the bed as Mercy rushed into the room and to Tedi's side. "I heard you call a code over the phone, Lukas. What's going on?"

"Anaphylactic shock," Lukas said. "Apparently from a bee sting. The beekeepers brought her in. She's getting air much better now."

Mercy bent over her still-unconscious daughter. "May I use your stethoscope?"

Lukas handed it to her.

"What happened?" Mercy asked as she listened to Tedi's chest. She glimpsed the tiny line of drying blood on her daughter's throat. "You started a cric?"

"She stopped breathing. I couldn't intubate her."

"Is that why you called the code?"

Rachel Simmons stepped up to the bed. "Funny you

should ask, Dr. Richmond. I wondered the same thing, since your daughter's heart never stopped. You're on the QA team; maybe you can explain to Dr. Bower what constitutes a code and what constitutes a violation of protocol."

Mercy straightened slowly and stared at Rachel in amazement. This nurse had always shown a decided lack of compassion for patients on the floor, but Mercy wasn't sure, at first, that she'd heard the woman correctly.

"Am I to understand that you're complaining because my daughter wasn't actually dead when Dr. Bower called the code?" Mercy's voice froze the air around them.

"Of course not. That's not what I mean."

For another moment Mercy didn't trust herself to speak. She continued to hold Rachel's gaze until Rachel looked away. She knew the woman had some grave personal problems and that it affected her work and her interpersonal relationships. No one wanted to work her shift. Mercy had often been irritated by her attitude, and sometimes she felt sorry for her. But this was inexcusable.

Claudia stepped up to the bed, glaring at Rachel. "Excuse me, Nurse, but weren't you the one who refused to send anyone down for us when we called upstairs for help?"

"We were busy. You're not the only department in this hospital."

"When it comes to little girls fighting for breath, we are!" Claudia snapped.

"I don't know if Dr. George will feel the same way," Rachel said, backing out of the room. She turned to leave.

"Come back here, Nurse," Lukas called before she could step out the door.

Her back stiffened. She stopped, but did not turn to look at Lukas.

"As Claudia has stated," he said, "were you not the one who refused my stat order to come to the trauma room tonight?"

She turned around and glanced at him with narrowed eyes, but didn't reply.

"In fact, I requested help twice and you refused twice," Lukas continued. "Your insubordination endangered this child's life. I had no choice but to call a code. If you have reason to doubt my professional opinion or skills, tell it to administration, and they can take whatever actions they feel are warranted. In the meantime you are to obey my orders when I am on duty. Is that understood?"

Rachel raised an eyebrow and stared at him coldly.

"If it is not," Lukas insisted, "I will request your immediate termination. Is that clear?"

She held his gaze for a moment longer, then looked away. "Very."

"Thank you. I am going to write you up for this, and if it happens again, I will request your dismissal from this hospital."

Rachel's face flushed bright red. "Dr. George may not agree to that, either."

Mercy stepped over to stand beside Lukas. "Rachel, the cessation of breathing constitutes a respiratory code. It is a protocol not subject to interpretation. You may go back to the floor…for the time being. I haven't decided yet what I'm going to do about this, but I, too, can request your termination."

They waited until the nurse had left the room.

"Wow." Claudia breathed at last, looking at Lukas with awe and respect. "I didn't know you had it in you."

Lukas grimaced. "Unfortunately, my temper surfaces

from time to time." He turned to Mercy. "I'm impressed. You really can keep your cool when you want."

"Really? I hadn't noticed. Thank you for your support, Dr. Bower. It's very comforting." She bent back over her daughter, whose eyes had begun to open.

The rest of the code team left the room, except for Claudia, who took Tedi's blood pressure once more.

"I'd've fired her on the spot," Claudia muttered as she smoothed Tedi's hair back and swiped at a smudge of dirt on the child's cheek. "She shouldn't have a license to nurse. She's rough on everyone. There's a bad morale problem on the floor because of her."

Mercy looked in dismay at the dirt covering her daughter's body. "Claudia, would you hand me some of those moist towelettes behind you? Where has this child been, a barn lot?"

"Exactly," Lukas said. "Don't ask me what she was doing there."

Tedi blinked and squinted. "Mom?" Her raspy voice barely reached them.

Mercy leaned closer. "Yes, honey?"

Tedi's eyes opened wider. "You're here?"

Mercy kissed her daughter's cheek. "Yes, Tedi, I'm right here. How do you feel?"

"Mom, I was so scared." Tears formed in Tedi's eyes and dripped down the sides of her face, forming dirty streaks that disappeared into her hairline. "I thought I was going to die. It was dark in the barn, and this big dog kept trying to get in." Her hoarse voice cracked.

"Try not to talk right now," Mercy soothed.

"But I have to, Mom. It was so awful. First Julie came and gave Dad some wine, then they started talking about marriage, then she told him I said you supported us, and

I had to leave because I...because I was scared. But I didn't want—"

"Tedi, honey, slow down." Mercy cleared some of the grime from her daughter's face.

"Mom, I swelled all up, and my lips got thick, and I couldn't breathe, and at first I couldn't find my way out of the barn. I thought that dog was going to eat me when I fell out of the doorway, but he didn't, and then some people came."

"She must mean the beekeepers," Lukas explained. "They're in the waiting room. They were the ones who found her and brought her in."

"Good." Mercy tossed away a soiled towelette. "I want to talk to them and thank them personally." She frowned and leaned closer to inspect Tedi's shoulders. Both looked as though they'd been bruised. She straightened and caught Lukas's attention, then jerked her head toward the bruises.

"Yes," he said softly. "I noticed those just a few moments ago."

"What do you think?" she asked.

"I don't dare make a guess."

"Mom?"

Mercy bent back down. "Yes, honey?"

"Grandma always said to pray when I got scared, and I did. Don't you think Jesus answered my prayer?"

Mercy hesitated.

"He sure answered ours," came a female voice from the doorway.

They turned to find the senior citizen beekeepers standing in the entrance, smiling.

"You don't look the same as when we brought you in," the man said, holding his work-stained bill cap in his hands.

The woman's iron-gray hair matched her friendly eyes. She stepped in ahead of her husband and approached the side of the exam table. "Looks like you've been cleaning out the barn, kiddo."

"Are you the ones who found me?" Tedi asked.

"Sampson's the one who found you," the woman said. She reached out and touched Tedi's arm, as if to assure herself the child was really okay. "He's our dog," she explained to Mercy. "He just wouldn't leave us alone tonight, growled and whined all during dinner."

"He barely ate his own food." The man stepped farther into the room. "That's when Goldy got worried." He gestured to his wife. "She insisted we follow Sampson and see what he wanted. I told her she'd been watching too many Lassie reruns, but she insisted." He shook his head and sighed. "I'm sure glad I listened to her."

"Now, Carl, you know you were worried, too." Goldy patted her husband's arm.

"I'm thankful to both of you," Mercy said. Tears welled up in her eyes, and she forced them back. "You saved my daughter's life." She took Goldy's hands and squeezed them gently. Her own hands trembled. "Thank you."

"And don't forget Sampson, Mom," Tedi said. "He didn't eat me. He saved me."

"We were just the tools, child," Goldy said. "The Lord was watching over you. He was taking care of you all along. We've been in the waiting room, praying, and we called some friends to pray, too. I want to go call them back and tell them our prayers have been answered."

"Yeah, just like Grandma says." Tedi smiled at the couple. "Thank you for saving me and for praying. Thank your friends, too."

Goldy bent forward and kissed Tedi on the temple. "You're so welcome, honey."

As the beekeepers left, Rita stepped into the exam room. "The bed is ready in ICU. We had to get parental consent to admit Tedi." She glanced at Mercy. "I'm sorry, but I had to call the legal guardian. Tedi's father is on his way down to sign the forms."

Mercy stared at Rita for a long moment. No, she wasn't a traitor. She was doing what she had to do. It was the law. Stay in control. "Of course you had to call him, Rita," she said at last. "We have to follow the rules."

"Dad's coming here?" Tedi asked softly.

"Yes, honey," Mercy said.

"But can't you just stay with me?"

"Don't worry, I'm not leaving this hospital." Mercy glanced down at her denim cut offs and stained T-shirt. Her hair hung around her shoulders in a tangled mess, and she hadn't even brought a comb. Too bad. The staff would handle it. Tonight she was a mother, not a doctor.

Lukas placed a hand on Mercy's shoulder. "Your mother's still in Colorado, isn't she?"

Mercy nodded.

"Is there someone I can call for you?"

Mercy looked down at her daughter. As Tedi's condition improved, Mercy's was deteriorating in direct proportion. She was letting down, but she couldn't let down too much. She shook her head. There was no one to call.

"Why don't I get in touch with your secretary so she can cancel your appointments tomorrow," Lukas suggested. "You'll be tired."

Mercy looked at Lukas and forced a smile. "I'm a part-time E.R. doc, remember? I'm used to doing without sleep. Besides, I'm off tomorrow morning."

"Good." Lukas leaned over Tedi to check her breathing once more.

Mercy gently touched Tedi's left shoulder. "Honey, what are these bruises?"

Tedi stiffened, and her eyes grew fractionally wider.

Lukas raised his stethoscope, then lowered it again. "Keep breathing for me, Tedi."

Tedi obeyed as she held her mother's gaze. Mercy saw fear there, and the fear she saw shook her badly. She waited until Lukas was done. "Tedi, do you remember how you got them?"

Tedi continued to hold her gaze and shook her head. "I…I guess tonight. I fell."

At the edge of her vision, Mercy saw Lukas shaking his head. She broke eye contact with her daughter and looked up at Lukas.

He mouthed the word *wait*.

As she stood there struggling for control, Theo's voice reached them from the central desk. "I'm here to see Theadra Zimmerman. I'm her father."

Mercy watched Tedi's expression grow even more fearful. "It's okay, honey, I'm here."

They heard quick footsteps, and both of them looked toward the doorway.

Theo came rushing in. "Tedi!" He stopped and glanced at Mercy, then Lukas.

For some reason, Mercy couldn't help noticing that every blond hair on Theo's head was in place. He was impeccably dressed in a blue silk shirt and black Levis. It was as if he'd taken time to groom himself before coming down.

"What happened?" His voice was surprisingly subdued for Theodore Zimmerman. "They wouldn't tell me anything when they called," he continued. "They just told me to come to the emergency room because my daughter was here." His eyes sought and found Tedi. "What happened?" He stepped to the other side of the exam table and laid a hand on Tedi's shoulder.

Tedi recoiled. Theo withdrew his hand. He shot Mercy a quick look of annoyance. His eyes were bloodshot.

Lukas stepped forward. "Mr. Zimmerman, I'm Dr. Bower. I'm the E.R. physician on duty. Your daughter was injured this evening. She's better now, but her condition is still serious. We want to watch her in ICU overnight, and we need your signature on the admittance forms."

"What kind of injury?" Theo asked. In such close proximity, Mercy could smell the booze, and Tedi probably could, too. "Tedi, where did you go? I couldn't find you."

"I got stung by a bee," Tedi said. "I swelled up and couldn't breathe. Some people found me and brought me here."

Once again Theo put a hand on Tedi's shoulder, and once more she withdrew. "You look fine to me." He looked at Lukas. "Why does she have to stay in the hospital overnight?"

Mercy glared at him. "Tedi went into anaphylactic shock, Theodore. They called a code on her and almost had to do a cricothyroidotomy. I'd say that warrants an overnight observation in ICU. Don't worry, my insurance covers it. You won't have to pay."

Theo returned her glare. "You really think I value money more than my own daughter? I would just like to know what's going on, why she left the house without telling me. Is that too much to ask?"

"Under the circumstances," Lukas said, stepping

forward, "I think the answer will have to wait. Tedi needs some rest."

"How much rest?" Theo asked.

"We'll keep her overnight and watch her," Lukas said. "Her family doc may release her in the morning if she's doing okay."

"Look, I can't stay here all night," Theo protested. "I'm already late for a meeting."

"I'm staying," Mercy said. "You would only upset her."

Theo glared at her. "Why? Because you intend to poison her mind about me?"

"Mr. Zimmerman." Lukas stepped around the exam table and took Theo's arm. "Please continue this conversation elsewhere." He glanced at Mercy. "I'll stay with Tedi."

Mercy squeezed her daughter's arm and gestured to Theo to follow. She led him to an empty trauma room and turned to face him. "The first thing that will upset her, Theo, is the fact that you're drunk. That always terrifies her, or didn't you know that?"

"Drunk! You think just because I've had a small glass of wine, I'm automatically drunk."

"I think you're drunk because the fumes from your breath make it dangerous to light a match. I think you're drunk because your eyes could pass for stop signals, and if you don't think Tedi can see it, you vastly underestimate her. Do you realize she almost died tonight because of you?" Mercy could hear her own voice rising, and she struggled for some of the control Lukas had praised her for earlier. "She left home tonight because she knew you were drinking, and she was afraid of you." She paused. "We found some bruises on her shoulders, Theo, and I want to know how they got there."

He grew still for a moment; then his face darkened.

"For Pete's sake, Mercy, your daughter almost died tonight, and you're worried about a couple of bruises? She probably fell—"

"They're not fresh, and they're not from a fall." She couldn't be sure of that, but she could bluff. Her voice took on the cutting edge of a scalpel. "She was afraid to tell me what happened, but I intend to find out."

Silence descended on the room.

"There's nothing to find out," Theo said at last. "I'm a good father. You wouldn't know about that. Just because your father was a drunk—oh, excuse me, I believe the polite term is alcohol dependent—you think you're an expert. Just because your father beat you—"

"What?"

"Don't you recall? Or maybe you'd had too much to drink that night."

"I don't drink."

"I remember holding you while you cried and told me about your father beating you."

"I never told you anything like that!"

Theo shrugged. "Selective amnesia? Your dad lost his temper and whipped you with the horse bridle. You had welts on your legs for days."

"How can you bring that up now?" What other things about their private moments together was he planning to spill to the whole world?

"Your own father abused you. That makes you more likely to be an abuser, too," Theo said. "Julie agrees with me."

"Or it makes it more likely to have married an abuser. And you leave Julie out of this. My life is none of that woman's business!"

"It will be. She's going to be Tedi's new mom."

The shock of the words struck Mercy speechless for two seconds. "I'm her mother."

Theo watched her face with a slow, taunting smile. "You're such a good mother, the courts made me Tedi's legal guardian."

"She won't be much longer."

"But that's why I'm here tonight, isn't it?" His voice was low and smooth. "They can't even trust you enough to let you sign the admittance forms. It's a good thing Tedi has me. Her mother did a stint in the psych ward, her grandfather was a drunk and a child beater, and her grandmother's out sleeping in the woods with her boyfriend—"

Mercy's fist connected with Theo's face before she even realized the cork had popped on her control. Her knuckles stung as Theo staggered backward in surprise and stumbled against a metal suture tray. The table fell sideways with a crash that echoed through the emergency department.

Theo scrambled to right himself as he glared at Mercy over the top of the table. Blood seeped from the left side of his mouth. He sprang forward, fists clenched.

"What's going on in here?" Lukas came running through the open doorway. "What are you doing to my trauma room?" He caught sight of Theo's face and stopped.

Theo kept his gaze trained on Mercy. He touched the blood on his mouth with his finger and held it out to look at it. A slow smile replaced the outrage on his face. "See, Mercy? Like father, like daughter. No court in the land would give you custody of an innocent ten-year-old child, and if you were to try to take her anyway, I'd have you thrown in jail so fast you'd never see your daughter again."

Every muscle in Mercy's body tensed. She lunged toward him.

"Stop it, Mercy!" Lukas grabbed her around the waist and lifted her bodily from the floor.

"He can't do this!" she cried, struggling. "Let me go!"

"Mercy!" Lukas held on more tightly. "Stop it. Tedi's crying in the other room. She heard you in here."

That worked. Mercy grew still. The tears came then, angry, frustrated, painful tears. She could barely see Theo through them, but that hateful smirk was imprinted on her mind. Lukas continued to hold her.

"I'll sign those papers now, Dr. Bower," Theo said.

"They're ready at the desk," Lukas replied coldly.

"You know where to find me if you need me."

"I doubt that will be necessary."

"Fine. I'll be back in the morning between nine and ten to get my daughter. She'd better be ready."

"That isn't up to you, Mr. Zimmerman," Lukas said. "Good night." Somehow the icy tone of his voice comforted Mercy.

Theo didn't even stop again to see his daughter before he left.

Chapter Twenty-Three

Theodore drove into the darkened parking lot of the Golden Lion.

He wasn't surprised to find it empty at eleven o'clock at night. Even the kitchen help had gone home. Okay, so Gordon and the clients weren't here, but Gordon might have driven them back to the office for a talk. Surely he'd tried to keep them occupied as long as possible.

"Should've called," Theo muttered as he turned out of the parking lot. He drove the short five blocks to the office and saw a light coming from Gordon's cubicle. His car sat out in the drive, but there were no other vehicles nearby.

As Theo pulled up, the front door opened and Gordon strode out, hands in his pockets, jingling his keys and loose change, an irritating habit of his when he was angry.

This did not look good.

Theo parked and got out quickly. "Gordon, I'm sorry. I've been in the emergency room ever since I talked to you last. Tedi got stung by a bee and had a bad reaction. She almost died." He said it fast, before Gordon could interrupt.

Gordon stopped in front of him, still jingling his keys,

anger and frustration plain in his eyes even in the dimly lit darkness. "You realize what this means, don't you? Century 21 has several places for them to see, and they won't give up."

"Did you show the place?"

"Oh, they saw the place, all right." The jingling continued. "You're the one who's been handling this, and they wanted you to be the one to show it to them. They couldn't understand what could be holding you up." He shrugged, then said sarcastically, "They liked all that telephone charm of yours, and mine just wouldn't do. Maybe they thought that since they'd flown all the way back here from California, you could take time out of your busy schedule to meet them. You're the only one with a smooth enough line to get that dump unloaded before it gets dangerous."

Theo curbed his own anger. "They'll understand an emergency, surely."

Gordon shrugged again. "You didn't even bother to call and let us know. You stood us up at the Lion after you'd promised to be there." He lowered his voice and glanced around. "Look, Theo, you'd better call them and get this straightened out, because you and I both stand to lose thousands on this deal if we don't sell." He leaned forward and tapped Theo on the chest. "Money we can't afford to lose in an investment we can't afford anyone to find out about."

"Don't worry, we'll make it back in time. We'll cover all the loans. No one will know."

"You may get to tell it to the judge if you can't get us out of this. If the boss hears about it, you're out of a job."

"We're in this together, Gordon."

"I'm not taking the fall for you."

"You keep the company books. You wrote the check."

"It was your idea to do this! You set it up, and you convinced me it would be okay. You've got to explain things to these guys and get rid of this property before the whole thing explodes in our faces."

Theo held his hands up. "Okay, okay. Relax. I'll call and give them the sad story about my little girl. We'll make another appointment for tomorrow and everything will be okay."

All was quiet, and Lukas knew he should be trying to catch some sleep, but he couldn't get certain people off his mind. Just to make sure about Tedi, he climbed the stairs and entered ICU. He nodded at the nurse who sat at the central desk, then spied Mercy sitting with her head bent by the side of her daughter's bed. She still wore her stained T-shirt and cut-off denim shorts.

Lukas stepped over to the nurse. "Don't you have a cot we can set up beside the bed for Dr. Richmond?"

"Yes, but I've been so busy here I haven't been able to leave, and we're short an aide tonight."

"Tell me where to find the cot."

She gave him directions, and he returned in a few moments with a narrow fold-out sleeping chair and a set of scrubs. He carried them to the end of Tedi's bed.

"Mercy?" he called softly.

She raised her head and looked up at him. Her eyes focused on what he held.

"You need some sleep," he said. "And since Tedi's out of danger, you can relax. These scrubs will be more comfortable than those clothes." He placed the scrubs on the arm of the chair in which she sat, then tossed down a comb that he had purchased from a vending machine in the cafeteria. "Go change while I set up this cot."

She didn't move. She stared at him. For a moment

tears filled her dark eyes, but they did not fall. Without saying a word she finally picked up the stack of items and walked out. Lukas folded out the sleeping chair closely enough to Tedi's bed that Mercy could reach out and touch her. He spread a sheet and a blanket over it, then grabbed a pillow from a nearby empty bed.

When Mercy came back in, she wore the blue scrubs and had combed the tangles out of her hair. She still looked pale and very tired.

"Thanks, Lukas. I feel a lot better."

"You don't look any better. You need some sleep."

"No wonder you don't date much." She sat down on the cot and watched Tedi's breathing for several moments in silence.

Lukas leaned against the next bed and observed the silence with her.

"I made a fool of myself tonight," she said at last. "I upset Tedi and I showed my weakness to Theo."

Lukas grinned at her. "Like a mama tiger. You should have seen Claudia. If I hadn't made her stay with Tedi, she'd have come in there and ripped into Mr. Zimmerman herself." He chuckled at the memory.

Mercy shot him a glance and a wan smile, then patted the other end of the cot.

He sat.

"What did you overhear?" she asked.

"Everything. You know there's no soundproofing in that E.R., and you didn't even shut the door. Tedi was the only one in, so…" He shrugged.

"There was no noise to cover it."

"That's right. So if we didn't already know what a nasty character your ex-husband is, we do now. I don't think it came as a great shock to anyone."

"Sometimes I hate living in a small town."

"Why? Because everybody knows everybody else's business? At least someone cares."

She shook her head. "They don't care here any more than they do in a big city. They just have less to keep them occupied, so they occupy themselves in the lives of others." She paused, glanced toward the nurse, and lowered her voice. "I have to make sure I don't take a vacation or medical conference break at the same time a male doc does in this town."

Lukas knew what she meant. "Gossip."

"You bet. I had my name linked to a very respectable, very married physician in the hospital just because I took off at the same time he did for a conference last year."

"How frustrating. Did it cause much trouble?"

"I didn't give it a chance. I threatened to recommend dismissal for a tech who couldn't keep her mouth shut or her mind out of the gutter, and then I warned the wife about it." She grimaced. "I found it extremely insulting and distasteful."

"Yes, you would. I know the feeling."

Mercy glanced at him. "You, too?"

"I was amazed at the rumors that circulated about women I supposedly dated or had secret affairs with, especially when it involved women I'd never even met." He glanced at her. "Some people in KC still think I'm a father, even though blood tests proved the child was not mine. The mother was a nurse I worked with when I started my residency, and for some crazy reason she decided I was going to be the one true love of her life. She was very insistent, and unfortunately, she was the daughter of the director of internal medicine. When I didn't see things her way, she complained to her dad and to my trainer about me. She said she thought I was manic depressive and accused me of sexual harassment."

"You don't seem bipolar to me."

"I was going through the grief process at the time, but no, I'm not bipolar. This nurse insisted that I was endangering the patients in my manic state. She even charted orders I never gave and had other docs questioning my judgment. They held a meeting and decided I was to be reviewed by a psychiatrist. I made the appointment, but then my trainer scheduled me to work that day and no one would cover for me, so I missed the appointment. I was fired soon after. When this nurse then turned up pregnant, she spread the word that I was the father and that I had seduced her."

Mercy shook her head in amazement. "You? Surely nobody believed— I mean, you're not…you know…the seducing kind."

"The hospital used it against me later when I took them to court. And as far as I know, there has only been one Immaculate Conception in history."

Mercy raised a brow at him. "I hope they realized you're no philanderer."

"I'm a normal, healthy male, who just happens to believe in purity before marriage and monogamy after."

"You're a Christian." She made it sound almost like an accusation.

"Yes."

"My mother's a Christian," she said. "She has been since my father died. She's always preaching to me about things she's read in the Bible, great 'spiritual truths' she's suddenly discovered. She doesn't push me too much, but I can tell I frustrate her at times because of my beliefs."

"What do you believe?"

She shot him a warning glance. "Don't you start, too."

"I'm not. I'm just asking what you believe."

"I'm not sure you would call it belief. Maybe you'd call it lack of belief." She glanced over at her sleeping daughter and shook her head. "I have trouble believing in a so-called loving God who would allow so many painful things to happen in my life and my daughter's."

"That's perfectly understandable. I felt that way after I watched my mother die of cancer, and I've been a Christian since I was ten years old. I argued with God about why she had to suffer. She was a great lady who helped half the people in town in some way or another over the years. It's hard to watch your loved ones hurting."

"Who won the argument you had with God?" Mercy asked.

"Well, it turned into something besides an argument. It turned into an intense conversation that involved several kinds of communication and several people." He shrugged. "I'm sure you don't want to hear my 'great spiritual truths' any more than you want to hear your mother's."

"I'll humor you just this once. What kinds of conversation?"

"It was a gradual thing. It took place over the months of grieving after Mom's death. As I searched the Scriptures and prayed, and continued to lay blame at God's door, I became aware of His loving patience with me—not only in the Bible verses He led me to read, but in the fellow believers in my church who continued to love and support me emotionally, even though I wasn't always very nice or faithful in attendance. God works through His people, and He shows His love, as well, through His people. I remember one elderly lady in my parents' church who came to talk to me one day when I was home visiting. I came straight out and asked her why a loving God would allow so much suffering."

"What did she say?"

"She asked if I would have preferred a dictatorship."

"Yes, yes, I've heard all about that from Mom," Mercy said. "Adam and Eve were given a free will and chose to sin. And now we're paying for their sin."

"No, we're paying for our own sin and just plain sin in general. Everyone but Christ has chosen sin from the beginning of time."

"So tell me, what do you call sin?"

"Do you want my own personal interpretation?"

"Yes."

"It's anything that shows lack of love for God or for my fellow man."

She raised a brow. "That's it?"

"To me, it's reasonable. All the laws are based on two rules, which are to love God with all your heart, soul, strength and mind, and to love your neighbor as yourself. If you do these two things, you'll never break any other of God's laws."

"So since we've broken these laws," Mercy said, "God's going to make us pay. He punishes us. We either love God or else." Bitterness laced her voice.

"I've felt that way before, too, especially when I thought I was being punished by Him for some reason. I've gradually come to the conclusion that love is an active thing, much the same as faith. You act on the basis of love and faith and don't worry about forcing the emotions to follow. God handles that part. And God doesn't punish for the sake of wreaking harm on us, but instead, He disciplines us for the sake of lovingly guiding us in His direction. He will do whatever it takes to teach us what He wants us to know."

"Even when it means suffering at the hands of an evil man?"

"I have to remind myself often that suffering was not in God's original plan," Lukas said. "Human beings were the ones who allowed sin into the world, and that is the cause of suffering. It doesn't seem fair, but as my father pointed out to me not long after Mom's death, we should look for God in the one who's hurting, not in the cause of pain itself. Because of our choices we separate ourselves from God's protection. I know God was there with Mom during her pain, even though she got cranky at times. During her lucid moments, near the end, I saw her become more and more eager for heaven. I think Mom learned something through her pain on earth that is now serving her in heaven."

Mercy watched his expression carefully. "You really believe that?"

"Yes, I do. Do you think I'm crazy?"

She thought for a moment, then shook her head. "No. I think I'd like to believe it myself. But what about my grandmother? Mom believed she wasn't a Christian. If you don't believe she went to heaven, do you think she's in hell?"

"Do you know for sure she was not a Christian?"

"Mom's pretty sure. That's why she didn't want Grandma's heart to stop. She wanted her to have another chance."

Lukas leaned forward. "Mercy, before your grandmother died, she spoke to me and told me to let her go, that she was ready. Only God can know for sure, but I had the impression she was at peace, just like Mom was when she died."

Mercy's eyes filled again with tears. "But you can't know for sure."

"As I said, only God can know for sure. I'm still learning to trust God during the times I have doubts, and I still fail, but God has proven that He has our ultimate good as a goal. Otherwise, there would have been no Christ, no death, no Resurrection."

Mercy glanced at Lukas. "You know, you seem to be a very honest person, especially with yourself. It's an admirable quality." She shook her head. "Thanks for telling me about your experience in Kansas City. I hate what they did to you. I hate politics." She sat in silence for a while, then looked back at Lukas. "Do you know why Theodore has custody of Tedi?"

"You were hospitalized for depression, and he used it against you in court."

Her eyes widened. "See what I mean about small towns?"

"Where were you hospitalized?"

"Lakeland in Springfield. My father had just died of alcoholic cirrhosis, and Theodore and I were going through a nasty divorce at the time." Mercy leaned forward to check Tedi, then sat back. "Another woman." She glanced at Lukas to judge his reaction, hesitated, then continued. "I wasn't just hospitalized for depression, I was forcibly committed for attempted suicide—which was a setup." She kept watching Lukas.

He held her gaze. He'd heard most of this—after all, as she'd said, the gossip mill was alive and well in Knolls. He'd like to hear the truth from her.

"I was depressed," she said.

"Who wouldn't be? You were going through a horrible experience."

"I suppose you overheard Theo's announcement about one of the beatings I received from my father. I had never come to terms with that. Also, Theo had run up some whopping bills during our marriage, and I was working all the shifts I could in E.R. so I could pay them off. When I caught Theo with the other woman—she dumped him after the divorce—I guess you could say I got a little depressed."

"Amazing that you would have such a reaction," Lukas said drily.

"But I didn't attempt suicide. What I did do was take a couple of extra Valium just to kill some of the pain. Unfortunately, in my drugged state I decided I needed help for depression and went to see the wrong doctor at the wrong time. He was a friend of Theo's." She spread her hands, as if the rest was obvious. "It was a divorce-court tactic. That doctor is out of practice now—he lost his license two years later for unprofessional conduct with a female patient. That's the kind of people Theo makes friends with. Unfortunately, there are a lot of corrupt people like that in the world, and they haven't all had their hands slapped yet for their corruption." She looked down at the comb in her hand, then raised her eyes to meet Lukas's gaze. "Thanks for getting all this stuff together for me. The comb, the bed, the scrubs—I appreciate it."

"Hey, it was my pleasure."

Mercy smiled. "Sorry if I sound as if I'm wallowing in self-pity. I guess I just wanted you to know the truth."

"I already know the truth. You're the kind of physician who was willing to answer a disaster code when no one else cared, and you spent your own money—which you probably couldn't afford—to help people in need."

She leaned back, as if to get a better look at him in the dim light. "Wow. Do you speak at motivational seminars?"

"I just tell it like I see it."

"I've been called a man-hater."

He reached up and felt the stubby growth of hair on his face. "I've always considered myself a man. You've never been hateful with me."

"You're…different."

"Would you have gone to so much trouble to treat Clarence Knight if you truly hated men?"

She seemed to think about it a moment. "I like Darlene. I admire them both because they want so badly not to be a burden on society."

"I don't think anyone likes the injustice you've experienced at the hands of Theodore Zimmerman. Anyone would be distrustful of men if he were a typical example. I hope he isn't."

"Would you think I was horrible if I told you I enjoyed socking him in the mouth tonight?"

"Only if you would blame me for wanting to do the same."

She grimaced. "I'll pay for that moment of glory, though."

"Do you think he'll file charges?"

"And cut off his gravy train? No way. Why else do you think he's keeping Tedi?"

"Maybe that's why he treats you so badly."

Mercy frowned, and Lukas continued. "Male pride. Have you always been the main provider?"

Her frown deepened. "All except for the first couple of years of the marriage."

"I realize this sounds archaic, but I believe most men still feel as if they should be able to support their families."

He cleared his throat. "The remark you made to him about your insurance covering Tedi's expenses made him angry, I could tell. If he feels dependent on you, he'll take it out on you, and maybe even Tedi."

Tedi stirred, as if in response to the sound of her name. Mercy stood and leaned over her daughter. "Okay, honey?"

"Yeah, Mom," Tedi said hoarsely. She raised her head and looked around the room, her dark eyes apprehensive. "Is Dad here?"

"No."

Tedi relaxed and lay back.

Mercy reached down and brushed a tendril of long, dark hair back from her daughter's face. Lukas marveled at how much alike the two looked. Tedi's eyes even held the same wary sadness in them as Mercy's did.

"Tedi," Mercy said softly. "Do you want to talk about why you were in that barn?"

Tedi lay there for a moment without replying, almost as if she hadn't heard the question. Then she said, "I can't."

"Can't?" Mercy touched her daughter's face. "You mean you're afraid to?"

Tedi didn't reply.

Mercy's face tightened. She glanced at Lukas, then back at Tedi. "Are you afraid of your father?"

Tedi's eyes filled with tears. She nodded slowly. "You can't say anything to him, Mom. Please. I don't want you to go back to the hospital, and I don't want to have to stop seeing you."

"Is that why you didn't want me to try to get custody?"

Again Tedi hesitated, then nodded.

Mercy touched Tedi's shoulder. "The bruises, honey. Did your dad do that?"

Tedi's face contorted with more tears. "Please don't ask me, Mom."

Lukas saw Mercy's fist clench, but her voice remained gentle as she spoke to her daughter. "Are you afraid he'll do something like this again?"

No answer.

"I can't let that happen, honey."

"Don't say anything, Mom. Please. He only gets mean when he's drinking and…sometimes I get mad and sass him. Then I'm scared."

"Did you sass him tonight?"

"No, but Julie…she told him something I said."

"Which was…?"

"That you supported us."

Mercy closed her eyes and took a deep breath, then glanced meaningfully at Lukas. "That's my fault, Tedi. You've heard that from me. I'm sorry." Her face puckered again, as if she might cry.

"It's not your fault, Mom." Tedi's voice was indignant. "They fought about it, and I knew I had to leave until Dad got sobered up. I fell asleep in the barn, and then I woke up in the dark, and the bee stung me, and I got really scared and started to cry, and I swelled up and—"

"Shh." Mercy's hand shook as she stroked her daughter's hair. "You're okay now. You're here with me, safe in the hospital." Her voice had lost some of its calmness.

"Mom, please don't tell Dad I told you. He got mad when that counselor guy, Nick, told him I wanted to live with you."

Mercy grew still. "The counselor told him?"

"Yes. That was why I called you and told you not to take Dad to court."

Mercy was quiet for a moment. "Do you still want to come and live with me?"

"Mom, I can't. Dad will ruin your practice and send you back to the hospital, and he won't have anything to lose, because if I live with you—"

"He can't ruin my practice, and he can't send me back to the hospital." Mercy's voice shook now as badly as her hands.

Lukas reached out and touched her shoulder gently. She stiffened and glanced at him, then took a deep breath and let it out.

"Tedi, all that happened five years ago, and it was because an evil man lied about me. He can't do that now. And your father can't get my license revoked."

"But he says—"

"He's trying to scare you. I can't take the chance that he'll hurt you. I'm taking him to court."

"No, Mom!" Tedi's hoarse voice was loud enough to get the attention of the nurse at the desk. "Please! I'll be good. I won't sass him anymore. I don't want you to take him to court."

"Why not?"

"Because…because I don't want him to hurt you because of me…and I don't want him to hurt me. I'm scared."

Once again Lukas touched Mercy's shoulder. For another moment she stood, looking at her daughter.

"Tedi, I won't do anything that will get you hurt."

"You won't tell Dad what I said?"

"Of course not." She reached down and tucked the blankets up around Tedi's shoulders. "I'm going to stay with you tonight. Try to get some sleep."

"You'll be here in the morning?"

"Yes, I'll be here."

Tedi raised her head and looked over the side of the bed at Lukas. "And you won't tell Dad what I said?"

"No, I won't tell him what you said."

Tedi lay back, relieved.

Mercy leaned down and kissed her daughter's cheek. "Sleep tight."

"And dream good dreams with all my might…" Tedi said, reciting a poem her mother must have taught her when she was little.

"And when the morning brings the light…"

"Everything will be all right."

Theo wished he had a drink, but with Gordon sitting in the chair across from him, watching him like some prison warden, a little liquid comfort would have to wait. For the fifth time, Theo picked up the phone and dialed the number of the hotel where their prospective clients were staying. At last someone picked up, a very sleepy someone.

"Harrison speaking. Is this an emergency?" came a man's raspy voice.

"Well, sir, there was an emergency tonight with my little girl," Theo said, "which is why I was unable to join you at the Lion. This is Theodore Zimmerman. I'm sorry about the lateness of the hour, but I just got here from the hospital emergency room. My daughter nearly died."

The man's voice softened. "What happened?"

"Well, it seems she was stung by a bee, and she had a bad reaction. She's fine now. I just left her with her mother at the hospital, but I'll be going back over to get her in the morning. I'd like to be able to meet with you if you can find it in your heart to give me another chance. I know this has been inconvenient for you, but I'm sure you understand how important my own little girl's life is to me."

There was a pause while Mr. Harrison consulted with someone else in the room. "Okay, Mr. Zimmerman, we have another meeting early in the morning, and we leave early afternoon. Why don't you just meet us out at the property at…say…ten-thirty?"

Theo grimaced. He had planned to pick Tedi up between nine and ten in the morning, but this could work out. "Yes, I'll be there at ten-thirty. Thank you for giving me another chance. See you tomorrow."

After he hung up, he turned back to Gordon. "Still think this whole thing will blow up in our faces?"

Gordon had stopped fidgeting. "Century 21 has them first thing in the morning, though."

"Don't worry. This is a great deal for them. They could expect to pay twice as much as we're asking."

Gordon shook his head. "We've been through this before. Maybe if they were from the East Coast. And we're asking many times what we paid. No one around here would pay that much."

"No one around here could afford it. I love these out-of-staters. I'm going home. Lock up, will you?"

"Zimmerman, no booze tonight. You've got to be fresh in the morning."

Theo ignored him and walked out the door.

Chapter Twenty-Four

At five-thirty Thursday morning Lukas walked out of his call room, still groggy from too little sleep, but glad of the three uninterrupted hours he'd received. Claudia met him at the desk.

"Sorry to wake you, Dr. Bower. The patient I just called about hasn't come in yet. He has a laceration from an accident at the shoe factory."

Lukas nodded. Graveyard special.

"Just to keep things interesting, though," Claudia continued, "we have a sixty-four-year-old Caucasian female on her way here by BLS ambulance complaining of chest pain and shortness of breath."

"BLS? For chest?" That surprised him. A BLS unit— Basic Life Support—could not administer nitroglycerin, could not start an IV and didn't even have a cardiac monitor on board.

"Yes, the ALS unit went on a transfer trip to Springfield. I have a room ready for each patient, and both are stable. They should be here in a few minutes. I have some good news for you."

"I could use some."

"Looks like we're going to be working together a lot more. Beverly traded some days for my nights, and they just happen to be on your shifts. I'm looking forward to it."

Lukas felt his shoulders slump. Beverly didn't like working nights. There went another nurse who didn't want to pull a shift with him. Either he was getting more difficult to work with, or Jarvis was causing more trouble.

"Do you want me to call a nurse down from the floor to help out down here?" Claudia asked.

"Let me see the patients first, since they're both stable."

Claudia grinned. "You just don't want to risk dealing with Rachel Simmons again on this shift."

He nodded. "I don't want to risk losing you to the police on assault and battery charges."

"You're right. All you'd have to do is request her termination. I'd have to kill her." Claudia turned toward the desk, then turned back. "I checked on Tedi Zimmerman just a few moments ago. She's sleeping peacefully, and so is her mother."

Lukas nodded. "Thanks."

Claudia held out a container of breath mints. "Want one?"

He took the hint. "Should I comb my hair, too, Mother?"

"Wouldn't hurt."

About three minutes later Lukas and Claudia heard a woman's voice before the emergency medical technicians wheeled her through the E.R. door. "Watch those turns! I don't want to go flying off this thing."

"You're perfectly safe, Mrs. Baker," the female tech assured her. "Just relax."

"Are you sure this oxygen tank is working? I'm not breathing any better."

"Yes, Mrs. Baker, I've check it three times."

Lukas recognized Mrs. Dondi Baker as they wheeled her past the desk and into exam room five, where he directed them. She had been a chronic complainer the last time she was in. Lukas had seen her chart in the stack on Estelle Pinkley's desk as one of the patient complaints. She'd been furious when Lukas gave her an inexpensive script for antibiotics and told her all she had was bronchitis after a chest X-ray and blood test ruled out pneumonia. She'd come in by ambulance that time, too.

"Did you get my overnight case from the ambu—" Mrs. Baker recognized Lukas in midsentence. "You again!"

"Hello, Mrs. Baker."

She tapped the male tech on the arm. "Excuse me, but I distinctly remember telling you to call Dr. George. He's my family doctor, and he's the one I want to see."

"I'm sorry, Mrs. Baker, but as we explained to you before we brought you in, Dr. George is not on duty here in the emergency room. Dr. Bower is, and he'll take good care of you."

"You didn't tell me Dr. Bower was on duty, or I would have waited to see Dr. George. I have an appointment to see him later this morning, but I just started feeling so bad…" She patted her chest.

Lukas braced himself and preceded Claudia into the exam room to help with the patient transfer. "What seems to be the problem this morning, Mrs. Baker?"

The gray-haired woman glared at him mutinously while they moved her from the cot to the bed. "I want to see Dr. George."

"How about we check you out and get you feeling better. Then I'll call and let him know you're here," Lukas suggested.

"He'll come for me."

Claudia put a blood pressure cuff on her arm. "Now, Mrs. Baker, do you really want to drag poor, hardworking Dr. George out of bed at five-thirty in the morning unless this is something serious this time?"

"I don't want all those tests again. Dr. George says they were completely unnecessary, and you know my insurance doesn't cover all this expensive stuff. I'm not a rich woman, and these bills are more than I can pay."

"Why did you call the ambulance if you're worried about expense?" Claudia asked. "That costs more than an entire E.R. workup."

Mrs. Baker patted her chest. "I couldn't breathe, and my daughter called for me."

"Where is she now?"

"With her children. She can't get a sitter this early."

Lukas stepped out while Claudia attached the monitor leads to Mrs. Baker's chest. For someone with breathing trouble, she sure talked a lot. He still heard her muttering to Claudia when the next patient came through the doors with his arm wrapped in gauze from a knife wound.

Lukas took the new patient's vitals and charted them instead of calling another nurse to help out. He started the patient on a Betadine soak, then stepped back into exam room five.

He glanced at the monitor and nodded. No irregularity. The vitals didn't look too bad, with normal blood pressure and heart rate. She did have a temperature of 100.6, tympanic. "How are you feeling now, Mrs. Baker?"

She took a deep breath. "Nothing's changed."

"Have you noticed if you've had a fever the past few days?"

"I don't think so. I haven't felt very well, but I didn't take my temperature. I'm not a hypochondriac."

"On a scale of one to ten, how would you rate the pain in your chest?" If he could get an idea about the pain, he could do a nitro challenge and see if it helped.

"I wouldn't call it pain, exactly, just kind of a tightness with a dull ache. Can't you do something to help my breathing? That's what bothers me most. I've been coughing a lot."

"Productive?"

"What?"

"Is it a dry, hacking cough, or—"

"No, I think I'm having a lot of drainage."

He looked at her chart and noted that she had no history of heart problems, but with her complaints he didn't want to take any chances. "Okay, Mrs. Baker, I'd like to do a chest X-ray and EKG to rule out any heart problems. Then I want to do a blood—"

"Just hold it right there." She paused to cough. "Didn't you hear what I said a while ago? I don't want you running any of those tests on me. Those X-rays are expensive, and some of that comes out of my pocket."

Lukas caught himself gritting his teeth and forced himself to relax and smile. "Mrs. Baker, I need to be able to find out what's wrong with your chest. The tests I want to do are routine for this kind of problem."

"Dr. George is right. You do run too many expensive tests." She turned to Claudia. "Call Dr. George. He'll know what to do."

Claudia shook her head. "Dr. George will want the same thing, Dondi."

"Why don't we get the blood test for now," Lukas suggested. "It won't cost too much, and it can tell us if there's infection. We can decide on the rest after the results of that come back. Meanwhile, we'll give you a breathing treatment and see if that helps. Then we'll put you on some oxygen."

"That's more like it," Mrs. Baker said.

While Claudia did the orders, Lukas went back in to see the laceration patient. It wasn't as bad as it had looked at first, but the stitching required some time. Claudia helped Lukas while lab took a specimen of Mrs. Baker's blood and respiratory therapy gave her a breathing treatment and put her on oxygen. Lukas heard the woman muttering about a doctor and a nurse who abandoned their patients. Sounded like Mrs. Pinkley was about to receive another patient complaint.

Lukas left Claudia to finish with the laceration while he washed and went in to check on Mrs. Baker. He picked up the lab report on the way.

"Sorry to keep you waiting, Mrs. Baker," he said as he walked into the exam room where the woman sat, still attached to oxygen. "We had another patient."

She grunted and nodded, still scowling.

"We have the results of your blood test," he continued. "You have a white count of 17,900 and 11 bands, which means you definitely have an infection. Without a chest X-ray I can't tell if it's pneumonia, and without that or an EKG, I can't tell if it might be your heart. How are you feeling now that you've had the breathing treatment?"

She nodded. "Better."

"Do you feel as if the oxygen has helped you, as well?"

Again, she nodded, but said nothing, as if she hated to admit he might have helped her.

He took a deep breath. "Mrs. Baker, I strongly recommend further tests, but since you have an appointment with Dr. George later this morning, I'll get you started on some antibiotics and let you go. That is, of course, with the understanding that someone will be with you to help in case you begin to feel worse."

"My daughter can come over, although the kids get on my nerves when I don't feel well."

"And you'll keep your appointment with Dr. George?"

"Yes, of course," she said irritably.

"Then we'll leave you on oxygen for a little longer, and you'll be free to go." Lukas turned and breathed a sigh of relief. In less than an hour his shift was over. No more of this until Monday.

Mercy awakened to the sound of Theo's voice, and at first she thought she was in the middle of an old nightmare. She opened her eyes, glanced over beside her, and saw Tedi still sleeping in the hospital bed.

Theo stood over in front of the ICU desk, arguing with the nurse on duty. "I made it clear to Dr. Bower last night that I would be picking my daughter up first thing this morning. He made no indication that this would be a problem."

Mercy stretched and pulled herself out of the cot. That was a barefaced lie, but she knew this nurse could handle him.

"I'm sorry, Mr. Zimmerman, but Dr. Simeon is Tedi's admitting physician, and he hasn't been in to see her yet."

Theo glanced impatiently at his watch. "How long is he going to be? I can't wait around here all day. I've got an important meeting in less than an hour, and I already missed one meeting because of this."

Mercy strolled toward the desk, attempting to paste a pleasant expression onto her face. "It's okay, Theo. I'll take care of her today."

Theodore turned around, eyebrows raised in surprise. "I thought you were a busy doctor," he said.

"I'm off this morning. They'll want you to sign the paperwork, of course, but I'll take her home, or to school, depending on how she feels." She kept her voice light and unchallenging. She had a quality assurance meeting this morning, but Tedi was infinitely more important.

Mercy could read the confusion in Theo's face at her sudden capitulation after last night. But he was too concerned with his own interests to realize she was doing this because of last night and all the other nights her daughter may have been frightened of him—too afraid even to tell her own mother.

He glanced at his watch again. "What if the doctor doesn't release her today?"

"I'll call you and let you know." She took pride in the evenness of her voice, even though she wanted to sock him in the mouth again, like last night. "You'll be at the office?" she asked.

"Probably not until later. I'm showing a place this morning."

Mercy nodded. If she played him right, she might be able to keep Tedi for the rest of the day, maybe even overnight. But her eyes flicked to the small bruise by his mouth, and she knew he wouldn't forget that right away. If Theo knew how badly she wanted to keep Tedi, he'd never let her do it. Play it cool.

"Okay, Mercy. Where are those papers?" He glanced again at his watch, and Mercy suppressed a smile of satisfaction.

* * *

Jarvis George felt better, thanks to the Demerol he'd finally decided to take. But that wasn't why he was grinning this morning. He leaned back in his leather chair and clasped his hands behind his neck. The papers on his desk told it all.

The fax from Ivy had arrived a few moments ago—a sincere, heartfelt letter questioning Bower's ethics. Jarvis felt a momentary pang at the way he had snapped at Ivy before she left on her trip, but it got the desired results, didn't it?

Mrs. Dondi Baker had been shipped out a few moments ago with an MI—something Bower had failed to pick up on in the wee hours this morning. The idiot hadn't even done an EKG or an X-ray. That oversight alone had sealed his fate, and Ivy's letter was just icing on the cake. The quality assurance committee meeting this morning would be a breeze.

The hospital board might even threaten to dismiss Estelle Pinkley for protecting Bower for so long. Bailey would probably push for that.

For a moment Jarvis hesitated. Should he give this information to Estelle? She was, after all, the administrator. Of course, she'd been nothing but a pain to him the past few years, changing everything here at the hospital so that they were computerized. Whatever happened to good old-fashioned medicine? And Estelle had been the one to hire Bower. If Bailey forced her out, that would be her problem.

Jarvis took another satisfied breath and smiled. He should have started taking this Demerol weeks ago.

Chapter Twenty-Five

Lukas awakened to the sound of the overhead intercom paging Dr. Richmond to call the switchboard. He glanced at the lighted dials of the clock, groaned, and tried to turn over and go back to sleep. It was only ten-thirty. He wanted to sleep until noon, at least.

Unfortunately, as he dozed off again, he remembered that Beverly was on duty this morning. He needed to talk to her before the noon rush hit.

Beverly stood in the trauma room when he stepped from his call room. She had her back to him, checking the defibrillator batteries. She was alone. Good.

Lukas stepped into the room behind her. "Beverly?"

She stopped working, but did not turn around or speak.

"Can we talk?" he asked.

She stood for another moment with her back to him, then slowly turned around, a wary expression on her face.

He strolled over and leaned casually against the cot. "How are things going with Cowboy?"

"Pretty good."

"Is he letting you drive his car?"

She flashed him a ghost of one of her old, teasing grins. "Now, Dr. Bower, you know I'm not going out with him just for his car."

"Of course not. I figured you wanted to get to know Leonardo a little better."

She shrugged. "He's a nice cat…in his place."

"Which is in a stainless-steel cage?"

"Exactly."

"Did Buck's wife ever forgive you for getting him into that mess?"

"She actually spoke to me at the grocery store the other day."

"Good. Then things are back to normal."

"If you want to call Cowboy normal."

"The animals seem to like him, and animals are supposed to be good judges of character. I'm sure they like you, too," Lukas added. "You've got character. Integrity."

Her expression froze. She closed her eyes and sighed, turning back to her work.

"Beverly," he said gently, "do you remember that AMA report you were going to do for me about Dwayne Little?"

She kept working and didn't answer. It was answer enough.

"It's protocol, Beverly. I need you to do the report."

She worked a moment longer, then said, "I'm sorry, Dr. Bower, but I don't feel right about it."

Lukas frowned. "You don't feel right about following hospital protocol?"

"I don't feel comfortable about the way you handled the case." She sighed again and turned around. "You threatened Dwayne. No wonder he left against medical advice."

"You know exactly what happened that day. Why have you changed your mind?"

"I've had some time to think about it. That medication could have killed him."

"Only if he were a drug addict, and you know I wouldn't have given it to him anyway. I was just trying to bring the problem out in the open. You were the one who alerted me to his drug-seeking behavior."

An expression of annoyance crossed her face. "Don't blame me for this. I didn't tell you to threaten him!"

"I did not threaten him. I even offered to get him into a drug rehab program. Come on, Beverly, Dwayne Little is in big trouble and everybody knows it."

She crossed her arms over her chest, refusing to meet Lukas's gaze.

He shook his head impatiently. "If you have a problem with the way I handled the case, then write me up, but do the AMA form. If you don't, it looks as if I turned away a patient without offering relief from his pain, and that's not true. It's a COBRA violation, and it could put my job and the future of this hospital in jeopardy."

She closed her eyes and shook her head. "I'm sorry."

Lukas waited for her to say something more, but she didn't. "Has Jarvis been threatening you?" he asked.

"No."

"Dwayne Little?"

She shook her head, still not looking at him.

"Bailey Little, then."

She turned away.

"He's threatening your job?" Lukas asked.

"He's saying I could be implicated with you if I do the AMA form."

"He's wrong, and you should know that. He's manipulating you. The AMA form simply states the circumstances."

"He's a powerful man, Dr. Bower. He could ruin my

whole career. If I sign that AMA form, I'll look as guilty as you, as if I were in agreement with your course of treatment."

"Your signing of the form would simply show that you know that Dwayne refused my proposal." He wished she would turn around and look at him. He took a step closer. "If you have a problem with the proposed treatment, you can write me up after you sign the AMA form."

"It's a little late for that, isn't it? If I did that now, he would just say I was trying to cover myself."

"His word is not law. Mrs. Pinkley will have something to say about this, and I won't let you take the fall. Beverly, you didn't do anything wrong. Neither did I."

She still didn't look at him, but paced restlessly across the room. "Do you know how hard it is to make a living for a family of three on a nurse's salary around here? I don't get child support, I don't get help of any kind and I have kids depending on me. If I cross the president of the hospital board, I can kiss my job goodbye without any hope of a good recommendation."

"That depends on whom you ask."

She shook her head in exasperation and glanced at him briefly.

"You're willing to help Bailey and his son hide the truth?" Lukas said it sadly.

She stopped pacing and stared at him as if he'd slapped her.

"You're going to let Bailey Little's threats prevent you from doing the job you were hired to do?"

"When you have a family of your own to support—"

"Is that going to be your excuse when someone tells you to start letting patients die because keeping them alive cuts into hospital profits?"

"Of course not!"

"Where do you draw the line between principles and a comfy home?"

"Where do you get off talking about principles? You got kicked out of your residency for endangering patients!"

Lukas returned her glare. So Jarvis had sunk to mud-slinging—Jarvis or Bailey, or someone else itching to get rid of him. What other rumors had been spread about him throughout the hospital, even the town? Mercy was right about Knolls.

"I was exonerated of all charges in Kansas City," he said quietly. "My name was cleared in court."

A voice from the hallway startled them both. "Should we don boxing gloves?"

They turned toward the door to find Jarvis George standing in the entrance, arms folded in front of him.

"You two were shouting loudly enough for me to hear you out at the desk."

Lukas refrained from telling Jarvis that Beverly had been the only one shouting.

"Sorry, Dr. George," Beverly said. She did not look at Lukas again but turned and walked out.

The older doctor smiled at Lukas. It was a smile totally without humor or warmth. "Trouble with the staff, Bower?"

"Trouble with empty rumors and poorly drawn conclusions."

The smile vanished. "You're not going to have to worry about that much longer. You cut your own throat with patient treatment this morning. Add to that a letter that was faxed to me by Mrs. Ivy Richmond, and you're out of this hospital."

"Which patient are you talking about?"

"Mrs. Dondi Baker. You gave her a breathing treatment

and sent her home with an acute myocardial infarction."
He drew the words out as if relishing the sound of them.
"No EKG, no X-ray—"

"She refused them. Where is she? How is she doing?"

"That's not your problem now, is it, Bower?"

He took a step toward Jarvis. "Of course it's my problem. What's going on with her?"

"On her way to Cox South. She came in for her appointment and told me you left her alone in the exam room for at least an hour while you treated another patient."

"You told her I took too many unnecessary tests last time, and she refused to let me do anything but a blood test, which showed—"

"I'm not really interested in that. The patient is not held liable where medical negligence is apparent. She shouldn't have to play doctor—that's why she came to the emergency room."

"Was I supposed to diagnose an MI with a stethoscope?"

A hint of the hateful smile returned. "A good doctor could do it."

Lukas shook his head. "Only if there's an S-4 murmur, which she did not have. I checked. Was I supposed to hold her down and do the tests by force?"

"If she had trusted you in the first place, she would have listened to you. I didn't have any trouble with her at all."

"I wouldn't have had any trouble, either, if you hadn't already undermined me. Was it really worth all this just to get rid of me? What if she dies? Will it be worth it then?"

Jarvis held up some papers, the top of which was an incident report on Lukas's treatment of Dondi Baker this morning. "When the quality assurance committee sees this in a few minutes, and when the hospital board reads the facts about you next week, Estelle Pinkley won't know what hit her. And then I won't have to worry about warning my patients about you." He pivoted and left.

Lukas noticed that Jarvis's footsteps faltered as he walked away.

Tedi had not yet been released when Mercy received the call from Colorado. Ivy's voice sounded weak and distant. Maybe the connection was bad.

"Mom? Where are you calling from? I thought you'd be out in the middle of the mountains by now. Don't tell me you took my advice and carried a cell phone in your pack."

"I didn't."

Mercy didn't like the sound of her voice. "What's going on? Is everything okay?"

"Just a little mishap, nothing for you to worry about. I'll be coming back home sooner than expected." Ivy sighed. "I'm afraid I've botched the whole trip for everyone, except maybe for Louise, Hugh Heagerty's old nurse. She hates Colorado and is coming back with me. I don't know how anyone could hate Colorado."

"Mom, what's going on?"

"You were right, honey. I had no right to disregard your feelings and come out here."

"What happened? You sound awful."

"I just couldn't take the high altitude."

"You had another bad rhythm."

"My heart acted up on the trail," she admitted. "Hugh had taken some extra precautions, thanks to you, and he broke the rhythm, then brought me and the rest of the gang all the way to Denver. I'm in the hospital now. He saved my life, Mercy."

"Is Hugh there? Let me talk to him."

"He's gone. I sent them all back, except for Louise. She's bringing me home Monday."

Mercy leaned back against the wall, overwhelmed.

"I'm fine, Mercy. There was no damage. It wasn't a heart attack."

"Who's the cardiologist treating you?"

There was a pause. "I don't know, Dr. Davis…something. I really didn't pay that much attention because it's no big deal. Hugh took care of everything."

"I want to talk to him."

"And I don't want you to. You have enough going on without taking this on. I told you I'm fine. Believe me, Hugh would never have left me here if he weren't convinced I'd be okay. And Louise will keep a sharp eye on me. Are you on rounds?"

"No."

"Oh? I thought you were off this morning, but you didn't answer at home. Can't you stay way from that hospital?"

"It seems I can't." Mercy hesitated. It didn't seem like a good time to tell her about Tedi, but Mother would be furious if she came back on Monday and…

"Honey?" Ivy prompted. "What's wrong? Are you okay?"

"I'm tired, Mom. I slept in the ICU all night on one of those hard cots."

"Babysitting one of your patients again?"

"We had a calamity last night. Tedi was stung by a bee, and she had a reaction."

There was a pocket of shocked silence. "What kind of reaction?"

"She went into anaphylactic shock. Dr. Bower almost

had to do a cricothyroidotomy before she started breathing again."

Ivy gave a sharp intake of breath. "I knew I shouldn't have come. I should have been there."

"It got a little ugly with Theo for a while, but Lukas managed to convince him he was not welcome here."

"Lukas?"

"I slugged Theo in the mouth. Lukas kept me from killing him."

There was a long pause, and Mercy could have sworn she heard a faint hum of reluctant approval. "Where is Tedi?" Ivy asked finally. "Can I talk to her?"

Mercy glanced toward the bed. "She's asleep again. Why don't you give me your number so I can call you later?"

It took a moment for Ivy to locate and read the number to Mercy. "So you're saying Dr. Bower was on duty last night?"

"Yes, thank goodness."

"Okay." There was a long silence, then, "Oh, boy."

"Mom?"

"He saved her life."

"Yes. He even came up to ICU last night to check on her. We had a long talk. Mom, do you know Lukas is a Christian?"

There was another long pause. "How do you know?"

"I accused him of it, and he admitted it. He's a very caring person. He said some things last night that really made me think."

"That doesn't prove he's a Christian."

Mercy bit her lip. This was not a good time for a fight. "If you had heard Lukas talking about his relationship with God, you wouldn't doubt his sincerity. Why are you determined to find fault with him?"

Ivy replied with a deep sigh.

Mercy glanced over at her daughter's bed and saw that she was awake. "Tedi, your grandma's on the phone. She wants to talk to you."

Tedi eagerly sat up, threw off her blanket and climbed out of the tall hospital bed. She looked pink and healthy and wonderful. Mercy held the phone out for her, and she took it gladly.

"Grandma? How's the hike going?"

Mercy couldn't help smiling at her daughter, at the expression of joy on her face, at the way she seemed to be bouncing back from yesterday's pain and fear. Now if only there was a way to keep the fear away....

Chapter Twenty-Six

Lukas took the stairs to the second floor, anger and frustration hitting him like salt in a fresh wound. It was happening again. He'd fought hard to earn a good reputation at Truman, so why had he left there? So a half-crazy old doctor and a drug addict could ruin him again?

"Why am I here, Lord?" he muttered. "I thought this was where You were leading me. Why can't I feel Your peace any longer? What have I done wrong?"

He stepped out of the stairwell and turned left toward Clarence Knight's private room. But instead of stopping there, he walked to the end of the hallway, where a window overlooked the staff parking lot.

"Are You trying to teach me some kind of new lesson?" he whispered to God. "Did You really want me to be a doctor, or did You just want to taunt me with the possibility, then let me fail?"

Why were Jarvis George and Bailey Little capable of wielding so much power over this hospital? And why did things always have to be so political? Since when did treating patients turn into a popularity contest instead of a career using finely honed knowledge and skill?

As if God had spoken, Lukas immediately recalled a simple passage of Scripture from the book of John: *In this world you will have trouble. But take heart! I have overcome the world.*

There was no true peace in this world, and he needed to stop expecting perfection from others. He did, however, need to start working harder on himself.

It occurred to him that if he had shown Jarvis George all the respect the man had tried to command, and if he hadn't told Ivy Richmond how he felt about her mother's code... If he hadn't written an incident report on Jarvis for the missed needlestick protocol and hadn't resisted Dorothy Wild about the disaster drill... But how could he, in good conscience, have continued with the drill when real patients needed him? Some things he would do again, and some things he would change.

"Help me, Lord. Show me what You want."

He caught sight of Mercy's ten-year-old Pontiac in the parking lot. She was still here. Good. He would check on Clarence, then find Mercy before he left. Then he would go home, pack and drive to Mount Vernon. That would give him three hours to think and pray about this situation.

A familiar deep growl reached him just before he walked into Clarence's room.

"I can't even get out of this bed to get to the john," came Clarence's deep, complaining rumble. "The bed's broken."

"You're not supposed to go to the bathroom," the nurse said. "You're supposed to use this urinal. We need to measure it."

"But I can't sleep! I'm tilted on my side."

"I can't help you right now, Mr. Knight. You can't expect me to lift you all by myself."

Lukas stepped to the doorway and peered in to see the nurse standing with her hands clutching her clipboard. The big guy looked pathetically back at her, his body scrunched onto a tilted hospital bed.

Lukas fought the rush of anger that hit him and tried to remind himself to stay calm. He cleared his throat. "Nurse, may I see you out in the hallway for a moment?"

When she joined him, he gestured for her to take a few steps away from Clarence's door. "Do you know what OSHA would say if they saw this patient in a broken bed?" He kept his voice soft, unthreatening.

The young, slender woman gave an irritated shrug. "I can't help it. Everyone else is busy right now. Surely you don't expect me to switch beds for him myself."

"Why not? He's ambulatory."

"He'll just break another bed. Do you know how much he weighs?"

"Do you know how much he's being charged for a bed in the stepdown unit? And at this moment he's listed as a cash patient. Let's give him some quality here. Clarence Knight is a human being and deserves to be treated with as much respect and kindness as you or I would want if we were sick."

She scowled and held up the chart. "See all this? Heart problems, diabetes, who knows what else they'll find, and he brought it all on himself."

"How do you know that?" Lukas demanded. "Are you familiar with his life history?"

She gestured toward the room. "Overeating has been his life history. I don't need a chart to see that."

"Did it ever occur to you during your years of nursing school that you would be dealing with real people who had real problems, many of which they'd brought on themselves? Would you react the same way with someone who suffered from anorexia nervosa? How about emphysema or heart disease from too much smoking?" Don't the schools teach compassion these days?

A deep flush rushed up her neck and face.

"Get a bed in here now," Lukas ordered. "I'm not leaving until Clarence Knight is comfortable, and I don't want to hear any more remarks about his weight."

Her eyes widened. She stared at him a second longer, then swung away and rushed down the hallway.

Lukas glared at her retreating back. Not only did this hospital not hire enough staff, the staff it did hire lacked compassion, even common human decency.

A moment later, he sighed slowly. This nurse was like millions of others who judged by appearance and not by the heart, but wasn't he judging, too? Why did he have to be so quick to condemn people? God loved people like this nurse, even as He loved Clarence. Jesus Christ would have found a way to be tender with her, to gently show her the error of her ways instead of wounding with harsh words as he had just done.

Of course…there had been the time with the whip in the temple. And Jesus had never been too tender with the religious leaders of His time. "White-washed sepulchers" and "vipers" had been a couple of His favorite terms for them….

"Hey, Doc, that you out there?" came Clarence's booming voice.

Lukas forced a smile and stepped back through the threshold to the room. The huge man lay on the drunkenly tilted bed, his sheet-covered body nearly enmeshed in the stainless-steel rails on both sides.

"How are you feeling, Clarence?"

"Feels like I'm in a vice."

"Do you want me to let the rails down?"

"No, I'll fall out."

"We're going to remedy that. Maybe we can try to get some padding over the rails when your new bed comes. Other than that, how are you feeling?"

"Fat. I don't think I've lost any weight yet." He gestured toward the door. "I heard what you said to that gal."

"Sorry you caught that. People surprise me with their insensitivity."

"Thanks, Doc. I thought you'd be mad at me 'cause I didn't listen to you when you tried to get me in here in the first place."

Lukas grinned. "It took a woman's touch. Dr. Mercy did all right."

Clarence growled.

"Give her a break, Clarence. Her heart's in the right place."

"You mean she's got one?"

"I'm pretty sure she has."

Clarence thought about it, then nodded. "Guess you're right. Guess she probably has a lot going on in her life right now, too."

Lukas blinked in surprise.

"I should've gone to school to be a psychologist." Clarence tried to shift his weight, got stuck in the bars, and gave up. "Take that nurse just now. Jeannie's her name. It was her first time in here, but I knew when she walked in the door that others had been talking to her about me. It was like she'd been warned not to react when she saw me, but she couldn't help it. Maybe I could pay hospital bills if I joined a circus."

"You won't have to resort to that," Lukas said drily. "Dr. Mercy has already made arrangements for a social worker to come in and talk to you on Monday."

Clarence growled again, but his dark eyes held no animosity.

"I know you hate the thought of accepting state aid, but we've been over this before."

"I know, I know."

"You're doing this for your sister."

Clarence nodded.

"She's worth it. You're doing the right thing. You'll have to improve your bedside manner, though, if you intend to become a psychologist."

"Nah. I'd be great with fat people. We could relate. You oughta take some pictures of me the way I look now. When I get this weight off, we could take more pictures and publish the before and after shots together. I'd be the most popular weight-loss guru of the year."

"Of the century. Start writing your memoirs." Lukas had never seen the big man so expansive. It was encouraging. Something was going right, for once.

The nurse arrived with a bed and an orderly. She avoided looking at Lukas while he helped Clarence out of the broken bed and into the new one, but her attitude with the patient, though still stiff, was better. As they finished up, Lukas followed the nurse out into the hallway again.

"Jeannie?" he said quickly before her escape pace took her out of earshot.

She stopped and turned back with obvious reluctance. She glanced at him warily.

"Thank you," he said. "I'm sorry I was so sharp with you earlier. I could have been gentler."

She hesitated, then took a tentative step back toward him. "I'm sorry I was rude with Mr. Knight. While I was getting the bed, I tried to imagine how I'd feel if I were him. It's got to be awful."

Lukas smiled, encouraged out of proportion to the incident.

"Thank You, Lord," he murmured as he went back into Clarence's room to say goodbye. After that he checked on Mercy, who was preparing to take her daughter home. Time to hit the road, and he was ready.

Theo lost the sale. He sat watching the men from the West Coast drive away in their rental car, back to Century 21, with whom they had decided to deal and for whom they had postponed their flight back. He pounded his fist against the steering wheel of his car and shouted curses at their brake lights as they stopped at the traffic signal two blocks away.

He'd busted his rear, called them over and over again, and abandoned his daughter so he could meet them and show them the place, and they'd shown no more appreciation for his efforts than if he'd been a mindless computer.

The door to the office opened and Gordon walked out, head down, hands in his pockets. It was a sure sign he'd been chewed out by the boss, and now it was Theo's turn.

Gordon looked up, saw Theo, and his eyes narrowed.

His hands came out of his pockets, and he strode down the sidewalk toward the car.

Theo was tempted to turn on the engine, put the car in gear and drive away.

Gordon reached the passenger door, opened it and stuck his head in. "Did they bite?"

Theo took a deep breath. "No."

Gordon glared at him. "You'd better do something, and do it fast. Johnson's looking through the accounts and making calls to the bank."

"Why is he looking through the accounts? You keep the books."

"I don't know. Just do something, Theo. Quick! How're we going to cover this?"

"Would you relax? You're being paranoid. He's not an accountant. You covered your tracks, right?"

"Yes, but I'm not an accountant, either. I've never done anything like this before. And tell me how we're going to make our money back on that investment. My loan's coming due, and I'm not going to get a second mortgage on my house."

"Gordon, use your brain. You've got a good pal at the bank. You can get the loan extended."

"No, I can't! I want out. You thought this was such a good deal, you come up with the extra cash and take care of this."

"How?"

"I don't care how, just do it!" He slammed the door and stalked to his own car.

Instead of going inside to face the boss, Theo started his engine and drove away. Johnson could hunt him down if he wanted to ask questions, and besides, it was almost lunchtime and Theo hadn't eaten breakfast yet.

The lunch crowd had not yet arrived when he reached the Golden Lion. That suited him fine. He wasn't interested in any company right now, except for good ol' Jack Daniel's.

He ordered a double with his lunch special and downed it before the food arrived. He ordered another to wash down the steak.

It didn't help. His head hurt. The food felt like sawdust in his mouth.

He raised a hand to gesture a waitress over. "This steak's overdone," he snapped, shoving the plate to the side of the table. "I ordered medium rare." He pressed the center of the steak with his fork. "Do you see any blood running out of that?"

She started in with her soft-voice apologies, and he held her hand up. "I don't want to hear it. Just give me my money back and get me another drink."

She hesitated, watching him warily, the way Tedi sometimes did when he was relaxing with a beer in the evening. He glared at her. She picked up the plate and walked away. When his drink came, a different waitress brought it along with a generous dish of their dessert specialty, bread pudding with whiskey sauce.

"On the house," she said, laying down a fresh spoon. "The chef apologizes for the mistake."

He didn't reply, just waved her away and glared at the dessert. They thought they were so cute, giving him something to fill his stomach so the alcohol wouldn't affect him as quickly. How stupid did they think he was?

He finished the drink in two gulps, threw some cash down on the table, and stalked out of the restaurant.

He was going to take the rest of the day off, and if Johnson didn't like it, let him yell.

Theodore picked up a fifth at the corner liquor store on his way home.

Chapter Twenty-Seven

Jarvis had a headache, but that was old news. He could barely remember a time when he didn't have one, or when the hospital staff didn't question his orders at every turn, or when he didn't have to take combined drugs—including narcotics—just to function. In fact, he could barely remember much of anything anymore. It seemed as if his short-term memory had vanished.

He sat back in his comfortable old leather chair and sighed, still irritated by Robert Simeon's attitude earlier today during the QA meeting. After Jarvis had presented his info on Bower—the loss of residency, the faxed letter from Ivy Richmond questioning Bower's ethics and the information about Dwayne Little's lawsuit and Dondi Baker's missed MI—the committee had voted to request the young, cocky doctor's termination from the hospital. The only dissenter had been Robert Simeon. It was almost as if he'd wanted to protect Bower for some reason. Good thing Mercy wasn't there. A very good thing.

Jarvis punched a button on his phone and picked up

the receiver. "Bailey, Jarvis here. We're getting the recommendation we wanted from the QA committee."

"Excellent. Good work. I knew they'd see things your
way."

"Ivy Richmond came through with a letter," Jarvis continued, giving Bailey all the information about this morning.

"Sounds as if we have enough to hang this guy,"
Bailey said.

"Except for one thing. I'm wondering about the one
nurse who was working with Bower when Dwayne
came in that night. She hasn't done her AMA report yet,
but if—"

"That's not going to be a problem. She's a single mother,
and that's expensive these days. She doesn't want to lose
her job because she really needs the income, and she may
not find anything else in the area. I've discussed the matter
with her. I think she's been reasonably convinced."

Jarvis blinked in surprise, then frowned and shook his
head. Sometimes, Bailey's methods chilled him. "She's
a good nurse, Bailey. Estelle wouldn't let her be fired for
something like—"

"Estelle won't be here to do anything about it if I have
my way. She willingly hired Bower, knowing his ques-
tionable background. The hospital board won't stand for
it, not when we get finished with them."

Jarvis thought about that a moment. This was what
he'd wanted, wasn't it? He wanted to get rid of Lukas
Bower, and he wanted life the way it was before Estelle
Pinkley complicated things with all the red tape and
computer talk and documented confusion. Of course,
things wouldn't change back just because Estelle was
out of the picture.

"Robert Simeon protested our vote," Jarvis said.

"The medical staff has not been informed of our decision, and he feels we should make the recommendation to them first. I told him it was not necessary protocol."

"Good work, Doc. I knew I could count on you. Talk to you later." Bailey disconnected.

Jarvis sat holding the phone, frowning. This was what he wanted. But was this the way to go about getting it done?

Tedi sat on the sofa in Mom's living room watching a video of her favorite old cartoons, eating chicken noodle soup and listening to Mom on the phone canceling her schedule for the afternoon. No school today and Tedi felt great. Her throat was kind of sore and her hand hurt where the bee had stung her, but the sofa felt so comfortable and the soup tasted so good, she couldn't help smiling. She loved Mom's voice. It sounded so safe and strong.

Mom hung up the phone and came into the living room from the kitchen. "More soup?"

Tedi held her bowl up. "Not finished with this."

Mom leaned over and felt for Tedi's pulse, then checked the bee sting on her hand. "Feeling okay?"

Tedi shrugged. "Yeah. Not swelling. Grandma says she'll be home next Monday. Do you think she's really okay?"

Mom raised Tedi's legs, sat down on the sofa and put Tedi's legs on her lap. "I think so, honey. I think she's finally decided to take better care of herself. She's just accepted the fact that her heart is slowing her down, and she wants to be healthy for us." She patted Tedi's legs. "Just like you want to stay healthy for your grandma, right?"

"Right."

"No more wandering into beehives and old barns?"

Tedi took a swallow of soup and didn't answer for a

moment. "I've got to start keeping my smart mouth shut, huh, Mom?"

Mom looked at her for a long time without saying anything. She looked as if she might cry. Then she picked up the remote and turned off the VCR, took the bowl of soup from Tedi and sat it on the coffee table and pulled Tedi up on her lap and cuddled her the way she used to do. She held her like that for a long time.

"It's my fault," Mom said at last.

Tedi, who had her ear against Mom's chest, felt the vibration of her voice. "It's not your fault I sass Dad."

"Yes, it is. You've heard me do it, so you do it."

"But I'll stop doing it."

"Good. I'll try, too."

"Mom?"

"Mmm-hmm?"

"You won't tell Dad what I said, will you?"

"No. At this point, I can't afford to make him mad."

"What if he marries Julie?"

Mom swallowed and took a deep breath. "How would you feel about that?"

"Yuck."

"Why?"

"She makes him drink. That was why he drank last night—because she brought wine over. It's really stupid, too, because I heard her fighting with him about his drinking too much."

"How does she treat you?"

Tedi thought about it, then shrugged. "I don't know. I get the feeling she wishes I weren't there."

Mom squeezed. "I can't imagine anybody not wanting you around."

"I think she wants Dad to herself."

"How do you feel about that?"

Tedi made a face. "You sound like that counselor."

"Oops. I'm a doctor, guess I can't help it."

Tedi continued. "I'm thinking maybe if Dad and Julie got married, they might not want me around, and he wouldn't fight you if you wanted me to come and live with you."

Tedi felt her mother smile. She felt her warm breath against her face.

"You're pretty smart," Mom said.

"Grandma says I take after you."

"Good for her." There was a long silence, then, "Tedi, I'm going to try to get you back."

Tedi stiffened, and her eyes widened in fear. "Mom, you said you wouldn't tell Dad—"

"I'm not planning to tell him anything. I'm going to talk to a good attorney, and I'm going to ask for custody. Your father can't hurt me now, and I'm not going to let him hurt you." She squeezed Tedi tighter. "You'll have to trust me, honey. I can't let him do what he's been doing to you. I know a court battle will be hard on us, but not as hard as living with your father has been on you." She kissed Tedi's forehead. "Please trust me."

Tedi sighed and hugged her mother hard.

The phone rang.

Mom didn't move. She just sat there, holding Tedi. "Let the recorder get it."

They listened to it pick up, heard Mom's recorded message, then heard Dad's voice.

"Mercy? This is Theodore. I want you to bring Tedi home. Now." The machine beeped, clicked and rewound.

Mom took a deep breath.

Tedi looked up at her. "I have to do it, Mom."

Mom nodded. "I know. I don't want you to go."

"I'll keep my mouth shut and be good, and if he gets drunk and I get scared, I'll call you to come and get me."

Tears filled Mom's eyes and dripped down her face. She didn't move. "You promise?"

"I promise."

Lukas was just preparing to lock the front door of his house when the phone rang. For a moment, he listened to it ring and considered ignoring it.

He picked up on the fifth ring. "Bower here."

"Yes." It was Jarvis. There was a long pause. "I just thought you'd want to know the results of our QA meeting this morning, Bower."

Lukas waited.

"We plan to recommend to the hospital board next Thursday that you be released from your contract with us and terminated from this facility."

Lukas's first reaction was to observe that Jarvis didn't sound like he was gloating. He sounded almost hesitant. Then the news hit deeper, and Lukas closed his eyes. "And why are you calling to tell me this?"

There was a long silence, then a sigh. "If you fight us, Bower, you'll drag Pinkley down with you, and possibly even this hospital."

"Is Bailey Little going ahead with the suit?"

"That's right."

"You and Bailey Little are after my job, and you won't be satisfied until I'm gone."

"We want what is best for the hospital."

Lukas allowed his temper to carry him for a moment. "That's an outright lie! Obviously you don't care who gets hurt as long as you get what you want. You sounded almost happy that Dondi Baker had that MI, because it meant more ammo against me. You don't even care if the poor woman dies! Bailey Little doesn't mind getting rid of an excellent hospital administrator, or even ruining the whole hospital along with hundreds of jobs, as long as his drug-seeking son is vindicated. He'll fake a claim of wrongdoing to COBRA. What happens to Estelle Pinkley, and to the lawsuits and to the hospital if I give him a letter of resignation?" Lukas was shocked by his own words.

Apparently, so was Jarvis, because he didn't answer for a moment. "I just want you gone. I have no intention of destroying the hospital." His voice sounded weaker, yet forced, as if he was struggling to keep up his strength. "Do what you want, Bower. By next Thursday, it won't matter, anyway."

Frankie Verris straightened from his weeding and put his hand over his chest. It didn't hurt, exactly, just felt like a gentle tug. He took a deep breath and wondered about putting one of those little pills under his tongue, but that stuff was used in explosives, for goodness' sake. The one time he'd used one the chest pain had gone away, but his head felt as though it might explode for a few moments.

He ambled over to an old tree trunk and sat down on it. The heart problem didn't bother him as much as it had at first. He even welcomed this reminder that he wasn't going to be stuck on this old earth much longer. He'd be seeing his sweet wife, Doris, soon, and since this sudden friendship he'd developed with Jesus Christ, he was eager to see heaven. A little pain was nothing in comparison.

Shelly would grieve, he knew. He'd talked to her about it—even had to fight her so he could fill out one of those DNR sheets so they wouldn't restart his heart if it stopped. She'd cried and he had cried. She'd said she didn't know what the kids would do without him. He loved those kids, and so had Doris. Shelly had been like a daughter to them for years.

After he and Shelly had finished their cry, he'd done something he never could have done before. He'd told her about his relationship with God. And she had listened. She hadn't listened to Doris, for some crazy reason, but when he told her what had happened to him, she'd admitted there was something missing in her life, too.

"Thank You, God," he whispered. "Thank You for giving me a life with Doris. Thank You for Shelly, who loves me and takes care of me, and thank You for Dr. Bower, who helped point me in the right direction that day in the hospital."

His chest had stopped cramping, but he knew it would come again.

Children's voices reached him from the side of Shelly's house. Her two oldest children, Jason and Jamie, came running toward him, trampling good dirt and young sprigs of corn in his garden. He smiled and held his arms out to them.

Chapter Twenty-Eight

Monday morning Tedi got up and made her own breakfast before Dad was even awake. He hadn't said much to
her since Mom had brought her home Thursday night,
probably because he had a hangover. He'd tried to call
Julie a couple of times, but she hadn't answered. Saturday
and Sunday he had worked, and Tedi had called and
talked to Mom on the phone three times on Saturday and
twice on Sunday. Mom wanted her to call as often as
possible, at least every day when Dad wasn't around, and
Mom was going to call the school every day to make sure
Tedi was there. She'd promised not to say anything to Dad
about the bruises, but she'd made Tedi promise to call her
any time Dad drank or even acted angry for any reason.

Dad's snores reached Tedi in the upstairs bathroom,
where she brushed her teeth. If she got lucky, like she did
Friday morning, she might slip out of the house before
he woke up. She would pack her own lunch so she
wouldn't have to ask him for lunch money.

Just as she stepped into the kitchen, the phone rang
once. She jumped and nearly dropped her backpack, but

the answering machine picked up and there weren't any more rings. She tiptoed into the den to listen.

It wasn't Mom. Some grouchy-voiced man demanded that Dad call back as soon as possible. He didn't even leave a name. How rude.

Tedi didn't wake Dad. She quickly packed a peanut butter and jelly sandwich and a banana, stuffed it in her pack and rushed out the door.

Theodore didn't awaken until the sounds of morning rush hour traffic—five cars from the neighborhood—echoed against the bedroom window. He checked his alarm clock and found that he hadn't set it. He stumbled downstairs to see about Tedi and caught sight of a neatly printed note stuck to the fridge with a magnet. Tedi had left early so she could walk to school, just as she had done Friday. He sighed, glancing at the rinsed breakfast cereal bowl and juice glass in the sink. He combed his fingers through his hair and stood at the sink, staring out the window at the old swing set. How long had it been since she'd played on that? Had he lost his little girl?

She'd been so distant lately, almost as if she were afraid to look at him. Did she think he was a monster?

What had she told her mother?

Obviously not much, or Mercy would have been camping on his doorstep with the National Guard, along with Ivy.

He walked into the den and listened to the recorder. Johnson was mad again.

Theo sank down into his comfortable office chair and buried his face in his hands. He'd shown six houses this weekend, and not one had sold. He'd called three banks Friday for a loan, and no go. Gordon was losing control and wanted out of the deal. Sure he did. He'd known it was a risk when he bought in, but now he wasn't as willing to gamble.

Julie wouldn't even answer her phone when he'd tried to call on Sunday. Why not? Just last week she'd been ready for marriage. Was she backing out now just because of a little fight?

Theo thought about the fifth of Jack Daniel's he'd bought last week. He hadn't opened it again since that day. He didn't even know why he'd bought it, really, because he was trying to stay off the stuff when Tedi was home. But it was there. He thought about it often.

He picked up the phone and speed-dialed Julie's number. No one answered. She'd probably already left for work.

He paced back into the kitchen and opened the top cupboard above the refrigerator. The bottle was still there in its plain paper bag, just as he had placed it. He wanted a drink. He could almost taste it, feel it warm his throat and coat his stomach.

But he wasn't going to drink it. He was not an alcoholic. He could control this. To prove it he closed the cupboard door and went upstairs to shower.

The cry of a needle-shot child followed Mercy down the hallway as Josie followed her orders in the pediatric exam room. The pain wouldn't last too long; Josie was the best in the business. She had the skill of a neurosurgeon when it came to giving shots to children. She was a wonderful asset to the practice. The only complaint most parents had with her was that she refused to give candy to children who were good. She handed out crayons or colored pens or even toothbrushes, but never anything she perceived as unhealthy. Mercy supported her.

A pink message note on Mercy's desk requested she call Dr. Simeon as soon as possible about the QA committee meeting they'd had last Thursday. She checked her schedule and found, to her surprise, that she had a few minutes. She punched Robert's number.

When she reached him, she apologized for missing the meeting.

"No need to feel bad," he said. "In a way, I'm glad you weren't there, but at the time I really wished you were."

"Why? What happened? Is Jarvis throwing his weight around again?"

Robert didn't answer for a moment. The child in the other room had stopped crying, and Josie's soothing voice echoed down the hall.

"The QA committee voted four to one to recommend Dr. Bower's termination to the hospital board at its next meeting this Thursday," Robert said abruptly.

Mercy caught her breath. "What?" She nearly shouted the word. "That's crazy! Why?"

"You already guessed it. Jarvis George."

"Don't tell me he used that ancient story about Dr. Bower's dismissal at Cunningham."

Robert was quiet for a moment. "Yes."

"He took them to court and cleared his name of all charges, even the paternity question. He's a good doctor, Robert, and a caring person. Kansas City was all politics." She frowned. "You said the vote was four to one. Were you the one?"

"Yes."

"Why didn't you stop it? You're the chairman."

"How was I supposed to do that, shoot everybody? They outvoted me, Mercy. Jarvis has clout and I couldn't stop them. And there's more than just the Kansas City fiasco. It seems there have been some patient complaints about Dr. Bower. One incident took place Thursday morning, when he allegedly missed an MI. We were given no particulars. Dr. George just expected us to take his word for it. I, for one, have not had a single complaint by any of my patients, and I won't take Jarvis's word for anything."

"More politics." Mercy leaned back in her chair and closed her eyes. "I think Jarvis is losing his mind. I've never seen him behave so perversely."

"He's always been perverse."

"I'm thinking mental dysfunction, Robert."

"You'd do everyone a big favor if you'd prove it and get him out of this hospital. Unfortunately, there's more, and you're really not going to like this."

Mercy opened her eyes and sat forward.

"Your mother," Robert said.

Mercy stiffened instinctively. "Mom? You've heard from her? Has she had another—"

"She faxed a letter here last Thursday."

Mercy sat back with relief.

"It concerns Richmond funds," he said.

"Oh, no."

"She's threatening to withhold a considerable amount of financial support from Knolls Community Hospital if Dr. Lukas Bower isn't completely investigated, then terminated if the results warrant it."

"She's blackmailing the hospital?" Had she lost her mind? Why hadn't she mentioned this over the phone? Probably because she wanted to live.

"I wouldn't put it quite so harshly. She means well."

"Then she'd better butt out of things she knows nothing about," Mercy snapped.

"I think that's your department. Can you talk to her?"

"I most certainly will. She's flying in today."

"Perhaps you should cool off a little before you speak with her."

"Thank you for the vote of confidence. What about the Dwayne Little fiasco?"

"Still going strong. I would be surprised if Jarvis and Bailey weren't working together."

"Me, too. Wish me luck."

"You'll need it," Robert said. "Remember who won the last argument you had with your mother."

"She lost in the end, Robert. They had to carry her off the trail and rush her to the hospital. It was her heart."

"How bad?"

"As I said, she's flying home today. It wasn't an MI."

"She should never have gone."

"And she should never have written that letter."

Monday's noon rush started early and ended early. By the time Lukas felt hunger pains, he was free to eat, much to his surprise. He left instructions for the secretary to page him if he was needed and hurried toward the cafeteria. This past weekend had been great. He'd had a long walk and a long heart-to-heart talk with Dad. They'd prayed together, read Scriptures together, and then prayed some more. By the time Lukas drove back yesterday, he was at peace again. He knew himself and his own willful heart well enough to know this probably wouldn't last for long, but he also knew that even when he wasn't faithful, God was. The decision he'd made this weekend reflected the trust he knew he could place in Christ.

"There you are," came a familiar female voice from behind him.

He turned to find Mercy rushing to catch up with him, and he felt the warmth of a welcoming smile on his face.

She held out a large, flat box. "Want some healthy low-fat pizza?"

He eyed the box skeptically. "Healthy?"

"It even tastes good." She pushed a door open beside them in the corridor. "Come on, we need to talk."

They entered a minuscule conference room with a small refrigerator. Mercy took two cans of Diet Sprite out of the fridge and opened them. She set them down on the table. "Say your prayers. You're going to need them."

Lukas pulled a chair out and sat down when Mercy did. "You've heard the rumors."

She held his gaze for a moment. "Tell me which rumors, and I'll tell you if I've heard them."

Lukas bowed his head and said a quick, silent prayer. He'd prayed a lot this weekend, and he felt as much at peace as he could humanly feel.

When he raised his head, Mercy opened the box and took out two paper plates and plastic forks. "Dig in. This is guaranteed not to give you heartburn."

The melted cheese looked real. "How can this be low fat?" he asked.

"Fat-free cheese mixed with reduced fat. The rest is veggies and superthin crust. They put lots of garlic on it, so your patients and staff will avoid you this afternoon."

"I love garlic."

"Then enjoy." She picked up a slice. "Quit stalling. What have you heard?" She bit into the slice without benefit of plate or fork.

He picked up his own slice. "I'm going to be sued,

possibly by two different patients, and if I don't quit the hospital, I could be fired."

Mercy stopped chewing, and her gaze shot to his face. She swallowed. "Hefty rumors. Who told you?"

"Dr. George." He took a bite of the pizza. It reeked of garlic and onion and herbs and yeast. It was wonderful. But it could definitely cause heartburn.

"Since when did you start listening to Jarvis?" Mercy asked.

"Since he threatened to dump Mrs. Pinkley for protecting me."

Mercy put down her slice. "When did he tell you that?"

"Thursday." He took another bite. "This is really good. Where'd you get it?"

"That jerk! Did he tell you about my mother's letter?"

"He told me the works, I suppose. Mmm...low fat, too. I can't believe it."

Mercy glared at him. "So what are you going to do?"

"Quit." He took another bite.

She shot forward in her chair. "No!"

He kept chewing.

"Lukas, I don't believe this! You've fought this kind of thing before. You've got to do it again."

He swallowed, took a deep breath and returned her gaze. "I can't in good conscience jeopardize other jobs to save my own." He was touched by her expression of outrage on his behalf. "I've done nothing but pray about it and think about it and talk about it with my family all weekend. It was not an easy decision, but I am offering the resignation to Mrs. Pinkley. What she decides to do with it is up to her. This at least gives her some leverage if she needs it."

"Let me have a talk with Mom."

"Eat your pizza."

"Lukas, at least allow me that. My mother is not a vindictive woman, and she's usually not stupid, just mistaken. She'll see reason when she understands the whole thing. Right now she just doesn't know."

He shook his head. "I'm sorry, Mercy. Your mother's letter isn't the only ammunition that's being used against me."

"I know about the missed MI, but Jarvis isn't sharing all the facts on that. If Mom's fighting for you instead of against you, people will listen."

"Because she has money?" he asked.

Mercy winced. "I know how that sounds, but yes. She helps support this place. The least she can do is try to reverse some of the damage she's done. You've at least got to let me try. Promise me you won't make a move today until I contact you."

Lukas hesitated. Her passion touched him. He put his food down and leaned forward. "Mercy, would you want me to stay and fight if it was going to cost you your job?"

"Right is right no matter what the cost."

He smiled as he reached out and touched her hand. "I appreciate what you're saying, and I believe you feel that way, but this isn't about my rights anymore. It's about doing the right thing after counting the cost to others."

"Estelle Pinkley won't be fired. She's too good to let that happen."

Lukas took a deep breath. "I'm presenting the resignation. In my court battle in KC against my former employers, three people spoke up in my defense. Before the trial was over, those people had lost their jobs. I won my case, but at what cost?"

"At least wait a day. One day, Lukas. Give me a chance to talk to Mom. Please."

He picked up his pizza and took another bite, chewed, swallowed, while she waited. "I wasn't going to make a move until tomorrow, anyway," he said at last.

Her brown eyes came alive when she smiled.

Chapter Twenty-Nine

Tedi walked home from school with a backpack of books slung across her shoulders. It was almost summer, and she was so sick of being in school. Mrs. Watkins didn't seem too happy about her being there, either. Why hadn't she tried harder these past few months? The homework would take her hours, if she did it at all, and if she didn't do it, Mrs. Watkins would probably call Dad in for another conference. He would call her an old cow again, and Mrs. Watkins would just get grumpier. Tedi really hated that. There were a lot of things she hated about him lately. Not everything.

He had always rebelled against his teachers when he was in school. He'd told her so one night when he'd been drinking just a little. His parents hadn't helped him with homework, either. They'd gotten a divorce when Dad was Tedi's age. His dad, Tedi's grandfather, had died before Dad graduated from high school.

For a moment Tedi felt sorry for Dad. His family had been really poor when he was growing up, and Dad was unpopular in school. His brothers, all three of them, were a lot older than Dad and had gotten married and moved away before Dad reached junior high. Then he'd been shifted back and forth from mother to father.

It was strange, but sometimes Tedi liked Dad better when he'd had a couple of cans of beer. It never lasted long, because he wouldn't quit once he'd started, but sometimes he would relax for a few minutes. For those few moments he was nice. He would talk about himself and his own childhood, even about having a crush on Mom years before she knew he existed—when she was hitting the books so hard she barely noticed boys at all and never dated because it might interfere with "real life," as Dad put it.

A car pulled up to the curb beside her. "How about a ride?"

Tedi stopped walking and turned slowly toward the voice. Dad sat in the driver's seat of the BMW, gripping the steering wheel as if prepared for impact.

Tedi shrugged, trying not to frown. "Sure, Dad."

His hands relaxed as she unslung the book bag from her shoulders and opened the door.

Trying not to be too obvious, she sniffed the air for the telltale odor of liquor breath. She didn't detect anything, but Dad's mouth was closed. She climbed in and put on her seat belt.

He pulled off slowly. At least he wasn't mad about anything.

Tedi cast a glance at him, pretending to look for a book in her bag. He was watching her. She looked away quickly. Why'd he have to come and get her? Next time she'd walk another way, maybe use the alleys or something. She didn't want him coming to get her or trying so hard to be nice, especially when that meant he would spend more time with her. He never seemed normal anymore. Nothing seemed normal. She was scared of what he might do, but even worse than that, she just didn't like him. The sudden thought scared her. She felt so mad at him. In a way, she was almost more afraid of her own anger than she was of his drinking. She felt as if her mouth might say something horrible to him before she could stop it, and then he might hurt her.

"Lots of homework tonight?" he asked.

"Yes."

"How about the Oriental Buffet for dinner before we go home?"

She looked at him and blinked. She didn't smell any booze, but didn't he realize it was barely past three o'clock? "I'm not hungry yet."

"Okay, then, takeout."

She shrugged. Why didn't he just stay at work?

"Does that mean yes?" he asked. His voice sounded impatient.

She took a breath and let it out slowly. "Yes," she said through clenched teeth.

She had to keep her mouth shut. She'd promised Mom.

Mercy stepped out of her car with her stethoscope draped around her neck and her doctor's bag in her hand. Mom would not push her attentions off today.

As Mercy's anger had seethed this afternoon, she'd rehearsed what she would say, keeping in mind the fact that Mom was sick. This would not be a good time for a fight or even one of their regular arguments. This was a time for tenderness and a good bedside manner.

Ivy opened the door before Mercy could knock. "I've been watching for you."

Mercy hid her dismay at Ivy's pale features. "Hi, Mom. How're you feeling?"

"Tired. Relieved to be home." She stepped back from the doorway. "Come on in. I guess I deserve this visit."

"What are you talking about? I'm just going to check you out for myself to make sure you survived the flight."

Ivy let her in, then closed the door and dropped into the nearest straight-backed chair. She gestured toward the stethoscope around Mercy's neck. "Don't strangle me with that thing."

Mercy lowered herself to her knees beside the chair in order to work better. She took the offending instrument from around her neck. "I'm not going to strangle you."

"You know about my fax to Jarvis, don't you?"

"Who doesn't? Be quiet for a moment." Mercy listened to the regular sinus rhythm of Ivy's heart, took her pulse, counted respirations. A little elevated, but understandable if she'd been expecting a fight. Mercy's own pulse was probably a little fast, too. She pulled the sphygmomanometer out of her bag and checked Ivy's blood pressure. Also a little elevated.

She put everything away and perched on the arm of the sofa across from her mother. "Relax, Mom, I'm not going to yell. I didn't find out about the fax until Dr. Simeon informed me about it this morning. Of course I was upset when I heard, but your health is of utmost importance to me right now."

Ivy smiled wryly. "So when you find out I'm perfectly healthy, that's when you'll strangle me."

"Am I that bad?"

"You can't help yourself. You take after me." Ivy leaned forward, elbows on knees, and fixed Mercy with an intent gaze. "I still act on impulse. That fax was pure impulse when I was in the Denver hospital waiting to find out whether or not I was going to die. I felt so guilty for behaving irresponsibly, ruining the first part of the hike for the others and endangering my own life. I thought about what that might have done to you and Tedi, and I knew I'd really blown it. I think, with the guilt and fear and continued grief over Mother, I wasn't thinking clearly. I could also blame it on remnants from the drugs they gave me."

"Are you saying you're sorry you sent it?"

"More so as time goes on, and I think about the damage I may have done to Dr. Bower's career, to the future of the hospital."

"When did you decide this?"

"On the flight back. I had a lot of time to think about it, and I realized you were right about my attitude weeks ago. I blamed Dr. Bower for Mother's death." Ivy sighed, leaned back in her chair and closed her eyes. "I was being spiteful and vindictive, and I tried to camouflage it as community spirit—seeing to the safety of our citizens. I didn't show a Christian spirit."

"As you said, you were sick and confused."

"I can't blame you for not listening to me when I talk about Christianity. I spout all this stuff about the love of God, and then sometimes I act as if I think *I'm* God. I'm sorry, Mercy. I'm failing you."

"That's ridiculous, Mom. You're human."

"I'm also a Christian, and my own daughter rejects God."

Mercy studied her mother's face for a moment. "Maybe not."

Mom's eyes widened. She didn't say anything, just held Mercy's gaze.

"That doesn't mean I plan to 'get saved' and join a

church. But, Mom, you really have changed. Five years
ago, you would've never admitted what you just did. And
you're more forgiving than you used to be, more patient
with Tedi."

"I really was terrible, wasn't I?"

"That's not what—"

"I know." Ivy smiled. "You don't know how much that
means to me." She studied Mercy's face for a moment
more, then said, "Dr. Bower's had something to do with
your change of heart, too, hasn't he? You told me on the
telephone the other day that he was a Christian, and I
didn't want to hear it."

"He is, Mom."

"What can I do to help him?"

"He's planning to quit the hospital."

"Why?"

"Lots of reasons. The fax was just one of them. Bailey
Little has a personal vendetta against him for reasons I
can't go into—"

"Dwayne Little tried to get drugs from the E.R. and
Dr. Bower was not compliant."

Mercy looked at her mom with renewed respect. "Yes,
and Lukas also missed an MI last Thursday, but upon re-
searching the case, I have discovered that the patient
refused any of the tests that would ordinarily alert him to
the problem. Lukas should have signed her out AMA—
against medical advice—but he didn't. Jarvis has been out
of line on this whole thing, especially when he spread
word about Lukas losing his residency position."

"I know. I allowed him to bully me into siding with
him against Dr. Bower."

"I personally wouldn't believe what Jarvis said about
anything right now."

Ivy shook her head. "I'll call Estelle and try to do some damage control."

Mercy smiled, then stood up and hugged her mom. "Thanks. If they'll listen to any one person, they'll listen to you. I'll call Lukas tonight and try to talk him out of resigning."

The young emergency room physician at Willow Springs reminded Jarvis of Lukas Bower, with his muscular build, light brown hair and glasses. Jarvis found this extremely irritating, and he hated the position he was in, needy, dependent. He had no choice. He was out of pain meds and could get no more without arousing suspicion. Jarvis had checked in here at least an hour ago using a fake name and offering to pay cash at the window. They had run tests, let him sit in pain and pretty much treated him as if he were a drug seeker.

"I'm sorry, Mr. Delaney, but your tests results aren't back yet," the young doctor answered in response to Jarvis's repeated plea for pain relief.

"What about the CT?" Jarvis snapped. "Surely that's been read."

"We want to run the films."

"I want to see them. What about the other tests?"

The young doctor sighed and explained slowly, as if Jarvis were of below average intelligence, "When we get the films, we would like to teleradiograph them to the radiologist on call. Then we'll consider all the results—"

"Skip the details!" Jarvis shouted. "I know the details!" His head throbbed so painfully that he grabbed at his skull and cried out and felt as if the lights had suddenly gone out. He heard the man's reply in snatches.

"…can see you're in pain…give you a shot…lie back…"

"I can't stay overnight," Jarvis managed to say as he

allowed unseen hands to help him lie down. "I've got work to do."

A few moments later he felt the prick of a needle. The relief, when it came, was not complete, but it was very precious.

Mercy had arrived home and was about to call Lukas when her own phone rang. Tedi's muffled voice reached her when she picked up the line.

"Mom, it's me. I hate him! I wish he were dead!" She stopped, and a sob echoed through the phone line. "I know I promised to keep my mouth shut, but it's so hard."

"What happened?"

"Nothing. He's just so hateful." Tedi's sobs grew in strength, and Mercy allowed her to cry. It was probably what she needed most, aside from a different father. When the sobs dwindled and stilled, Mercy asked gently, "Where are you calling from?"

"Home."

"Where is your father?"

"He's not a father. He's a horrible—"

"Where is he?"

"He went out for a while. Probably to drink." She sniffed.

Mercy wanted to drive over immediately and take her daughter out of that house, drive away into the night and never bring her back. "Tedi, has he been drinking?" She braced herself for the answer.

"No, Mom, I don't think so."

"What has he done today?"

More sniffing. "Nothing. He picked me up on the way home from school, and we got something to eat, and then he tried to help me with my homework."

"He did?"

"But he couldn't. He's dumb."

"Did he help you with English or math?"

"English and history."

"Let him help with math. He can do that."

"I don't want him to help me with anything! I want him to stay away from me. I don't want him to even talk to me. I kept thinking about what he's done and I hate him!"

Mercy recognized the signs. She'd felt the same way, when she couldn't stand the sight of Theo even when he was trying to be nice, because she knew it wouldn't last. All the kindness he could dredge up wouldn't erase all the pain he'd caused.

"I know, Tedi. I understand how you feel." A ten-year-old little girl should never have to feel that way. "Do something for me, okay? Just go to bed. Try to be asleep when he comes home. That way you won't have to talk to him again tonight."

Tedi was silent for a long time, and Mercy heard soft sniffling again. How much longer would this go on?

"I love you, Mom."

"I love you, too, honey. We're going to get you out of there, but I want to do it legally so it'll stick. Please do as I ask."

"Okay. I'll try."

"And, Tedi?" She couldn't believe the words that came to her mind, but she knew Tedi needed to hear them. "Remember the night you got stung by the bee?"

"Yeah."

"Remember that you prayed?"

"Yeah."

"Pray again."

* * *

Lukas read and reread his short letter of resignation. It simply informed Mrs. Pinkley that he wished to be released from his duties as of this coming Thursday morning. It was an offer that came after hours of prayer. That would give Jarvis Tuesday and Wednesday to find someone to take his place Thursday, and it would meet the deadline for the hospital board committee meeting, therefore not endangering Mrs. Pinkley's job. He added no stipulations about liability.

The phone rang, and Lukas reluctantly picked up. He knew who it was. He knew what his answer had to be. "Yes, Mercy." He listened. Bless her. "Thursday, Mercy. Unless something happens, Wednesday will be my last day at Knolls Community."

Chapter Thirty

At eight o'clock Thursday morning Theo sat across the desk from Mr. Johnson, his boss. Gordon slumped next to him, eyes averted, while Johnson threw down some copies of transactions that had taken place at the First State Bank months ago.

"Can either of you explain these to me?" the boss growled.

No one said a word.

Johnson sat back in his seat, crossing his hands over his midriff. "Ever heard of a paper trail?" His eyes simmered with anger. "Gordon? You write all the checks—or you did until now. Tell me what I've got here." He picked up the papers and waved them.

Gordon cleared his throat and shot Theo an unholy glare. "You tell him, Theo. This was all your idea."

Theo took a deep breath, wishing he were any place else. "That property we told you about back in—"

"I know which property you're talking about!" Johnson spat. "I told you not to buy it, remember? I knew it would cost too much to fix up, then be impossible to unload. You not only disobeyed a direct order, you used company money—money from *my* company!—to gamble on something I'd already told you was a lost cause."

"But we contributed, too!" Theo exclaimed. "The price was—"

"That place was worthless at any price!" Mr. Johnson tossed the papers back down and shoved himself away from the desk. The rollers of his chair took him backward several inches. "I can have you arrested for embezzlement right now. You didn't think I could follow your juggling act, did you, Gordon?"

"It was temporary." Gordon's voice held a definite whine. "We were going to pay it back."

"You'll pay it back, all right." Johnson stood to his feet and placed both hands on his desk. "You'll have thirty thousand dollars here in this office by Monday, or I'll press charges and this will be in the hands of the police. I imagine the state Board of Realtors will also have some input."

Theo also stood, determined not to be intimidated. "Where are we going to get that kind of money?"

Johnson's eyebrows shot up in amazement. "I don't think I heard correctly. Are you implying that's my problem?"

"I'm simply stating that you're not giving us much time to—"

"Shut up, Zimmerman," Gordon snarled. "He doesn't have to give us till Monday."

Johnson stared at Theo for another moment. "Your little buddy here is right, Theodore. I could have had the police waiting for you this morning when you walked in. Count your blessings." He shook his head and turned to walk out the door. "You're both fired," he said over his shoulder. "Get out."

* * *

At eleven-thirty Thursday morning Jarvis sat at the nurses' station in the center of the emergency department, grimacing every time the baby screamed in exam room three. He was ready to strangle the baby, the mother and the nurse, Claudia, who seemed to contradict every decision he'd made this morning.

There had been few patients so far, none with high acuities, for which Jarvis was thankful. Thanks to narcotics his pain was manageable, but barely. He did not want to have to make snap decisions about human lives under these conditions, and he cursed Lukas Bower for not being here to do his job. While he was at it, he decided to curse Bailey Little, as well. His threats were the reason Bower had handed in his resignation. Estelle Pinkley deserved to be on the list, too, for suspending Bower's privileges so he wouldn't be on duty today. The woman had the audacity to refuse the resignation! After tonight's meeting they could set about hiring someone to take Bower's place, but that didn't help now.

The ambulance speaker sparked to life, spewing information about an elderly man in apparent cardiac distress. They were on the scene and would be en route in a few minutes. The patient apparently lived close to the hospital.

As soon as the report ended, Jarvis turned toward the desk and spied Dwayne Little sitting out in the waiting room. He motioned to Claudia. "Is Little here as a patient?"

She glanced at Carol, the secretary, and they exchanged a meaningful look. "Yes, Dr. George. He says he has a headache."

Jarvis felt a flash of irritation. "Is there some reason he hasn't been taken care of yet? We've got several empty exam rooms."

"He was low on my triage list," Claudia said tiredly.

"Since when is pain a low triage? There's nobody else waiting out there, is there?"

"No, but I'm getting ready for our cardiac patient."

"Fine, you do that, but take care of our other patients while you're at it. Get Dwayne back here."

Claudia took a step closer to Jarvis and lowered her voice, glancing over her shoulder at Dwayne's head resting in his hands. "You realize he's here seeking drugs?"

Jarvis's irritation turned to anger. "Nurse, almost every patient who steps through those doors is here seeking drugs in some form or another. If you're implying, as Bower did, that this man is a drug addict and a drug seeker just because he's been here more than once for intractable pain, then you can join Bower in the unemployment line. Otherwise, get that patient to a room and get him taken care of!"

Claudia held his angry gaze for a moment, her own eyes flashing. He hoped she would say something, just one more thing. Then he'd have a good reason to get rid of her. He'd had all he could take of this bossy woman today.

She didn't say another word. She picked up a chart and walked out toward the waiting room.

"Call a nurse down from the floor," Jarvis ordered Carol. He needed as much backup as he could get. He turned to glare at the secretary. "Or are you going to argue with me, too?"

Carol shot him a resentful stare, but said nothing. She picked up the phone and dialed upstairs.

A few moments later Jarvis stepped into exam room six, holding a thick file on Dwayne Little.

"Hi, Uncle Jarvis." The slender, fair-haired young man sat rubbing his forehead. His shoulders were bent forward and his face held a grimace of pain.

"You don't look too happy." Jarvis tossed the chart down on the desk, then leaned back against it with his arms crossed over his chest.

"I feel awful. I know I shouldn't be coming back in here, but I've got to get help. I know I should get some tests to find out what's wrong, and I will. But right now I just hurt." Tears formed in the young man's eyes.

Jarvis could identify. His own head ached a little more, in spite of the narcotics on board, just from the stress of the morning. He listened to Dwayne's chest, checked his eyes, then took out a prescription pad and wrote on it. "I'm going to give you some relief, son, but you've got to promise me two things."

Dwayne looked up, his eyes hopeful. "Anything."

"No driving under the influence. I know you love that hot rod of yours, but morphine does crazy things to the mind. You can't drive. Call your father to come and get you." He felt like a hypocrite. What about practicing medicine under the influence? "Same with the prescription. No driving."

"I know. You won't see my car out in the parking lot, either. I've got a friend I can call."

"What about your father?"

Dwayne grimaced and shrugged. "Dad's too busy. So what's new?"

Jarvis smiled and patted Dwayne's arm. "Call your friend. I'd take you home myself if I weren't stuck here." He wrote out a note. "I also need you to promise me that you'll find out what this problem is. I'll make an appointment for you with a good neurologist, and I want you to be sure to follow up. You need to find out what's going on. It could be dangerous."

Dwayne's eyes widened. "You think it really could be?"

"Ever heard of brain tumors? Strokes? Son, this could be anything. I don't want to scare you, but you've got to start taking this thing seriously." Jarvis frowned. His own tests had turned out negative so far, but he knew he had to keep trying, too.

"I'll be good. I promise." Dwayne's eyes grew slightly moist again, and he held his hand out. "Thanks for believing in me, Jarvis."

Jarvis reached out his own hand, but it suddenly went numb. Dwayne's face fuzzed out of focus. The room tried to spin, but he closed his eyes.

"Jarvis?" A hand touched him on the shoulder. "Uncle Jarvis? Are you okay?"

In the distance the sound of a siren echoed.

Jarvis took several deep breaths, forced his eyes open and gripped the edge of the cot for support. The brightness of the room hurt his eyes for a moment, but everything gradually focused again.

"Jarvis?" The boy's voice was gentle, worried.

Jarvis nodded and straightened. He reached up and patted Dwayne's shoulder. "I'll be okay. You just see to it you keep your promises to me." He turned and walked out the door, issuing orders to the nurse for Dwayne's shot.

Frankie's chest hurt worse than ever before. The nitroglycerin helped some, but he almost wished he hadn't let the paramedic give it to him. If Shelly hadn't found him… He reached his hand out and felt her grasp it as they turned into the hospital ambulance entrance. This time she wasn't crying.

"You're going to make it, Frankie," she whispered.

"Somebody's watching the kids?"

"Yeah, Mrs. Mahurin from across the street."

He smiled and closed his eyes. The kids liked Mrs. Mahurin. She would be good to them. "You be sure and give them that DNR sheet, okay?"

There was a long pause. "The paramedic has it."

Frankie nodded. "Good. Thank you, Shelly." He knew that had been hard for her to do.

"I don't feel right about it. It's like I just told them to kill you."

"You told them not to fight God's decision if He wants my heart to stop beating. That doesn't mean it will stop today." The chest pain hit him again, and he grimaced. Shelly's hand tightened over his; then they heard the sound of the ambulance doors opening.

"Okay, Mr. Verris, we'll be inside in a moment," came the paramedic's voice.

"Who…" he gasped, "who's the doc today?"

"Dr. George."

Frankie nodded. Not Dr. Bower, but it didn't matter now.

He fought the pain as they wheeled him out into warm, fresh air, then through a sliding glass door into cooler temperatures, beeping machines and muted voices. In spite of the nitroglycerin, he hurt worse now.

He groaned and clutched his chest. The voices swirled around him. He thought he heard the doctor….

"Good, you've got him on oxygen. Get me an EKG and draw blood for a cardiac panel, and I'll be in. Claudia, do you have that morphine ready?"

"Yes, Dr. George. His BP is a little low, and he's having some PVCs on the monitor. Do you want me to start another line?"

"Just follow my orders! Give him 2 milligrams every five minutes."

"Yes, Doctor."

The voices faded out while Frankie waged a physical battle with the demon in his ribs. Later, he felt something burn a little down his left forearm. Sometime after that the pain eased. But the demon hovered nearby. Frankie could feel it.

He kept fighting, but his time was almost up and he knew it. They chased Shelly out of the room, but he heard her crying in the hallway over the beeps and voices and movements of the people that surrounded his bed.

One voice rose above the others, and he thought he recognized the nurse who had helped him when he came in. "Dr. George, the morphine's not helping. He needs Tridil. What rate do you want me to start at?"

"Just give him another sublingual nitro."

"His BP is too low for that. He needs IV nitro."

"I know what he needs!" the doctor's voice snapped. "Stop…stop telling me how to do my job! I can't think with you nagging me—"

"What rate, Dr. George?" She spoke more sharply.

"The EKG doesn't show anything…."

"The monitor is showing more PVCs and some couplets. He may need lidocaine, too. Do you want me to start a heparin drip? Five thousand or 10,000 bol—"

"Stop it!" the doctor snapped. "Stop…"

"Doctor, are you okay? Doc—catch him, Carol! He's going to—"

"Leave me alone! I don't need you hovering over me! Help me with this patient. Get me another line. Repeat EKG…."

Frankie groaned with pain. The doctor sounded drunk.

Where was Dr. Bower? Why couldn't he have been here when the time came?

More hands moved over his chest and arms.

"He's got ST segment elevation. It's an MI."

The pressure grew beneath his ribs with sudden intensity.

"V-tach! He's in V-tach!"

He couldn't breathe.

"I can't get a pressure!"

He couldn't think.

"We're losing him!"

The voices faded once again.

"He's in V-fib!"

The pain released him. The darkness disappeared. Another voice reached him, a long familiar voice. Frankie felt a rush of joy unlike any he had ever known.

He was going home.

Jarvis pronounced the death of Franklin Verris, then set the wheels in motion for cleanup. He glanced into the waiting room to see if Dwayne was still out there. He wasn't. His friend must have come to pick him up while they were busy. Claudia wouldn't be too happy about that. She'd warned Jarvis that Dwayne hadn't called anyone to come and get him. Now she would probably insist that the kid had driven away while their backs were turned.

Jarvis passed by the open door of the extra call room, and to his surprise, he saw Claudia standing by the desk with her back to the door, holding the telephone receiver to her ear, talking softly.

Now what was she up to?

He stood there for a moment, but couldn't hear what she said. Frustrated, he went to his room and lifted the receiver. Line two was lit, and he quietly punched the button and listened.

"Well, you may fire me for this," came Claudia's calm, matter-of-fact voice over the telephone, "but I'm worried about Dr. George. He's made some pretty…indefensible decisions this morning, and he's not getting any better. I think he's sick. He almost passed out on us down here in the E.R. while we were working on a cardiac patient. The patient died on us, Mrs. Pinkley."

"Are you saying the death was due to lack of good medical judgment?" came the administrator's grave question.

Claudia cleared her throat. "Yes. Dr. George is sick, but he won't admit it." Her voice grew softer still. "I'm in the E.R. and he might overhear me. I've got to get back to work."

"Wait a minute. You're saying there have been other instances this morning?"

"More than one. Dr. George gave morphine to Dwayne Little and just let him go. We got busy with the cardiac, and Dwayne disappeared while I wasn't watching."

"You think he drove?"

"I sure do, Mrs. Pinkley. Dr. Bower was right about Dwayne."

"Claudia, are you suggesting I remove Dr. George from duty and bring in another doctor to take his place?"

Claudia did not hesitate. "Yes. Preferably Dr. Bower. I'd better go. Bye."

There was a click and a dead line.

Lukas had just laced up his hiking boots and pulled on a T-shirt when the telephone rang. He trekked across the bedroom floor, scattering the carpet with dried flecks of caked mud left over from his last hike.

"Dr. Bower?" came a familiar voice when he answered. "This is Lauren. I heard you weren't at work today."

"That's right." Considering the town grapevine, he didn't doubt that every citizen in Knolls knew he had turned in his resignation. Did they know that Estelle had refused it?

"So how are you enjoying your suspension?" Lauren asked.

Lukas chuckled. "How do you keep up with everything?"

"Sorry. I've told you before, I've lived here all my life and everyone knows me. When I was in high school, I was the editor for the school paper. It comes naturally. But there are certain things that I care about more than others. Are you doing okay? I've been praying for you."

He had no doubt that Lauren was sincere. "Thank you, Lauren. I've been doing a lot of praying, too, and I believe I'm doing the right thing."

"Good. My offer to go fishing still stands—no strings attached, honest. You just need a friend right now to—"

"Sounds great."

"Huh?"

"When can we go? I'm all dressed for the outdoors, but I'm warning you I'm not much of a fisherman." He could almost hear her grinning over the phone line.

"I'll get my poles and be over in fifteen minutes."

"How about I drive? I've got this great Jeep that knows how to hit the potholes. I'll pick you up. What's your address?"

Shocked by his own sudden impulsiveness, he had to ask her to repeat her address; then he had to ask directions since he didn't know his way around town yet.

When he disconnected the phone, he grabbed his jacket and keys and walked out of the house before he could change his mind. This was crazy! Lauren's chatter would probably drive him nuts and scare off the fish. But at least he knew there was probably nothing anyone could do to hurt his career at this point.

He heard the distant ringing of his telephone as he opened the door of the Jeep. He paused and turned to go back into the house, but changed his mind halfway back. It wouldn't be the hospital, since he was on suspension. It might be Dr. George calling to issue more threats or taunts, and Lukas didn't want to deal with it. He let it ring and switched off his cell phone before stepping into the Jeep.

Chapter Thirty-One

Theodore Zimmerman sat with his shoulders hunched over the desk in his office at home. He'd been there at least two hours, drinking, belching, swearing and sometimes crying. Why he was crying, he didn't know. The booze should be making him feel better by now. He hadn't cried since high school.

He should be scrambling to dig up the money to pay off Johnson. Gordon had called three times and had left increasingly angry, desperate messages on the recorder each time. Theo had sat and listened and poured another drink. His stomach burned and he knew he needed to eat lunch, but Jack Daniel's was all he could swallow right now.

He picked up the telephone to call Julie's office number. For a moment the numbers danced on the dial pad, then swam back into focus. He hit a wrong number, disconnected, tried again, missed, cursed. Finally he got it right, and relief poured through him. He needed to talk. Had to get some of this stuff off his chest before Tedi came home.

Thoughts of Tedi brought tears to his eyes once more. "What am I doing to my little girl?" He'd been so hard on her the past few months, taking out all his problems on her, leaving her at home alone too much, yelling at her…and worse…when the pressure got too bad at work. And all for what? Now he didn't even have a job. And Tedi wouldn't speak to him.

He wiped the fresh moisture from his cheeks and waited for Julie to pick up.

She did.

He cleared his throat. "Hello, uh, Julie? Sorry to bother you at work." Had to keep his voice steady. She didn't need to know how much he'd had to drink.

"Theo? What's wrong?"

The instant concern in her voice warmed something inside him. "I've had a rough morning. Got some time to talk?"

He expected an immediate reply, but instead there was a long hesitation.

He frowned. "Julie?"

"Theo, this isn't really a good time. Can we meet for dinner or something?"

His tears dried up, and he felt a shaft of anger, swift and strong. "I need to talk now. Can't you just—"

"Theo, it's really hectic here right now, and if this isn't an emergency—"

With another surge of anger he slammed the phone down and shouted a curse. So much for a listening ear from a loving woman.

He tried to stand, but the wheels of the chair rolled sideways and he stumbled against the desk and fell back. He pushed back from the desk with another curse, and one of the wheels caught the edge of the small recorder he'd hooked to the phone. He'd placed it on the floor the other day when he was working on some files.

He stopped and stared at the small light on the machine. He hadn't listened to it since last week. He reached over and took another swallow of his drink, then bent down and punched Rewind and Play. Might as well see what had been happening around here the past few days.

Tedi's voice reached him, then Mercy's. It was a new message.

As he listened, he felt as if his life were draining out on the floor.

By three o'clock Thursday afternoon Jarvis couldn't concentrate on anything for more than a few seconds at a time. His headache had returned with such force that he was tempted to take the remainder of the morphine that had been intended for Frankie Verris. Unfortunately, Claudia was on the ball, as usual. She had poured the drug into the hazardous waste container, with the other nurse as a witness, and they had both signed off; then Claudia had gone to lunch and left the other nurse, Tish, to take her place.

Jarvis still seethed at Claudia, both for her actions in the E.R. and for her betrayal of him to Estelle. The problem was he couldn't afford to just fire her right now. Hard as it was to admit, he needed her today. Badly. If not for the DNR sheet on Mr. Verris, this death could have turned into a lawsuit. Claudia had been an E.R. nurse for so long she could probably run a code single-handed, and she knew it. Bossy was better than dim-witted like her lunch replacement. Tish was a young, inexperienced nurse who didn't even know how to deal with the funeral home director who came to pick up the body of Mr. Verris.

They were wheeling him out on the black shrouded cot when the ambulance radio blared.

"This is Knolls 832 to Knolls Community. Knolls Community, come in, please."

Jarvis groaned inwardly, then gestured for Tish to answer. He turned to walk toward the call room. He had to lie down just for a few minutes.

He took some more Ultram when he reached the room, even though he knew they wouldn't help. Maybe combined with the narcotic…

The telephone rang by the bedside before he could even sit down, and now there would not be time. The ambulance was a block away. He could hear it as he walked back out the door.

Tish came running toward him. "Dr. George, they're bringing in a trauma patient in his early twenties. He's unconscious and has an obvious injury to his head and his right leg, but his blood pressure is okay."

Jarvis stopped and stared at her, not wanting to comprehend what she was saying. Another serious patient? "Why didn't they fly him?" he snapped.

She stared at him helplessly. "I guess they didn't think he was hurt badly enough. Should I page Claudia?"

He shook his head in annoyance. "If you're not qualified to take care of this, you shouldn't be here in the first place."

They both looked up when the entrance doors slid open and the attendants came through with a gurney.

"Hello, Dr. George," Connie said as she led the way toward him. "This one flew his Porsche off the side of an embankment, no seat belt. He was thrown clear and landed on the ground. He has a large contusion to the forehead with an overlying stellate laceration. We have him on 100 percent nonrebreather and have run two large bore IVs. While we were at it, we drew lab for a trauma work-up. He has limited response to pain."

Jarvis bent to look at the pressure dressing on the patient's forehead, then stopped suddenly. He recognized those polo shorts. He took a closer look at the patient and nearly lost his balance. His whole body went numb.

It was Dwayne.

"Dr. George?" Connie stepped toward him.

He straightened, still staring at the young man. Had to stiffen up. Had to do this right. Dwayne was…his life might… This was horrible!

He reached into his pocket for his penlight, then pulled the young man's lids back one at a time to check for signs of a blown pupil. None. That was good, although the morphine Dwayne had on board from his injection could have something to do with that, couldn't it?

For a moment Jarvis couldn't think, couldn't concentrate.

No, the eyes were good. Time to check the rest of him out.

The attendants had adequately placed him in full c-spine immobilization on the long spine board. At least they knew what they were doing. He wouldn't worry about the neck right now. Maybe he could get Dwayne shipped out before he had to think about that.

"Carol?" Jarvis called over his shoulder as he directed the attendants to take Dwayne to the trauma room. "Get ahold of the surgeon on call. We need a consult as soon as possible."

He pulled out his stethoscope and listened to Dwayne's chest for breath sounds. His eyes teared up as he stared at the boy's bruised and cut face. Breathing sounded good.

"Dr. George," came Carol's voice from the doorway,

"the surgeon can't be here for thirty or forty minutes. He's at his office in Willow Springs."

"What!" Jarvis straightened and was immediately sorry. The room spun around him. He grabbed the cot and steadied himself. "Of all the irresponsible—" He broke off, glaring at Connie. "You should've airlifted him." He turned to Carol. "Call a chopper. We've got to get him out of here."

He bent back down over Dwayne's body, noting the Harris traction splint on his right leg and abrasions on the left knee. He stared at the splint, confused. Normally it was the driver who suffered a tib-fib fracture from standing on the brake during impact. But Dwayne's friend had picked him up.

Jarvis turned to Connie. "What happened to the driver?"

The paramedic stared at him blankly for a few seconds, then shook her head. "Dr. George, he was driving. He was the only one in the wreck."

For a moment her words did not register. When they did he first felt a deep sense of disappointment that Dwayne had not listened to him. Then more fear hit him. He'd been the one to prescribe the morphine after Claudia had warned him not to.

What was he supposed to do next? He couldn't think. What had he already done? Should he have Tish page Claudia to come back to the E.R.?

The only other thing he could think to do was check for a pulse distal to the fracture site. With hands that had begun to shake, he held his fingers to the top of Dwayne's right foot. There was a pulse. At least he thought he could feel a pulse, but could he be sure? Maybe he was imagining something that wasn't there. Maybe he was hoping for it.

He would have to trust his instincts.

"Okay, Tish," he called. "Let's get a head CT on this patient before the chopper arrives."

Was he forgetting something?

He'd been treating patients for over thirty years, and he'd seen his share of traumas in this E.R. Surely he could trust himself by now. A CT was the way to go. It would save a lot of time when Dwayne reached Springfield for neurosurgery.

Ozark green had deepened with the maturing of spring into summer, and the vibrant colors of purple, yellow, pink and blue wildflowers dotted the shore of Piney River in a scene that could have been a Thomas Kinkade painting. Regrettably, the incredible beauty sure hadn't improved Lukas's fishing any. Nor his coordination. He'd already managed to tangle his fishing hook—complete with worm—in Lauren's ponytail. And they'd only arrived an hour ago. He'd also stepped into a muddy river sinkhole up to his right knee and had apparently frightened off all but one striper, which Lauren had caught and put on her stringer.

True to her word, Lauren did not put any moves on him, and she had obviously not dressed to tempt him. She had no makeup, her hair had not been washed, and she wore baggy overalls with an old blue chambray shirt underneath. She laughed at him a lot, chattered as incessantly as he had feared and managed with all those words not once to bring up the subject of Knolls Community Hospital.

Okay, Lord, he prayed in his head during one of her rare silent moments, *You were right, as always. I needed a friend.* She was definitely turning out to be a good,

Christian friend—still a little deeper than he intended to take it, but the companionship was nice. He didn't feel quite so lonely.

Thursday afternoon Tedi walked all the way home from summer school by way of alleys. She never saw Dad's car, but she didn't want to take any chances. It was kind of fun finding her way through new territory, trying to recognize where she was from the backside of the houses she knew so well. Everything looked so different this way. It almost felt as if she were in a new place, a new town. It would be easy to imagine she was headed toward a new home.

When she came out to Tenth Street, she paused and glanced down toward the circle drive where Grandma lived. Wouldn't it be great…? But she couldn't. Dad would come looking for her there, and he would blame Grandma and Mom.

Time to go home and be good and shut up and let Dad do the talking. Maybe he would get tired of the silent treatment he'd gotten the past few days and ship her to Mom's.

When Tedi arrived home she felt a great surge of relief to see that Dad's car wasn't parked in the drive. The past few days, he hadn't driven out to find her when she'd walked home. Maybe he'd finally given up on his efforts to be pals. That would be good; it wouldn't be so hard for her to keep her mouth shut.

She pulled the house key out of her pocket and stuck it into the front door lock. It wasn't necessary. The door was already unlocked. Tedi shrugged and went on in. Dad was probably so out of it this morning that he hadn't remembered to lock the door. He always nagged her about security, but then he didn't listen to his own warnings.

She swung the book pack off her shoulders and turned the corner to go upstairs, but the sound of a footfall reached her from the shadows at the side of the staircase. With all of the drapes closed, little light ever seeped into the hallway even when it was bright daylight outside. Tedi stared hard into the dimness.

The darkness moved toward her, just like the monster in her nightmare. She stepped backward. He came faster, with a heavier step. Tedi jumped back and screamed, shoving the book bag toward the shadow. He knocked it aside and kept coming. She pivoted toward the door and tried to open it.

A big hand grasped her arm and jerked her back around. She caught her breath to scream again, but she stopped. It was Dad.

"Why are you running from me?"

His voice sounded slurred, and his hand continued to grip her arm too tightly.

"I d-didn't know it was you, Dad. It was dark."

He squeezed her arm tighter. "Come with me."

"Why? What's wrong? What are you—"

"Shut up."

He jerked her forward and dragged her through the house toward the office in the back. She could smell the booze more strongly than ever, and she suddenly wished it had been a stranger who had broken in.

He shoved her through the office door and forced her into a chair.

"Dad, what's—"

"I think we need to spend some quality time together, don't you?"

She was too scared to answer.

He sat down in front of the desk and picked up a small

oblong recorder from the floor. He punched a button, set the recorder on the desk and waited, watching Tedi. "I think we've had some trouble with communication lately, just like your teacher says. I want to take care of that problem right now."

The fumes from his breath washed across her in a wave.

She recognized her own voice—she'd heard recordings of it at school when Mrs. Watkins let them listen.

"I hate him! I wish he were dead!"

Tedi gripped tightly to the arms of the chair on which she sat. She forgot to breathe as she listened to a playback of her phone conversation with Mom from the other night.

She listened to her own sobs, to Mom's reassuring voice, and now she concentrated on that voice.

What was Dad going to do? He'd already been listening to this, she could tell by a quick glance at his face. What would he do this time?

Mom's recorded voice returned. *"Where is your father?"*

"He's not a father. He's a horrible…"

The next few phrases washed over Tedi, but she couldn't hear them—her heart was beating too hard and fear gripped her too tightly. She couldn't look up at Dad. She heard her recorded voice telling Mom again that she hated Dad. She heard Mom telling her to go to bed. And then she heard Mom telling her to pray.

She started praying now, silently and quickly. *God, help me! Please, help me! Please save me!*

Dad took a deep, long breath and rested his elbows on the desk for a moment. He buried his face in his hands, rubbed his eyes, exhaled. He shook his head and turned to Tedi on the swivel chair.

"You just can't leave it alone, can you?" he snapped, his eyes blazing blue fire.

She didn't answer. She didn't know what he was talking about.

"You've got to keep running to your mommy with everything, as if she's the only one who can make things better. You didn't ever consider the fact that she's the one who started all the problems in the first place."

Tedi stared at Dad. With the fear, a little anger now mingled.

"It's her fault we're divorced."

That wasn't true, but Tedi stayed quiet. She hoped her growing temper didn't show in her face.

"You've let her twist your mind against me until I'm some kind of monster in your eyes." He paused and his eyes narrowed. "Apparently, a stupid monster! I don't even have the brains to help you with your homework. But you didn't tell your mother that you wouldn't even let me try!" His voice grew louder, filled with more anger. He wheeled closer to her, bending forward until his breath burned her eyes. "You didn't tell her that, did you? Why not?"

She couldn't keep sitting there. She felt as if she were being swallowed by the anger in his eyes. Slowly she stood, but he stood, too, blocking the door.

She tried to speak, but her voice caught. She swallowed and tried again. "I didn't want you to help me," she answered honestly. She couldn't think of any quick lies, and he wanted an answer.

"Why not? Aren't I good enough? Are your mom and your grandma the only ones who know enough to help you?"

She swallowed again and started to nod, but stopped

at the flare of fury that crossed his face. He took a step toward her. She couldn't step back. She knew she couldn't get away, but she had to try. She jumped to the side and tried to duck past him, but he grabbed her.

She screamed and tried to wrench from his grasp. She couldn't. His hand came up.

"Daddy, stop!"

He smacked her sideways, snapping her head back. She felt herself falling, felt her head hit something hard. Everything disappeared....

Chapter Thirty-Two

"Code orange, CT. Code orange, CT." The announcement came through the overhead speakers, blasting Jarvis where he sat at the desk with his head in his hands. He looked up with a frown as Tish dropped what she was doing and rushed out the door toward radiology. Why were they calling a code?

Radiology. Dwayne. He was crashing.

Jarvis forced himself to his feet, stumbled against the chair, righted himself and rushed after the nurse. This could not be happening. The chopper would be here any time. Dwayne couldn't die. He'd been stable when they wheeled him out.

Nurses, techs and aides rushed toward the CT room from every direction, but they gave Jarvis right of way. He was the E.R. physician. He was the one in control.

He reached radiology to find others converging on the room that held the patient. Though the red warning light was still on above the door, no one paid attention as they rushed past the CT computer and circled the gantry on which Dwayne lay. Claudia already stood beside him, re-

leasing the clamps from the IV tubing and calling for help
to lift him off the gantry and onto the wheeled cot. He was
still strapped onto the backboard with the c-collar around
his neck. He looked so young and helpless.

Jarvis groaned. This was a horrible place to try to do
a code, and as more people rushed into the already-
crowded room, shouting questions and getting in each
other's way, the level of confusion grew.

"Let's get him back to E.R.," Jarvis said.

"You heard the doctor," Claudia said. "Rachel, put
him on an ambu bag." She helped them transfer Dwayne,
then led the way out of the room and down the hallway.
She glanced at the automatic pressure cuff on the patient's
arm. "Doctor, the BP is 45. He's in shock. He needs
blood. How much do you want?"

"Four units." Jarvis gestured toward the lab tech. "Do
you have him typed yet?"

"No, Doctor. We'll have it soon."

"No time," Claudia snapped. "Doctor, what type do
you want?"

"O negative." He had to concentrate, couldn't stum-
ble now.

They wheeled Dwayne into the trauma room.

"How fast do you want it?" Tish asked.

Jarvis turned and glared at the young woman. "He's
bleeding to death, Nurse. Put it in a pressure bag and get
it in him as fast as you can."

"O_2 sat is only 76 percent," Claudia warned.

Jarvis couldn't show any weakness in front of this
crew. "We'll have to intubate. Get me a 7 tube and a
curved blade." He'd done this before lots of times, but not
working around a c-collar and not when he was in so
much pain he could barely concentrate.

While Tish hung the blood, Claudia handed Jarvis a curved plastic tube with a 12-CC Luer Lok syringe attached. "I've already checked the bulb and lubricated the tube, Doctor. Everything's ready." She snapped open a laryngoscope and instructed a tech to raise the bed.

Taking the scope, Jarvis leaned over Dwayne's mouth and gently pried between the teeth. He slid the laryngoscope blade down the right side of the tongue and used it to push the tongue up and to the left to get it out of the way. With light from the scope, he tried to get a view of the vocal cords. Nothing. He couldn't even find the epiglottis. He pulled up as much as he dared, but still got nothing. His hands shook and his head pounded with pain so sharp it blurred his vision. He couldn't do this.

He had to do it.

He must have overshot. He pulled back up. There! He saw the epiglottis, but still no cords. They should be right beneath. He raised the blade a little more, prying forward.

A tooth snapped.

He muffled a curse. He couldn't get it. But he had to keep trying.

"Doctor, O_2 sat is 72 percent," Claudia said.

He pulled back the scope. "Bag him."

Tedi lay on the living-room sofa where Theo had carried her from the office. Her face glistened with moisture from the wet cloth Theo was using to try to wake her. He bent down and listened for a heartbeat again. It was still there. He couldn't tell if it was slow or fast. He could barely hear it over the roar in his head. He could hardly think over the voice that kept telling him he'd killed his little girl. He'd hit her. Hard. There was probably a place

at the back of her head where she'd smacked against the edge of the bookcase.

But she wasn't dead. Not yet.

"Tedi!" he shouted, grabbing her hands and squeezing them tightly in his own. "Tedi, please wake up. I'm sorry. I'm so sorry." His eyes and nose dripped from tears. He couldn't believe he'd hit her.

She didn't move. He leaned forward and felt the faint whisper of her warm breath on his face. He should be the one lying there unconscious and broken. What had he done?

He glanced toward the phone. He should call an ambulance. He had to get help for her fast. But he could get her there faster himself.

He ran into the kitchen and grabbed the keys to his car, shoved them into his pocket and ran back into the living room.

Gently he lifted her into his arms and carried her out to the garage. "Tedi, please don't die on me, baby. Please don't die."

Sweat from Jarvis's hands made the laryngoscope hard to grip. He wiped first one hand, then the other on his shirt. It wouldn't work. He couldn't get it.

"Dr. George, the O_2 sat is 69 percent," a respiratory tech announced.

He gave up and straightened. "Bag him again. Claudia, get that c-collar off the patient."

Her eyes widened in surprise. "That could paralyze him."

"Don't you think I know that?" Jarvis snapped. "The collar is blocking the intubation. He'll die if we don't—"

"Dr. George," Carol announced from the door. "The flight crew is here for the patient."

The two newcomers, a female paramedic and a male

nurse, were not shy. They stepped into the room and walked to opposite sides of the bed.

The paramedic, a seasoned veteran familiar to Jarvis, studied the situation and stepped up beside him. "Any luck?"

"Not yet."

"Let me try," she said. "I've done quite a few of these."

Jarvis nodded and stepped back, too relieved to be offended, too weak to argue. His hands continued to shake. Even as he watched the paramedic work, his vision blurred once again. He slumped against the counter, hoping no one would ask him any more questions.

They got the tube in place, repackaged the patient for shipment, and cleared the room. Jarvis heard himself thank the flight crew as they wheeled Dwayne out toward the chopper.

"Jarvis."

The voice came from somewhere beside him, but through the growing murkiness he couldn't tell who it was except that it was female.

"Jarvis."

This time Estelle's face floated into view. "Jarvis, how's our patient?"

"Stable, I think." He heard the tremor in his own voice.

"I'm not talking about Dwayne, I'm talking about you."

He raised a brow and looked at her. "I'm not—"

"You're relieved of duty," she said. "I want you to see a doctor. Today, if possible." She glanced at her watch. "It's five o'clock. Dr. Simeon should be off duty soon. I'll call him to come over and check you."

"No."

"I'm not asking, Jarvis. You *are* off duty as of now, and you need—"

"I've seen a doctor." His voice grew weaker. He felt weaker all over. "Ran tests." He gave up and leaned against the wall.

Estelle gently took his arm. He didn't fight it because he didn't have the strength. He even allowed her to help him walk toward the call room.

"What were the results of those tests?" she asked.

"Negative CT."

"That's all? A CT isn't the only test they can run, you know." She turned and called over her shoulder, "Claudia, I need you to get some vitals for us over here. I think Dr. George has finally—"

The E.R. doors flew open, and Theodore Zimmerman stumbled in carrying Tedi in his arms.

"Help my little girl!" he cried.

Lukas unlocked the door to his house, feeling more relaxed than he had felt in months. It was great. He glanced down at his feet, then bent over and untied his hiking boots. They were caked in good old Missouri mud and river water. Wonderful mud. His jeans still smelled like fish, although he hadn't caught a thing. Fishing wasn't as much fun as hiking, but it wasn't bad. Being out there in the beauty of God's natural creation always helped put everything else into perspective, and he no longer worried as much about what was going to happen to his career. God would be faithful. He always had been.

Lukas had made it halfway across the bedroom floor in his double-stockinged feet when he caught sight of the flashing light on his answering machine. He punched the play button as he passed the machine on the way to the kitchen to get a tall glass of lemonade.

The sound of Estelle's voice stopped him in his tracks.

He raced back out the door, into his mud-caked boots, and off toward the hospital.

"Put her in two," Jarvis said as he pulled from Estelle's grasp and wearily turned to meet Theo and Tedi at the room.

Estelle did not protest. She couldn't and Jarvis knew it.

"What happened?" he asked Theo, giving the younger man a sharp glance.

Claudia immediately came into the room and started taking vitals.

"She hit the back of her head on the edge of a book-case." Theo wiped at his nose with the back of his hand. He was a mess and reeked of alcohol. "It knocked her out. I couldn't wake her up."

Claudia glared at Theo, suspicion obvious in her eyes. "Why didn't you call an ambulance?"

Theo stared at her dumbly. "I…I didn't think it could get her here as fast—"

"How long has she been out?" Jarvis asked.

"I don't kn-know. Maybe twenty or thirty minutes."

"Why did it take you that long to get here?" Claudia demanded.

Theo's face crumpled and he dissolved into sobs.

Jarvis motioned to Estelle, who stood at the doorway. "Get him out of here. He's not doing us any good like this."

As the administrator began to coax Theo toward another room, Jarvis turned to her again. "Estelle, get another doc in here now."

Jarvis pulled his penlight out of his pocket and gently lifted Tedi's eyelids. His hands continually shook now, and the ends of his fingers felt numb. Tedi's pupils were equal and reactive. The light did not wake her up. He checked for a wound and found a large contusion at the right parietal-occipital region of her head.

Claudia finished her vitals. "Dr. George, her BP is 110 over 75, heart rate's 85, respirs 18, no temp. Her O_2 sat is 96 percent. Do you want oxygen?"

Jarvis hesitated. The nurse's words seemed to blur together. He looked at her. "What?"

"Oxygen, Doctor. Do you—"

"Yeah." He glanced down into Tedi's face. "I can't do this," he muttered, pulling over the stool to sit on.

"You've got to," Claudia snapped. "We don't have another doctor yet." She opened the glass cabinet and took out a c-collar from the supply. "Do you want an IV?"

He looked at the nurse again. "What did you say her BP was again?"

Claudia placed the c-collar on the child's neck, then reached for an IV tray. "It was 110 over 75. I'll do a heplock."

Claudia raised Tedi's left forearm, prepared it with an alcohol wipe, and expertly slid a 20-gauge needle through the skin into the vein below.

"Ow!" came the sound of the little girl's voice.

The sudden cry startled Jarvis. He scooted the stool forward and leaned toward the child as Claudia continued to work.

Tedi's eyes slowly opened; then she squinted in the light, focusing on him. "Jarvis?" She reached out her right hand and touched his face. "Jarvis?" She looked around, her dark eyes gradually filling with apprehension. "Why am I here again?"

He nearly cried with relief. "Sweetheart, it's okay." He patted her arm. "It's going to be okay now."

"Did I get stung by another bee?"

"No. You bumped your head." Jarvis leaned forward and rested his forehead against the edge of the cot. She was safe.

He heard Claudia talking to Tedi, but he only picked up snatches of the conversation as his vision blurred in and out of focus.

"We were wondering if you might remember what…"

"I just came home from school. Someone was inside…"

"It's okay, honey. Don't force…"

He heard Claudia ordering a head CT, and then he felt hands helping him move sideways until his head and arms rested on something harder and flatter. There was silence, and he allowed himself to sleep….

"Jarvis?" The voice was Estelle's. He heard her footsteps draw near, and the echo of them pounded in his head, which he could not raise from the desk for the moment. She laid a hand on his right shoulder.

He forced his eyes open. His whole body trembled as he made himself straighten in the chair.

"How are you feeling now, Dr. George?"

"I'm okay," he heard his own voice croak. He blinked and glanced around the room. "Have they taken Tedi to CT?"

"They did that ten minutes ago. Jarvis, you're sick. Dr. Bower is here now, and I've asked him to check you out."

"I told you I've been checked out," he growled, sudden irritation giving him momentary energy. "I don't want him touching me." He struggled to his feet, then walked unsteadily past her out the door toward the central desk. He knew she was following, but he didn't care. "Claudia, have you heard anything about Dwayne yet?" he asked.

The nurse turned and looked up at him, then glanced at Estelle.

"Go ahead and tell him, Claudia," Estelle said.

"Yes, Dr. George. I called Cox South as soon as I made sure Tedi was going to be okay."

"How is he?"

Estelle laid a hand on his shoulder. "Dwayne coded about five minutes out, Dr. George. They did a hot offload, but they couldn't get him back. I'm sorry. He died."

Jarvis could not respond. He stared at Estelle for a long moment. Then the room went black. He felt himself topple forward.

"Help me, Claudia!" Estelle cried as she caught Jarvis and eased him to the floor.

A full-body spasm caught Jarvis in its relentless grip.

"Where's Dr. Bower?" Estelle demanded.

"He's in room six," Claudia said.

"Get him now!"

Chapter Thirty-Three

Lukas heard Mrs. Pinkley cry out, and he rushed out of exam room six to find Jarvis on the floor, his hands and legs flailing in a classic seizure. Mrs. Pinkley knelt before him, watching helplessly, but wisely not restraining him.

"What happened?" Lukas asked.

"He just passed out and started seizing. What should I do?"

"Make sure he doesn't hit his head against the desk." Lukas walked over and grabbed a cot. "Claudia, get out the Ativan."

The severity of the convulsions slowed, and in thirty seconds they stopped. "Did he hit his head when he fell?" he asked.

"No," Mrs. Pinkley said. "I was able to break his fall."

"Good." Lukas reached beneath the doctor's arms, lifted him from the floor and manhandled him onto the cot. "Claudia, is that Ativan ready?" He pushed the cot into exam room two.

"Coming."

"Good. Grab a gram of Dilantin on your way. Put it in 100 CCs of normal saline. We want to get this in by IV if possible. We'll need extension tubing. I don't want him pulling the IV out if he seizes again. You concentrate on the IV. I'll take care of the rest."

He had Jarvis hooked to oxygen and had padded the bed rails with blankets by the time Claudia walked into the room.

"Do you want blood drawn?" she asked.

"Yes, but do it fast. We want to be able to break the next seizure if there is one." He applied monitor patches and attached the leads.

"How fast do you want me to give it?" she asked.

"Fifty milligrams per minute. You're just in time," he said as he watched her secure the IV with tape. He stepped to the door and called out to Carol for stat blood work. Jarvis's arms and legs had begun to tense for another round. "Claudia, hold the Dilantin. Give the Ativan—2 milligrams per minute should break it."

Jarvis jerked violently and it started again. Claudia pushed the drug Lukas ordered, and the length of extra tubing prevented the IV from being pulled out. Within two minutes the seizure broke.

"It's working." Lukas watched as the spasms once again grew less intense. "That's enough Ativan. I think we can start the Dilantin now."

"Gotcha." Claudia switched the medications quickly. She shot Lukas a broad grin. "Good to have you back. I can't tell you how much I've missed you."

Lukas reached over and straightened Jarvis's oxygen mask, which had slipped sideways during the seizure. "I haven't even been gone a whole day."

"It's been a rough day." She lowered her voice. "We've

lost two patients already. Sweet old Mr. Verris had an MI, and he had a DNR sheet, so we couldn't code."

Lukas felt a swift rush of pain. "Frankie?"

"Sorry, Dr. Bower. I know you really liked him."

Frankie had been looking forward to his reunion with his wife, and he was ready. That knowledge brought Lukas peace. It must have upset Dr. George to lose a patient, especially considering the mental state he'd been in recently.

"Let's check for vitals since we didn't get a chance to do so earlier." Lukas reached for an ophthalmoscope and shined the light into Jarvis's eyes. They were equal and reactive, and thanks to the seizure, there would be no question about the movement of all four extremities. "You say we lost two?" he studied the patient. "Jarvis? Dr. George? Can you hear me yet?"

No reply.

"The other one was Dwayne Little," Claudia said softly.

Lukas jerked around and stared at her. "What? How?"

"He came seeking drugs again, and he got them this time, then drove away while we were busy with Mr. Verris. Wrecked his car. Jarvis seized when he got the news about Dwayne."

Lukas felt another rush of pain, and no peace followed this one. Another human life, a human soul, lost.

Mercy pushed through the emergency room doors and saw Mrs. Pinkley coming forward from the desk to meet her. "Thanks for calling me, Estelle. Where's Tedi?"

"She's in CT right now." The administrator's deep, familiar voice conveyed a sense of calm as she laid an arm across Mercy's shoulders and walked with her, keeping up the brisk pace without apparent effort. "She was awake and talking when they took her over, so it looks as if the worst has passed."

Mercy took a deep breath and willed herself to slow down. She headed toward radiology. "What happened?"

Estelle pressed her lips together thoughtfully. "She doesn't remember it yet. Her father says she fell and hit her head against a wooden bookcase."

Mercy raised a brow at the older woman. Estelle caught the look and returned it. "I'm glad Carol was able to reach you. I'd been trying for some time."

"Oh? Why?"

"Dr. George has fallen ill, and I needed someone to fill in for him. Dr. Bower came in just a few moments ago."

"Good. Where's Theodore?"

"I left him in the private waiting room."

"Has he been drinking?"

Mrs. Pinkley nodded.

Mercy didn't say another word. She would deal with Theodore later. Right now Tedi needed her.

When she stepped into the CT room, she caught sight of her daughter's brave expression where she lay in the center of the shooting match. It made Mercy want to cry. The technician completed her final orders and gave Tedi some encouraging words. The press of a button slid Tedi out from beneath the X-ray cameras.

"Can I talk now?" Tedi asked.

"Yes, go ahead. We're finished here," the tech said, nodding to Mercy. "You can come and get her if you want, Dr. Richmond."

Mercy stepped around the lead-lined partition and bent down to kiss Tedi, taking care not to move her any more than necessary. She still wore the c-collar. Mercy studied

Tedi's skin for signs of abuse and found nothing. No marks. Still, children often failed to show signs of trauma.

"How are you feeling, honey?"

Tedi blinked and yawned, then raised her hand and touched the collar. "My throat hurts."

Mercy's interest sharpened. "You have a sore throat?"

"No." Tedi tapped the collar with her fingers. "It's my neck, right here." She indicated the left side of the collar.

Mercy gestured toward the tech. "Ann, has she shown any physical changes since they brought her in?"

Ann shook her head. "She's been perfect. She did everything I told her to do, didn't cry, didn't complain. I wish all my patients were so good. Time to get her to the plain film room so we can clear that c-collar. Maybe her neck will feel better then."

Fifteen minutes later, Tedi continued to pick at the c-collar with her fingers. "This thing really hurts, Mom." The X-ray tech had just finished with the final shot, and Mercy stood brushing the hair from her daughter's eyes and watching her face.

Something didn't seem right. Tedi did not seem to feel as well as she had earlier. She should be getting more alert, not less alert.

"Mom, that machine's still buzzing in my ear. It's too loud."

Mercy frowned and glanced at the tech. "Buzzing? I don't hear anything."

Tedi looked around and pointed toward her left. "It's coming from over there."

"Are you hurting anywhere besides your neck?"

Tedi yawned. "My head hurts." She raised her hand toward the right back side of her head and blinked sleepily.

Mercy checked the movement of her daughter's pupils.

They were fine. Mercy turned to the tech. "Please have Dr. Bower come over here for a stat exam. Something's wrong."

The tech brought Dr. George's lab printouts to the exam room. Lukas studied them, frowning. "I don't see an obvious explanation here. We'll have to do a CT of his head." He stepped toward the door to give Carol the order.

"No."

Dr. George's sudden, gruff voice startled Lukas and Claudia. Lukas turned back toward the bed. The lids of Jarvis's eyes were half-open in a struggle for more complete consciousness.

"Dr. George, you've had a seizure," Lukas explained. "The blood work shows no obvious cause for it, so a CT scan is the next step."

"Done it," Jarvis growled.

Lukas blinked at him in surprise. "When?"

"Monday." His eyes opened farther, and he turned his head to glare at Lukas.

"What did it show?"

"Nothing."

"Then we'll need a lumbar puncture. You're in trouble, Dr. George. We've got to find out what—"

"Not here, and not by you." Jarvis struggled to sit up. Lukas laid a hand on his shoulder to stop him, and Jarvis knocked it away. "Get me to Springfield!"

"Jarvis, you're already seizing, so you know time could be—"

"Dr. Bower." Carol rushed into the room. "Sorry to interrupt, but Dr. Mercy's calling for you over in radiology. She thinks there's something wrong with Tedi."

Jarvis lay back against his pillow. "Get over there and take care of that little girl, and get me an ambulance."

* * *

Theo was slumped at the end of the sofa in the private waiting room. His head hurt so badly he could barely hold it up, so he sat with his face buried in his hands, tears dripping between his fingers. He heard the door open and heard footsteps on the carpet, but he didn't look up. If it was Mercy, he'd rather not see the attack coming.

Nobody hit him, but someone sat down beside him, then reached down and patted his knee. He opened his eyes and looked at the hand without raising his head. The hand had deep veins and liver marks and wrinkles. It was feminine, but not Mercy.

"How are you feeling, Theodore?"

He recognized Estelle Pinkley's voice. "How's Tedi?"

"Not doing too well at the moment, I'm afraid."

He raised his head, sniffed and wiped the moisture from his face with his sleeve. "What's wrong with her? What's happening? They said she was conscious. Is Mercy here yet?"

"Yes, she came in a few moments ago. Tedi isn't feeling as well as she was when she first woke up."

Theo's head didn't swim now, but his stomach churned with nausea and fresh fear. What had he done?

Estelle grabbed some tissues from the box beside the sofa. She laid them in Theo's lap. "Here you go. I know that sleeve's awfully handy, but it's already a mess."

He took the tissues and wiped his face with them. "What're they doing with Tedi?"

"All they can do. You know, Theodore, although I've been blessed these past forty-five years to be married to a strong man who knows how to be tender, I grew up with three testosterone-ridden brothers and I know the hazards of male pride. Some men would rather die than admit they have a problem. But what if it kills someone they love?"

The words struck him like a railroad tie in the gut. He sucked in his breath as he looked into her all-seeing eyes.

"Tedi is still going through some tests. But, Theodore, tests are subjective," she said quietly. She held his gaze.

He blinked at her.

"We've got good doctors here, but they aren't God. They x-ray what they think might be damaged, just as they run blood tests for particular needs. They can't find every little thing if they don't know what to look for."

Slowly Theo realized what she was saying.

She continued to watch him, as if studying every move of his face for signs of weakness. "I've worked with people a lot of years, Theodore. I've learned to depend on my ability to read people, and I think I've become quite good at it. Can you honestly tell me that Tedi is suffering from a simple bump on the head?"

He looked away, looked down, then buried his face once more in his hands.

Tedi sighed with relief when they finally took that big, hard collar from her neck. She tried to concentrate as Mom talked to the radiologist and to Dr. Bower. The CT was normal, whatever that meant. They said she had a large contu…something on the back of her head. What in the world were bone windows? Anyway, they were normal, too. Why did doctors have to speak a different language from other people? Didn't it just confuse things worse?

With another yawn, Tedi closed her eyes and tried to sleep. Her neck still hurt, though, and that buzzing still bothered her, even though Mom said she couldn't hear anything. Maybe something was wrong with Mom's hearing.

The radiologist left, and Tedi listened to her mother's worried voice float over her.

"Something else is going on, Lukas. I don't like this."

Gentle hands touched her face, and she opened her eyes to find Dr. Bower bent over her.

"Tedi, how are you feeling?"

"Weird."

"Describe that feeling to me."

"My neck still hurts, and can't you hear that sound? Mom can't hear it."

"Which direction is the sound coming from?"

Tedi glanced around toward Mom. "That way somewhere."

"And show me where your neck hurts."

She raised her left hand and touched her neck, then frowned and held her arm out. She couldn't see it very well. It looked fuzzy. She looked up at Mom's face. It looked fuzzy, too. That was when she got scared.

"Mom, what's happening to me?"

Theo wished he could die. Mrs. Pinkley's words kept running through his mind, and he couldn't make them stop. The doctors didn't know what to look for. They were treating Tedi for a bump on the head. What if he'd done worse damage? What if he'd broken her neck or something, and they overlooked it because they didn't know?

He picked up the cup of coffee Mrs. Pinkley had brought him and downed it with one swallow. It was lukewarm. He choked on the dregs. He couldn't let anything happen to his little girl.

With heart pounding, he stepped out of the waiting

room and crossed the hallway to the E.R. He heard Mercy's voice mingle with others, and he walked in that direction.

He stepped into the exam room where Mercy stood. The voices fell silent.

He looked into Mercy's accusing gaze, and then glanced down at Tedi. Her eyes were closed and tears moistened her cheeks.

Theo still felt woozy from the aftereffects of the booze. He had to tell them.

"How is she?" he asked.

"Worse." Dr. Bower held a stethoscope to Tedi's chest. "Claudia, check her BP again, and do an O_2 sat."

"Keep looking," Theo said. "Is her neck okay?"

Dr. Bower glanced up at him sharply. "Why do you ask?"

Theo grimaced. He had to say it. Out of the edge of his vision he saw Mercy take a step toward him. He had to tell them, anyway.

"I hit her."

"How?" Bower demanded.

"What do you mean, how?"

"Where did you hit her? How hard? Which hand did you use? Which way did she fall?"

He looked at Mercy then. "I'm sorry. I didn't mean to do it. I just—"

"I don't care why you did it!" Bower shouted. "Just tell me how!"

With a feeling of unreality, Theo told them. To his surprise, Mercy did not lunge for him, but bent down over Tedi again.

Dr. Bower turned to the nurse. "Catch the radiologist before he leaves. We need him to read a stat Doppler ultrasound." He bent down and gently placed his stethoscope against Tedi's throat, listened, looked at Mercy. "I don't hear a bruit, but that doesn't mean anything. Look at her left eyelid. Ptosis."

Mercy leaned closer. "You're right, it's drooping. We've got to get her out of here."

Bower called to Carol. "Call for an airlift. She'll need an emergency arteriogram and maybe surgery. She's got a carotid dissection."

Theo watched them work over his daughter for a moment, then turned away and opened his cell phone. He dialed 9-1-1.

"Hello, I need to report a child abuse case."

The chopper lifted off with Tedi as the police placed her father in the back of a squad car.

Epilogue

Saturday morning Estelle Pinkley sat in her quiet study, barely aware of the low hum of the air conditioner, of the rays of sunlight that escaped the vertical blinds of sliding glass doors that led out to her spacious deck. Her sweet, understanding husband always gave her as much quiet time as she wanted on Saturdays to regroup, especially after a difficult week. This past one had probably been the worst of her career at Knolls Community Hospital.

The sound of her doorbell echoed in the distance. She didn't look up until the study door opened and Bailey Little stepped through the thickly carpeted threshold. For the first time since she had known him, he looked disheveled. He wore no tie, his hair was not combed, and he had not shaved for at least a couple of days. His eagle-eyed sharpness had deteriorated to a grief-stricken, teary-eyed mess.

"Bailey," she said as she stood up from her easy chair. "Come on in. I'm so sorry—"

"I don't want to hear it." The glare he leveled at her was filled with anger and pain. He held up some papers. "Do you know what these are?"

"Bailey, come and sit down. We can talk about—"

"I'm finished talking." He stood stiffly in the middle of the room, right hand fisted on the sheets he carried. "I got this fax from the coroner thirty minutes ago. Do you want to guess what it is?"

She sat down with a resigned sigh. She knew it was Dwayne's autopsy report. "I don't need to guess, Bailey."

He threw the top page down on the coffee table in front of her. "This shows clearly that my son died of a ruptured spleen and a lacerated liver. The CT showed a skull fracture but no bleeding." He let copies of other reports drop to the table on top of the first. "These are Dwayne's medical records from Knolls Community Hospital. You're a sharp woman. I bet you already know what they say."

"Yes, Bailey." Not only had Jarvis George given Dwayne morphine and a script for more, but he had let the boy drive away high on drugs. And when Dwayne had been brought back to him, battered from the wreck, Jarvis hadn't even checked for internal bleeding. He'd concentrated on the head.

"Your doctor killed my son," Bailey snarled. "My only child is dead, and Jarvis George and Knolls Community Hospital are going to pay for that death!"

Tedi Zimmerman switched the channels on the television control at Cox South pediatrics unit in Springfield. The Saturday morning cartoons bored her. She preferred playing with the bed controls, and the nurse had reprimanded her for it twice already. Tedi grinned to herself, then shot a surreptitious glance at Grandma Ivy sitting at the bedside chair. Grandma had her head back, her mouth open, and she was snoring softly.

Eventually, Tedi switched off the television and lay back against her pillow.

The sudden silence woke Grandma. She snorted, then straightened in her chair. "What's wrong, sweetheart?" She pulled herself up stiffly to her feet and stepped over to the bed. "Not feeling well?"

Tedi reached up and touched the gauze that covered her neck. She sighed heavily. "I'm bored."

Grandma smiled. "Child, you haven't even been out of surgery for thirty-six hours, and you're already feeling as well as if nothing ever happened."

"When will Mom be back?"

Grandma glanced at her watch. "In a couple of hours. She'll drive back as soon as the funeral's over."

Once again Tedi reached up and touched the bandage at her throat. "Grandma, is it a sin to think something bad if you don't actually say it?"

"That depends on if you dwell on it or not. We can't stop some bad things from entering our minds, but as soon as they do, we've got to confess them. Tell it to God. He'll help you control those bad thoughts."

Tedi sighed. "Okay, then I'm sorry I wished it was Dad's funeral Mom was going to."

Grandma didn't act shocked; she just nodded. "I know the feeling. And if it's that hard for me to control my feelings about all this, I can imagine how it must be for a ten-year-old. Does this mean you remember what happened Thursday?"

"He hit me." Tedi fiddled with the bed controls again. "That's why I'm here, isn't it?"

"Yes. He admitted it. That's how they knew what was wrong with you."

"What did Mom do when she found out?" Tedi asked.

"She did what any good mother would do. She took care of you and let the police handle Theodore."

Tedi gaped at Grandma. "The police?"

"Yep. He called them himself."

Wow. "Is he in jail now?"

"Yes."

"For hitting me?"

"Yes, Tedi. There are laws against things like that."

Tedi frowned and gazed out the window for a moment. "Grandma, does this mean I'll get to live with Mom when I get out of here?"

"Of course. You can't live with your father in jail." Grandma took Tedi's hand and squeezed it. "Your mother already has custody, and your father hasn't fought her at all. He's requested hospitalization for his alcoholism once he gets out of jail."

"I hope he never gets out. I hope he dies there."

"What your father did was bad, Tedi. He's done a lot of bad things, but he's still your father. And in spite of the way he acted, he loved you enough to tell the doctors what he did."

"But he did it in the first place, didn't he? I could have died, couldn't I, Grandma?"

There was a long hesitation. "I don't even want to think about that, Tedi. I can't stand the thought of it."

"But I could have."

"You didn't. Tedi, have you ever done anything bad?"

Tedi shot her a quick look. "Yeah."

"So have I, and I felt awful afterward. How did you feel?"

"Terrible."

"Do you think God was strong enough to forgive you?"

"Yes. Do you think He's going to forgive Dad?"

"Don't you think He can?"

"Yeah, but I'm not as strong as God."

"You don't have to be, Tedi."

Lukas allowed the organ music to melt over him as he
sat near the front of the funeral home. He couldn't play
backseat Baptist today, because there weren't enough
people to stretch that far. Frankie didn't have any remaining family, and so Shelly and her husband and kids sat in
the recessed section reserved for special guests. Shelly
did the part justice.

That strange combination of sadness and joy pervaded
Lukas as it always did when he attended a Christian
funeral. It was a loss, but it was also a final triumph in
the knowledge that the person who had lived in this
earthly shell would no longer suffer pain.

Maybe, as some said, it was a simplistic way to look
at life and death, but Lukas didn't care. He believed it,
and he'd never been proven wrong—not about that.

Lately he'd been wrong about a lot of things, but for
some reason only God knew, Lukas had been reinstated
in the E.R. at Knolls. Not only that, he was now the
acting director as long as Jarvis was in the hospital. That
would be a while. Jarvis was battling TB encephalitis in
the Cox South ICU, brought on by a certain needlestick
incident.

Six months ago Lukas would have felt exonerated,
maybe even gloated a little—as soon as he knew Jarvis
was out of danger, of course. Now he didn't feel exonerated. He felt sad for Jarvis and grateful that the old trou-
blemaker was still alive.

Lukas smiled to himself. The turning point had been
the resignation he'd offered Mrs. Pinkley. He would never

have done that before, would have considered it stupid and wimpy. Now he didn't. Maybe he was maturing.

Sure had taken him long enough.

"Mind if I sit here?"

He glanced up in surprise to find Mercy standing in the aisle, grinning at him. He stared at her for a moment before scooting over. She sat down beside him and took his hand, then bowed her head for the opening prayer.

* * * * *

QUESTIONS FOR DISCUSSION

1. Dr. Lukas Bower came to work at a place completely different from his last job in a large hospital in Kansas City. He was disillusioned by the way he was treated by people with political clout, and yet encountered it in Knolls, as well. How would you feel if this happened to you? Would you be as determined as Lukas to follow hospital protocol, even after the director tried to ignore the needlestick? What could Lukas have done differently?

2. Two of Lukas Bower's first patients introduced in *Sacred Trust* were Frankie Verris and Jane Conn. Frankie tried to kill himself, and Jane signed a form instructing medical personnel not to resuscitate her should her heart stop beating. Do you see a difference between the two? Could you identify with either of them? Could you understand why Ivy was so reluctant to let her mother die?

3. Lukas discovered he had a couple of tough allies in Estelle Pinkley and Mercy Richmond. Do you think he might have had a little trouble depending on women to rescue him, or did he come across as a man who is comfortable in his masculinity?

4. Lauren McCaffrey made it obvious that she admired Lukas, and her friendly personality could have made it easier for him to be more attracted to her than to Mercy Richmond. Why do you think he was more drawn to Mercy? Do you think Lauren was too pushy?

5. Tedi Zimmerman lived in fear of her father, and yet she was also afraid of what he might do to Mercy if she fought him for custody. Would it have helped if Tedi had been more adamant about her fears? Would anyone have listened who could have done anything about it?

6. Mercy's helpless rage toward her ex-husband affected her life in so many ways. Can you list some of those ways?

7. Ivy Richmond was determined to retain her independence and normal activity level despite an apparent heart problem. Do you think she should have slowed down, or should she have pushed on and lived life on her terms as long as she could? What would you do? Do you know anyone like Ivy?

8. Darlene and Clarence Knight were in a situation they couldn't escape on their own, though they'd tried to do it for years. Some people may look at Clarence and their first opinion may be one of disapproval. Does your opinion of Clarence change when you discover the trail of inevitable failures he suffered on his way to this place in his life? What would you do in his place? In Darlene's?

9. Jarvis George's situation worsened as time went on, and yet he continued to clash with the man who might have helped him prevent the problem in the first place. If you were in Jarvis's shoes, when would you admit you were in trouble and ask for help?

10. Lukas had two women interested in him. One was a Christian who shared his beliefs, and who was obviously a kind and good person. The other woman had suffered some major heartbreaks in her life, and had a darker outlook. She is not a Christian. Do you think Lukas is wise to continue a friendship with Mercy as it becomes apparent that his affection for her is deepening past friendship? Do you think people have the ability to make a choice about whom they will and will not love?